Calling

Bernadette's

Bluff

2552-MCGO

Calling Bernadette's Bluff

A Novel

DALE MCGOWAN

To order additional copies of this book, contact:
Xlibris Corporation
1-888-795-4274
www.Xlibris.com
Orders@Xlibris.com

Acknowledgements

I am grateful to many people for input ranging from unreasonable praise to bilious contempt to deep, professional editorial indifference. Special thanks to Theresa Ostrom and Cecilia Konchar-Farr for expert reading and commentary. Thanks also to David Foster Wallace, Voltaire, and Kurt Vonnegut for writing so damn well, and to T.H. Huxley, A.N. Wilson, Carl Sagan and Richard Dawkins, each for "sitting before the fact like a little child" and putting it in writing so the rest of us could imagine what intellectual integrity is really like. Deepest thanks to my sweet, smart, beautiful kids, Connor, Erin and Delaney, to my mother Carol Hanewinkel, and to my awe-inspiring wife Becca, who improved the book repeatedly and who rocks my very casbah.

Note

The very suggestion that the College of Saint Bernadette, a fictional Catholic women's college in Minnesota, is intended to depict the College of Saint Catherine, the non-fictional Catholic women's college in Minnesota where I teach, is ridiculous and bizarre. St. Bernadette's, you see, is in St. Philip, and St. Catherine's is in St. Paul. More important still is the recognition that though several of the fictional characters herein bear a passing resemblance to non-fictional characters hereout, they are, in fact, fictions. Example: my dear wife of ten years is named Becca, but she is *not* a journalist, has *not* left me, yet, and is *not* a sex addict, yet. She *inspired* the character in certain respects, you see, but they are far from equivalent. Neither should fictional sociologist Brian Finnegan be confused with actual sociologist Brian Fogarty, Lily Galen with Lily Goren, and so on. Least of all can fruitful parallels be drawn between fictional college president Wanda X. Streamley and non-fictional college president Andrea Lee. Just one example of the many, many differences between them is the fact that Sister Andrea Lee signs my annual contract. Ahem.

The character of Scott Siberell is, however, disturbingly similar in type to one Christopher Perkins—except for the redeeming features, which are Scott's alone.

I

The Land of Nod

Philosophy is questions that may never be answered.
Religion is answers that may never be questioned.

Author unknown

I should've been a nun, he says, half aloud,
as his feet leave the ledge. *Old style.*
Pre-Vatican II. Full habit. That idiotic, beatific half-smile, which,
as he thinks of it, blooms imperceptibly on his lips.

Why, I'd look like Sister Bertrille up here right now,
wind in my hair,
hand up to my winged hat. Sister Bertrille
in a bad air pocket.

Of course—not a priest. A nun.
What a role that would have been!
How stupid of me not to have thought of it sooner.

Too late now.

But no, not Sister Bertrille, anyway. Quieter. Some anonymous
pawn in a remote, contemplative order of paired, gliding,
nodding chesspieces. That would have been the life. Untroubled by
mental racket. Worry about nothing but which bead I'm up to.

He whistles appreciatively at the ascending earth.

"All hail to thee, Saint Bernadette
Our patroness and friend
We kneel before the works of heav'n
And to our fellow men.

"Dear Saint Bernie, guard our College,
Bless us all where e'er we roam,
Saint Seraphic, hear our pleading
Watch our ways and guide us home."

Sister Anita Margarita releases the final chord from her grip, gradually straightening to a less severe curve over the piano keyboard as her performance squint softens to a lowered smile. Sister Annabella's handkerchief, clutched at arm's length, steadily lowers, the *mmm* of her last word spreading to an identical smile as she sweeps the Mother Teresa Board Room with a beatific gaze. A few empty seconds pass before the sisters realize that no applause is coming. And, at the same moment, the committee members realize that the sisters had expected applause, had probably hoped for it, relished the thought of it—and that it's now way too late to pretend the silence was just a spellbound moment of audience rapture.

An awkward cough.

A woman of evident authority sits up in her chair and clears her throat. "Ah, thank you so much for your assistance, sisters."

Uncomfortable smiles and nods, followed by another pause that makes it clear there has been no discussion of their departure, if any.

Smiles without end.

"Now we wouldn't want to bore you by asking that you stay for the actual discussion." It is Genevieve Martin, chair of the committee and Dean of Education. The same sentence spoken by, say, Maya Angelou would cast a calming mist over the room. But coming from the Dean it has the gentility of a starter's pistol, and neither nun is visible by the time the final word arrives.

Dean Martin is used to the fear she inspires. Never considered it a problem, frankly. Some in fact consider it to be the trait that propelled her to her current position and drives her through each day and every crisis with none but the most quailing and temporary of opposition. It's never an issue of *what* she says, since her written words are generally judged on mere merit. But say the same thing in person, she's found, and questions of merit shed their relevance, padlocks fly open, and underlings collide headlong, Stoogelike, in a frenzy of wish-fulfillment tinged with an inexplicable but highly motivating terror of consequences.

Lovely thing, really.

For anyone who has heard her speak, her written word packs the same punch. Her voice seems then to leap from the page and, bypassing the ears, plunge straight through the forehead, deep into primitive places. *Ohhh yeah*, says the brain stem. *Be afraid.*

She scans the room, running her fingers down the lapels of her suit like a gunfighter blowing smoke from a muzzle tip, taking a silent census by type. Seven Nodders, four True Believers, three Men, and herself. Depending on her own intentions, Dean Martin can play these factions any way she wants. Today it is her desire that the Nodders succeed so thoroughly in conflict-avoidance that nothing of any substance will actually happen.

Since things do tend to happen when the Dean speaks, she nods control to Professor Kassel. Jack takes a deep, careful breath and begins.

"Well then, we meet again to discuss changes to the college fight song." Audible gasps around the table. Jack's eyes inflate as he realizes what he's done. "I mean, the college *song*," he sputters in a rush. "The *song*. The *Hymn to Saint Bernadette*." Oh goody, he thinks. Now I get to start in a hole. Shit on a *stick*.

Jack Kassel's seen the inside of The Hole before. Every man at St. Bernie's Catholic College for Women is presumed male unless proven otherwise, and the smartest know enough not to confirm the presumption too early or too well. Nod a lot. Be quiet. Seize upon all moderate feminist statements as insufficiently committed to The Cause. And never use words like "seize." Just unlearn all language with any kind of ass-kicking, name-taking flavor. If ever possessed of a deathwish, refer to the school song as a "fight song" in a committee meeting, especially one attended by Leslie Erickson Mitchell-Robbins Moore, whom Jack now eyes nervously. *Be nice now, Leslie. I didn't get lunch today. My mind's not right.*

All eyes, in fact, have gone straight to Leslie, who leans forward on tweed elbows and erupts.

"Well, gosh, folks, let's think about this. What might we like to celebrate in a school song? Hmmm . . . it's a college for *women*," she says, drawing out the words as if pondering a real stumper, ". . . devoted to development of leadership qualities and independence and self-respect . . . Why, what could be better than a lot of *pleading and kneeling*—especially kneeling to *men*. Good stuff."

Nodding all around.

"Sarcasm there, people."

Nodding all around.

These nods, it must be said, indicate neither assent nor dissent. They are meant to *encourage* the speaker, to *celebrate* the speaker, to honor the speaker's unique voice, and nothing more. Someone has spoken, goes the rule: nod, nod goes the head. Someone else speaks, in utter contradiction to the previous speaker: nod, nod. Since there's no consensus, as someone will eventually say—and since truth is relative, everyone knows without saying—nothing to do but table the topic and move on.

Each meeting at the college, then, consists of True Believers firing at each other from behind the plywood figures of the Nodders and leaping over the prone figures of paralyzed Men until someone yells Time.

Leslie, satisfied for the moment, leans back. She's in her happy place. There is a world to be remade. So long as there's a red cape to charge, Leslie knows she is awake. Pleasantries are make-believe. IF YOU ARE NOT OUTRAGED, her Beetle bumper screams, YOU'RE NOT PAYING ATTENTION.

Leslie tries hard to pay attention at all times. And just as Dean Martin disarms and confuses with a combination of Brains plus Voice, Leslie too has a powerful Brains Plus combo, but her plus is pure visual. Something indescribable spreads across the front of her head whenever she delivers her verbal napalm—a spectacular, face-rending Grin that has the effect of convincing the victim he's been kissed and kissed well.

Tina-something from theater arts breaks the spell. "I've never been sure why she's called 'St. Seraphic'. We should lose that. That's always bugged me. 'St. Seraphic'. Is that supposed to be her last name, married name, what?" Blank stares. "What?"

"Uh, may I?" quavers Leonard the Poet. "Well, it means 'like unto a seraph.'" Leonard, the tiny, stooped medievalist, is more deeply saddened with each new appearance of *obs.* after a word in the Oxford English Dictionary. Total nod moratorium in effect until further notice. "A seraph . . . singular of 'seraphim.' Six winged angels, I believe. The term itself is a back-formation, and a charming one, back through Middle and Old English to Late Latin and . . . well," chuckling, "I'm not sure you want the whole . . ."

"Is this really what we're going to deal with here? *Back-formations?*" Leslie has pitched forward again, getting happier. "Anybody else notice Rome burning out the window there?"

". . . the whole derivation—though it is a particularly vivid one, but more to the point, it connects directly to the original Hebrew, which provides a . . ."

"Big flames. I'm going for water."

". . . connection to the past, especially to Judeo-Christian roots that might be . . ."

"Good night *nurse,* somebody pull out his batteries, take his little bass drum away, *something!*" Leslie looms over the table and grins hard at Leonard, who giggles.

A wave of squirming discomfort sweeps the boardroom, neatly skipping Leslie. Dean Martin watches quietly over half-glasses as her goal of ultimate inaction wends its way home, then speaks.

"The seraphim are the highest of the nine orders of angels. They guard the throne of God. Good strong image. It stays."

The committee members one and all take a sudden, quiet interest in the tabletop.

"Yes, um . . . all good points." Linda Near, theology, referring to everything and nothing. "I myself have always found it more of a problem that we call a saint by her diminutive name. (Nodding.) I mean, 'Saint Bernie' is a fine . . ."

"And that's up there with removing patriarchal implications?" Leslie cries. "Hello. Come on now." The many heads pause in confusion as to whether nodding silent assent or shaking a silent 'no' would be the more supportive gesture. A few diagonal twitches.

"I'm with Leslie on this one." Tina again. "This is nothing more nor less than an ode to male domination. It's just like *history.*" Very blank stares. Tina's voice climbs two rungs. "His story! HIS-story. And this is the HYMN to Saint Bernadette. Don't you see the subliminal message? The HIM." Stage whisper: "The *him.*"

Leslie tips her head sideways toward Tina and stage-whispers, "By that logic, Ben-*Hur* must be a feminist epic."

Tina's hand rises to her open mouth as she considers the implications.

"Uh, there's also the music itself." Another male, one Dr. Robert Frapples of Music. Pretty risky for someone littered with y-chromosomes to follow feminist commentary with a topic change, but Bob Frapples is tenured and just don't care. "Bad melody without a real climax . . ."—one gasp to his left at the use of *climax* — "and some really dated harmonies. Three bars in and it's 1895 all over again . . ."

". . . which is when the College was founded," intones Sister Joan Krenek, IHM. "It is thought that conservation of tradition should retain some inherent value in our deliberations." Vigorous nods. Sister Joan, reigning queen of passive voice, all vertical lines, and flanked as always by two silent anonymous nodding sisters Kassel calls Thing One and Thing Two.

Leslie's eyes roll hard and close. "Sister. Slavery was a tradition. Witch burning was a tradition. Not all traditions deserve to be sung about."

Pretty long pause. Sounds of distant field hockey.

"Then, of course, there's the, uh . . . the metrical foot," whispers Leonard the Poet. "Iambic in the first stanza, trochaic in the second."

Slow nodding.

Jack Kassel strokes a sideburn distractedly as he takes a reading of the room. His stomach grumbles in protest over the brain's decision to skip lunch, and Jack makes silent promises to it. "So . . . any chance we can come to a consensus on which of these many items to put first?"

Leslie's face lights up. "Oh, the metrical foot, of course! Let's do iron that out."

Leonard becomes dangerously smaller in his chair.

A decision has been called for. The Nodders sit paralyzed.

Dale McGowan

The Men crouch in their various holes. Tradition and Revolution, having spoken, perch high and unflinching. Fear and Loathing quietly cha-cha down the table's length.

A distant referee's whistle.

"Well then, it looks like we're not going to achieve consensus today." It is Dean Martin, so it is so. Relieved nods dribble like basketballs on various necks. "Let's table this for the time being, keep in touch with each other, and reconvene when we can . . ."

"Dean Martin!" It is Latifah Woo-Murphy, Executive Assistant to the Dean, bursting breathlessly through the door. "Dean, I'm sorry to interrupt, but . . . Father Hillerman is *dead!*"

Personal diary of Josiah Putter
4th of April, Year of Our Lord 1871

Today I note with all sadness that full three years exact have past since the date of the Great Sckism that rent the fabric of our Congregation sorly asunder. For it was on the 4th of April in the Year of Our Lord 1868 that my brother Zebulon T. Putter and the company of his followers walk'd from the arms of the Grace of God westward into the uncharter'd wilderness of the Minnesota prairie and on to theyre most probable demise and Judgment. Many times have I pray'd and wonder'd what greater guidance I might have shown that would have prevent'd the great clash of theologys that shutter'd dear Zebulons very eyes and heart from the Truth of our Lord and caus'd him to seek his salvation in false doctrins. His journey into Iowa on poor advise of our nephew Henry Grantwell was the source of all the Trouble I am assurr'd for it was then that he came upon these wick'd deceptions of what has been call'd the

Reform'd Lutherans. These falshoods, bro't to us from Foreign Hessian lands, work'd a powerful cunning on my dear brother's open heart and led him to preach wick'd mistruths about our Missouri Synod traditions that peirc'd my very heart. For several months did I attemt to remind Zebulon my dear brother of the inerrent words of the Lord as our great founder Martin Luther himself nail'd to the door of that church in Hessia many years past when he creat'd the Missouri Synod but no. Zebulons was a clos'd heart then. When so many of our fellows here in Saint Philip—the bless'd town that together we built as brothers in the Lord full seven years past—when many heard his words and were Deciev'd as he had been, then was my heart sorly brok'n further. And when at last he made the Fatefull deciding to tear the fabric of our belov'd Saint Philip— yea as in the days of the prophets when they rent theyre very garments in hearing blasphemey—when he took his gathering and left Saint Philip to go into the wilderness then the wrath of the Lord was on his head for not five days past until a powerful storm come upon our land and surely wip'd out the wand'ring rabble as they roam'd unprotect'd by God or man. And sure as we have never heard tale from any traveller about theyre Fate, sure as that is the Missouri Synod rightly but sadly aveng'd low these three years hence.

Personal diary of Zebulon T. Putter
April 4 in the Year of Our Lord 1871

It is hard to believe that three full years have now passed since we left St. Philip to establish a new Reform congregation here in St. Jude. The first year was difficult as we built the town from nothing, founding a new community based on the firm foundation of our Lord's mercy and grace. I remain saddened but not surprised at my brother's apparent refusal to reach out in reconciliation across the three-and-one-half prairie miles that separate our villages. His old resentments of me are reborn—that it was given to me to better my education at University and Seminary and his to remain behind, caring for our Mother and sister and homestead. It is perhaps not surprising, then, that he clings to the old religion while I see my way to the new. Perhaps I shall attempt someday to overcome my own accursed pride and extend my hand to him. Though we find our God in different religions, perhaps we can learn that there is not so much distance between us as it may seem.

Jack Kassel steps out of Hildegard Hall into what no self-respecting liberal any longer calls Indian Summer, turns east and begins the steep walk down The Wedge toward the prairie beyond the gates.

Saint Bernie's is located on the dun-colored plains of southwestern Minnesota and built—for reasons known only to the dead—on a one-of-a-kind land formation that has captivated the imaginations of at least, oh, three geologists in the past century: a wedge of earth, tapering downhill from the top of a forty-two foot clifflet to prairie level over the uneven course of 645 feet, apparently overlooked by the glacier that razed everything else as flat—though not a bit as green—as a pool table. The grade's a good five percent, which in prairie terms is straight up. State records have no specific name for the place, but generations of Bernies have lovingly or cursingly dubbed it The Wedge. Then-college president Sister Esther Kester tried feebly in the 40s to impose the name used by the neighboring Philippians and Judeans: "Bernadette's Butte," a fine alliteration which she dropped in appalled dismay when the obvious mispronunciation proved irresistible to students and faculty alike. She finally settled on "Bernadette's Bluff," resolutely, unshakably, as the informal nickname of her choice—and out of respect for her, until the very afternoon she died, everyone tried hard to use that name in her presence.

But otherwise they all called it The Wedge. Still do. It's a wedge, after all. Just look at it.

Jack has the sun at his back as he walks the daily mile each way to and from his home in Saint Philip Township. Every morning his heart pumps and pits glow as he reaches his wedgetop office near Saint Jude's Leap. Afternoons are a roll downhill, fun and easy—until about early December, when it turns into a fight for friction to avoid becoming a projectile down J. Putter Road headed straight for Saint Philip Town Hall.

Jack holds the endurance record for non-nuns in the Philosophy Department at twelve years, twelve long years. Colleagues hire in for a few terms, then are somehow catapulted to greater glories by hidden forces Jack has yet to channel for his own escape. His predicament was actually predicted twenty-two years ago by well-known sociologist/philosopher/man-about-town Sinclair Reynolds in his 1980 book *The Coming Malthusian Crisis in American Philosophy*.

A ten-pound doorstop of a book, Reynolds' tome was in four massive parts. In Part I, the childhood years of every major philosopher from Descartes to Russell were examined for similarities of experience. Lots and lots, as it turned out. Part II took those similarities and laid out an elaborate hypothesis, sprinkled with references to Freud and Erickson, suggesting that any child who underwent the same set of key experiences at critical points in personality development—a very precise timetable of existential angst, confrontation with mortality, experience of unbounded wonder, and disillusionment with pronouncements of authority—that any such child would be virtually predestined toward philosophy as a vocation.

Part III—the only one the media had any fun with—claimed that just such a set of precisely-timed circumstances had actually occurred in recent American history in a way that potentially affected hundreds of thousands of youngsters, a whole swath of the social fabric: the set of all American children born into or above the middle socioeconomic class in the year 1962. As a result, Reynolds posited that an absurdly large percentage of American children born in '62 would flock to philosophy as a life's calling.

Born in the belly of the Cold War, their earliest memories would have been of the Cuban Missile Crisis—or more precisely, of their parents' anxious reactions to it. Dim recollections of air raid siren testing and duck-and-cover drills, viewed through confining cradle bars, were indelibly etched on these most fragile little minds while utterly dependent on the very people who seemed most fearful and out of control. Issues of existence and nonexistence were thereby thrust before the embryonic consciousnesses of the smallest infants. Their earliest memories of television included stark images of the dead and dying in Vietnam, bringing questions of mortality to an individual level long before it is usually confronted. Then the Apollo program arrived right on schedule as the group reached elementary school age, the Age of Wonder. The first photograph of the earth taken from the moon, Reynolds argued, would have impressed no one so much as a first grader. It must have seemed simultaneously an explosion of radiant hope in the midst of the Cold War's existential angst and a deeply disturbing view of our own impermanence and frailty.

Reynolds produced admittedly anecdotal but compelling evidence drawn from the notes of first grade teachers during the late 60s:

Mavis Trembly, first grade teacher, Walker Elementary

School, Bally, Pennsylvania, 1964-1977: "You can see the change in the records I kept for parent conferences. I always kept very good records, mind. I always asked the children what they liked to think about. I told them to include happy thoughts and even thoughts that might be kind of sad. I always promised them it was just between us, of course, so they'd feel safe, then when parent conferences arrived I'd give them the scoop. Well 1967, 1968, they're thinking about puppies, about Mom and Dad, about their new shoes, about the choo choo they rode on ... then boom, 1969. Let me read a few I wrote down word-for-word. Oh yes, here: 'I think about what if time was in a circle, not going in a straight line.' And 'I think about whether my brain can ever stop thinking and if everything is really still there when I close my eyes.' 'I wonder if my awake time is really a dream and my dreams are really awake.' They're all like that! And I was supposed to read The Little Gingerbread Man to these kids. I tell you, it was a tough year. I'm ashamed to say I drank a bit. And all I ever thought was, just imagine what they'll be obsessing about by the time they get to Bally High! I'll admit I was troubled by it. Then boom, the next year, back to puppies and choo-choos for the next group. Damndest thing, excuse my salt. Oh crap, is that mike on?" (Reynolds 1980, pp. 642-3)

The immediate falloff the next year fit Reynolds' prediction, since that birthyear was post-Missile Crisis. The preteen experience of disillusionment with authority during Watergate solidified the final philosophical destination of the 1962 cohort, and in 1980, as the group prepared to depart for college, Sinclair Reynolds predicted a glut of philosophers the likes of which the world had never seen. Pundits and fellow academics fell over each other to shower Reynolds with scorn. But within three years he was vindicated as the cohort entered college, wandered through a variety of unrelated majors—classic pre-philosophy behavior—then dutifully and inevitably lept to their destiny. Grad school was preordained without pause, and in 1989 the Ivy League alone turned out an unprecedented 3,094 Ph.D.s in philosophy—including one Jack John Kassel, post-Hegelian neo-Kantian rationalist with a twist of Aristotle and an eye on the moon. Nationwide the total was a staggering 27,348.

Even if these newly-minted doctorates were only competing with each other and not with the unemployed Ph.D.s floating in any given year, securing one of the 56 truly desirable positions available in university philosophy in the Fall of 1989 carried odds of one in 488. A young buck philosopher had to have been dubbed "the New Voice of Neo-Platonic Idealism " or of some other school of thought to make it to academic paydirt. In a world awash with *summa cum laudes*, mere *magna cum laudes* were hidden on résumés like felony convictions. Multiple article publications prior to graduation were laughed to shame in favor of jobseekers with multiple book publications. University philosophy scouts crept into the backs of Big Ten lecture halls, scoring grad student lecturers like Olympic gymnasts, thrusting contracts and autograph books at only the biggest stars.

Which brings us to the fourth and final section of the book: even extending down into mail-order diploma mills, no more than about 2% of the Ph.D. Class of 1989 could expect work in their field the first year—and far fewer each subsequent year. Reynolds was an unheeded Cassandra:

> This phenomenon will then have created a deeply-indebted, over-educated, seriously under-employed and profoundly alienated subculture of ten thousand existential philosophers with time on their hands and

chips on their shoulders. They will rightly consider
themselves the creations of a society that in turn denied them the means to survive. The threat to national security could rival or exceed that anticipated
after the Second World War as three million armed
men returned from Europe and the Pacific to find
their jobs had been filled. A quick-thinking Roosevelt
Administration created the GI Bill in 1944, neutraliz-
ing a potentially volatile set of circumstances. Will
we respond as quickly to the current situation, or sit in
idle complacency as the nine-year gestation of a mon-
ster of our own creation ticks inexorably by? (p. 1493).

As for Part IV—well, nobody read Part IV. Okay,
Reynolds probably did, and his editor, and three grad students at Penn. And there was at least one more, a political
newcomer running for Congress in 1980 from Minnesota's
Second District, which just happens to include St. Bernie's.
His name was, and is, Peter D'Angelo—now eleven-term
Republican Congressman Peter D'Angelo—whose campaign
manager, one of those three Penn grad students, saw an opportunity in Part IV. D'Angelo saw it too, a big-government
idea so obscure it just might serve as the straw man he needed
for his campaign. A GI Bill for philosophers! *Welfare for
headscratchers*, he called it, and catching the electorate in a
properly foul mood, he showed what would become a lifelong talent for galvanizing the voters in opposition to
boogeymen of his own choosing. Now Reynolds wasn't even
running for the office himself, of course, but D'Angelo's op-
ponent *was* an academic—and we all know what *that* means,
he'd wink. In a blistering six-week campaign he effectively
tarred the bookish Democratic incumbent with the label of
"liberal elite academic tax and spender," connected him unreasonably to Reynolds, and soundly carried the election and
ten more over the course of two decades.

As luck would have it, Jack never needed to look into assistance for philosophers-without-portfolio. And he knew he was lucky to get any position anywhere in 1989, but after twelve long winters in the outback of North America, the glow of good fortune starts to dim and one's sights turn to greener, less-severely-inclined pastures.

He passes the field hockey pitch—which conforms rudely to the grade in a way just one team at a time appreciates— then Cady Stanton Hall. Cady Stanton is sinking in front for reasons no one can figure. The building had thirty-nine front steps when Jack arrived in '89; he counts thirty-four as he passes.

Why, here comes Brian Finnegan.

"Jack." Nod.

"Brian." Nod.

Not the mindless, acquiescent nods of the meeting-drones, these. These are knowing nods of the silent men of Gynotopia, intentional minimalism, blips of unfathomed meaning enjoying the silence they preserve around them.

"LITTLE HELP!" A field hockey ball skips by into the opposite lawn. Jack scoops it up and pitches it back inexpertly.

From the air, St. Bernie's is just close enough to symmetrical to make it awkward that it isn't. Admin backs up to the Leap at the top of the Wedge, facing onto a long, narrow central green. Long sightlines into Greater St. Philip. And centered at the top of the green is a spectacular, mythic-looking hundred-year old oak tree, visible all the way from the hog dung lagoons at the far side of Saint Philip. A ways down from the oak, the green becomes the hockey pitch, then back to green on the other side and on down the wedge. Five buildings on the south flank of the green, six on the other, all built at ten-year intervals with an apparent terror of architectural continuity. Hildegard Hall, the music building, begins the south row, just off the corner of Admin, followed by the foundering Cady Stanton (social sciences) and Curie Hall (physical sciences). The English and Languages building—which to Jack always begged a certain question—is named for the best-known Bernie in the wider world, pulp fiction author Elizabeth Caldwell Monty, whose bequest to the college of the entire proceeds of her potboiler Oprahbook *Sighs Don't Matter* earned her eponymous honors in the very building where she toiled as staff gossip columnist for the campus weekly *The Wedge Issue.* Just down from Monty Hall is the Steinem Residence Hall, completing the southern row, every building facing into the green and generally leaning oh-so-slightly forward.

Top of the North is Humanities and Arts, Jack's building, (named Bronte Hall, no one knows which one), then the Student Union, the Catherine of Alexandria Library, an unnamed, hellacious catch-all referred to as You Know, the Other Building, the Schlafly Residence Hall, and at last the college chapel, just inside the gates at the bottom of the wedge, the last vestige of any sort of elevation for 118 miles. Wide flagstone walks running down the sides of the green keep the hockey teams a safe distance from any falling buildings.

Since the western edge of campus is a cliff, it is the chapel, flush with the wedge bottom, that is the first and last thing everyone sees of Saint Bernie's. Jack always enjoys the sight of it for the latter quality, in addition to an austerity he finds weirdly comforting.

Most every building at Saint Bernie's goes nameless for its first several years as a howling tempest of controversy rages around it. Tempests aren't all that surprising in a college that tries to be both Catholic and feminist—strange bedfellows if every there were—and most campus decisions muck up the swimming hole of one or the other. Even within a single swimming hole there are snarling factions, like the conservative Catholics and liberal Catholics flinging mud in each other's eyes. Women's issues suffer the same ism schisms, resulting in tense compromises like Steinem and Schlafly Halls leaning menacingly toward each other across the green.

Once in a great long while, a naming is neat and tidy, like Curie Hall—who can fault the Madame, after all—and the Library. And Hildegard of Bingen was a strong pious musical female Catholic nun, so the music building had a natural patroness. But every other building stands for a while at the vortex of a whirlwind, each with its own unforgiving partisans dug in deep, years after the brass nameplates finally go up.

If ever they go up at all, that is. Admin, poor Admin, still stands in quiet mortification high atop the wedge, known only by its function. Every generation or so a new campus optimist, ignorant of the gruesome history of past Admin Naming Committees, blunders into the crosshairs by volunteering to head up a new one. How hard can it be to find someone to honor, after all.

After a hundred years and a half dozen disemboweled optimists, the name remains generic.

And so it nearly went for the Chapel. Before the roof was finished in 1922, the search was on for the available public domain name of a churchgoing American feminist woman. An anonymous donor had been lined up to fund a naming, but only with those precise stipulations.

The committee began its deliberations—True Believers, Nodders, and Men. And in the meantime, penicillin was discovered. Earhart flew the Atlantic; the atom was split and the Empire State Building built; fascism and the sound barrier were defeated. And still the committee met.

Every name proposed had Cheerleaders on one side and an Over-My-Dead-Body lobby on the other. Amelia Earhart was a frontrunner in the thirties—until she was lost over the Pacific. Along with her went any chance of Earhart Chapel; naming a church after someone who was lost and never found sent the wrong theological message, went the reasoning.

Emily Dickinson? Too "lusty." Nellie Bly? Too "unseemly." Annie Oakley, Willa Cather, Mary Cassatt? Too secular. Susan B. Anthony? Too political. Saint Frances Xavier Cabrini, the first American saint, now who could argue with that? No, people will see 'Saint Frances Chapel' and think it's just 'Saint Francis' misspelled. Girl Scouts founder Juliette Low? Judge Constance Baker Motley? Suffragist Lucy Stone? Pioneering feminist Catherine East? Well, it actually is a low, motley, stone chapel, east of campus—so any one of those would read like a description, not a name. A subtle undercurrent of racism in the forties kept Sojourner Truth out of the running—despite the gorgeous glory of the name *Truth Chapel.*

Friendships strained and snapped, the committee dissolved, reconstituted, redissolved. The UN Charter was written and ratified, polio conquered, DNA discovered, Everest summited—and still the chapel was just The Chapel. Until one evening in 1953 when *The Crucible* premiered on Broadway with Sister Mary Evangelina Whittaker, reigning campus optimist of Saint Bernie's and chair of the sixth incarnation of the Chapel Naming Committee, sitting ninth row center—and vibrating with excitement as the first act neared its end. By the time the lights came up for intermission she was galloping for a lobby phone, habit flapping, beads wildly clattering, to call Saint Bernie's with the news that she'd found the perfect name at last.

Rebecca Nurse.

Rebecca Nurse: tried, convicted, and hanged as a witch in 17th-century Salem. Puritan, granted, not Catholic . . . but then the Puritans were anti-Anglican, right, and the Anglicans were anti-Catholic if *anybody* was, so went the thinking . . . and the enemies of my enemies are my friends, are they not. And it was men men men who did the hanging in Salem and women who hanged. And so, after 25 unnamed years, Nurse Chapel took her post at the gates.

Jack likes the chapel, the name and the story.

Once in a while an eastbound hockey ball will get enough spin on it to skip all the way into the labyrinth mowed carefully into the grass at the bottom of the green. Placed into the floors of the European churches of Crusader wannabees around the 12th century were beautiful multicolored mazes of tile and stone and glass. Those unable to make the trip personally to free the Holy Land and gut the heathen Moor could walk the labyrinth, making a virtual pilgrimage of a sort to Jerusalem, represented by the center. Rosily redefined, washed clean of any nasty historical context, the labyrinth gradually found its way into the better homes and gardens of modern Catholicism. For American Catholics it has become a symbolic walk through earthly life to eventual salvation in Christ. For New Agers it is an opportunity for meditation and symbolic rebirth and the focal point of an energy vortex. For Carl Holtz of CSB Maintenance it's one more damn thing to mow.

At any given moment in any given day, one or two women—only ever women—can be seen gliding silently around the Bernadette labyrinth, deep in contemplation, slowly advancing one foot, then the other, stepping over or around the odd hockey ball, eyes downcast or upraised (depending on how many times they've made the trip), arms at the sides or crossed on the chest. Students assigned to walk the labyrinth for theology classes are easy to recognize, tearing through it impatiently like the halls of Curie between classes, passing the nuns and local farm women regulars like Manhattan cabs.

At the dedication ceremony for the Bernadette labyrinth, college president Wanda Streamley was positively transfixed, deep in ecstasy about the spiritual symbolism and potential for personal transformation inherent in such a thing.

Leslie Erickson Mitchell-Robbins Moore spoke last among the faculty presenters, laying confident claim to the labyrinth as a feminist icon as well. Gesturing mightily toward the scattering of leather projectiles strewn across the labyrinth, she declared to the nodding throng, "Let this labyrinth stand as a powerful metaphor for a woman's journey through a man's world. To make it through the maze of this life, a woman's got to be prepared to kick some balls." The wall between the east gates is ankle-deep on the inside with a wedglet of balls. Once in a while, a ball will roll with such conviction and plumb that it finds its way directly past Nurse Chapel, straight through one of the gates and into the greater world.

Lucky ball.

Jack is slapped to consciousness by the approach of Marilyn Sherwood-Forrest, all teeth and heels, accompanied as always by a never-explained giant poodle. She comes to a halt with a doubleclick and beams carnivorously at Jack. Marilyn does the same doubleclick-and-beam for all nineteen men on campus, so Jack knows not to read anything in.

"Jack John Kassel, how *are* you doing!"

Marilyn Forrest's recent remarriage, this time to Doug Sherwood, smacks of shameless namebuilding to key campus mutterers. Her new hyphenated name should have been "Forrest-Sherwood," the classic "hers-his" construction, they mumble. At least she's consistent, they allow grudgingly— she followed the same "his-hers" name order in her first marriage to the doomed Dr. William Black.

Anyone crossing her view with a name like Frank Enchanted or Samuel Deepdark would certainly be jumped by Marilyn inside of a week. And more than a few credible witnesses swore that Marilyn Forrest was uncommonly preoccupied and brow-knitted during the brief tenure of adjunct math professor Judith Gump.

The namebuilding theory got a big boost when Marilyn submitted her engagement announcement to The Tonight Show for a cheap timefiller gag Jay Leno does with serendipitously funny engagement name combos. And to this

day, Jack's noticed, she finds a way to mention her nine seconds of national prominence in every conversation.

"Oh, just fine, there, Marilyn, how are you doing!!" Ser-
endipitous my eye, he thinks. *Namebuilder.*

"Well, just trying to get home sometime today! Nothing
to write Jay about! Say, you headed home?!"

"Sure am!!" A tightness cinches the back of Jack's head.

"You lucky duck! Say, how's Connor!!! Is he three now!!"

"He's five, actually, and doing just great!"

"Five!! Oh good deal! Gosh, I haven't seen him in ages!
He must be getting SO BIG!"

"He's a big guy!!" Not *whether* to kill her, he thinks, but
how. *How.*

"Oh that's so fun!! Well, see you Monday! Oh wait, not
Monday! I've got an appointment in Mankato! Maybe Tuesday!"

"Okay, see you then maybe!"

"Good deal then! Bye bye!"

"Bye bye!"

Jack lets his face fall into a deathmask and intentionally
lopes, letting gravity do the work of getting him home.

One more, at the gate.

"Jack."

"Tim."

Jack passes the wedglet of balls, fumbles in his jacket
pocket, lights and draws on a Salem, and walks through his
own tiny, intermittent clouds toward the red brick and white
clapboard of twilit Saint Philip.

*Lessee . . . a little rush of blood to the head . . . a little shifting
of organs. Earth stops ascending, aaannnd . . . recedes. Ascends.
Recedes. Ascends. Gee, the cords held. How nice. And that's it, I take
it. My damn collar didn't even crimp.*

(Calliope music and the smell of sunburned children.)

There's the dirtbag carny, grinning stupidly as they lower me to him. Asshole. I want my money back.

"Heck, Father, you don't even seem shook! Lotta first-timers just about wet theirselves 'til them cords grab. You's jist smilin' peaceful straight through! Power uh prayer, eh Father?"

Okay, the dirtbag deserves a thrill, even if he can't give me one for twelve bucks. "Son, at this point in my life you'd have to soak me in diesel fuel and drop me through a cloud of flaming dog shit to get a reaction from me. And don't think that fact doesn't piss me off on a daily basis."

And there it is, the gaping look of shock and astonishment. Goddam cretin. You'll get mileage out of that story for years. I get nothing.

2

The Book of Jude

And the LORD said unto Cain, "Where is your brother Abel?" And Cain replied, "I do not know. Am I my brother's keeper?"

Genesis 4:9

A Centennial Celebration of Saint Jude, Minnesota
One Hundred Years on the Prairie

© 1968 by Margaret Feldenhook and Daniel G. Howser.
Part IX: The Story of the Founder's Statue

It was in late March of 1872 that the Reverend Zebulon Putter made the trek back to St. Philip to reconcile with his brother Josiah. It had been a particularly bleak and difficult winter, and the absence of a path or road of any kind between the two towns made late winter traveling especially arduous. But Reverend Putter managed the three-and-one-half mile distance in an afternoon, just as the first settlers of Saint Jude had done four years before in the opposite direction. Zebulon found his brother with two neighbors, cutting wood behind his house on the western end of St. Philip Township. It is the accounts of these neighbors, Grover Howser Sr. and Walter Quick, that have come down to us through family histories.

Grover Howser III grew up in St. Philip but emigrated to Saint Jude in 1887 at the age of fifteen to work as a jerky cutter. Grover recalls his family story:

> I remember FarFar—that's what we called Granddad, a Swedish thing, I think—I remember FarFar telling this story over and over, especially to me since that was the year I was born, about how Zebulon come out of the scrub with his arms outstretched, either like to hug you or like a ghoul or some such, and how Josiah fell back over the cutting stump like he seen a ghost. When Zeb started in to explaining the whole thing, how they was living just more than three miles to the west, well old Josiah went and clamped his hands over his ears, like this here *[Mr. Howser demonstrates by clamping his hands over his ears]*, then rushed into the

house and closed the door. Well, FarFar and Mr. Quick spoke kindly to the Reverend, since them and lots a other folks never did figure them Reformers for dead anyhow, and so wasn't about to go falling over no stumps when they met one of 'em. Zebulon he says he hoped his brother would consider visiting Saint Jude and that he wouldn't bother him no more in the meantime and then he waves at the house, since Josiah's hair and eyes was peeking up over the windowsill of the back window, right up til Zeb done waved and they popped right down out of sight. Well, my Farf . . . my Granddaddy knocked and went into the house and he tells Josiah what Zeb done said and Josiah, well he says Zeb couldn't never have said no such things to you, he's four years dead, and anyhow there weren't no town right out to the west or they could sure see it, it's just flat prairie after all. And Granddad and Mr. Quick says they couldn't very well have both had a vision, the same one, and you saw him too Josiah don't say you din't, and Josiah says yes two men could share a vision don't you read the prophets and no I din't see any such thing, now leave my home.

Later that summer the town of Saint Jude put on a festival to celebrate the construction of Main Street in the center of town, with six storefronts, the First Lutheran Reformed Church of Saint Jude (now a National Historic Landmark) a water tower and a livery. There was a morning parade, an afternoon dance and dinner, and an evening performance of a dramatic play, written to depict the brief history of Saint Jude to that point. The Reverend Zebulon Putter had been asked to portray himself, an invitation he had graciously and humbly accepted. The townspeople gathered enthusiastically in the schoolhouse, cleared of desks for the occasion. The

men of the town had built a small but ample stage to elevate
the players. Now the townsfolk watched with rapt attention
as their history played itself out before them. Men and women
alike wept and cheered, laughed at the reenactment of the
now-famous molasses barrel incident, shouted a giddy "That's
me!" when they recognized themselves being portrayed, and
joined tearfully in the solemn prayer of thanksgiving that
Reverend Putter had offered up upon their arrival, grateful
for a safe afternoon's journey. And then, just as he had done
over four years earlier, the Reverend proposed to God and
the assembly that the town be named Saint Jude, after the
patron saint of lost causes. *(The discovery two months later by
Luther Turner's daughter Paige, the town librarian, that Jude was
in fact a Catholic saint and not recognized by the Lutheran Church—
and therefore a less-than-ideal namesake for a town with the particular founding impetus this one had—that discovery went
undramatized this particular night. Eds.)*

The crowd roared with approval as the makeshift curtain
was pulled across a suspended rope. One by one the actors
stepped through the opening in the curtain and took their
bows. Not until the end did the Reverend Zebulon Putter
step slowly through the curtain to receive the adoring cheers
of his fellow Judeans. Looking out over the crowd, he raised
his hands high, then bowed long and low. The applause continued for over two minutes as Reverend Putter remained
low in his bow. Only after another full minute went by and
the applause began to thin did Mrs. T. F. H. Olafsson, a trained
nurse, suspect that something was amiss. All were silent as
she stepped up onto the makeshift stage and placed her hand
on the Reverend's back to ask if he needed assistance in right-
ing himself. The weight of her hand was all that was needed
to topple the frozen pastor forward off the stage. Women
screamed, men cursed mildly, and children strained to see.
Saint Jude had received the most cruel blow of its history, for

the Reverend had suffered a massive heart attack in the midst of his genuflection. Zebulon T. Putter was dead at fifty-one.

Early the following morning, a party of three aldermen on horseback assembled on the east end of Main Street with full kits of provisions for the journey to St. Philip. It was only fitting, the council had decided, to attempt once more a reconciliation with Josiah Putter and his townsmen. They would make the trek to St. Philip and ask Josiah Putter to preside over his younger brother's funeral. After a full hour's journey, the three aldermen arrived at the home of Josiah Putter and delivered their awful news. Erin Gaulding, granddaughter of one of the aldermen, tells the story:

"They go on up to his house and says 'Joe, we're sorry to tell you your brother is dead.' And Josiah says 'See, what did I tell you!' and he slams the door in their faces. So Grampa and the others come back home."

After three days of tearful mourning, Reverend Putter was laid to rest in the little cemetery on the east end of Saint Jude, only the fourth resident of the town plot. The church secretary performed the service.

But after another week had gone by, the townspeople began to discuss the need for a greater monument to their town's founder. Someday, they said, the great cities of the East will beat a path to our door. Saint Jude, Gateway to the Northwest! A grand road will roll in from the East, bypassing St. Philip, and enter our town, bringing prosperity for all its citizens! Those visitors must know who founded this great town: Zebulon T. Putter! A monument of epic proportions was called for.

And so, a committee was formed to decide on the design of the monument. Many meetings were held without progress as all members had their own ideas of what was important. Friendships were sorely tested. Days stretched into weeks, and weeks into a year as the church secretary toiled to reconcile the schedules of the committee members. At last, in a meeting in February of 1873, it was decided that a statue of the founder himself was the best possible monument, right at the east end of town—right over his grave. In a moment of great creativity, it was further agreed that Zebulon Putter would be depicted in the deep bow which was his last act, facing his beloved town, locked in an eternal, humbled curtain call before the upturned faces of the grateful townspeople whose applause was the last sound he heard on this earth.

A fund was established and the money raised quickly from the generous townsfolk, greatly assisted by a bequest from an alderman who closely followed the Reverend in death. The total collected, in fact, greatly exceeded the projected cost, so the project was enlarged to consume the funds available. A sculptor from Saint Paul was brought to town, who toiled from morning to night, late March to late July. At last, as the town bean crop reached its peak and the summer sun blazed, the great statue was completed. Even in its bowed position, from toes to the top of the great figure's back measured a full 32 feet of magnificent bronze. Add to this a pedestal of fifteen feet and the dimensions of the work can be imagined even by those who have not seen it. This forty-seven foot high masterpiece (now a National Historic Landmark) put Saint Jude on the map of southwest Minnesota. We think we speak for all residents of Saint Jude, past, present, and future, when we speak of the burning pride we feel in this monument to humility.

July 30, 1873
Personal diary of Josiah Putter

Of all the foul and despirate provications imaginable, this must surely be the greatest. For as I trained my spyglass West to prove to my townsmen that no such abomination exist'd as a town found'd by my hifalutin brother Zebulon, I beheld not just the town itself but the foullest of offenses in

Creation. For my brother, in apparent spite and perhaps in the thrall of Lucifer himself, did construct and build a gigantic statue of a man bending over with his great metal arse in my direction. What deviltry could possess even so misguid'd a soul as Zebulon to cast in steel his lowest thoughts of contempt towards me and his former town? All his booklerning together shant save him from judgment at the Throne! Gods wounds! Are we to live forever in the shadow of this monstrous butt? Shall the sun forever set on the upturned rear of this enormity??

August 2, 1873
Today, by the Grace of the God of our Fathers, our holy retribution is under way! Saint Philip is mobilis'd in a unity of rightious indignity regarding the profane arse of Lucifer point'd at our very community. We have begun the construction of a Great Wall to obstruct the befouling ediface from our Christian gaze. At a point one mile in the direction of my brother's Sodom-on the-prarie, a Great Wall of earth and tree and bush and cast off items and sundry personal goods now rises. A mighty line of men and horsecarts winds from our western limit to the site, and even today our progress is evident. Over two hundred of our Godly men have devot'd themselves to this task. By the first snows, a great structure fifty feet high shall render theyre unChristian gesture invisable to the good people of Saint Philip.

"And, indeed, by the third of October in 1873, a tremendous mound had grown up, sufficient to obscure the offending statue from the Philippians' view. The final form was not so much a wall as an irregular bluff or butte, for it proved difficult both to build straight upward and to convince the increasingly-exhausted townspeople of Saint Philip to carry their loads of fill all the way to the dump point. As time progressed, they unburdened themselves and their animals earlier and earlier still, until a vast tapering butte of earth-covered refuse was formed, pointing toward Saint Philip like a tremendous wedge. In the final weeks of construction, ever more desperate for fill materials, the Philippians began to include old wagon wheels, lumber, corn stalks, used bottles, and any other bulk materials they could lay their hands on. Two of the residents of the town, an elderly husband and wife by the names of Engebret and Margret Bergseth, died within a month of each other in the last weeks of building and, to contribute to the cause, were buried with solemn ceremony in the depths of the massive formation. Over the next twenty years, much of the surface fill naturally composted into a fine topsoil, and poplars, cypress, wildflowers and grass created the beautiful natural surroundings that were to inspire Mother Anna Cordion to found The College of Saint Bernadette on the site." (From *In the Shadow of Bernadette's Butte: A Centennial History of Saint Philip, Minnesota* © 1964 by Leonard Holdenmiller, incomplete and unpublished).

"If that's a butte, I'm the King of the Jews."
Penciled margin note in the Minnesota State Surveyor's Report of the proposed site of The College of Saint Bernadette, west of St. Philip Township, Minnesota, May 11, 1894

3

Jack and the Pulpit

We have this curious spectacle: daily the trained parrot in the pulpit gravely delivers himself of ironies, which he has acquired at second-hand and adopted without examination, to a trained congregation which accepts them without examination, and neither the speaker nor the hearer laughs at himself. It does seem as if we ought to be humble when we are at a bench-show, and not put on airs of intellectual superiority there.

Mark Twain, *Thoughts of God*

There's perpetual climatic combat in Leonard the Poet's office in mid-third floor pitchside Monty Hall. Multiple unspecified frailties of Leonard's are kept at bay by two pale green institutional humidifiers, one in each of the inside corners of the room. Refilled remotely twice daily by the department secretary via aquarium tubes that exit through a small hole in the wall, the humidifiers have run continuously since the Carter administration.

Papers cling fearfully to each other on Leonard's massive oak desk. Regular droplets of condensation fall from the front corners onto the sopped orange brown shag, *tick-tick-tick*, measuring the passage of decades. The walls are ever-so-slightly alive.

Each night one Gerard Mulryan of Maintenance wet-vacs the carpet and carefully dries every surface with terrycloth, humming "Wade in the Water" in a gravelled baritone. One Saturday morning in the depth of each January, Gerard opens Leonard's window for precisely five minutes—just enough time for the breath of winter to dispatch the green colonies on the walls—and leaving Leonard the Poet, once more, for a short while, the sole representative of the living in his tiny office.

Leonard's beloved books line the short side walls from floor to ceiling, stiffbacked with age and authority. The pups of the collection, barely twenty years older than Leonard himself, date to the First World War. The eldest, an original King James Bible of 1611 and a 16th century edition of the Canterbury Tales lie thick and still, sheathed in chamois, on the highest shelf of the northern case. And the whole collection, 842 volumes averaging 203 years in age, sits encased in two hermetically sealed glass-fronted bookcases, kept dry as Chaucerian wit by two expensively-humming dehumidifiers.

The college administration balked at buying the dehumidifiers at first, and Leonard never forgets. He was on the brink of a lawsuit alleging inadequate accommodation of his disabilities—for it was the humidifiers that started the combat, and they are necessary for his own survival while a simultaneous threat to the survival of the books that are the heart and substance of his work—when the college relented, and, in the midst of a national economic malaise and declining enrollments, purchased what in 1978 was $2,366 worth of defense appropriations for the dry side of Leonard's conflicting needs. When one of the machines started rumbling and squeaking two weeks ago, Leonard shot off a sabre-rattling memo to the Dean demanding its replacement. He enclosed a photocopy of the 1978 litigation threat, just to be nasty. Flirting with personal power gives Leonard a little tickle in the loins whenever he manages to do it.

He remembers the original victory with a disheveled grin each and every time he pulls the release lever and hears that hiss of decompression. Returning from the song meeting, he secures his office door and walks directly to the lever. *Sssshhhooooooo.* He retrieves an old cutting board from the lowest shelf and places it on his desk, straddling a scatter of moist papers. Slowly he climbs the ladder to the uppermost shelf and ritualistically lifts a tan chamois bag from its resting place. Inching back down, he recesses the lever, grins at the swallowed hiss of closure, and walks to his desk, placing the bag on the bone-dry board like the head of John the Baptist. He turns to the small table at the end of his desk and tinkers with a Sputnik-era RCA turntable. One minute later the sounds of David Munrow's classic 1968 recording of His Majesty's Sackbuts, a medieval brass consort, are issuing from the attached speakers. Leonard reaches into the bag, pulls out his 400-year old volume of the Tales, carefully lays it open, and reads, lips moving, nose and glasses inches from the yellowed page of The Miller's Tale.

Hir mouth was sweete as bragot or the meeth,
Or hoord of apples leyd in hey or heeth.
Wynsynge she was, as is a joly colt,
Long as a mast, and upright as a bolt.
she baar upon hir lowe coler,
As brood as is the boos of a bokeler.
Hir shoes were laced on hir legges hye.
She was a prymerole, a piggesnye,
For any lord to leggen in his bedde,
Or yet for any good yeman to wedde.

(Her mouth was sweet as bragget or as mead |
Or hoard of apples laid in hay or weed.
Skittish she was as is a pretty colt |
Tall as a staff and straight as cross-bow bolt.
A brooch she wore upon her collar low |
As broad as boss of buckler did it show;
Her shoes laced up to where a girl's legs thicken. |
She was a primrose, and a tender chicken
For any lord to lay upon his bed |
Or yet for any good yeoman to wed.)

Now, sire, and eft, sire, so bifel the cas,
That on a day this hende leonard
Fil with this yonge wyf to rage and pleye,
Whil that hir housbonde was at oseneye.

(Now, sir, and then, sir, so befell the case |
That on a day this clever Leonard |
Fell in with this young wife to toy and play
The while her husband was down Osney way.)

At each mention of the clerk Nicholas in the original text,

Leonard substitutes his own name—but stretched to fit the heroic pentameter, *LEE*-oh-nard. Leonard rolls and pleasures the syllables in his mouth:

> As poets ben ful subtile and ful queynte;
> And prively he caughte hire by the queynte,
> And seyde, ywis, but if ich have my wille,
> For deerne love of thee, lemman, I spille.

> *(Poets being as crafty as the best of us /*
> *And unperceived he caught her by the puss,*
> *Saying: Indeed, unless I have my will /*
> *For secret love of you, sweetheart, I'll spill.)*

Queynte. "Quaint." *Queynte*, he whispers. The erotic word-play, the lost and ancient dance of meaning. The sackbuts roar their approval.

> And heeld hire harde by the haunchebones,
> And seyde, lemman, love me al atones!

> *(And held her hard about the hips, and how! /*
> *And said: O darling, love me, love me now!)*

Leonard begins breathing rhythmically and slow.

> Or I wol dyen, also God me save!
> And she sproong as a colt dooth in the trave,
> And with hir heed she wryed faste awey,
> And seyde, I wol nat kisse thee, by my fey!
> Why, lat be, quod she, lat be, leonard,
> Or I wol crie ** out, harrow ** and ** allas! **
> Do wey youre handes, for youre curteisye!

(Or I shall die, and pray you God may save! |
And she leaped as a colt does in the trave,
And with her head she twisted fast away |
And said: I will not kiss you, by my fay!
Why, let go, cried she, let go, Leonard! |
Or I will call for help and cry 'alas!'
Do take your hands away, for courtesy!)

He catches a droplet with a quick hand just as it leaves the
tip of his nose, then reaches for a handkerchief to dry his
face.

This leonard gan mercy for to crye,
And spak so faire, and profred him so faste,
That she hir love hym graunted atte faste,
And swoor hir ooth, by seint thomas of kent,
That she wol been at his comandement,
Whan that she may hir leyser wel espie.
Myn housbonde is so ful of jalousie
That but ye wayte wel and been privee,
I woot right wel I nam but deed, quod she.
Ye moste been ful deerne, as in this cas.
Nay, therof care thee noght, quod leonard.

(This Leonard for mercy then did cry,
And spoke so well, importuned her so fast |
That she her love did grant him at the last,
And swore her oath, by Saint Thomas of Kent |
That she would be at his command, content,
As soon as opportunity she could spy |
My husband is so full of jealousy,
Unless you will await me secretly |
I know I'm just as good as dead, said she.
You must keep all quite hidden in this case |
Nay, thereof worry not, said Leonard.)

"She hir love hym graunted atte laste," he intones, "and swoor hir ooth, that she wol been at his comandement . . ." Leonard's voice trails to a whisper as his eyes roll back and close. She spoke to him again, even smiled at him in that hard, ruthless way, not an hour ago. "Leslie leslie love, leslie legs, leslie lips, leslie leslie leslie . . ."

A poet hadde sitherly biset his whyle,
But if he koude a carpenter bigyle.
And thus they been accorded and ysworn
To wayte a tyme, as I have told biforn.
Whan leonard had doon thus everideel,
And thakked hire aboute the lendes weel,
he kiste hire sweete and taketh his sawtrie,
And pleyeth faste, and maketh melodie.

(A poet has lazily employed his while /
If he cannot a carpenter beguile.
And thus they were agreed, and then they swore /
To wait a while, as I have said before.
When Leonard had done thus all to tell /
And patted her about the loins so well,
He kissed her sweetly, took his psaltery /
And played it fast and made a melody.)

"And thakked hire aboute the lendes weeeeeeeel." He lets the book slap carelessly shut. "Lendes lendes weeeeeeeel. Leslie leslie lovely lendes loins leslie lendes *weellllllllllll* . . ."

Leonard the Poet walks transfixed to the fresh air of the open window to clear his small, round glasses of their fog. Hum of riding mowers crossing the hockey pitch to prep for the evening match. Long shadows, lovely long leggy shadows. And in the midst of the pitch, a large swath of dandelions, late-season, second-crop dandelions. The lion's tooth, *dent-de-lion*, middle French, in yellow and white. Curious thing, thinks he, wiping his glasses, looking again. Very curious. The dandelions seem almost to form an image, feminine, perhaps medieval. Beautiful. *Jaune et blanc.*

"Leslie?" he whispers as the twin mowers enter the dandelion patch from east and west.

"Dad?"

"Yeah, Con."

"Dad, I was wondering something in Mom's house."

". . ."

"Dad?"

"Yes, Con, what were you wondering in Mom's house?"

"I was in my bedroom upstairs and I was wondering why the floor doesn't just fall down into the living room 'cause there's nothing under it to hold it up."

"Good question. The walls are holding it up on the sides."

"Dad?"

"Yes, Connor."

"Dad, look at those clouds. Why are those ones pink and those aren't?"

"Uh, it looks like the . . ."

"OH, *I* KNOW! It looks like the pink ones are blockin' the other ones from the sunset."

"Looks like it."

Four beats.

"Dad?"

"You know, Con, we're the only ones in the car. You can just start talking without saying 'Dad,' okay? I promise I'll answer."

"Okay."

". . ."

"Dad?"

"You can just start talking, you know."

"I'm well aware."

"Excuse me?"

"Dad, you kissed Mom pretty long tonight when you got to the house."

"Uh, hmm. Well, she was kissin' back too, don't you think?"

"Big time. So how did that make you feel?"

"Excuse me?"

"You don't have to keep saying 'Excuse me,' Dad, just talk."

"How was kindergarten today?"

"Are you uncomfortable talking about your feelings for Mom?"

"Exc . . . well, your Mom and I love each other, you know that."

"I think her *neighbors* even know after that kiss. Holy Moses."

"Can I see some ID, please?"

"Dad?"

"YES, Connor."

"How come you call her 'my Mom' now? When you guys were still married you just called her Mom."

That's true. Never thought of that. "So how was kindergarten today?"

Exaggerated sigh. "Fine, Dad."

Five minutes of rhythmic radial thrum.

"Dad, how did the whole universe get made?"

Okay now. Teachable moment, Jack, don't screw it up. "Well it's like this. A long time ago—so long ago you wouldn't even believe it—there was nothing anywhere but black space. And in the middle of all that nothing, there was all the world and the planets and stars and sun and everything all mashed into a tiny, tiny little ball, smaller than you could even see. And all of a sudden BOOOOOOOM!! The little ball exploded

out and made the whole universe and the world and everything. Isn't that amazing!"

Beat, beat, and . . . *action*. "Why did it do that? What made
it explode?"

"Well, that's a good question. Maybe it was just packed
in so tight that it had to explode."

"Maybe?" His forehead wrinkles. "So you mean nobody
knows?"

"That's right. Nobody knows for sure."

"I don't like that."

"Well, you can become a scientist and help figure it out."

". . ."

". . ."

"Dad, is God pretend?"

"Well, some people think he's pretend and other people
think he's real."

"How 'bout Jesus?"

"Well, he was probably real for sure, one way or the
other."

Pause. "Well, we might never know if God is real, 'cause
he's up in the sky. But we can figure out if Jesus is real, 'cause
he lived on the ground."

"You're way ahead of most people."

"Uh huh. Dad?"

"Yeah, Con."

"Would you still love me if all my boogers were squirtin'
out at you?" Pushes up the tip of his nose for maximum *verité*.

"No, Con, that'd pretty much tear it. Out you'd go."

"I bet not."

"Just try me."

Two tiny nasal exhales as he takes a quick inventory. He
shifts sideways in his seat and is asleep in three minutes.

Saint Philip to the Twin Cities, 226 miles roundtrip two
Fridays a month, and again on Sundays for the return. When
Friday afternoon is free of some asinine meeting, Jack can

make it to Becca's by dinnertime, eat and have Connor back to St. Philip by nine.

(612) 588-9085.

"It's me. He's asleep at the wheel. Send help."

"Hey, it was good to see you, Jack. Great kiss too, by the way."

"Yeah, Connor mentioned it. Doesn't miss a thing, that kid."

"Well it's hard to miss a 45-second pause in conversation, Jack."

"I guess. So what do you want?"

"You called me, Jack."

"That's not what I meant."

"Oh. That. So how was your day?"

"Yeah, I tried that one on the boy, too."

". . ."

". . ."

". . ."

"Sorry about being late tonight. I had another meeting about the fight song . . ."

"Jack, I'm not seeing anybody else, and I'm not a lesbian. I am a journalist, and I need to work. Wee Saint Philip is not the place for me. I just can't do it anymore. We've been through this."

"It isn't the place for me either, Becca. Yeah, you're right, I remember this tape loop. I'll let you go and just play it back in my head."

"I'm still hot for your bod."

Jack smiles a little. "What kind of thing is that to say? I'm supposed to be the horn dog in this relationship."

"You teach on Monday?"

"Two o'clock."

"Then bring Connor back Sunday night and *stay*."

"Don't you think that will confuse him a little? And yow, by the way."

"Can you recall the last time he was more confused than us? Sex on Sunday, yes or no."

"Let me get back to you."

"Liar."

"Harlot."

"Stud."

"Please, girl, I'm driving. I'm likely to hang a sudden U-turn at seventy-five."

"Hold on." Muffled conversation off-mike. "Oh, uh, Jack . . . my mom wants to know if you've been taking Connor to church Sunday mornings."

"Ask if she got the memo that Christianity has been canceled due to lack of interest."

"Jack."

"Becca."

"Jack, come on. She's concerned that he's only getting . . ."

". . . indoctrinated twice a month? Scared out of thinking for himself twice a month? You come on, Becca. Talk about conversations we've *had* before . . ."

"Not that we've ever finished one of them."

"True. Here's the end of one coming now, so don't blink. No, we're not going to church, this Sunday we're going to the Cottonwood River. If God's there we'll say hey."

" . . . "

" . . . "

"Mom wants to talk to you."

"Uh-oh, I'm going into a tunnel!! *Kccccccchhhh* . . ."

"You little *chickenshit*," she whispers.

Okay, now he's happy. He could hear her smiling as she hissed that through those spectacular teeth he was just sucking on an hour ago. "Oh dammit, all right. Tell her I will take him to King of Glory, but he sits right by me in the sermon, not in Sunday School with a Fable Funnel in his ear. Delmore's sermon'll put him off his feed for awhile. We'll hike in the afternoon and deprogram."

Mufflemuffle. "Not King of Glory, Jack. She wants you to take him to the Baptist church." Harsh background whisper, foreground sigh. "The *Southern* Baptist church."

"Oh that's rich. She might as well ask me to take him to the First Orthodox Druidic Temple. This is Saint *Philip*, Becca. Do I have to remind you what that means? One bar, one gas station, one church. King of Glory or nothing."

Muffle. "Well, she's not happy about that, but..."

"Hey, me neither! Perfect, no church. That was easy."

"I don't appreciate being in the middle here. Take him to King of Glory."

"Fine."

"I love you, Jack."

"Cool. Will you marry me?"

"Bye Jack."

"Becca?"

"Jack."

"Thanks for pretending Saint Philip's the only problem." Liar. Harlot.

"Bye Jack."

Jack decided to shift the Cottonwood hike to Saturday so on Sunday he and Connor could see to the reinforcement of God's self-esteem. *You are Most Glorious, Lord, we worship Your name, and no you don't look fat in that.* Seven months have flown since last Jack's great arse connected with a King of Glory pew. Why, that's just the amount of time since Becca left, he reckons. Fancy that.

And on Saturday, verily, it rains like hell. Sunday—the day of the original hike plan, remember—dawns bright and warm and clear, putting Jack in the most worshipful of all possible moods.

They sit pressed and silent in the back left pew, six empty pews between them and the nearest neighbors in front of them. That'll work out fine for the "Peace be with you" greet-yer-neighbor deal, thinks Jack. We can just wave.

Uh-huh. When that moment comes, and Reverend Delmore invites the assembled to turn to the persons seated around them and wish them Peace and Love, Helen Bettencourt turns with a huge smile and, aghast, finds no one behind her—and her with all this peace and love to give—pokes her husband, whispers in his ear, hits him when his eyes roll, drags him to his feet, and leads him by the elbow all the way back to vigorously Peace-be-with-you the Prodigal Kassels.

The church is pure country simplicity, a lovely white box with matching white pews, white pulpit and parishioners, regular glass in the windows, felt banners with block letters assuring those present that God is, in fact, love.

Jack's heard spectacular sermons in his thirty-nine years, sermons that have moved him deeply, that have made him think in new ways, that have challenged him to become the kind of a person he always knew he could be. He's even heard a few sermons that made him wish there *was* a God. This is no such sermon. Delmore seems nearer death each time he approaches the pulpit and nearer still as he steps down from it at the end of the address. The only drama in the message is the ever-present possibility that he will make it to his reward before the preposition at the end of a given sentence. Not that too many congregants would notice: of thirty-six people present, fourteen are men, leaving just twenty-two who could even *possibly* be listening. And of those twenty-two women, no fewer than nine are in a deep rapture of nodding throughout the message, eyes closed, hands crossed on the chest. Of the remaining thirteen, six are knitting (and nodding attentively, liars) and six are kept busy full-time poking their husbands or someone else's. Which leaves only Mrs. Geraldine Larsen, deaf as a hobby horse and therefore free to imagine a sermon of soul-rending magnificence. Such sermons have been delivered. Jack has heard some. Jesus delivered some. Lucian B. Delmore has not.

Jack envies the deaf in church.

Well, there was in fact that one moment of memorable content in this otherwise unmemorable morning, Jack recalls as they leave, when the pastor told the tale of the Christian (the "*KRISSST*–ee–inn," says Delmore) and the atheist who meet and discuss their respective worldviews:

> *And the Christian said, "When I die, if I am correct in my theology, I will go to a greater reward than I can imagine. If I am wrong, which I am NOT, I will have lived my life the best I could with the information I had. I will have treated others like I would wish to be treated, lived humbly, loved mercy, and praised a God of justice and forgiveness. What better way to live? What better way to die?"*

> *And the atheist reflected, "If I am correct in my theology, the universe is meaningless, Man arose from the slime, and there is no right or wrong. If I am wrong, I go to an eternity of unending misery." And lo, the scales fell from his eyes, he realized the hopelessness of his beliefs, and he accepted the Lord into . . ."*

"HOW DO YOU KNOW?"

"Oh my gosh, Dad, sit down."

"How do you KNOW that, Delmore? *Reverend* Delmore. How on Earth do you know that that is what an atheist would say?"

Oh now the men were listening, sure. The congregants were all turned around in the pews with looks ranging from horror to amusement to Aw-I-was-just-about-to-sneak-out-to-pee-and-now-this.

"How do you know he wouldn't find great satisfaction in having divined a truth hidden by two thousand years of potent mythologies . . ."

"Dr. Kassel!" The Reverend stepped away from the brink of demise for the moment. "Sit *down*, sir!"

High drama is always enhanced by small spaces, Connor noted to himself.

"I will not sit down! Answer my question! I could never get away with this level of protection from challenge in my classroom. You said something preposterous, now defend it! So I ask again: How do you know that is what an atheist would say?"

"Sir, I'll have you know this is a sermon published by the distinguished Calvary International Publ . . ."

"Might he instead challenge the Christian to read his own Book? To find the glaring inconsistencies and internal contradictions and rape and murder and genocide and slavery in it, all condoned by God? Might he not point out that the biography of Christ as imagined by the evangelists bears a striking resemblance in almost every major detail to the alleged life of Mithras, a Persian god some six hundred years older, who was born of a virgin on December 25th, healed the sick, performed miracles, was executed and entombed, only to rise on the third day and appear to his twelve disciples before ascending into Heaven to join his father? Might he point out that most Christians conveniently fail to 'live humbly and love mercy,' preferring instead to use their alleged divine knowledge to hate and divide and judge—us and them, us and them—all in the name of God, and to threaten with hellfire those who use their minds to discover the actual *truth* of who we are and what this glorious universe is really all about? To stand in the way of every major advance in our self-understanding from medicine to astronomy to biology to psychology, murdering hundreds of thousands who dared to think for themselves, who dared to question what was handed to them by their fearful, unschooled, backward ancestors? Might he have noted that evolution not only dispenses with the Creation story, but also with the concept of an immortal soul, since there was no single moment we became human, but rather a gradual series of minute changes, starkly evident in the fossil record despite see-no-evil Christian assertions to the contrary, so that the real division between us and the 'soulless animal' is non-existent?"

Pause . . . and with a lowered voice, almost beseeching, "Might he not have offered the suggestion that knowing the truth, even if disconcerting, is always, always better than a comfortable self-deception?"

Ah, that would have been great, thinks Jack, but once again it had taken place only in his mind—as on every previous churchbound, nonhiking, pointless Sunday. Chickenshit. Becca was right.

4

Job

The LORD said to Satan, "Have you considered my servant Job? There is no one like him on the earth, a blameless and upright man who fears God and turns away from evil."

Then Satan answered the LORD, "Does Job fear God for nothing? Have you not put a fence around him and his house and all that he has, on every side? You have blessed the work of his hands, and his possessions have increased in the land. But stretch out your hand now, and strike all that he has, and he will curse you to your face."

The LORD said to Satan, "Very well, all that he has is in your power."

Job 1: 8-12

And so it appears that, on a bet with the Devil, God said, "Take this, Job, and shove it."

Author unknown

552-MCGO

A dditional short-term emergency budget requests, academic year 2001-2002

- Cady Stanton hall cellar bracing reinforcement/jacking $ 372,000
- South walk flagstone repairs $ 11,000
- Hockey pitch weed treatment/aeration/reseeding $ 4,000
- University of Minnesota Raptor Center extension station $ 55,000
- Exploratory drilling/surveying for tunnel construction $ 120,000
- Replacement of (1) bookcase dehumidifier $ 3,200
- Repair of broken section of westside ("Jude's Leap") fence $ 8,700
- Admin Building recarpeting, levels 1-2-3 $ 22,000
- Goose poison (liver, brie, and smoked salmon flavors) $ 2,400
- Window replacements (7), Alexandria Library and Curie, $ 2,100
  pitchside

Dean Martin works on Sunday because no one else does. The silence is complete, the parking off the point of the wedge empty, and it turns every Monday into a Tuesday, which is just plain better. Friday, then, becomes Saturday, of course, and Saturday Sunday, so she goes to church then, on what others call Saturday, alone and happy, because of course no one else in the town of Sleepy Eye does the same. She arrives at work at five a.m. every day in time to enjoy the prairie dawn from her third floor window, lunches at nine-thirty, and (in the absence of the odd school song meeting) leaves by 2 p.m., missing whatever semblance of rush hour might run between Bernie's and Sleepy Eye. No one on campus has ever precisely figured out her schedule; she is simply never where it seems she should be, which works out very well indeed.

- Cady Stanton hall cellar bracing reinforcement/jacking $372,000

Good gravy. Well, that's non-negotiable, I suppose. Who'd
dare ask for that amount unless the sky were falling. And I'd
swear another step has disappeared this week. She prints [OK]
in the margin, reaches to switch on Yo Yo Ma's recording of
J.S. Bach Suite No. 1 for Unaccompanied Cello and pulls a
jerky stick out of her desktop canister.

　　Oh, Sunday, you are my sweet Number One.

　　• **South walk flagstone repairs**　　　　　　　　　$11,000

Glances out the window. I just came up the south walk. Looks
fine to me, Carl. [DEFERRED] To seal the deal, she leaves
a quick voicemail message in case his brain stem needs a
reminder.

　　• **Hockey pitch weed treatment/aeration/reseeding**　　$4,000
　　　　　　　　　　　　　　　　　　　　　　　[JUSTIFY THIS]

　　• **University of Minnesota Raptor Center extension station**　$55,000

In the margin is a Post-It with "Believing is Seeing!" embla-
zoned across the top and a note from Wanda Streamley,
president of the college. "Gennie dear," she writes, "this
sounds like a WONDERFUL opportunity to support our spiritual mission! Let's do fund this."

　　Now Genevieve Martin has known Wanda for seventeen
years, so she knows what to do: become the Wanda. Think
like a Wanda. See what the Wanda sees . . .

　　"University . . . of . . . . . Minnesota. . . . . . ."

　　A moment's pause—then it hits her: *Rapture* Center.

　　Tact is not a skill for which Dean Martin is well-known.
Tact is a needless grace when you get your way anyhow. But
Gennie Martin has developed an impressive ability to both
prevent making the college president appear foolish when
she makes this kind of error (daily) and then to actually make

Wanda feel she has gotten her way. No small feats. The U of M Raptor Center Station, a breeding, care, and observation facility for birds of prey, turns out to be something various schools are *applying* to host. Within an hour Dean Martin has written the crappiest possible host application and dropped an e-mail to Wanda expressing her *own* deep joy at the prospect of its success.

- **Exploratory drilling/surveying for tunnel construction**   **$120,000**

Certainly this would have been in the initial budget. A glance at the appropriate file confirms that it was. A quick, terse phone message to Gustafson and Son Construction ensures that nothing further will be double-billed, ever. Monday/Tuesday morning, in fact, it lands a fruit basket on her desk.

- **Replacement of (1) bookcase dehumidifier**   **$ 3,200**

Leonard, you disturbing little screwball. I am going to pour red pepper flakes into your water supply, don't think I won't. [LATIFAH: HAVE ED TAKE A LOOK AT THIS THING BEFORE WE JUST WRITE A CHECK.]

Yo Yo's on the third movement and Gennie's on her third jerky. Starting to get jerkymouth pretty darn bad.

- **Repair of broken section of westside ("Jude's Leap") fence**   **$ 8,700**

Who exactly are we keeping out? Rockclimbers? Cliff-dwelling prairie dogs? [NO]

- **Admin Building recarpeting, levels 1-2-3**   **$ 22,000**

Oh, that'd go over well, especially snuck in outside of the regular budget. [NO]

- **Goose poison (liver, brie, and smoked salmon flavors)**   **$ 2,400**

What the hell? Brie? Is the $2,400 to serve it French-style? Jesus GOD this place. [OK]

- **Window replacements (7), Alexandria Library and Curie,**   **$ 2,100**
  pitchside

Well, that's Katie Jackson, the freshman hockey studette, I suppose, putting her shoulders into it. Coach Phaire says they've got a shot at the tournament title this year. We'll buy her a few windows. [OK]

Now that's $700,400 whittled down to $476,500. A fine morning's work, with Mr. Ma still on the first suite.

Oh, wait a minute.

- **Repair of broken section of westside ("Jude's Leap") fence**   **$ 8,700**

I see. The fence is to keep *us* from falling *off*. [DO IT FOR HALF]

Gennie Martin stretches and does her cocky-budgetcutter-all-alone-in-the-buildin' strut to the restroom to brush her teeth.

"Good afternoon, sisters and brothers!"

A delighted Wanda opens another Tuesday morning all-campus faculty meeting. Members of the faculty, crammed into a small theater-in-the-round in the basement of Hildegard Hall, work hard to keep their own enthusiasm in check. Various campus buzzers suggest this meeting might be a tad intense, for President Streamley has promised a "major policy address" regarding the growing frustration over faculty salaries, frozen for three years running.

She beams the murmuring assemblage into silence, then introduces the opening prayer.

"Let us begin our time together by turning our gaze westward to greet the rising sun as it begins its journey across the heavens." The members of the faculty shuffle to face a total of seven directions in the windowless room before turning at last to see Wanda, eyes closed in blissful contemplation, facing true North. All turn to join her as Thing One and Thing Two begin an unaccompanied hymnlet of their own composition, sung in "Spanish Eyes" parallel thirds:

> *Sun and moon and glorious stars*
> *Winds of Pluto, frost of Mars*
> *Saturn with its fiery rings*
> *Watching over everything*
> *Help to make our futures bright*
> *Constellations of the night.*

In an uncommon and unplanned display of unity, the faculties of Theology, Astronomy, Poetry, and Music emit simultaneous shudders and soft, injured moans.

Last month's minutes are approved on a head-nod vote, minor issues and announcements dismissed indifferently.

Tina-something announces impending auditions for what she calls a "feminist reimagining" of the play *A Man for All Seasons*. All characters, she says with eyes the size of personhole covers, are being rewritten as women. "Imagine the empowerment!"

The room, all a-nod, imagines.

And the moment arrives. President Streamley rises again, redolent in a muu-muu of many, many colors, and glides beaming to the podium. Wanda is honestly, sincerely, absolutely filled with joy to be here, regardless of where "here" is or who or what stands before her. The college trustees are transfixed by her every word; alumnæ praise her, and the campus sisters speak of her as the living embodiment of the Mother of God. Our Lady of Many Colors. In short, those whose devotion to the president actually matters are deeply devoted to her.

The faculty is not.

To Dean Martin, Wanda is simply a force to be reckoned with. President Streamley has her foot on the accelerator of the college, shooting down the fast lane, waving elatedly at slack-jawed passersby and cops scrambling for their keys. All is jubilation so long as the freeway stays straight and clear and Wanda doesn't step out the car door to hug somebody. It is Dean Martin's job to ensure that no such thing happens. This occasionally entails distracting Wanda with a shiny object so the Dean can grab the steering wheel herself for a moment. She will not deny the power and effectiveness of Wanda's life force, properly channeled, but neither will she allow the crash to occur.

Genevieve loves dear old Wanda and she loves the college. And she lives every day in the hope that their needs will not collide, yet certain in the knowledge that if they ever do, and Wanda grabs that steering wheel a tad too tightly, Dean Genevieve Martin will not hesitate to open the driver's door herself and give a quick but loving shove. It is the college, and the protection of the college, that motivates the Dean's every thought and action. So long as Wanda's lucky magic moves it forward, Dean Martin will willingly copilot.

The crowd stills and the President remains silent, scanning the room like a searchlight of pure delight.

"My dear family, my good sisters and brothers of Saint Bernadette's, I have been asked to address the issue of faculty salaries and am proud and honored to do so today." Silent beams of satisfaction. "But as I prepared my remarks, it occurred to me that words alone . . ."

"Oh God," whispers Leslie. "Here it comes."

Jaws slacken. Expectations dim.

"... are insufficient to convey my deep affection for each of you and my appreciation for all that you do for this college—and to communicate my devoted intention to bring us all to agreement and to move forward to a new day of spiritual rebirth. And so, in lieu of my planned remarks, I will perform an interpretive dance to the indescribable music of Yanni."

Something begins to flow from hidden speakers, a hash of synthesized strings and rhythmic radial thrum. Bob Frapples lets out an involuntary hoot. But Wanda, alone in a fog of rapture, moves into the center circle and begins a sort of Dance of the Seven Veils, gesturing at the crowd, retreating, advancing, spinning and spinning. Minutes pass, Yanni does his Yanni-thing. Wanda's expression flashes from brow knitted concern to stalwart determination to a sudden breakthrough of joy, arms waving, torso undulating madly, at which point Marilyn Sherwood-Forrest's poodle shoots under Marilyn's chair with a yipe. President Streamley, it should be noted, is a dancer only inasmuch as she does in fact dance, but there are a few admittedly interesting moments when certain gestures, somehow expressive of difficult budgetary intangibles, flicker by. As the music builds to a climax that can only be described as eventual, Wanda spins into a tight circle and collapses to the floor. Several people burst into applause, more than enough to maintain Wanda's rapture. She rises, bows low, and exits the circle, the floor, the room.

A full minute ticks away before the faculty realizes the meeting is over. Slowly they begin to stand and look around, muttering to shrugging companions, then gradually filter out of the room in rumpled clumps. Marilyn babytalks her trembling pooch into the open and out the door. Jack remains staring, glued to his seat, as the crowd thins around him. Somehow the muu-muu is still spinning, the music still playing. The discussion is still underway.

It takes more than a few shoulder taps before Brian manages to break the spell. He leans to Jack and whispers, "Oh, now I get it. I was a little confused when she got to the part about waving your arms around, but the spin at the end brought it all together."

Jack, still in a trance of disbelief, continues to stare at the empty floor.

"Brian," he mutters. "Why exactly are you here?"

"Faculty meeting, Jack. I'm on the faculty. Plus you can't beat the floor show."

Jack snaps out of it and turns earnestly to Brian. "No, I mean why are you *here*, why are you at Saint Bernie's? You're a hell of a sociologist. Why in the name of God are you at a college where the president responds to faculty demands with choreography—*and the faculty applauds and leaves!*"

"Well, as you know, I am not here in the name of God. I am here because I cannot find my résumé."

"I'm serious for once," says Jack. They exit into bright sunlight, walking slowly. "That was a defining moment for me in there, somehow. Brian, I hear tell of a world where questions are answered with *answers*—and when something weird happens people stand up and say 'Hey wait a minute! That was *weird!*'" He stops walking and grabs Brian's lapels. "Take me to that place. Take me there, Brian."

"Oh get off me," Brian says, sweeping Jack's hands away with a grin. "If you're so miserable, get your résumé out there. Somebody'll . . ."

"Aack!" Jack staggers backward, clutching his chest. "You did not say that, Brian, did you? *Jesus!* My résumé IS out there, sitting in a slush pile in every philosophy department at every level school in the country, eleven in Canada and one in the Cayman Islands! I've got them pasted up in every stall of the men's room at Macy's. Biplanes rain them down on think tanks and coffee houses in the great cities of the Eastern seaboard." He sighs hard and starts walking again. "It's just that everybody's basic philosophical needs are being met and overmet . . . you're a sociologist, haven't you read *any* of Reynolds? There're an awful lot of peripatetic philosophers now—but nowadays that just means they're walkin' around. My new television cable package includes The Philosophy Channel and 'A&E II: Angst & Existentialism.' Unemployed philosophers are working up personas and wrestling each other on Pay-Per-View! I saw The Mad Materialist absolutely *slaughter* The Logical Positivist last night. What a farce."

"What's your point?"

"Well, I think it was fixed. Mad Mat told LP this folding chair wasn't really there, see, and then he hit him with it."

"The larger point, Jack."

"Oh, that." Jack pinches the bridge of his nose. "I'm *afraid*, Brian. I'm afraid of staying here any longer. I'm losing my grip. I've gotta get some real students, a real *challenge*. I need some excitement. I need some *conflict.*" He stops and faces Brian. "I wanna hear someone other than Leslie Erickson Mitchell-Robbins Moore actually disagree intelligently, then work something out to a conclusion. I need to *think*—and the longer I stay here the more I feel that ability slipping away. This is not a thinking place, Brian, did you notice? It's not a college any more than the thing it's sitting on is a butte. Esther Kester had it right: St. Bernie's is one big bluff, but nobody here has the nerve or the brains to call the bluff. Am I right, or am I missing something?"

"..."

"Brian!"

"Oh, I'm sorry, were you talking to me?"

"You know what somebody said in my Epistemology seminar this morning?"

"Yes I do."

"We're dealing with theories of knowledge, doing Berkeley's 'objective existence in the eye of God' thing and Russell's notions of our indirect experience of the world and she raised her hand. Ten years ago, even eight years ago, I might have brightened to the possibilities in that moment. Now I darken. She looked at me, eyes half closed, and asked 'How am I going to use this in my life?'"

"An optimist would say her eyes were half open."

"Exactly. All I could do was tell the Newton story."

"Fig?"

"Isaac. A tutoring pupil asked him that precise question, and Newton had this sudden reaction, laughing audibly for the first time in his life. Got to laughing so uncontrollably he had trouble breathing and had to stand and motion the student out of the house."

"Newton, reaction, motion. I get it."

"Will you focus, goddammit. Anyway, I told the story to make the case that knowledge is its own reward, and do you know what she said?"

"How does that story make that case? That story doesn't prove anything except that Newton was a little screwy."

"No, that was Archimedes. Anyway, I provided context. And do you know what she said?"

"Yes I do."

"She said, 'And how am I going to use that *story* in my life?' And feminist pedagogy tells me what I'm supposed to say to that, doesn't it: 'Good point. Good question. Terrific insight . . . ' and then I'm supposed ask if anyone else in the room can help her find an answer, since I am only 'the guide on the side, not the sage on the stage.'"

"So you interested in drinking like a poet?"

"It's eleven-thirty in the morning, Brian."

"Your point was?"

Jack has no idea what his point was. "Cascade at four."

He watches Brian shuffle away toward Cady Stanton, then drags himself to Bronte and through two insufferable hours of Philosophy of Ethics, thinking only of beer.

At precisely four o'clock, wondering why he hadn't said three, Jack walks through the door of the Guinness Cascade with a sigh of relief. Compared to the mumblings of his Ethics class, the enthusiastic bell of the aging pinball machine sounds like Socratic discourse to Jack. Ding ding ding. Deep stuff.

Brian, sitting wrinkled and spent in a rear booth, watching his first pint cascade, looks up.

"Are you better company now, Kassel?"

"I am exactly as good as I was, thank you."

"Oh. That's too bad. I might stay anyway."

Jack drops his jacket on the bench and walks to the bar for a Black and Tan. By the time he returns and slides into the booth he has a nasty comeback ready.

"So how's your sabbatical application going, there, Brian?" A cheap shot, but hey.

"Asshole."

"Oh, I'm sorry. I didn't know." Like hell. Jack just wants a friend down in the hole with him. He knows the committee just nixed Brian's application, and he knows why.

Jack pauses. "So . . . ya wanna talk about it?"

"My project was 'insufficiently feminist in its perspectives.' They canned it."

Jack feigns surprise. "Oh. I'm sorry." He slaps the table. "So, Brian! Why don't you 'get your résumé out there'?"

"My, my, but we're the peevish little philosopher today. You think *you've* been here a long time? I came in '82. That's nineteen years in a place that slowly dulls every edge you came in with. I'm not employable anywhere else anymore. You got maybe three years before it's true for you, too." He lifts his glass off the table and swirls the contents, watching the head build. "I read your piece on Jeremy Bentham."

"Oh, you little *prick.*"

"Oh come on, admit it. That's not the way you were writing when you got here. Twelve years in the Land of the Headbobbers seriously screws your ability to think and communicate. You gotta sharpen your mind on the opposition or it goes flabby, and Jack, that was a flabby piece."

"It was published, thank you! And that's such a male statement, anyway, 'sharpen your mind on the opposition' indeed."

"It was published in *The Thinker's Forum*, Jack! Come on. That's the *People Magazine* of humanities and you know it. The fact that you'd even pretend otherwise proves my point."

Steady thunk of darts missing a dartboard.

"And your point was?"

Brian leans in, putting an index finger and a cloud of beer breath in Jack's face. "You know who you remind me of?"

"Yes I do."

"You are Brian Finnegan circa 1993. I hit the same wall then that you're hitting now—and you know what I did? Nothing. Jack, drink that beer, then drink another one, then walk home and plan your escape. 'Macy's men's room' is fine schtik, but you've gotta get serious, not just jaded-chic. And you *know* how I love jaded-chic."

Jack knows. He adds one beer to Brian's suggestion and trudges home to bed.

5

The Parson's Prologue

A priest is a man who is called Father by everyone
except his own children, who are obliged to call him
Uncle.

Italian saying

Delivered-To: postmaster@CSB.mail-stphil
Date: Wed, 3 Oct 2001 06:59:15 -0500
From: ministry@sacredheart.org
To: kasseljj@stbernie.edu
X-Lotus-FromDomain: CSB
Subject: attach
Mime-Version: 1.0
Status: U

Dear Dr. Kassel:

Please help. I'm a frightened young man with no place to
turn. I just found out I'm pregnant and I don't know who
the mother is. Oh, stop it, you whining ninny! Be a man!
Be two! Be still my beating heart, for an attractive orangutan has just wistfully entered the dance floor! Now is
my chance! Where is that damn banana? Oh, I guess THIS
will do! Look at that specimen, his orange hair flowing in
the air conditioning with every hideously awkward movement, torturing every fiber of my tormented soul until. . . .
but wait! I reveal too much!

.

.

.

www.sacredheartoakland.org

_____

"What the . . ." Jack blinks at the screen, then clicks on the
website button.

```
┌─────────────────────────────────────────┐
│  Father Scott Francis Siberell welcomes you to │
│     🐾 Sacred Heart Parish 🐾              │
│            Oakland California              │
│            (510) 459-1092                  │
└─────────────────────────────────────────┘
```

THIS WEEK'S MASS ✝   ✝ DEVOTIONAL

MESSAGE FROM FATHER SCOTT! ✝   ✝ NEWS FROM THE HOLY FATHER

VISITATION WATCH ✝   ✝ PRAYER REQUESTS

CONTACT US!

Jack nearly sprays the screen with a mouthful of coffee. He grabs the phone and dials caffeinatedly.

A pastoral baritone answers. "This is Father Siberell. How may I help you?"

"You may not hump me at all, thank you, but I *will* have that banana."

"JJ! What took you, I sent that e-mail six minutes ago."

"Look, we'll riff in a minute. Answers first."

"What . . . oh, the orangutan? That's all over. We're still friendly, for the kids' sake."

"Scott, you're a *priest. You are a priest!!*"

"Prove it."

"'Father Scott Francis Siberell welcomes me to Sacred Heart Parish.' So which is this, practical joke or scam?"

"Now watch yourself, atheist-boy. I know some people. One phone call and your car has God-shit on the windshield. Just try to get *that* off."

How ironic. Thirty seconds on the phone with Scott Siberell makes him feel *more* sane. Six years have passed since their paths last crossed and nineteen since they shared a dorm room at Berkeley. Scott lives in five dimensions, spinning like a thrown mower blade through one unsuspecting tableau after another. The thrill has always been the thing for Scott—

which, to Jack, would seem to make the Roman collar more than a tad tight.

"Okay then, you were called to the priesthood by conscience. The next question is where you shoplifted a conscience."

"Brrrrring. 'Yeah, hey Jehovah. Scott. Bombs away, big guy.'"

"Uh huh. Real altar-talk there, Father. Now what the hell is going on?"

"Let's save it for Friday night when I get to town."

"Get to . . . What? Get to *what* town? Are you coming through the Twin Cities?"

"Saint Philip, JJ! Quarter to four this Friday I land in Minneapolis, you pick me up at the airport and drive me to your couch in Saint Philip where I'll sleep the night before my Saturday morning interview at your very own St. Bernie's. Next time you pass your campus chapel, see if you don't catch a whiff of dead priest."

Oh, *right*, thinks Jack. Latifah bursting into the song meeting. Father Edmund Hillerman's ancient body had indeed followed his mind to eternal rest at last—and the college put an immediate announcement out to seminaries and parishes nationwide, including, apparently, Sacred Heart of Oakland, present venue of Scott 'Francis' Siberell.

Too much too fast. Jack is sitting ten squares back, head spinning. "I don't believe this. Tell me this is an elaborate gag."

"Oh I'll never tell."

Jack sighs, then chuckles in familiar surrender. "All right. Sure, fine, I'll play along. I'll get you at the gate. Scott . . . just in case this is for real, I hope you know you'll never get this job. You're not gonna strike them as Saint Bernie's material—and that's a compliment. But I suppose it'll be fun to show you around my corner of hell."

"I'll get the job, all right, my Nubian love-lynx. Too long

have you been away from my charms." Jack hears that broad smile. "I get what I go for."

Scott does have a talent for getting what he wants, Jack well knows, and what he wants is generally the least gettable thing in view—which is precisely why Scott wants it. The realization sweeps over Jack that the Wedge is about to encounter something for which it is wholly unprepared.

What *fun*.

When Friday afternoon arrives, Jack is standing at Gate 57 with pink Mylar balloons that say "Happy Bat Mitzvah." A hundred passengers deplane and stare at him lovelessly before Scott steps off the jetway at last, in full priestly garb, grinning widely. Definitely older. He walks directly to Jack, embraces him, then engages him in a passionate simulation of a French kiss that few in the gate area will ever forget. Try though they may.

In 30 minutes they are coursing through farmland. The three-hour ride to Saint Philip is more like their early twenties with every mile, Jack as straight man again and Scott as Scott. Just outside of Rockford, Jack decides to start the long, probably futile process of mining for straight answers.

"So do I want to know why you are a priest, or do I want more riff?"

"I do think you want an answer, Jack, which would usually send me the other direction, but I'm tuckered out. I became a priest for the same reason I joined the Marines."

"You were in the Marines!?"

"Still in the Reserves now, technically. Chaplain, you know. I mostly do confessions by phone now to fulfill my gig. And I joined the Marines for the same reason I streaked that Oakland A's game and did competition motocross at the age of nine and mainlined heroin only *after* Nancy Reagan said no."

"You became a priest and did heroin for the same reason. I can't wait."

Jack knows a lot about Scott, but nothing that seems to explain what brings him to Saint Bernie's. Scott is a hilarious

comic dissector of life and a brilliant dramatic actor with some
serious off-Broadway credits. He hates all seafood. He has a
longstanding schoolboy crush on Ally Sheedy. He is a positively psychotic thrillseeker. He decorates every square inch
of his living space in black and white with a single touch of
red. He reads philosophy like most people read cereal boxes
and has a bone-crushing intellect. And, in the nineteen years
Jack has known him, he has displayed not the slightest positive interest in religion or spirituality except as lush comic
fodder. So the question remains.

"Okay, Jack, this takes a few steps, so try to stay awake.
Also because you're driving."

"Uh huh."

"Remember your first solid food?"

Jack looks over, amused.

"Okay, you don't remember, but you can guess. Strained
carrots or something, right?"

"Or something."

"And it's nasty. You've had breast milk for a year, high-
quality nuzzle-time, and now this."

"Nasty."

"Right. Until you get used to it. Then it's the best solid
food you've ever had."

"Well, sure. It was . . ."

". . . the only solid food, exactly my point. So it's the best.
Until you have something else the next day, maybe strained
peas."

"This is riveting. Wake me up at age six."

"And the world of food is divided in two. Peas and carrots. You like one better than the other, so one becomes The
Best Damn Food on Earth and the other The Worst. Then
day three, green beans, and things are getting complex. By
the time you're two, you're insisting on *that* cookie, Mommy,
no not that one, *that* one, and *those* noodles, the bendy ones
not the straight ones. At four you have your first hamburger

and it's the best fucking burger you've ever had. Until you have a better one, and eventually you know you like them grilled, not fried, and medium-well, with *Dijon* mustard and dill pickles and Vidalia onions on a bun that is not stale and has no damn seeds. And then you discover actual steak, and that's a whole new area of likes and dislikes and by the time you're thirty it's duck in that particular plum sauce they can only do right at Narsai's, not the one in Berkeley, the one in Kensington, dammit, and you can only afford it once a year but every year there you are, on your birthday, different date but the same duck, and the same wine, what was it, Domaine of the Romulans, '79 . . ."

"It's Domaine de la Romanee-Conti La Tache. And '78, not '79."

"Exactly, the '78 Romulan Candy My Tush—when you could afford it, which was about twice ever. And why the '78 instead of '79, Jack?"

"There's a huge difference! The '78 has that incredibly long finish, and there's a . . ."

"There's a blah blah blah blah blah, I know, I don't care. But *you do*, and that's my point. There is a difference, you know the difference, you have a preference. And boom, in half a lifetime you go from carrots-yucky-peas-yummy to 'oh, no, Monsieur, zee '78 she ees *much* prefaired to zee '79.' People who haven't taken the same path from strained peas to strained grapes think you're a pretentious geek. They just don't get the difference. But you've experienced that path, so you can feel the joy and reality of the difference between '78 and '79. And you can't go back to the thrill of the peas."

"Oh. I see where we're going."

"*Pfft.* Since when. Now what's beyond that particular '78 bottle of hooch?"

"Well, there's nothing beyond it, as far as I'm concerned."

"Okay, the '78 Romanee-whatever is the ultimate for you. And it still does it for you, every year?"

"You think I've had a $115 bottle of wine since I started teaching? That was student loan money, my friend. Pell Grant."

"Ew. Okay, different approach. Remember the first time you read Hume?"

"Sure. 'Of Miracles,' I think."

"And you liked it."

"Like finding a long-lost brother who farts in the same key." Jack glances over at Scott, sees the collar, the crow's feet, the graying temples, and suddenly wants to call back the fart reference. No matter what's going on, things are certainly not as they were.

"Lovely simile. And did you read any more Hume?"

Jack knows very well that people who ask questions they already know the answers to are laying mines. Lawyers. Teachers. Scott. "Yes, I read more. Went at it like a crackhead."

"Well, like a Humehead, no different. And what was that like?"

"You know how I love Hume. It's like having an 18th century Woody Allen walk you through the human head."

"You and the witty similes today, you droll bastard! But reading Hume was never *quite* like that first Hume again, right?"

"Well of course not, not exactly. I kind of knew what to expect after the first few times. Still always great, though."

"Uh huh. And have you read everything of his now?"

Jack ponders. "Yeah, I think so. Last year I realized I had skipped 'Of Greatness of Mind' from the *Treatise*, so I picked that up. I'm pretty sure that's the last of it."

"So no more new Hume for you."

"Right."

"And that feels how?"

Jack takes a beat. Frowns. How *does* that feel. Never thought about it before. No more new Hume. And Hume's not writing much anymore these days. That discovery is all in the past.

"Reread all you want, JJ, but there's no more new Hume."

"Okay, thanks dickweed, now I'm depressed. Is there a point here?"

"No no, not yet big fella, one more step to take. Sex. Remember the first time?"

"Gosh lemme think yes."

"Who was it?"

"Your mother. Oh no, wait, that was last week. Okay, Keely Larsen."

"And every time you think of sex, or have sex, there's a little Keely Larsen in there somewhere, right? And every time you think of Keely Larsen, even twenty years later, you recall that certain wa-*chung* you have never quite felt since."

"Okay."

"'Yes, Father Siberell,' you say. Not 'okay.'"

"Yes, Father. I feel wa-*chung* for Keely Larsen and never quite since."

"So?"

"Did I miss something?"

Scott leans over meaningfully. "I became a priest to get back the wa-*chung*."

"Oh, I see. What?"

"When you're a teenager, sex is forbidden. It will screw up your life. As a result, wa-*CHUNG*, am I right?"

"You are hereby prohibited from talking to my son."

"Forbidden fruit. Once you're an adult, not nearly as fun, then married sex, well, squeak-squeak-squeak, *huuuunhhh*, ni-nite."

"Divorced sex is actually pretty good, I can vouch."

"*Now* you're getting it."

"As a matter of fact, yes I am."

"Well, when you're a priest, it ain't just Mom and Dad.

God *Himself* is telling you to knock it off. The thrill is back, Jack."

"You became a priest for the sex. What would your mother say?"

"My mother is dead, thank you."

"Well what would she say if she were alive?"

"She'd say 'AAAAAAHHHHH!!!! GET ME OUT OF THIS BOX!!!!' But you miss my point. It is not just the sex. It's the wa-*chung*, Jack. I live in search of the ever-evasive wa-*chung*. Thrill. Newness. Felt reality, living-in-the-moment, not living every moment filtered through a thousand past ones. It is a drug, and not exactly a drug of choice."

"The exceedingly rare rubythroated rufflecrested wa-*chung*."

"Not just rare, Jack. Endangered. Decreasing in population. That's the horror of it. For you it's wine and philosophy; for me it's Life Itself. Aliveness, my friend—a much more dangerous passion to get tired of. No new Hume, no wine beyond the '78, that's a drag, sure. But I've developed a highly discriminating palate for the actual experience of Life." He's looking hard at Jack for clues of comprehension. "Think about that, Dr. Kassel. What do you do when you've exhausted *that* spectrum?" He turns to stare out the window. "I don't just need another thrill, I need a *greater* one, Jack, ever greater, more refined, more complex and original. Once you've done what I've done, you can never go back to the peas and carrots of life as usual. And you start to wonder what's left."

"Have you tried bungee-jumping?"

Scott *pffts*. "See, that's the kind of amateurish question that shows that you can't *begin* to understand what I'm talking about. No offense. And yes, I just tried it last month. Twelve mothergrabbin' bucks. What a *scam* that is."

"Rollercoasters?"

"Jack, you're embarrassing yourself. *Maybe* leaving the platform on a downhill rollercoaster and hearing someone on an open mic yell, 'Oh God, we forgot to put half the wheels on and DAMN we forgot to remove that pile of blasting caps from the tracks! The priest and that axe-murderer sitting next to him are gonna die!' *Maybe* then. But after that, what?"

"All right, now I get the Marines thing too."

"Oh you wish. I joined the Marines so I could dramatically 'come out' to my platoon in the middle of a boot camp parade ground drill." He smiles, remembering the general shit storm of confusion that followed. He recanted halfway through the discharge process, then accepted a quick, puzzled transfer to Reserves.

"I didn't know you were gay."

Scott sighs. "Please follow the bouncing ball, J. The professorial life has dulled your edge. I happen not to be gay— unless and until it becomes cutting edge again." Disgusted exhalation. "It is *so* not cutting edge lately."

"What about skydiving?"

A quick, high voltage pulse rips through Scott's expression, the sure sign of a hit nerve. "Don't even *say* that." He inhales and holds it, then blows out. "Okay, so you're on to something there." He looks out over the deepening purple landscape. "I will admit that skydiving, high-altitude skydiving . . . yes, there is still *skydiving*. Skydiving would get my juices flowing hard."

"So skydive."

Scott looks over with an expression of pity and mild contempt. "Jack, you are so. . . . you are so *Jack*. I must never, ever jump from a plane. Not because I'm afraid of dying— although I *am*, of course . . ."

"You, afraid of dying? Please."

"Terrified, sure. I mean think about it: oblivion must be the ultimate boredom, don't you figure? The opposite, in fact, of skydiving, which *has* to be life brought to the present in the most intense way possible."

Jack is regaining his old ability to wait for Scott to spin out a thread without help from the studio audience.

"No Jack, the fear as I fall out of that plane . . ." He closes his eyes a moment and enjoys the image. "The fear would not be of landing ahead of schedule. It would be a fear of the next morning, waking up with life's ultimate, unsurpassable thrill behind me. Sure, I could jump again, but we've just been down that road with sex and philosophy, haven't we? Every intensely original experience is followed by a parade of pale, drooling imitations wearing T-shirts that say 'The Guy at the Front of the Parade Got to Be a Real Experience and All I Got was this Lousy T-Shirt.' So no, no skydiving."

They go silent for awhile, and Jack stares out at the black horizon ahead. He catches sight of a trio of radio towers against the darkening sky, red lights blinking in a neat pattern—the left two, then the right one; the outside two, then the inside one; right two, left one; outside two, inside one.

When Jack was a kid his dad would ask him if he knew what the towers were for. No Dad, he'd always say. What are they for.

"To hold up the red lights so airplanes don't run into the towers."

After the first time Jack always knew it was a setup, but he always lied and said no I don't know, what are they for, because he loved his dad.

Jack and Scott drive in muffled thrum for a good ten minutes.

Once they arrive in St. Philip, Jack knows, there'll be so much new material for riffing that the obvious remaining question might never get an answer. He opens his mouth to ask it just as the spotted buck flashes into the headlights. Jack pulls hard at the wheel, veers in front of an oncoming van—first car in five minutes, of course, he manages to think—which swerves and corrects, tires screaming, as all four wheels of Jack's car go airborne over the side. Oh, the sun hasn't quite set, he notices from his new altitude. The wheels find soybeans and the car bumps and lurches, ripping a one-eighty through the crop as it comes to rest.

True silence.

Scott turns to Jack, smiling. "Jack, *thanks.*" Pats his arm. "That was so *sweet* of you."

"Good morning, Dr. Kassel."

Jack squints hard out of early-morning habit, then realizes the room is completely dark, with the sole exception of three red fives on the clock.

"Who the hell is this?" Jack has no special affection for pre-dawn phone calls, especially on Saturday.

"I'm the byline on page three. Bye bye."

Ex-wives. How does Mickey Rooney get any sleep. Jack pulls on a robe and shuffles to the porch, grabs the paper and bangs the screen door for spite.

"Hey-ZEUS! Some people have interviews today, ya damn hick." It's the couch. A light clicks on and Scott sits up. "Oh, I get it. Milkin' time, eh Jed?"

"Becca got a byline that isn't behind the classifieds, so she reached across Dirk and gave me a call." Jack drops into the recliner and snaps the paper open.

Wisconsin School Board Rejects Evolution

By Rebecca Kassel • Minneapolis *Ledger-Domain* Staff Writer
Saturday, Oct. 6, 2001; Page A3

MADISON, WI–The Wisconsin Board of Education rejected evolution as a scientific principle today, dealing a victory to religious conservatives who are increasingly challenging science education in U.S.

schools. The 10-member board, ignoring pleas by educators and established scientists, voted 7 to 3 to embrace new standards for science curricula that eliminate the teaching of evolution.

Son of a *bitch*. There is just no end to this stupidity. And Wisconsin, that's just way too close to home.

"What is it?"

"End of the damn world."

"Cool. Oh, ya know, I think I get raptured up first. If you hear brass, grab on to my belt."

Wisconsin joins Louisiana, Kansas, Mississippi, Alabama, Oklahoma, Texas, Tennessee, and North and South Carolina for a total of ten states that have now removed biological evolution from their curricula. Four of the ten have additionally moved to institute the teaching of the Biblical Creation story in its place.

"Evolution has been removed," board member Evelyn Simmons, who opposed the new standard, said in a packed conference room at the State Capitol. "Instead of Wisconsin's curriculum having more and more credibility, it will have less and less. One hundred and forty years of science in a dozen disciplines has provided a complete foundation of concrete evidence for the fact of evolution. It is as firmly established as the Earth's orbit of the Sun. Arguments to the contrary rely on clear and outrageous distortions of fact."

Okay, that's my girl. Reason speaks first.

Prior to Friday's vote, the presidents and chancellors of Wisconsin's public universities wrote a letter saying that the new standards "will set Wisconsin back a century. There is no knowledge more important or more exciting that we can give our children than an understanding of our own origins and development as human beings. Evolution also provides the essential perspective that all life on Earth is directly related, a view that has staggering implications for our treatment of the environment and of our fellow creatures."

Wisconsin is the first non-"Bible Belt" state in the current reactionary wave to ban the teaching of evolution.

Oh sweet. How'd she get "reactionary" past her editors? Now I'm getting all tingly.

"I'm so excited," said Phyllis Rolley, mother of three school-aged Wisconsinites. "All that talk of evolution was causing my oldest to ask a lot of uncomfortable questions about Scripture. I believe the Board saved the souls of my kids, I really do."

Can't have those uncomfortable questions, can we? Becca, this is a first-rate piece of pinko journalism.

Many religious groups have argued that evolution cannot be proven, and some feel that evolution is not in accordance with Biblical teachings regarding the origins of life. Teaching evolution misleads students, said Joshua Turner, director of the Creation Association of Mid-America, which helped write Wisconsin's curriculum proposal. "It's deception," Turner said prior to the vote. "You can't go into the laboratory or the field and make the first fish. When you tell students that science has determined [evolution to be true], you're deceiving them."

Wisconsin Gov. Phil Graves (D) warned board members not to adopt the anti-evolution curricula, and has said he would support an effort to abolish the Board of Education.

"Excuse me while I fall on my sword," Jack says, tossing the section to Scott as he walks into the kitchen.

Scott reads in uncharacteristic silence. "Oh." He lowers the paper. "Well relax. This'll turn around. Stuff like this goes in cycles. Always turns around."

Jack opens the refrigerator door and leans heavily against it, staring at the bright bulb. He closes his eyes tightly and still sees it, the impression of light burning in the darkness. Twenty years fall away, and Jack is looking into a different refrigerator, much smaller. Nothing but beer and ketchup.

"Just imagine that, Jack! Once in my life, just once if I could deliver a line like that, God *damn!*" Jack follows the voice around the corner to find a very different Scott Siberell, younger by half, who looks up. "Find me a better line than that anywhere, J."

"Uh . . . what line again?"

Scott looks amused. "Hello, JJ, keep it in focus here! Huxley, Thomas Huxley, reads Darwin's theory for the first time and says 'How extremely stupid of me not to have thought of that.' One time in my life I'd like to say something like that. So simple and honest it's profound."

"Oh, Huxley, sure. A great line."

"The biggest question of them all, sitting there for thousands of years. Darwin finally figures out the mechanism of natural selection, boom, right on the mark—*here's where we came from, and here's how it happened*"—Scott is rattling at light speed, gesturing wildly with each word, as if Jack needs convincing—"and it's so obviously the right answer that Huxley thwacks himself on the forehead and says that great thing." His expression goes puzzled. "Hey, where's the beer?"

"Oh, your beer. Right." Jack turns back to the kitchen in a daze.

It was a great line, Jack remembers. And a great time, the long nights sprawled on their dorm room floor amid piles of open books, the two of them getting up to pace intensely, smoking like camels, shouting over each other like pork belly traders as they try to shred each other's arguments, getting riled up in that pretentious undergrad way, playing out every last wrinkle of the Theory—and when the smoke cleared, and the Theory still stood there, gleaming like polished chrome, they'd hoot like hell and pound the floor with their fists. Natural and gorgeous and elegant and simple and true. What a *sexy* thing, he'd always think, getting lost in the reverie of realization. Takes the complexity of life on Earth and snaps it into sharp and stunning focus with a CRACK that sends ducks skyward and caribou stampeding.

Jack opens the refrigerator door again and peers in. "We drinking Bud or Coors today?" he yells to Scott.

"Your call, J, it's your flashback."

True enough. He stares again into the bright bulb.

"Just the thought of it gets me all tingly," Scott continues from the next room. "Not too many things like that, JJ. Damn thing flings itself across your lap, says *Truth is beauty, babe, and here's real beauty. Go ahead, deny it*, and you just can't. Well *I* can't."

Jack closes his eyes tight. I hear you. Euclid is that kind of beautiful. Copernicus. Newton. Ravel when he's simple, Bach when he's not. I suck them up like mother's milk, always have. Gibbon, Hume, Voltaire. Thomas Paine. Thomas Jefferson. Thomas Huxley.

Darwin.

His eyes open to a full-sized refrigerator with all the food groups. He walks slowly back to the present and looks at Father Scott Siberell, wandering the living room, absently picking up photos and trinkets. He was there with me, thinks Jack. *Now* look at him.

"So tell me," Jack says, picking up the paper. "What's the view like from the Dark Side?"

Scott *pffts* without turning around to face him. "Oh what is that supposed to mean? Time for a lecture from the Perfessor?"

"Twenty years ago I knew somebody who looked a lot like you, but he was on the right side of the barricades on this one."

"Oh don't even try that. Catholics aren't behind this anti-evolution crap, Jack, you know that. They had their fun with Galileo and the heretics. Now they're much better housetrained. No," he starts pacing, holding a framed picture high like the Good Book, "it's Bible-thumpin' Protestant fundamentalists doing the legwork on evolution, always has been. Baptists, like Pat Robertson . . . and closet Baptists, like gosh, come to think of it, Peter D'Angelo, who I believe is your very own congressman, is he not? He's been beatin' this drum louder than anybody, and you're paying his salary." He glances sideways at Jack as he sets the picture down. "And anyway, don't you presume to know who's on what side."

Jack *pffts* himself and walks back into the kitchen. "Yeah, that's much better. Be a closet atheist in a priest's collar. That helps a lot. Still one more pulpit to outyell."

Scott scowls and farts, his old signal for the end of a discussion. Jack farts back hard from the kitchen.

I do not appreciate the idea of a Saturday interview, thank you very much, driving all the way in from Sleepy Eye, especially since it is my Sunday. Jerks the whole next week off-kilter. But we've got to get Hillerman replaced before Advent or the whole calendar gets fritzed. A little odd to have this guy from Oakland apparently so hot to dump the parish he's in now—but the priest crop is sparse anymore, and his references were just plain over-the-top. Everybody at Sacred Heart loves him like—well, like a father, I guess.

A little suspicious to pull in that kind of adoration, if you ask me. If he's a damn charismatic, I swear I'll cut him off at the knees. Got to plan for that, since Wanda and the damn bishop will both be there . . . oh, I have just got to stop with the damn *damns*.

Okay, say he starts in with serious mystic revelation stuff. I'll quiz him on Scripture, pull him back to earth, keep him in the left-brain for the rest of the interview, then boot him in committee.

Precisely halfway down the south walk from her office on the way to Nurse Chapel, dead even with the midfield line of the hockey pitch, Dean Martin is airborne. Yes, the pitch is weedy, she notices from her new altitude. She lands with an impressive skid and comes to a hard stop courtesy of her outstretched palms.

She takes a breath, then rolls over to a sitting position, retrieves her fallen glasses and looks up the path with a scowl. A single bit of flagstone juts sharply two inches above the others, a tiny pyramid. She walks back to frown at it, then notices several other cracked and uneven stones around it.

Fine, Carl. Fix the south walk.

She leans over to tug at the protruding stone, stops, steps back. Leans in and squints. Well would you look at that. Fascinating. A credulous eye might see a face there. I tripped on the nose, there, and see, right there, two eyes, and even a crooked mouth. Severe-looking female, almost medieval. Just the kind of Rorschach test that can smell out a damn charismatic. Hey, I should bring our interviewee out here to see if he sees the Mother of God in our sidewalk cracks. Save a lot of time.

She kicks the little pyramid free, pauses, looks again, then reaches down to scatter a few more stones.

This interview will be your standard walk in the park. I am possessed of serious off-Broadway credits, remember. You need fear the audience only when you don't know what they want, or you *do* know but can't give it to them, or they have plenty of better options for entertainment. And I've got all three of those wired up tight. Couple hours in the car with Jack and I got all the character sketches, so I know what they're after, and I know their favorite book like a script, though I have to figure out where they are on the scale. If the president's any indication, from what Jack said, and the bishop's a bishop, I'll just fade in and out of Marian rapture as I speak. As for their other options—well, priests are as scarce nowadays as philosophers are plentiful, so like they're gonna find someone else to come out here to the North end of nothing.

Jack says Streamley's a classic fuzzyheaded New Age crystal-wearing mystic. I came across a paper of hers on the Internet, "The Place of Joy in the Worship of God." The bishop has to be there, O'Donoghue I think it is, for clerical interviews, ever since *Ex Corde* came down. And they've got to have a theologian to preserve the illusion that theology and the church are somehow connected—might be Joan Krenek, Jack says, who comes with a couple of nuns as her personal Greek chorus. And an administrator, probably Dean Martin, Jack says. Maybe Sammy Davis will sit in, too. Deano's a bit of a mystery, apparently makes Jack wet his pants a little, so I can't wait to meet her. Add a couple of campus ministry guitar-strummers and we've filled the room with enough jerkable chains to get me the gig.

Ah yes. These just *have* to be the guitar strummers. Yes, I'm Father Siberell, very nice to meet you too. What a wonderful space, this chapel, what a blessing. Snap, snap, and perfect acoustics for guitar. I love the guitar in worship, oh yes there they go, lighting up like Nativity Jesus bulbs—oh, *you* play guitar? You *both* do?! What a delight, what a blessing. Back into the sacristy, no that's fine, I'll stand for now, thanks. I'm at the window gazing out while they get coffee going and get some tittering done. In a dark space, always stand at the window and gaze out. Looks downright beatific, and sure enough, here comes the audience. Pause by the window as if in deep contemplation of the, oh, hello, President Streamley, of course, and yes, Your Excellency, an honor and a pleasure to be here together this day. If I may ask, President Streamley, are you one and the same as the author of that marvelous paper on joy in the—oh, what a delight to meet you at last! That paper transformed my ministry in Oakland, it really did, Good Lord she's *buying* it, give me some *challenge* here, folks. Small talk, small talk, another arrival, oh Dr. Krenek, yes, thank you, pleased as well. And sisters, yes, a great blessing. Dr. Krenek, I don't know if you know of a composer by the name of Ernst Krenek, might you be relat . . . no, oh I didn't suppose so but it is never to be known by one, and yes there's her light, thank you Jack, I guess she *does* love extreme indirection in language. We sit in a tight circle of folding chairs. And you must be Dean Martin, you and Jerry Lewis should never have broken up I did *not* say, and yes she is one scary-looking woman. And what about that *voice*. Seems a little rumpled and even has a torn sleeve and oh my my my, what do you say when you meet someone with STIGMATA? This is a wrinkle I hadn't, oh you *fell*, oh my heavens, I do hope you're all right, oh of course, please take your time and take care of those hands, you poor soul. More small talk with the

Greek chorus, then Deano's back and joins the circle. I'd like to begin with a prayer that we may seek the Lord's guidance and that His will be done in these proceedings. Oh, big hit. Hands clasped around the circle, Eternal God, please bless our deliberations here as we seek to determine if our paths, now crossed, shall linger in this place, in Your service. We gather in the shadow of our dear departed Father Halloran, *Hillerman*, excuse me, now gone to his rest in your glorious Presence. Bless all of Your priests, who represent You on this Earth. Make them more greatly aware of the grace that You pour out through them when they minister the sacraments, *now at this point my eyes are closed, see, but I was in this play once in this divey dinner theater in New Jersey, just a complete hole, but I played this homicidal sleepwalker, so I had to get all around the stage and even kill three people all with my eyes apparently closed and I learned how to close them just to the point that they look closed from the outside but I can see just fine through the lashes, you know, and that's what I'm doing now to see the play-by-play reactions of my new friends* and help them to fall more deeply in love with You after each and every Mass that they celebrate. Please strengthen our priests, who shepherd your flock, when they are in doubt of their faith, that they may be examples of Your Truth and guide us always on the path to You. We ask these things of You our Eternal Priest *and they're lookin' for more, so let's try* and Hail! holy Queen, Mother of mercy, hail, our life, our sweetness and our hope. To thee do we cry, poor banished children of Eve: to thee do we send up our sighs, mourning and weeping in this vale of tears. Turn then, most gracious Advocate, thine eyes of mercy *uh oh, Deano just dark-ened six shades—but ho, Wanda's glowin' like a rod of uranium, let's try a little social justice* uhh, to teach us to be generous, to serve our God as He dost deserve, to nourish the bodies, minds and souls of the hungry, to give without counting the cost, to fight injustice without fretting at our wounds, to la-bor without seeking rest, to spend ourselves without looking for any reward other than that of knowing that we do Thy holy will. Amen.

Okay, the Dean's back to pink. That was a tight little tailspin, but now I know. Deano don't dig the fuzzy stuff. She and Wanda must have an interesting time of it. The next half hour is standard, the six basic questions and their corollaries. I see this ministry moving beyond the gates, becoming a regional beacon of hope and light, Okay, there's a glimmer in the Dean's eye, so she likes exposure, that works out well for The Plan. We can put Saint Bernadette's in the center of a movement to love mercy and live in Christian fellowship to spread the best intentions of our hearts and minds in the glory of the word of God and the goodness that is *Dark Dean Warning, abort string of words, recover syntax* the heart of our mission here.

At some point Joan Krenek shoots an eyebrow well up above the hairline and looks at me like Miss Hathaway at Jed Clampett. "As regards the ideas for outreach expressed in your letter of introduction. They are . . . well, let me say they are very *unusual*. Very interesting but unusual. What could one infer regarding what may be your intentions toward the campus population itself?"

Well put, Joanie. A very valid question. Although I do intend to maintain a high level of activity outside the gates, it will be central to my mission at Saint Bernie's to touch as many students as possible on a daily basis.

"You did not say that."

"I did. And they lit up like a Reno Keno board, Jack. I got the job on the spot."

"I think it's just possible that they did not interpret that line quite like you meant it. The campus priest is not typically encouraged to boink the student body."

"So to speak. Not even missionary position?"

"If I thought you were serious, I'd squeal to the Dean, I swear I would. I will. Scott, look me in the eye and tell me that isn't why you took this job."

"To be surrounded by 800 young women ages 18 to 22 with whom I am forbidden by God and the bishop to have sex? Naw. No wa-*chung* there." Scott grins; Jack stands suddenly and stalks to the kitchen, Scott at his heels. "Look at you defending the chastity of the Catholic virgins of the prairie. How *Christian* of you." Jack is seriously darkening. "Okay, okay, Jack, relax. That is *not* why I took the job. Look at you all glowery. I would not move 2000 miles just for a new flock of veal to nibble. That'd be fun for about six months—well, eighteen months, tops—then here I'd be."

Jack wheels around. "Then why? It doesn't make sense for you to be here, of all places, you and your thirst for life's maximum. I've been here a long time, Scott. There's no maximum here. I can see you in Beirut, Paris, New York maybe, Calcutta somehow, I could make sense of lots of destinations for you, but not St. Bernie's, *Jesus.* So give me a straight damn answer for once in your life. How does a hard-farting, thrillseeking atheist end up a priest at a little pissant college in the middle of the *Mondo Nada?* It makes no sense. You tell me how it makes sense."

An idiotic, beatific half-smile blooms imperceptibly on Scott's lips. *Tabula rasa. Tabula rasa del Norte.* He ends the conversation in his singular way.

6

On This Rock

The fundamental cause of trouble in the world today
is that the stupid are cocksure while the intelligent
are full of doubt.

Bertrand Russell, "Christian Ethics"
from *Marriage and Morals*

Representative D'Angelo's office, Paula speaking, how
may I direct your call? Okay, let me transfer you to
Mike Lutz, he's doing scheduling today, hold on.

Mike, it's the guy from the VA.

Representative D'Angelo's office, Paula speaking, how
may I direct your call? I'm sorry Mr. Robertson, he's in committee right now, may I take a message for him? Okay . . .
okay . . . okay I'll give him the message. You're very welcome. Bye bye now.

Representative D'Angelo's office, Paula speaking, how
may I direct your call? I'm sorry Mr. Heston, he's on the Hill
in committee right now, may I take a message for him?

Okay . . . uh huh . . . okay. I'm sure he'll get back to you this afternoon. You're very welcome. Bye bye now.

Representative D'Angelo's office, Paula speaking, how may I direct . . . Matt, where *are* you?! I don't care, you have *got* to come in, I am getting *killed* here with calls. I can't do it by . . . wait, hold on . . .

Representative D'Angelo's office, Paula speaking, how may I direct your call? No, Mr. Robertson, that won't be necessary, I am *quite* sure he has your number. Absolutely. He will. Good deal. Okay. Bye bye.

I'm back. That was Pat Robertson *again* Matt, get in here *now*. You sound fine to me. No, D'Angelo's golfing with you-know-who, and Mike and I are here alone. This is nuts. Hold on . . . no, don't you *dare*. You *wait*.

Representative D'Angelo's office, Paula speaking, how may I direct your call? No, the congressman is not making a statement at this time. No, there's no comment . . . Well, that would constitute a comment, wouldn't it? That's fine, you do that Phyllis. Or better yet, wait for the press conference next week.

That was Phyllis from the Post, Matt. *Matt!!!* . . . oh I thought you hung up, you would be *so* dead. Get *in* here, Matt. Hold on . . .

Representative D'Angelo's office, Paula speaking, how may I direct your call? I'm sorry, he's in committee right now, may I take a message for him? No, Ms. Kassel, there is no statement at this time. The regular press conference is next . . . no, no comment. No, let's not play that game, please. I'm snowed under here. I can . . . oh, all *right*, hold one minute and I'll give you something . . .

Representative D'Angelo's office, Paula speaking, how may I direct your call? Oh gosh, hold on sweetie, I've got three more lines flashing . . .

Representative D'Angelo's office, Paula speaking, can you hold please?

Representative D'Angelo's office, Paula speaking, can you hold please?

Representative D'Angelo's office, Paula speaking, can you hold please?

Okay I'm back, punkin-butt.... oh my God, I'm sorry, Ms. Kassel, no, I thought ... oh yeah, you wanted me to throw you a bone. Let me dig up my canned stuff here, Okay, here's one: "Congressman D'Angelo fully supports the right of any American citizen to engage in the democratic process, little d, by seeking public office, and that includes Jesse Ventura." Right. No, I can't give you anything on his own plans. No. You can certainly wait for the press conference if Pat Robertson can . . . oh shit, don't you *dare* print that, Rebecca. No, I absolutely deny that I said we have received a call from Pat Robertson. I . . . oh *hold on*, I'm gonna have to put you on hold again . . .

Okay, Matt, just get in here or you are stone cold dead. Goodbye.

Sweetie, I have to call you later. Thanks. No, I'm fine, it's just insane because Ventura just announced for Senate and the whole right wing of the GOP is on the horn to get Peter to run against him. Yes. Okay, see you by seven, I hope.

Thank you for holding, can I help you? Yes, Mr. Robertson, I think the committee meeting is over at three, but let me check, hold on . . .

Thank you for holding, can I help you? No, this is D'Angelo's office. D'Agostino is, lessee, 3206. Sure.

Thanks for holding Mr. Robertson, I've got my calendar now, and it looks like he'll be back at . . . oh *crap*. Ms. Kassel, for your information it is a different Mr. Robertson. Fine, you believe what you want. That's fine. Goodbye.

Mr. Robertson?

A rolling stone grows no grass under the feet of a man with a mission impossible.

Scott Siberell is such a man, whatever that means, and the mission begins at the stroke of the Monday after the interview. He lights into that mission, whatever it is, with the vigor of a man born again (in a Catholic sense, of course), arriving on campus at five o'clock in the pre-dawn morning, rubbing elbows at the gate with a startled Dean Martin on her way to Tuesday. By nine o'clock there are no fewer than thirty two pieces of introductory correspondence in the outgoing chapel U.S. Mail basket. By noon he has hoofed it through Admin, knocking on doors, shaking hands, making contact with a warmth and sincerity that is decidedly female and therefore met with positively sweaty enthusiasm.

More than one passerby is heard to suggest that the chapel building itself seems simply set aglow by the presence of a priest who might just be at liberty to devote personal energy to tasks beyond the maintenance of his own heartbeat. President Streamley has ordered the resumption of the tolling of the chapel bells at nine, noon, three and six, a sort of Angelus-plus tradition discontinued nine years earlier at Father Hillerman's request. The ringing, as it happened, never failed to catch Hillerman by stark surprise. As the first bell sounded, the old priest would invariably leap from his chair with an involuntary *ah!*, clutch his chest, then realize the benign source of the disturbance and slowly drop back to his seat. He would tremble visibly for a good piece and often lamented the failure of his nerves to completely recover for as long as three hours afterward—at which point, of course, the bells would ring again.

At this point in mid-October, the wedge is suffused in a yellow-orange leaflight that defies description, even for the most dedicated campus cynic. With each tolling of the bells, a glorious shower of leaves is set free, delivering a multimedia event in four showings a day. Most impressive, as always, is the massive oak at the top of the green, a spectacular sun on a stick pitching soft orange flamelets at the earth.

By three p.m. Father Siberell has visited every faculty and staff office on campus, pressing flesh and taking names. By six he has knocked on every dorm room in Schlafly and Steinem, personally greeting no fewer than two hundred students. At 6:15 he joins the campus ministry staff for a prearranged welcome dinner in the cafeteria. And at 7:30 p.m., he walks out the east gate, the single most beloved human being at St. Bernie's ever to do so.

Six days later, attendance at his first Sunday Mass is eight times Hillerman's average, which is to say about twenty-four bodies. By the second week, evidence of geometric progression is in the air as each member of the first congregation has apparently returned with two friends. There is talk of intense drama in the young priest's homilies, of pathos writ large, of subtle but appropriate humor, and of the discernable presence of an electrifying something that is identified at last in excited whispers amongst the congregants.

Content.

Within three weeks of Scott's arrival, Sister Joan and the rest of the theology department are suiting up for holy war. Regular memos begin to arrive in the Dean's mailbox bemoaning what the theologians call "a disconcerting change of focus" in the liturgy. "It is not to be wished that a change should be effected from attention to the feast of Communion with our Lord to a glorification of the waiter." By week four Joan's memo language has become almost direct. "The Eucharist itself, which should be the heart of the service, has been reduced in importance to the level of refreshments after a rock concert."

The Dean has especially little patience for severe drifts

into arcana. She stops well short of the end of Joan's fourth
memo, which dredges up canon law and papal instruction,
the Dean's least favorite trappings of the faith: "Among our
more serious concerns are the invitations he has extended to
laymen to provide 'faith stories' or even scriptural comment
during the Mass. Canon 767 of the Code of Canon Law clearly
states, 'Among the forms of preaching the homily is preemi-
nent; it is a part of the liturgy itself and is reserved to a priest
or to a deacon. Furthermore, the instruction *Inaestimabile
Donum*, issued by the Sacred Congregation for the Sacraments
and Divine Worship and approved by Pope John Paul II on
April 17, 1980 also condemns homilies given by lay people.
Under the section on the Mass, subsection 3 states that 'yak
yak yak yak yak yak yak . . .'"

I don't give a Pharoah's fart, thinks Dean Martin as she
lets the memo float into the trash bucket. He can raffle off
Precious Moments figurines as long as he is filling those pews
and not doing it with mystic hoohah. To delay the inevitable
tussle over the issue, the Dean institutes a personal policy of
Joan-avoidance.

By his fifth Mass, Father Scott Siberell, vigorous, debo-
nair and devout, presides over an SRO chapel audience,
450 strong, drawn perhaps by the simultaneous clarity and
mystery in his announced series topic, "God is God." The
parking lot looks like a WalMart the day before the fish-
ing opener. No less than a dozen plates from South Dakota and two from Iowa. Wanda Streamley stands elated
at the main entrance each Sunday in her best goin'-to-
meetin' muu-muu, enveloping each visitor in a warm fuzzy
hug and a glow of sincere welcome. Dean Martin is impressed enough with the numbers to switch her service
attendance schedule from Sleepy Eye to Nurse Chapel
and from her Sunday to the actual one, interrupting paperwork precisely at 8:15 for the 200 yard walk downhill.
Even Jack Kassel attends the first five of Scott's Masses,

including two with Connor, until the overflow crowd of the sixth and every subsequent Sunday leaves latecomers quite literally out in the cold. Jack is equal parts impressed, relieved, puzzled and pissed to see the Scott 'Francis' Siberell he has known for so long standing with evident devotion at the altar-helm of a Christian juggernaut, finding the lost and saving the damned of the featureless northern plains.

102-10/3A ONTARIO PROVINCIAL POLICE
STATEMENT OF CONFESSION

Suspect: Margaret Mary Sellars   DOB: 2/28/08 Sex: F
                                      Eyes: GN Hair: RD
                                      Hgt: 155cm Wgt: 138 kg

Occupation: Cook/Housekeeper
Employer: St. Ignatius Convent of the Order of the Radiant
          Hope of Mary
Home address: 302 Plothar Hwy, St. Ignatius, Ontario, Canada

Charge: Attempted homicide   Count(s): 27
Charge: Count(s):
Charge: Count(s):

Date of arrest: 03 Mar 1970
Date of statement: 05 Mar 1970
Date of typed transcription: 11 Mar 1970

Witness(es) to statement: Mr. Haviland DuPre, attorney
                                         for the defendant
                                       Sgt. Major Franklin Haas OPP
                                       Lt. Michael Coultier OPP

TRANSCRIPTION OF WRITTEN
NARRATIVE STATEMENT

I AM BLESSED TO SERVE AS EVENING COOK AND TO DO
LIGHT HOUSEWORK FOR THE SISTERS OF THE ORDER OF
THE RADIANT HOPE. I KNOW THAT THE LORD MY GOD
THROUGH THE INTERCESSION OF HIS MOTHER MARY
QUEEN OF HEAVEN BROUGHT ME TO BE IN THEIR SER-
VICE AFTER MY HUSBAND AND DEAR SISTER PASSED INTO
GLORY BOTH ON THE SAME NIGHT FOUR YEARS AGO NEXT
MONTH, LEAVING ME ALONE IN THIS WORLD OF SORROWS.
IT HAS BEEN THROUGH THE MERCY AND DISIPLINE [SIC]
OF THE SISTERS THAT I HAVE FOUND THE ESSENCE OF
CHRISTIAN GOODNESS AND SALVATION, TURNING AT LAST
FROM THE DIRTY, SINFUL, PRIDEFUL BEAST I HAD ONCE
BEEN TOWARD THE LIGHT OF GRACE AND FORGIVENESS
THROUGH OUR LORD. THE SISTERS KNEW OF MY LUSTS
AND OF MY AVARICE AND STILL THEY LOVED ME ENOUGH
TO MORTIFY MY FILTHY FLESH AND TO BRING ME INTO
THE RAPTURE OF THEIR SPIRITUAL DISIPLINE [SIC] TO
TEACH ME CLEANSING PAIN. ALL I HAVE BECOME I OWE
TO THEM. ONLY WHEN I LEARNED TO SHED MY GLUT-
TONY, TO FEED ONLY UPON THE WORD OF GOD, TURNING
FIRMLY AWAY FROM THE BASE FEEDING OF THE SINFUL
BODY, ONLY THEN DID THE GLORIOUS VISIONS BEGIN. AT
LAST WAS MY SPIRIT PURIFIED AND MY BODY FREE OF
EARTHLY POLLUTION, FREE TO SERVE THE WILL OF OUR
MOTHER OF HOPE. I LONGED TO REPAY THE SISTERS FOR
THEIR PRICELESS SALVIFIC GIFTS TO ME. THOUGH I LIS-
TENED TO THEIR HOURLY PRAYERS, MY MIND WAS WEAK
AND STUPID AND FAILED TO HEAR THEIR PLEAS. I WISHED
WITH ALL MY HEART TO GRANT THEIR SOULS DESIRES A
THOUSANDFOLD, BUT MY EARS WERE STOPPED BY MY SIN-
FUL NATURE. I BEGGED MOTHER MARY TO MAKE ME
THEIR SERVANT AND AN INSTRUMENT OF THE WILL OF

GOD. IN VISIONS SHE BADE ME GRANT THEIR EVERY WISH
BUT MY MIND WAS WEAK AND STUPID. I COULD NOT HEAR
THEIR PLEAS THOUGH THEY RAINED DOWN ON ME. AT
LAST I COULD BEAR MY FAILURE NO LONGER AND ASKED
SWEET SISTER THERESE MARTIN WHAT IN THIS WORLD
SHE WANTED MOST OF ALL IF ANYTHING COULD BE HERS.
MARGARET, SHE SAID TO ME, MARGARET LOOK NOT TO
THIS VALE OF TEARS FOR ANYTHING OF WORTH. I REMEM-
BER HER WORDS EXACTLY. MARGARET, SHE SAID, THIS
WORLD IS NAUGHT BUT PAIN AND SORROW. ONLY IN THE
NEXT WORLD IS OUR SORROW RELIEVED AND OUR SIN PUT
BEHIND US. THE DOOR TO OUR TRUE REWARD LIES BE-
YOND THE THRESHOLD OF DEATH IN LIFE EVERLASTING.
HER WORDS WERE SO BEAUTIFUL, AND NOW I COULD RE-
CALL THEIR HOURLY PRAYERS. I WANTED TO GIVE THE
SISTERS THEIR GREATEST DESIRE. THE VISIONS OF OUR
LADY GAVE ME STRENGTH TO FREE MY BELOVED SISTERS
FROM SORROW AND PAIN. BUT I ONLY INCREASED THEIR
PAIN. THE LYE I USED WAS NOT ENOUGH FOR THE SIZE OF
THE SOUP TUREEN. I WANTED TO FREE THEM FROM SOR-
ROW BUT I FAILED ONLY BECAUSE MY SPIRIT IS FOUL AND
SMALL. MOTHER MARY DESPISES MY STUPIDITY AND WEAK-
NESS. I AM SMALL AND SHE IS IN GOD. HER VOICE IS THE
VOICE OF THE ANCIENT OF DAYS. HER VOICE IS SHADOW
AND THE ANCIENT OF DAYS. I AM BECOME THEIR SORROW
AND THEIR PAIN.

"I must admit I'm pretty surprised."

"Well, he's all Bridget Nelson and the rest of the Religion staff writers are talking about lately. And *oh* did *you* score
points with Mom when you took Connor out there not once
but *twice.*"

"So she grudgingly lets me drag him to a Lutheran service but she's thrilled when I take him to Mass? I don't follow."

"It's not the denomination, Jack. It's your friend Scott. Mom's Bible study group has been all a-twitter about him for weeks. Three of them drove all the way out there last Sunday and came back just brimming with the Spirit, she says. It's really a Baptist kind of outreach he's doing. Mom's going next week. She already has her dress laid out and it's *Tuesday*. I haven't seen her this excited . . ."

". . . what, since our divorce, maybe? Look, I can't tell you how weird all this is for me, Bex. Scott's just not the type to be leading tent revivals. I've known him for years. You remember all the stories, don't you?"

"People change, Jack. Pretty central to the whole Christian thing."

"Yeah, people change, manna falls from the sky, prophets rise from the dead. All equally true. People don't change like *that*. Scott is a brilliant, profane thrillseeker, and three out of three of those things don't line up with his current job. I'm telling you, something's not right."

"You don't think it's thrilling enough for him to see this thing exploding like it is? To see his name and picture in the Ledge almost *every day?* To walk into a dead ministry and give it the Lazarus treatment?"

Now Jack wants to say, "Becca, you are so *Becca*. That's the kind of amateurish question that shows that you can't *begin* to understand what I'm really talking about," but only Scott has the moxie for that kind of line.

"Maybe you're right, maybe that's enough. Hey, how's school going for the boy?"

She pauses, a little too long to be good.

The Pause, Jack knows, precedes The Revelation. Becca's Post-Pause Revelation Hall of Fame already includes I'm Pregnant, I Found A Lump, There's This Guy, and We

Need To Talk, so Jack's hackles rise higher with each silent second.

"Well Jack, you could ask him yourself once in awhile, show a little interest."

He blinks. "Wh . . . where the hell did *that* come from!? Hey Ruth, put Becca back on the phone so I can . . ."

"Jack, he's not at Lakeview."

A remote glimmer of where this is going shoots through the back of Jack's skull. He pats his empty shirt pocket. "Uh, where is he going to school, Rebecca?"

" . . ."

"Rebecca? Tell the boy's father where he is going to school."

"Jack, do not freak out. He's at Calvary Lutheran Day School."

" . . ."

"Jack, it's fine. It's a good school and it makes Mom happy. You know, she actually wanted him to go to Holy Spirit Baptist, but I put my foot down. She's covering the tuition, by the way. Look, Connor's a smart kid. He isn't going to suddenly turn into some 'passive receptacle,' I think that's your phrase, and he might even get something good out of the exposure to the big questions, don't you think? Jack?"

" . . ."

"Jack?"

" . . ."

The Story of a Good Brahmin
Voltaire

On my travels I met an old Brahmin, a very wise man, of marked intellect and great learning. Furthermore, he was rich and, consequently, all the wiser, because, lacking nothing, he needed to deceive nobody. His household was very well managed by three women who set themselves out to please him. He passed the time in philosophizing. Near his house, which was beautifully decorated and had charming gardens attached, there lived a narrow-minded old Indian woman: she was simple of mind and rather poor.

Said the Brahmin to me one day: 'I wish I had never been born!' On my asking why, he answered: 'I have been studying forty years, and that is forty years wasted. I teach others and myself am ignorant of everything. Such a state of affairs fills my soul with so much humiliation and disgust that my life is intolerable. I was born in Time, I live in Time, and yet I do not know what Time is. I am at a point between two eternities, as our wise men say, and I have no conception of eternity. I am composed of matter: I think, but I have never been able to learn what produces my thought. I do not know whether or no my understanding is a simple faculty inside me, such as those of walking and digesting, and whether or no I think with my head as I grip with my hands. Not only is the cause of my thought unknown to me; the cause of my actions is equally a mystery. I do not know why I exist, and yet every day people ask me questions on all these points. I have to reply, and as I have nothing really worth saying I talk a great deal, and am ashamed of myself afterward for having talked.

'It is worse still when I am asked if Brahma was born of Vishnu or if they are both eternal. God is my witness that I have not the remotest idea, and my ignorance shows itself in my replies. "Ah, Holy One,"

people say to me, "tell us why evil pervades the earth."
I am in as great a difficulty as those who ask me this
question. Sometimes I tell them that everything is as
well as can be, but those who have been ruined and
broken in the wars do not believe a word of it—and no
more do I. I retire to my home stricken at my own
curiosity and ignorance. I read our ancient books, and
they double my darkness. I talk to my companions:
some answer me that we must enjoy life and make
game of mankind; others think they know a lot and
lose themselves in a maze of wild ideas. Everything
increases my anguish. I am ready sometimes to despair when I think that after all my seeking I do not
know whence I came, whither I go, what I am nor
what I shall become.'

The good man's condition really worried me. Nobody was more rational or more sincere than he. I
perceived that his unhappiness increased in propor-
tion as his understanding developed and his insight
grew. The same day I saw the old woman who lived
near him. I asked her if she had ever been troubled by
the thought that she was ignorant of the nature of her
soul. She did not even understand my question. Never
in all her life had she reflected for one single moment
on one single point of all those which tormented the
Brahmin. She believed with all her heart in the metamorphoses of Vishnu and, provided she could obtain
a little Ganges water wherewith to wash herself,
thought herself the happiest of women.

Struck with this poor creature's happiness, I returned
to my wretched philosopher. 'Are you not ashamed,'
said I, 'to be unhappy when at your very door there

lives an old automaton who thinks about nothing, and yet lives contentedly?'

'You are right,' he replied. 'I have told myself a hundred times that I should be happy if I thought as little as my neighbor, and yet I do not desire such happiness.'

My Brahmin's answer impressed me more than all the rest. I set to examining myself, and I saw that in truth I would not care to be happy at the price of being a simpleton.

I put the matter before some philosophers, and they were of my opinion. 'Nevertheless,' said I, 'there is a tremendous contradiction in this mode of thought, for, after all, the problem in this life is how to be happy. What does it matter whether one has brains or not? Further, those who are contented with their lot are certain of their contentment, whereas those who reason are not certain that they reason correctly. It is quite clear, therefore,' I continued, 'that we must choose not to have common sense, however little common sense may contribute to our discomfort.' Everyone agreed with me, but I found nobody, notwithstanding, who was willing to accept the bargain of becoming a simpleton in order to become contented. From which I conclude that if we consider the question of happiness we must consider still more the question of reason.

But on reflection it seems that to prefer reason to happiness is to be very senseless. How can this contradiction be explained? Like all the other contradictions. It is matter for much talk.

"Okay, who wants to start us off?"

". . ."

". . ." ['Female students tend to spend more time in the processing and formulation of answers in group situations, often resulting in more accurate and well-formed responses. Teachers at all levels must become comfortable with an average 6-8 second buffer of silence after posing a question to allow this process to occur.' Heinlein, Janet. "The Gender Differential in Response Styles in Class Discussion." *Journal of the National Education Association*, Spring 1998, 122-29.]

Six . . . seven . . . eight. One of the shapes begins to stir, sends up an appendage. Speaks.

Shape 1: "Voltaire was a philosopher who lived from 1694 to 1778."

Oh, for the . . . "Uh, yes . . . he was indeed. Good start. Okay, now how about the central question in the story? What's the main question here?"

Pause.

Shape 2: "Why learn anything when it just makes you miserable. I mean, this guy is totally miserable because he spends all his time thinking about stuff he can never know for sure, so what's the point. I agree with him. It's stupid."

Jack feels the darkening. The shapes undulate.

He continues. "Okay, first of all, you say you agree with him. Are you sure he's agreeing with *you*? Is he taking the position that it is stupid to think about things that may never be resolved? What would he say if he were in the room now?"

Silence. Silence. *Seven . . . eight . . . nine. Uh oh. Bad teacher. Answer not written on board, answer not obvious, Kassel, possibly even several answers possible, DO NOT ASK QUESTION IF ANSWER IS NOT ABSOLUTELY . . .*

Shape 3: "Well, he says he wishes he was never born, so yeah, he thinks thinking is stupid."

Introduction to Philosophy. Jack feels another small part

of his vital life force drain away. Jack thinks it is stupid. Jack wishes he was never born.

"Okay. Other comments. I suspect there are some . . . equally good points out there."

Shape 4: "I felt so sad for him. I just wish he could know what I know and what the Indian woman knows."

Jack hears the spring of the trap and moves in before she can gnaw her leg off. "And what is it that you and the Indian woman know?"

"Well, we have *faith*. He'd be happy if he just knew the Truth of Jesus."

"Like the woman in the story does."

"Yes. She's simple, but she's happy because she has faith, so she *knows* the Truth."

If this were a cartoon, Jack thinks, and it is, I could see that she is capitalizing Truth. Betcha. "Okay, she knows the truth, which is . . . ?"

"I'm sorry?"

"You said she knows the truth. She's Hindu, remember. She believes in the metamorphoses of Vishnu. Do *you* believe in the metamorphoses of Vishnu?"

"Well, no, I . . . I don't. Of course not. Well, I don't know what that is."

"So there is in fact a contradiction between *her* 'certain' truth and *your* 'certain' truth, no? Isn't that precisely the sort of thing that would concern the Brahmin?"

"I was thinking she believed in the *real* God. I guess I didn't read that page."

"This essay is two pages long. Which page *did* you read?"

Ohhhhh, Jack. The shape becomes more opaque. Blobs of cloudy matter appear in its liquid filling. "I . . . can somebody else talk?"

Jack steps back. Careful not to Marginalize and Silence. "Okay, let's step back. It was suggested by Shape . . . by, uh,

Brenda, that the Brahmin thinks thinking is stupid. But his student argues with him on that point, does he not?"

Silence well past eleven.

Shape 5: "Yes, but only because the student sees reason as a self-evidently high value. The Brahmin probably felt the same at one time but is past that now and sees a contradiction between reason and happiness." Pause, glance around, glance down. Resume apologetically, eyes focused on the desktop. "He has always taken the value of the search for truth on *faith*. Once he questions that assumption, he sees that the search for truth threatens happiness, which most would agree is the basic goal of life. The student says—here it is, at the end, 'it seems that to prefer reason to happiness is to be very senseless,' but the philosophers can't even see the unreasonableness of their dogmatic addiction to reason itself."

Jack squints in the light. Why, look. It's the shape of a human person, gradually coming into focus. "And remind me of your name, please?"

"Uh . . . Amanda. Amanda Corelli."

"Thanks, Amanda Corelli. So who wants to follow up on what Amanda Corelli said?" as if anyone will, as if you could, as if I *care*. Go ahead, you damned evil amoebas. Follow *that*.

Shape 3: "So yeah, all the other philosophers are as stupid as the Brahmin but they're so out of it they don't even *know* it. And he shouldn't call her an Indian woman anyway, it's *Native American*."

Noooo, life force, come back. Come back, life force.

Jack summons maximum restraint. "Except that this takes place in *India*."

Shape 3, after a dim pause: "Well, still. That doesn't make it okay to be prejudice." Assenting murmurs from neighboring shapes.

Jack walks slowly to the desk of Shape 3, leans over and grabs it by the ankles and begins swinging it round and round, round and round, until every other shape in the room has been flayed apart. Except Amanda, the shape of a person, of course, who has the brains to duck. True silence, lasting silence. The passage of shapeless time.

"Dr. Kassel?"

" . . ."

"Dr. Kassel?"

"Yes."

"Dr. Kassel, are you all right? You just sort of went blank there for a few minutes, so everyone got up and left. Should I get some help?"

Jack is sitting at the front of a room empty of students and free of bloodstains. Oh. Good. All the catharsis with none of the jail time. "No, no Amanda, I'm fine. I just . . . I don't know what that was. But yeah, I'm fine. Thanks."

"Okay, I just wanted to make sure. Oh, and I didn't mean to dominate the discussion back there."

Jack looks up in disbelief. Is it possible that she just apologized? I do believe she did. She apologized for *not* draining my life force.

"That's right, Amanda," he says. "You've got the message. Hide your light, Amanda. Lo, see how it makes the shapes blink and squint, they are afraid. Don't be so *mean*, Amanda. It might make the shapes realize that they are shapes and that you are a . . . a *being* of some sort. Apology accepted."

All sorts of light in her eyes. "Shapes, eh?" A smile of mild discovery. She had the concept but not the word before.

"Sarcasm there."

"I'm well aware. I'm also aware that you are cracking up and that I get to watch."

Aha, says Jack to Jack. Kindred. A sentient. A sentient, wiseacre kindred person-shape, right here in his very classroom. Ah *ha*. "I'm sorry, Amanda, but you ruined it. You pulled me back from the ledge." He reaches into his shirt pocket for a cigarette, then remembers the year. "Now I have to endure at least one more day before my official psychotic break. Thanks for nothing."

"Oh, don't put it off on my account. I think you *need* a good break."

"Well, what I don't need is an audience, especially not a clever one. Thank you for your concern—and, if I may say so, for your complete shapelessness."

"In another context," she says, smirking, "I'd be insulted."

Jack remembers a time before the Darkenings. Long, long ago, he was the undisputed campus darling. Barely twenty-eight when he arrived, just six years older than the seniors, a perfectly polished apple of youth and zeal. Coat and tie everyday. Shiny-shaved face every day. He came to work with a sobering daily fear that he just might not be up to the job. Came early and stayed late. His hand waggled in the air every time a faculty committee had an opening. Voice mail messages were answered the same day they arrived. Each semester he would scour his syllabi for neatness, accuracy and font selection. He did mid-semester "how'ma doin'?" surveys in every class, with yes, *that* title at the top. Student opinion was guide and master. Fairness and empowerment were his watchwords. Every student was an individual with a powerful story, full of value, full of worth, full of potential. He listened to countless hours of heartrending personal tragedy in his office. He nodded. One Family Size box of Puffs Facial Tissues sat on his desk, and he gladly paid just that little bit extra for the ones with quilted pillowing and a touch of Aloe Vera.

Deans pinked up at his approach. The Kassel name was invoked every time a minor deanship vacated. He was twice considered for Dean of Health and Human Services, a well-worn steppingstone to the Top of the Wedge. Students saw

him more as *confrere* than instructor, calling him Jack or even
JJ at his insistence. Eventually the familiarity began to feel
less and less warranted. He finally began requesting "Dr.
Kassel" after a persistent student-fan found herself on the
same Phoenix-bound flight with him, shouting a familiar "Hi"
followed by his first name, over and over, with increasing
urgency. Jack's earphones were in, so he didn't realize he
was being called until an emergency landing amidst flashing
lights was well under way.

In 1996 Jack was named Teacher of the Year. Three hundred bucks and a plaque.

And then it began. To this day Jack is simultaneously confused about why it began and why it took so very long *to*
begin. It started when he noticed students going a tad fuzzy
around the edges. Their personal tragedies and inanities
started to run together into a single, sustained whine—no,
it's more of a drone, really, like the continuous middle of a
goose honk. The salary began to seem rather insulting.
Friends from Berkeley were dot com millionaires, broadband
millionaires. His weak affirmation that hey, *he* gets summers
off had begun to sound just plain sad even to him. One too
many darkenings, one too many workshops with titles like
Neo-Feminist Pedagogy, Celebrating Diversity in the Classroom, Teaching to Divergent Learning Styles, Avoiding
Heterocentricity in the Workplace, Incorporating Lesbian
Authors Into the Curriculum, Incorporating a Celebration of
Diverse Feminist Learning Styles Into a Pedagogical Model
For Tolerance of Divergent Lifestyle Choices by Differently-
Abled Women of Color. Too much New Age Catholicism.
One too many labyrinth walkers, presidential dances, nod-
ding heads.

Jack lives and breathes deep in the political left. Brought
an impressive arrest record with him to graduate school, all
from properly radical protests. He went to the mat against
UC's investments in apartheid South Africa, against nuclear

rearmament, against deforestation. As a young philosophy major Jack spent six days and nights chained to the right side of a bulldozer blade in Sequoia National Park. (Fortunately, one smart and gorgeous young journalism major by the name of Rebecca Maples was chained to the left side.) He was self-consciously proud of the ruminating philosopher in him, which made him a chronic pain in the ass to the Doers around him, the ones who thought and acted from the gut. Jack had complete contempt for the gut sense, railing against his own fellow protesters when they spouted unthinking rhetoric and screamed mindless bumper stickers across the police tape. Scream an *argument,* for God's sake, he'd yell in their ears. Make them *think.* Reason supports justice; otherwise we're just yelling at them and they're yelling back. Reason is on our side here. Injustice isn't only immoral, it also *does not make sense.* Racism, inequality for women, environmental degradation, none of them stand up to critical scrutiny. They're all houses of cards. Reason is the only real difference between us and them, it's our ace-in-the-hole.

Nooo, they'd respond. Your ass chained to that *machine* is our ace-in-the-hole.

"Utilitarians!" he'd yell.

"Pencilneck dipshit!" they'd yell back.

By 1998, Jack felt deadened and disconnected. He'd walk up to Saint Jude's Leap at the end of each day and lean on the fence for hours, watching the sun melt into the prairie, trying to recover the feelings of purpose and principle that had come so easily at first. Just to feel a touch inadequate instead of so damned superior, so terribly underemployed. What a self-righteous *schmuck.* But with every passing semester the students had become more amorphous, less human, undulating in their seats like squat columns of lamp lava and emitting that . . . that *drone.* And Jack is just rational enough to know that it is he changing, not they, and that it isn't in the least attractive or sustainable.

The following year Jack began to float the résumé around, realizing after a few months that no one out there gave half a rip. The future stretched out endlessly before him, countless years ahead as a darkening husk stuck tight to a remote wedge peppered with squealing blobs that he periodically flayed into silence.

And then Becca left. Just because of Saint Philip, you know.

Jack longs for a bulldozer to chain himself reasonably to.

Saint Bernie's loves unrestricted giving but will take what it gets, heck. And in Fall of 2000 it received an anonymous gift of 1.2 million smackers to put an underground system of tunnels in the wedge. *Pfft.* Oh, everyone agrees the grade is tough to negotiate in the winter, which is to say seven of the nine months school is in session, but to hear the mutterers tell it, not a soul on the campus would have spent that kind of cash on *that*, of all the white elephants. The library roof is near collapse, and Hildegard Hall and faculty salaries are beginning to sink in sync. But the gift was indeed restricted, and from an undisclosed benefactor, so around the time Scott Siberell's ministry begins to catch fire, tunneling has begun in earnest.

Gustafson decides to dig in winter when the ground is firmest, since core sampling had shown the whole formation to be loose as English trifle. November 3rd is groundbreaking day, and eleven deans, six trustees and three construction supervisors pose in flurries for that annoying sham tradition, the hardhat, suit, and Gold Shovel photo. The opening of the main tunnel is to be in the middle of the bottom of the wedge, from which point it will run just over 600 level feet until it is 35 feet beneath Admin. The building elevator and stairs will extend down to meet it. Four branch tunnelettes will extend off the main line to the basements of the Student Union, the Library, and Cady Stanton and Curie Halls.

By April, so they say, the tunnels will be finished, just in time to not need them for another five months.

Eastbound in light snow.

"Ya know, Mom's really wanting to know if you're seeing somebody, but I'm not supposed to say that." Clamps his hand over his mouth in mock dismay.

"If she asks again, just tell her I said you're not supposed to tell."

The boy smiles. "Oh, you wanna jerk her chain a little."

"Connor, she's your mom. She doesn't have a chain." *Yeah, right. She's a regular Jacob Marley.* "Where'd you ever hear of jerking somebody's chain, anyway?"

"From Allison. She's one of the other divorced kids at school."

". . ."

"Dad?"

"Yeah, sweetie."

"Dad, what would happen if two bullets ran right into each other?"

"I have no idea. Let's try it."

"Dad, another thing I was wondering. I know there are planets and that they go around the sun, and I know there are stars further out, and I know those are suns, too. But what's out *past* the stars?"

"Nobody really knows. Maybe someday you can be a scientist and help figure it out."

"Rrrrgh."

Hmm. "Hey Connor, I have a question."

"What, Daddy?"

"It really bugs you, doesn't it, when I say nobody knows the answer to something."

"Well, yeah, 'cause I wanna know the answer."

"Okay, how about this . . . would you rather ask questions and have me say 'Nobody knows the answer,' and be annoyed, or just make up your own answers and be happy?"

Connor grabs his nose, a sure sign of a stumper. "I don't get it." An oncoming truck passes close to the line; the car shimmies slightly.

"I mean, what if you could just be happy making up your own answers and not find out if we really know the truth?"

"That doesn't make any sense, Dad. What if I'm just makin' up answers that sound right but aren't really?"

Where did I *get* this kid. A warm glow from the paternal side of the car.

Flashing radio tower lights on the horizon—and a full moon, Jack thinks, hanging above the towers like a round tuit.

Jack's dad used to keep a little round wooden chip in his pocket with TUIT printed on it in block letters. Every morning the chip went into his pocket with the keys and nail clippers. And James Kassel would wait, sometimes for weeks at a time, for someone to say, "I'll do that just as soon as I get around to it," and he'd plunge his hand into the pocket, grab the chip and thrust it at the guy, saying "There, now you got a round TUIT" and they'd laugh, partly in amazement that anyone could be so dedicated to pulling off a one-scenario gag as to carry this thing around every day of his life, waiting for that one line. That was the gag, really, Jack had eventually realized —not the pun itself, which just isn't *that* funny— but that it was just amazing that anybody would do that. And then James Kassel would have to ask for the chip back, which always took a little steam out of the joke there at the end, but not so much that he'd spring for a full box of chips or anything. "Money doesn't grow on trees," he'd sometimes have to say, palm up, to get the chip back from somebody dense.

Rhythmic radial slush.

"We didn't get a chance to talk about your school this weekend, Con. You liking it?"

"Yes, I am. I'll tell Mom you asked. She said that would be big points for you."

Jack's jaw cinches up a notch. "Not actually after points, Con. I'm *interested*. And be sure to tell her I said that. More points."

"Well, school's pretty good. Some of the kids are kind of mean, but I have three really good friends, Allison and Davy and Isaiah and Callie." He thinks. "And Ben."

"How about the teachers?"

"Oh they're good. They're really nice. But you know, sometimes they give a different kind of answer when I ask a question."

Jaw set. "Like what?"

"Well, like the thing about what's past the stars. Mrs. McInerny says we don't have to worry about that because God knows it *for* us."

Cinch. Clench. "And you said?"

"I didn't say anything, Dad. It was snack time."

"Of course. But if it wasn't snack time, what would you say?"

He hmmmms. "Well, there isn't another question to ask if she says that."

Indeed. The boy's last sentence finds its way through Jack's ears and into the brain, collecting significance as it goes. Somewhere deep in Jack's mind, a tiny electrical charge skis across a snowpacked mountainside. And well below the surface of the snowpack something slips, then something else. By the time the tiny pulse of meaning has cleared the slope, a spectacular avalanche is underway.

Jack smiles and breathes deeply as he feels it give way, at long last.

He pulls into Becca's driveway at six, turns down dinner, kisses the loved ones, backs out of the driveway and drives three hours straight through light sleet, breathing deep and even, right past Saint Philip to Saint Bernadette's. A slushy walk up the dark wedge and a jingle of cold keys in the building door, then up to the second floor.

In five minutes, Jack emerges from his office with a half sheet of paper. He tapes the carefully-laserprinted quote to the door:

> The world would be astonished if it knew how great a proportion of its brightest ornaments, of those most distinguished even in popular estimation for wisdom and virtue, are complete skeptics in religion.
>
> John Stuart Mill

Jack Kassel has one toe out of the closet.

By late October, Brian and Jack have made Tuesday afternoons at the Cascade a regular thing. On the first Tuesday of November, Leslie Erickson Mitchell-Robbins Moore and Lilly Galen of English spot the guys and leave their booth at the back to join them, and Tuesday grows to four.

Jack and Leslie have been great friends almost as long as they've been pissing each other off. They invariably end up on opposite sides of campus issues, but they both recognize an edgy kinship that has drawn them progressively together, a sort of horrified fascination with each other. It's that Grin, he thinks as she works her way across the room. Look at people as she walks by, diving for cover from that *Grin*. And Lilly Galen is one of those likeable sorts, animated and intense but not annoying, who drifts between and among social circles with ease, like the high school kid who managed to hang with the cheerleaders and the geeks without being either one. The author of the 1998 novelette *The Rise and Demise of Guys*, which the New York Times called "a merciless but fun-packed romp through postmodern post-feminism," Lilly is the closest current thing to an in-house celebrity at St. Bernie's. The book neared runaway best-sellerhood and was oh-so-close to beatification by Oprah when Jane Smiley and Barbara Kingsolver simultaneously published merciless but fun-packed romps through postmodern post-feminism and swept Lilly to the clearance table. Rumor has it she's now working on a satirical novel about Saint Bernadette's, so everyone works very hard to be fictionworthy when she's around.

Father Scott joins the next week. At four-thirty that same day, Leonard the Poet alights for ten minutes, right next to Leslie, then drifts away without a word.

Scott is intrigued. "Uh, was that a known person?"

"Leonard. Leonard the Poet," Lilly says, absently, as her eyes follow him out the door. "Odd man, a little off-center, I think. Every time I see him he looks like he just came out of the rain. In winter I swear he has this thin coating of ice all over him—he actually *crackles* when he walks."

"Has a last name, does he?"

Lilly pauses. "You know, I have no idea. I never thought about it, but I guess he *has* to . . ."

"Well, no—Cher, Madonna, Liberace, Jewel, Winona, Prince. Guess you just have to be an *artiste.*"

Heads shake around the table. "Everybody just calls him 'Leonard the Poet,' no last name." Lilly's voice trails off. She pulls out a steno pad and scribbles as everyone pretends not to notice.

"So Leonard needs a name, does he," Jack says into his beer. "Maybe he can borrow a couple of yours, Leslie."

The Grin bores through him. "Watch it, oppressor-boy. Keep your manpaws off my feminames."

"Yeah, about those *names.*" It's Scott, apparently thrillseeking. Jack shoots him a look of warning, which Scott ignores. "I'm usually way too socially adequate to ask this sort of thing, but: Leslie, Erickson, Mitchell, Robbins . . . *Moooore,*" he says, drawing out each name. "Do let me guess." The spectators wince as one. "First name . . . maiden name . . . first husband, second husband, current husband?"

All other chairs scoot back two inches, their occupants going silent in a way that suggests the good Father is about to be violently defrocked. If this were a Western, Brian thinks, the piano would go silent and the barkeep would slowly drop out of sight.

Lilly's almost entirely inside her steno pad, veiled in a thin graphite haze.

Leslie locks eyes with the new guy. "*Leslie* is my given name. *Erickson* was my mother's family name before she married my father and rejected her own unique identity by allowing herself to be swallowed in *his. Moore* is in fact my father's name, but it is also *mine,* thank you, because I was born to it. We call it my *birth* name or my *family* name, of course, not my 'maiden' name. I was never a damn maiden any more than you ever were, 'scuse me, Father. And *Mitchell* and *Robbins* are the family names of my maternal and paternal grandmothers, respectively, both of whom were similarly stripped of their individual personhoods when *they* were married. I reclaim their names to honor them and to remember their loss."

"And your husband's name then, is . . ."

"Bill."

Scott gives a low whistle. "Seems like people around here either have too many names or too few."

"It seems to *me,* Father, that everyone has precisely the number of names they require." Leslie leans across the table to Scott, without menace but also without mercy, and whispers, "Never underestimate the importance of the *names* of things . . . Father."

A smile spreads over Scott's face. Oh how he does love the odd chance to tilt with a surefooted zealot. She returns the smile and the unspoken sentiment.

Two pints later it is close to six o'clock, and aside from Lilly, who has drifted, scribbling, to a back booth, Scott and Jack are the only gown survivors as the town begins to filter in for the six-to-two shift.

They sit in silence for a few minutes until Jack, as usual, breaks it.

"So Scott."

"So Jack."

"It seems you are the Second Coming."

"Sure looks that way, don't it?" Scott becomes very interested in the contents of his glass.

Jack pretends to be equally intrigued by his own. "Well hallelujah then. And how does that make you feel?"

"Why, Messianic. Saviourial. Positively *KRISSST*–ee–inn." Scott seems self-satisfied in a way that makes Jack's stomach tighten. "The bishop, dean, and president are happy, and the theology department has its knickers in a serious twist. So I'm one for four."

"You know, when you entered the city on your ass, I actually worried that I was bringing my strangest little friend into a place that wouldn't have any idea how to deal with him. Now the place is kneeling at your feet and I sit here like I'm having a drink with someone else's celebrity. Very weird."

"Try being *me* for a day! The whole thing's bizarre, just clicking along in hyperdrive. It's like I'm on the outside looking in. This place was a little too ready for a savior." He drinks deeply and licks the bronze foam from his lip. "Gotta be the way Jesus felt. So hey, bring on the Second Coming references. Good for attendance."

"Although Christ probably wasn't licking beer foam from his lip as he mused about his ministry."

"Oh don't you bet on that. I figure Jesus for a pretty regular guy, actually, if you can get around the Gospel hagiographies. If there was beer there, he quaffed. Look, either he's doing the human experience thing or he's not, right? I figure he'd have done it right."

Jack rocks back in his chair, slack-jawed. "So this is a real deal, then. Listen to the WWJD talk coming out of you! You're an upgrade of the shell-game, keeping it flashy and current for the kiddies." His tone darkens three clicks. "Scott, look at yourself. You're turning into what we used to hate the most, the *most!*" Jack slams his hand down on the last word for emphasis, which draws the momentary attention of the bar townies.

He switches to half voice. "Remember, back in Berkeley, the preacher guy in Sproul Plaza? 'Bob God,' we called him?"

Scott smiles and nods. "How could I forget Bob."

"Out there with drawings of a half cow, half whale, front legs on land, tail in the water? Saying 'Look at what the evolutionists say happened. How could you have a half cow and half whale?' Remember this guy?"

"No Jack, I've forgotten since nine seconds ago."

"When you tilted with him every day for two weeks— well, it was the best two weeks of my senior year. Beautiful thing. People brought popcorn and big foam fingers. Remember the day you tore the historical assumptions of the New Testament to shreds? Bit by bit, book by book? 'Jesus was born during the reigns of Quirinius in Syria and Herod in Judea, right Bob,' you'd say, and he'd say yes, and you'd say 'And during the universal census of Caesar Augustus,' and he'd say 'I'm impressed at your knowledge of the Gospel truths!', and you'd say 'But it turns out Quirinius and Herod never ruled at the same time, and Augustus Caesar conducted not a single universal census,' and what did he say?"

"Lessee. He said 'Omigosh, you're right! Bring on the sexy bellydancers.'"

"And the Old Testament. You used *Age of Reason* as a guide, I remember, but a lot of it was original and *brilliant*. Remember how you argued him into a corner about the stated dimensions of Noah's Ark? Every known species of *beetle* wouldn't physically fit on the Ark, you said, much less the aardvarks and bats and elephants and eleven million other species on Earth. You did the actual math. You had color flipcharts! And when you asked if he was suggesting the whole Ark thing was allegorical, he said 'No, it happened just the way God said it did,' and you asked how, given the obvious impossibilities, and he said what?"

"Jack, you're spitting on me."

"And the contradictory genealogies of Christ, and the translation snafus, and the perfect resemblances of Christ's life story to Mithras, and on and on and on. And what did he say, Scott, every time you backed him into a logical corner?" Jack is half standing. "What did he say to you?"

"He smiled at me and said, 'The Lord moves in mysterious ways.'"

"And you'd just about *spit blood*," Jack rasps, poking his finger in Scott's face with each word, then dropping back into his chair.

Scott's expression is far away. "Yeah, those were good times. Big crowd everyday at noon—especially when I could get enough blood to come up."

"Gosh, big crowds, just like now, eh Scott? Except oh! now *you're* Bob God and there's no Scott Siberell on the other side." Jack's good and wound up and sure of himself. "Yeah, that's it, isn't it: it's the *crowd* that gets your juices going. You don't care what hat you wear."

Scott's look is now one of dimpled amusement, one he

knows infuriates Jack. "Look, is this going somewhere? 'Cause I've got to go home and do my devotional."

"No," Jack replies, rubbing his eyes, "it certainly isn't going anywhere, Scott, any more than the Bob God debates went anywhere. I'm just walking around a little mental maze. Just tell me more about my Savior and I'll be fine."

"Well, tell you what, I'll *be* your Savior instead. I saw that little Mill quote on your office door and gosh, as much as I like fireworks, I thought I might advise you to take that down for awhile."

Jack looks up at his friend with a mix of sadness and disbelief. "Oh, here it comes. And from you, that just corks it. Why should I take it down, Scott? Complicates your mission, does it?"

"Jack, calm down. Boy, for a philosopher, you've sure got some unexamined assumptions going. I am not trying to piss you off. I just wanted to warn you that raising a little atheist flag at this precise moment might complicate your life in a way you don't want. You familiar with *Ex Corde Ecclesiae?*"

"Wait, don't tell me . . . didn't they do 'Inna Godda Davida?'"

"See, you *don't* know, so I'm doing you a favor, chump. *Ex Corde Ecclesiae* is a very recent attempt by the Vatican to whip Catholic colleges and universities back into line. It was implemented two years ago by almost every Catholic college in the world, including our Saint Bernie's."

"And it deals with what, the number and dimension of votive candles in the sanctuary?"

Scott shakes his head in amazement. "You see? You don't have a clue. Do you even *read* campus memos? *Ex Corde* says, among other things, that all other professors at Catholic colleges are to respect Catholic doctrine and morals in their research and teaching and are to make *no public statements* that contradict, challenge or 'disrespect' Catholic teachings. You can see that's pretty broad, so it depends on whose watching the store, right? Turns out it's the local bishop's responsibility to monitor the 'Catholicity' of Catholic colleges in his diocese. For us that means O'Donoghue, who'd just love a chance to show the Vatican what a good soldier he is. Your weak little statement of principle can get you kicked out of here with no place to land."

Jack glares hard. "Just another brick in the wall, Father. Like hell I'm gonna take that quote off the door. It's the only reminder I have that I'm still alive above the neck." He downs a half pint in one go. "You heard about Wisconsin, but did you know Minnesota's talking about dumping evolution from the curriculum too? It's expected to fail, but they're *considering* it, Scott, right here. Not that it matters to me, since my son, *my son* is in a Lutheran grade school. We're buying a Fable Funnel on the installment plan. And *I'm* stranded for the rest of my career in a Catholic college that was at least tolerable before you, Scott, started making it a damned holy pilgrimage site. And now this *Ex Corde* thing."

"Jack, look at me. Lighten up. Remember when I got here last month and you were all suspicious about my unholy intentions?"

"I do. Relax, you are vindicated. You're a good little apostle."

Scott chuckles. "*You* relax. When was the last time you were so much as half a step ahead of me?"

"Well let's see, that would have been . . ."

Scott interrupts with a wave. "Whenever you think it was, you're wrong. You're great at the post mortem, JJ, always have been—but let's face it, you generally don't know what's happening until it's over, am I right? Look at Daddy, Jack—am I right? You and every other headscratcher of your generation."

Jack hates it when somebody pegs him, especially when it's done so calmly and he's so riled up. "I'll just wait and respond when it's over, since I probably don't *get* it yet. So enlighten me. What is it that's happening that I cannot see?"

Scott grins. "Oh no. Still not ready to feed it to you. There's more fun to be had with your head, apparently. But I have faith in your potential to one day figure something out before the postgame show. So let me just say *Abbe Meslier.*"

Abby Mezliay? "You won't be surprised that I don't know who the hell that is."

Okay. Jack quickly works up a pretty plausible theory in his head. Abby is some hot young Bernie that Scott intends to bag. Here's the scenario: Scott met Abby at some youth evangelism conference, found out she goes to Saint Bernadette's, which, gosh, is where his friend Jack Kassel teaches. He developed a sort of long shot, I-can-get-any-thing-I-want-no-matter-how-remote infatuation that lingered long after he'd returned to Oakland. Then boom, the job posting comes across his desk and the last puzzle piece falls in. That's gotta be it. This whole exploding mega-ministry is a cover for a seduction. That's as Siberellian a scenario as Jack's ever heard.

Scott continues, eyes closed and smiling. "Abbe Meslier is the answer to every burning question, a balm for the troubled heart. Abbe Meslier is the key to the kingdom."

7

The Bones of Contention

Good friend, for Jesu's sake forbear
to dig the dust enclosed here.
Blest be the man who spares these stones
And curst be he who moves my bones.

Epitaph of William Shakespeare

This has got to be the weirdest damn thing I've ever been a part of. Who would give thumbs-up to building a school on top of a trash heap I don't know. It isn't sound. It isn't solid. We have to shore up the sides as we go like we're digging in a sand beach, the ground is so damn loose. Nobody even knows what this hill-thing is, but I'm getting a pretty good idea. The plan has us digging an eight-foot diameter tunnel 600 feet from near the bottom of the formation right up under the Administration building at the top, and so far we've run into, listen to this, chairs, clothes, wagon parts, a roll of barbed wire, barrels, buckets, fence slats, an iron pump, a trough, two doors, and a china doll. Then today,

Bill's working at the tunnel head section about 15 yards in when he comes up with an *actual human leg bone*. Well didn't that stop the whole works dead in its tracks. Tom says we're likely to be hung up for weeks while the state archaeologist, which I didn't even know there was any such damn thing, while he comes out and figures whose leg it was.

Word of the found femur goes from Workman Bill to Foreman Tom to Workman Steve who tells a cute student cafeteria staffer, who still doesn't agree to go out with him but repeats it to her professor Brian Finnegan, who tells one Jack Kassel over a Guinness, who tells his five-year old son just to get him to say *"Wo!"*, who tells Mom, who just happens to need a story. Four well-placed phone calls later, she has stirred the pot enough to generate a bona fide bread-and-butter series.

Gruesome Find Beneath CSB
WORKMEN UNEARTH HUMAN REMAINS
Rebecca Kassel • *Ledger-Domain* staff writer

ST. PHILIP—Bernadette's Butte. Bernadette's Bluff. The Wedge. The Ramp. The peculiar western Minnesota earth formation on which the College of Saint Bernadette is built has gone by many names and perhaps fostered even more speculations about its origins. One theory, long dismissed by geologists and historians, received new fuel today with the discovery by workmen of a human femur during the digging of an underground pedestrian tunnel. A local Lakota Sioux tribal band has long maintained that the site is an ancient Lakota burial wedge. The discovery of the bones brought construction to an immediate halt so

State Archaeologist Dr. Leigh-Ann Bedford could determine the nature and age of the remains.

"It is unlikely that the remains date from the period prior to European settlement, but that's what we're here to determine," Bedford said.

William Kravitch, an employee of Gustafson and Son Construction, was the workman who found the bone. "It wasn't hard to find, it just sifted right out of the fill into the shovel of my loader and set there gleaming white as pitch."

Running Deer Shaw, a leader of the local tribal band, voiced anger at the state agencies that have ignored his contentions for years and at what he sees as their continued skepticism. "At last we will have proof that this college stands on the graves of our sacred ancestors. When this formation is verified as a sacred burial wedge, the college will be removed from this site, one way or another."

Informed that no wedge-shaped burial mounds have been reported anywhere on Earth, band leader R. D. Shaw replied, "Well, that makes it all the more precious, now doesn't it?"

Dean Martin is already ten minutes late for a meeting with the Lakota and Gustafson and Son Construction when she steps into the first floor elevator and into the smoldering presence of Sister Joan Krenek, IHM.

The Dean manages recover from a small heart attack enough to compose herself for a nod. "Joan."

"Genevieve." Her triumphant eyes make it clear that she has been lying in wait.

They've ridden in silence for about twelve feet when the elevator suddenly crunches to a halt between floors. The Dean swears inwardly and reaches for the emergency phone.

"Yes, Latifah, this is Dean Martin. Please tell Carl that the Admin elevator is stuck again. Yes, there are people aboard. Yes, I am one of them. Thank you, Latifah."

The two women stand engulfed in that peculiar, close silence found only in elevators and coffins.

Sister Joan clears her throat. "Surely it is not silence in which we are to find ourselves standing in this situation."

The Dean sighs. "No, Joan, I didn't imagine so." She allows her weight to fall back against the brass handrail.

"My several recent memos have gone ignored by you."

Oh here we go, thinks the Dean, her irritation beginning to simmer. I'm in just the mood for a damned liturgical debate in a little wooden box with a pissed off nun. "Now Joan, your memos have not been *ignored*. This has been quite an unusual Fall, I think you'll agree. I just haven't had a spare moment to consider your . . . *concerns*."

"It seems we find ourselves in mutual possession of a spare moment."

"Indeed."

The moment attempts to tick away quietly, but Joan seizes it. "Indeed. Yes, I will agree that this Fall is an unusual one," she says, pausing to flare her nostrils for dramatic effect. "It is the first in which the Lord's Table has been overturned by a huckster."

"Now, sister. He is a priest. Certainly we can give him the benefit of doubt before calling him a *huckster*. Father Siberell is obviously filling some unmet need in our community. Wanda is absolutely elated . . ."

". . . and I think we both know what it takes to do that, Genevieve. A cool breeze on a warm day. Weren't you present last month for the dedication of the new St. Francis sculpture by the pond?"

"Well no, I wasn't, I had . . ."

"In the middle of her speech Wanda caught sight of a formation of geese overhead and ran after them, clapping and squealing—in the middle of a *sentence*, mind you—and never came back." She pauses to enjoy the Dean's attempt to disguise her dismay. "So please don't use Wanda's elation to signify *anything*."

"Well then let Bishop O'Donoghue's enthusiasm signify something."

"I assure you a letter has been mailed to him as well. He has not attended the services in question, he's only seen the numbers and heard the publicity. He doesn't know we've got a Baptist revival tent opened up. Gennie, this is just not *us*, what's going on."

The Dean pounces. "No, you're right, Joan. It isn't us. It is *successful*, it is larger-than-life. It paints with bright colors. It reeks with imagination. Father Hillerman going through the motions for three nuns each Sunday, *that* was us. I thought it time to do something wholly uncharacteristic by hiring this man. And it has worked beautifully."

Joan squeezes the rosary in her pocket and closes her eyes. "Genevieve, listen to me. I was drawn to the service of Christ through the power and mystery of the Eucharist. There is nothing I do that is not informed by the truth and love of that moment. It is my reason for being. It is my greatest joy." Suddenly annoyed with herself, she swats a tear from each eye and stiffens. "I cannot bear to see it overshadowed by this man's self-serving showmanship."

Gennie extends a hand toward Joan's arm. Joan bristles and the Dean withdraws. Their acquaintanceship of a dozen years has been friendly in a stiff and formal way. Comfort with physical contact, Gennie figures, is another twelve years off. "Joan, I do understand what you are saying. I just don't agree that Father Siberell has diminished the Eucharist. His homilies are just so much more effective by comparison to Father Hillerman's that it *seems* the Communion has dimmed. It hasn't."

Sister Joan concedes nothing. "There was a time when you couldn't bear this kind of cult of personality yourself. Am I incorrect?"

"Oh it was never personality that bothered me, Joan, I assure you. I don't need things flat and lifeless. Scott has charisma, yes, but he's not a *charismatic*, if you catch my semantic distinction. And much of his charisma comes from the meaningful, sensible message he puts forth." Okay, let's get right to it, she thinks. "It's woolly mysticism that I cannot brook, Sister. What I despise is reliance on cheap spiritual gimmicks and supernatural stunts, like apparitions and holy spirit possessions and saints manifesting themselves in soap bubbles and walls and pancakes. Scott has none of that, so I have no complaints."

"I don't recommend keeping mysticism at arm's length, Genevieve. A lot of the enduring mystery of the Church comes from these kind of recurrent, inexplicable wonders. *That* should be the personality we're looking for, not this, this *tapdancing*. The Eucharist itself is part of that mystery tradition. Don't push mysteries away just because they defy explanation."

"Don't you assume to know why I push mysteries away, Sister." It is the Dean's turn to bristle. She exhales, then continues. "Joan . . . I come from a family that built ever day around mysteries. Every room a shrine, every act a ritual. Every part of our lives had a patron saint to implore. No childlike foolishness was innocent; it was all profanity to the name of God."

Three bangs from a wrench on the third floor startle both women visibly. "Ya down there then, are ya Dean Martin?"

"Yes I am, Carl," shouts the Dean, eyes closed. "Sister Joan as well. Not many other options, Carl."

"I suppose not, Dean. We're workin' on ya, okay there?"

"That would be okay, Carl. Could you get word to the meeting in the boardroom that I am unavoidably detained?"

"I can do that, sure."

"I appreciate it, Carl."

"Good deal then."

After a proper pause, Joan continues. "I'm certain your parents thought they were doing the best for you and your . . . do you have siblings?"

The Dean hesitates. "Why yes, as a matter of fact, I once had two sisters." This is none of her damn business, Genevieve thinks—then decides the whole story is her best shot at silencing Joan's litany. "Two sisters. I was in the middle. My younger sister Angelique was an early beneficiary of the mystic Christian spirit. Born with a light around her face, everyone said the same thing, 'A light around her face.' She looked like a holy vision herself—and she saw them on a daily basis." She gazes into her reflection in the brass button panel as she recalls. "Our parents treated her like a living saint. She fasted once a week at Mother's encouragement and mortified her flesh with a six-lash whip that Father made for her eighth birthday. She slept on a board. Spoke to angels. If it happened now instead of the 50s . . ." Deep breath. "Well, now they might see she needed help. But then—well, she was the answer to my parents' prayers, Angelique was.

"Summer of 1952, New York State Fair, Angelique is eleven. She and I ride the Ferris Wheel together. Our seat stops at the top. She cries out in ecstasy that the angels are calling her and walks off into their arms." Joan gasps in shock, hand to her open mouth, and Genevieve continues. "I was always prone to rationalism, more partial to Thomas Aquinas than Thomas à Kempis, so Mother put all her hope and spiritual energy into my older sister."

Joan's hand drops slowly from her mouth. "Oh Gennie,

I'm so sorry. But . . . *surely* you'll agree that your sister's terrible tragedy is an extreme example, not representative of mainstream mysticism . . ."

"Well, as I said, I'm not out of sisters yet, Sister. And I'd suggest quite frankly that 'mainstream mysticism' is an oxymoron." Tilt with me about religious fanaticism, Joan Krenek, and I will bury you, thinks the Dean. "After Angelique's 'rapture'—yes, that's what my parents called it, and after the initial shock they were overjoyed—my older sister Therese joined the Order of the Radiant Hope of Mary." Joan shudders visibly. The Order is well-known for an extreme rule and an almost unspeakable discipline. "She felt incredible pressure to live up to Angelique's example, you see. Therese once told me she felt Mother's daily disappointment at her stubborn insistence on clinging to life when martyrdom was waiting so patiently."

"Oh Genevieve, you simply *must* be reading a great deal into this."

"Am I? I don't think I'm reading terribly much into things when I say that our faith can lose itself in an obsession with death, and it is that obsession I resist."

Joan leans forward, imploring. "Not *death*, Gennie . . . eternal *life*. The difference is *complete*."

"The difference, Joan, is *semantic*. I am sickened by any tendency to deflect our attention from the here and now into some mystical unknowable existence after death."

"Genevieve Marie Martin!!"

"March 3rd of 1970, 4:45 p.m., Therese's entire convent finished their grace, crossed themselves and picked up their spoons to begin their dinner of thin broth, only to be thrown to the floor in agony. The cook told the police that Mary Queen of Heaven had instructed her to poison them, to grant the sisters entry to paradise by ending their lives. But she put too little lye in the soup, Joan, so they got the consolation prize: an increase in their purifying pain. They all suffered severe esophageal and tracheal burns. Most of them cannot speak at all. Some must be fed through stomach tubes for the rest of their lives. Therese can be understood if she presses her lips to my ear and expends all of her energy in a single sentence." The Dean meets Joan's stunned gaze directly. "You may suggest, if you wish, that hers is yet another extreme example, but eventually we'll have to deal with all these 'extremes.'" She punches the 3-button six times and sighs. "My point is that unfocused, undisciplined mysticism can produce wonderful imagery to fire the spirit, but it also fuels the darkest, most disturbed aspects of human nature. In a perfect world we can invoke all the spirit and power of the unknowable wonders without fear." One more punch to the 3. "This is not a perfect world, so I prefer some sober rationality. Father Siberell may be a bit flashy, perhaps even young and vigorous, but if you listen to what he says, it actually makes sense, and it's about life, not death. That's about all I can ask. He speaks my language *and* he packs them in while doing so. That's a rare combination. We'll keep him."

Joan Krenek pauses to fully accept the impossibility of continuing the discussion, then reaches over and throws the emergency stop switch back to RUN.

Dean Martin enters the shamelessly ornate and inappropriately named Mother Teresa Board Room at a brisk clip, joining a meeting that has needed her. Twenty minutes without her steady hand on the rudder has resulted in several smoldering constituencies without the saving option of tabling the topic until next year. Around the immense square of the table are arrayed the thirteen players. Most decidedly present is one Olaf Gustafson Jr., walrusine president of Gustafson and Son Construction, with two pinstriped attorneys and one herringboned accountant. Off her father's starboard side is the critically pale Olaffe Gustafson III. It is Olaffe who constitutes the "Son" in Gustafson and Son. Thirty-two years ago, upon hearing of his wife's new pregnancy, Olaf descended on City Hall in New Ulm with cigars and decrees that onto each and every occurrence of his company name in city files the suffix "and Son" be appended. The paperwork for the name change took three months and cost Olaf over six thousand dollars all told. No matter, he crowed. Olaf III will be born with his shining future laid out before him.

When the doctor announced to the waiting room that a girl had been born, early and small and pale, Olaf froze, a gargantuan smile pasted across his face, for eight seconds of intense, silent rumination. "Splendid!" He bellowed. "Bring him out!"

From that day forward Olaf treated his daughter with the greatest of kindness, love and respect, but managed somehow to avoid so much as a single gender-specific pronoun. "Someday," he would proudly aver, "the company will be hi . . . her . . . uh, Olaf(fe)'s."

Directly across from the Gustafson contingent sits Helen Highwater, Dean of the Interior, and Bruce Everell-Beers, a temp. Bruce was called in as a temporary replacement for Sullivan Reeves, Vice-President of Finance, who was out sick and subsequently died. Bruce is twenty-two. Bruce can file, answer phones, and type 80 words a minute if there's no radio going. His eyes adopted a look of stricken horror when he heard the nature of the position he was filling for two days. Now, five months later, the look has taken up an apparently permanent residence on his face—coupled horribly with an intense, frozen smile below an earnest attempt at a dignifying moustache. Upon first meeting him, his facial dissonance has led more than one new secretary to flee the office weeping.

Bruce and Helen look up at the Dean with unmistakable relief as she enters and sits between them.

The third side of the table is underpopulated, consisting of a single representative of the anonymous donor without whom even the merest thought of tunnels would never have seen the light of day.

On the fourth side sit Running Deer Shaw, Lakota band leader; his wife, Fog-in-the-Valley-Makes-for-Dicey-Hunting; his son, Gorge-Burn-Hard; and two very pleased-looking tribal attorneys. Their collective posture and attitude make it clear to the Dean that theirs is the upper hand at the moment.

Seated in the far corner of the room so as not to appear allied with any one side is Dr. Leigh-Ann Bedford, Minnesota State Archaeologist.

"Please forgive my delay—I hope you received word of the reason," says the Dean.

"Well, no, actually we were wondering." It is R. D. Shaw. "We hope you don't mind that we started right in."

"Not at all." Dean Martin makes a mental note to murder Carl. "So where are we?"

Bruce surprises everyone, especially himself, by jumping in. "Well, we started by having everybody say what they thought about stuff, and then we started talking about stuff."

"We had established, I believe," interjects one of the Gustafson attorneys, "that the Gustafson and Son company contract specifically releases Gustafson and Son from any liabilities resulting from unanticipated discoveries of this ilk, and that Gustafson and Son shall retain the contract for the duration of this project, and furthermore that since Gustafson and Son has not *caused* the delay by its actions, said company will not incur any contract penalty from the delay, which is to say that the company is still on the clock during the delay whether shovels are lifted or not."

The donor's rep takes the floor. "My client has made it clear to me that the amount of the gift is final, meaning that no additional funds are available for this project. Any cost overruns generated by this delay must be covered by the

College. And since $305,000 of my client's gift has already been spent on the initial phase of the excavation, it is her intention . . . it is his or her intention that the project be brought to eventual completion—that it is not terminated, in other words— or that the $305,000 be returned to her, to him or her, *molto pronto.*"

"And those funds would come from where, sir?" asks the Dean.

"Not my client's problem."

"And we had also agreed, I thought," interjects Running Deer Shaw, "that these are secondary issues that can be dealt with when I and my family and attorneys are not sitting here waiting for our ancestors' spirits to be properly honored."

"Just bringing the Dean up to speed," says Helen.

"Yes, well, now that we're all 'up to speed,'"—he shows himself to be among those people who bracket the air with quotes to signal contempt—"let's continue where we left off with your," he brackets, "'State Archaeologist.'"

"Yes, Dr. Bedford, please continue."

Dr. Bedford rises from her chair. "I would prefer to remain neutral in all but the scientific decisions here. The state mandates that found remains of unknown origin and evident age be examined by my office to avoid disturbance of historically-significant sites that may be of interest to the State Historical Society."

"Not to mention others," fumes R. D. Shaw.

"The State Historical Society exists to serve the needs of all communities in the state, including Native American bands and tribal units, so no exclusion was implied."

"But you will certainly admit that a 'State Historical Society' is primarily interested in issues related to the 'state' as a political entity."

"Its founding charter states otherwise. 'State' refers only to the modern boundary itself, but the Society and my office are concerned with anything and everything that has happened within that boundary. If our concern was only the actual State of Minnesota, for example, our interests would not reach back prior to 1859 into territorial days and earlier still. But they clearly do."

"Where is the bone now, by the way, and by what authority have you taken custody of the bone of our ancestor?"

"The bone was removed to my lab in Saint Paul by authority of the state. The bone was not found on tribal land, so no tribal jurisdiction is even implied."

"What you mean is the bone was not found on the land to which our people have been unlawfully confined for one hundred and forty years," inserts Fog-in-the-Valley-Makes-for-Dicey-Hunting. "But all of this land was ours for forty thousand years before the white man came. The bone should remain near its resting place until it can be examined by your office and by our healer."

Bruce blunders in. "Uh, your *healer?* I think it's a little late for that." He laughs nervously and repeats "Get it?" several times to an unreceptive audience.

Carl suddenly pokes his head in the door. "Excuse me, folks, ah, Dean Martin says to tell you she's gonna be late, she's . . . oh, hello there, Dean! Good deal, then."

Carl's head vanishes. The Dean mentally commutes his sentence from death to dismemberment.

Gorge-Burn-Hard Shaw answers Bruce with a cold stare. "The healer is what *you* might call a 'shaman' or 'medicine man.' He's our most highly respected elder in the spiritual realm. He dreams realities that are hidden to us and communicates with our ancestors."

"And he will examine this bone in the only place where the truth can be revealed," says Running Deer. "Its resting place. When you removed it from the site you disrupted its connection to its own story. That will have to be restored, then our healer will determine its true origin."

"Now, I am the first to respect diversity and to celebrate

difference," pipes up the Dean of the Interior, "but let's be rational here. If this was an ancient Indian burial site, do you really think Saint Bernadette would have appeared to Mother Cordion and asked that she build the College here? It strains credulity to think the saint would make such an error."

"Well it will all be made clear once a proper examination has taken place," Shaw says. "Then we'll all know the truth."

Dr. Bedford responds with a hint of lost patience. "And if your healer's findings contradict those of my office, Mr. Shaw? Then what? I too value input from all corners, but I must insist that science be the last word in this. The findings are not likely to be ambiguous."

Shaw leaps to his feet. "Your findings are *already* ambiguous! The bone you have found is not even a leg bone, as you've claimed—it is an *arm bone!*"

Somewhere a wavering organ chord is struck. A confused sort of minigasp goes up. Eyes dart back and forth in unmoving heads.

Dr. Bedford blinks, weighs her options. "Mr. Shaw, with all respect . . ."

"Your error was revealed to two of our elders in dreams last Wednesday night. How do you account for the simultaneous dream that an arm bone, not a leg bone, was found? How do you account for that with all your (bracket) 'science'?"

He continues with mounting confidence and pique. "I think we can safely say that enough questions have been raised regarding the accuracy of your methods to demand that our healer be permitted to examine the bone and to announce what is thereby revealed to him. We will expect word from you within 48 hours as to how, not whether, this will be carried out."

Shaws and company are up and gone.

❧

"Hi, can you tell me if it's a good day for James Kassel in 212? This is his son."

Four minutes of Marilyn Manson in soft orchestral arrangements.

"What is it. Whaddaya want."

"Hi Dad, it's Jack."

"Uh huh. He's not here."

"This is Jack calling you, Dad. Happy birthday."

"One-of-a-kind, real quality, top-notch! No markup whatsoever. My word's my bond."

"Dad, I . . ."

"Cheery cheery cheery cheery cheery-beery Edelweiss."

"Okay Dad, can you put the nurse back on the . . ."

"Jack."

"Yeah Dad. Hi."

"Hi Jack."

"Happy birthday Dad."

"Happy birthday Jack."

"You having a good morning?"

"Yeah, it's a good one. I've been pretty clearheaded all day."

"Good to hear, Dad. So, seventy-five, eh?"

"Yep, seventy-five. Seventy-six next week."

"So you still having those problems with your leg?"

"You know, everything is just so interesting here. We went on a bus trip yesterday."

"Oh, where'd you go?"

"Africa. And you know, Jack . . . they have the *nicest* kitchens there."

"That's great. Dad, I'm talking to the home again about moving you here but they said you're doing well enough that they need you to sign off on it. I think it'd be a good . . ."

"I am *not* moving to Minnesota. I just can't keep the walks clear like I used to, Jack, I just can't *do* it anymore. No snow in Arizona, you know."

"Dad, they'll do that for you here. I found a really good place in Mankato, you can just have time for your woodwork and your Mickey Spillane. You don't have to shovel snow."

"I'm well aware, Jack. What, do you think I'm a damned idiot?"

"No, of course not, Dad."

"You do."

"I don't! Look, I just want you closer to me so I can see you more often."

"Like that would make a damn bit of difference, I haven't seen you in twenty years."

"Dad, I was there for three weeks in August."

"Like hell. You ought to spend your time looking for a job instead of trying to get me to shovel your sidewalks. Have you even *tried* to find a job, Jack?"

"I'm a college professor, Dad. Twelve years now."

"Oh sure, teachin' what? Philosophy. What the hell is that supposed to do for anybody? What a damn waste, Jack, you'da made a hell of a salesman."

"You were a great salesman, Dad, but it's not for me."

"Puttin' things into people's hands that they can use, that makes their life better than it was the day before, that gives 'em time with their kids, time to read and garden and make love . . ."

"See Dad, *you* were the great salesman. I'm a great philosopher."

"Oh what the hell is that supposed to mean? Great philosopher. Fill your head up and then you die. What the hell *is* that? When you're layin' down in a pine phonebooth and people try and figure out if they give a rat's damn you ever lived, what do they look at? Your damn full head? Put things in their hands they can use, son, you do somethin' *useful* for people an' they'll remember you. You better believe they remember *me*, Jack. They'll remember you."

"I'm not sure that's the most important thing to me, Dad."

"Uh huh. Mm hmm, mm hmm, cheery cheery beery."

"Becca says hi."

"Oh Becca! How's she doin'? Jack, I gotta tell you, I'm surprised you haven't screwed that one up yet. She's a helluva good woman."

"Yeah Dad."

"Really good pair of tits, too."

". . ."

"And Connor, how 'bout my grandson?"

"Yeah Dad, he's doing great. He's actually starting to read for himself."

"No kiddin'! That's fantastic. Five years old, right?"

"Yes! Yes, he is, Dad. He's five."

"And *reading* already! It's 'cause he's got a damn genius for a father, Jack! He sees you readin' and thinkin' everyday and it rubs off. Just make sure he does something *useful* with it, Jack, not fritter it away."

"Like I did, you mean."

"What?"

"Well, it was nice talking to you. I hope you have a good birthday, Dad."

". . ."

"I love you."

"Hey Lou, looks like I got one of Jack's fag Berkeley friends on the phone here makin' a goddam faggot pass at me!"

Louise Kassel, 1700 miles away and twenty-seven years dead, declines to dignify this with a response.

Students returning from Thanksgiving break pass a seated huddle of protesters, mostly Lakota, cloaked in grey and brown blankets against the freezing wind, positioned between and outside the entrance gates. A single drum maintains a steady rhythm as the small group intones a wailing chant of anger and despair. Hand-lettered signs held in laps read LEAVE OUR ANCESTOR SPIRITS AT PEACE and CLOSE THE COLLEGE and REMEMBER THE *FIRST* THANKSGIVING? Running Deer Shaw and his son hand out leaflets to whatever students, faculty, and staff will take them from their outstretched hands. A film crew is on hand, recording the scene for a news update. Though the story is three weeks old, this is the first appearance of an organized protest and hence the first good televisable visuals since the bone itself.

Leslie Erickson Mitchell-Robbins Moore's heart jumps as she spots the protest through the windshield of her approaching Bug. She dismounts and beams as she walks toward campus, step quickening, leaning into the wind.

She walks so directly to R. D. Shaw that he startles.

"Tell me your story."

"I'm sorry?"

"No, *please* don't be sorry. Oh my word, don't be sorry for *anything*. Tell me about your struggle."

R. D. warily enters into a discussion of the excavation and the find, somewhat thrown off by the intense receptivity of the audience, finally concluding, "And so, it comes down to whether or not we, as living representatives of our ancestors, are to fulfill our obligations to their spirits by honoring the remains of their living flesh."

Leslie stands spellbound. "That is so beautiful. So very beautiful." She grabs his hand in both of hers and vibrates it rapidly. "I am with you. I am *with* you and your people.

We *will* win this fight." She continues through the gate, then returns to R.D., takes half of his flyers, beams hard, and retreats to the campus.

Subsequent excavation by the state archaeologist's office has now unearthed two complete human skeletons, both of which had been gradually pulled apart by the shifting soil of the unstable ground. In order to maintain order at the site and to allow the investigation to proceed, these additional discoveries have not yet been made public.

Dr. Bedford looked over each of the skeletons for five minutes before turning over responsibility for the mind-numbing detail of an actual report to two young interns in her office from the University of Minnesota. The findings, as she had predicted, were unambiguous: two Caucasians, one male, one female, both in their late sixties or early seventies, both dead of natural causes in the mid-to-late 19th century, originally buried side by side in their Sunday best. Case closed.

Coming up the walk from the parking lot shortly after Leslie—perhaps suspiciously so—is Leonard, hands thrust deep into his coat pockets, nose and ears swimming in a knit muffler. He veers away gradually as R. D. Shaw's outthrust flyer approaches him, then reluctantly removes one hand from his pocket, snares the flyer, and thrusts it back into his pocket. A few feet inside the gate he retrieves the crumpled flyer from his pocket and pauses in the clouds of his own breath to read:

THIS COLLEGE IS BUILT ON NATIVE GRAVES!!!

The recent unearthing of a native arm bone confirms what we, the Lakota Sioux peoples, your friends and neighbors, have long known: that the formation on which the College of Saint Bernadette is built on is an ancient burial wedge containing the sacred remains of our revered ancestors.

This issue, long a source of grief for our Lakota people, gained greater urgency when our resting dead were disturbed by the construction of your underground tunnel.

THEREFORE:

WE DEMAND that the College allow our Lakota healer Edward Moon-River to examine the bone to determine the identity of the Lakota ancestor to whom it belongs;

WE DEMAND that the College cease and desist all construction of underground tunnels;

WE DEMAND that the College be removed from this site or pay 17.6 million dollars in compensation to the members of the Lakota band for the desecration of our heritage.

TELL PRESIDENT STREAMLEY WHAT YOU THINK!
CALL (507) 220-3400 or email
wxstreamley@stbernie.edu

Leonard turns to look back at the protesters, then at the flyer, then at the tunnel entrance and idled equipment. He retraces his steps back to Shaw, leans in conspiratorially, and whispers:

"Not what happened, you know."

"Beg pardon?"

"It isn't true. No native bones in the wedge. I know."

"What do *you* know about it?"

Leonard's lips slide across his teeth into something of a

smile. "I even know their *names*." He nods meaningfully, then walks back through the gates and up the Wedge.

The last two weeks of the semester are always grueling, and Dean Martin begins to extend her days and her week. The controversy over the excavated bone has managed to add some complicating wrinkle to every item in each day's agenda. There are reporters to duck and constituencies to stroke. The cost overruns resulting from the month-long delay in work on the unwanted tunnel require cutbacks in other areas. Leslie Erickson Mitchell-Robbins Moore, president of the Faculty Senate, has taken to tying bone-related amendments to every item under consideration.

The Dean makes her way down the slope slowly at the end of the first Thursday in December. "The end of Thursday" is closer to literally true than ever before, for it is 11:15 p.m. before an exhausted Genevieve Martin finds herself stopping halfway down the hill, peering out over the most remarkable bit of snow-art she has ever seen. Someone somehow has managed to make an exceptionally lifelike rendering of Mary, Our Lady of Sorrows, in a monumental likeness spanning the entire width of the snow covered hockey pitch, sparkling in the glow of the globe lights along the flagstone walks. The shading, proportions, and expression are absolutely breathtaking in their attention to detail. Dean Martin notes with interest that the artist has chosen a beautiful but slightly severe style to mimic, almost medieval . . . and has managed the entire portrait without leaving a *single evident footprint* . . .

She stands in a spell of genuine awe and reverence combined with a growing concern, first slight, then more pronounced. It is so very skillfully done, even a little *too* well done for comfort. Suppose the artist, just for fun, remains anonymous, and a passing . . . well, a passing *Wanda* sees this in the morning . . .

A quick glance around, then Gennie Martin hikes her coat and skirt and tromps out into the snow field, decisively though not without a tinge of regret, and obliterates the lovely image.

"And then this one kid named Cooper, he broke the top off it and he told Mrs. McInerny he didn't and he said Callie did it and Callie got in trouble and that wasn't fair at *all* 'cause Callie is my friend."

Jack switches the phone to his right ear. "And did you tell Mrs. McInerny what really happened?"

"I couldn't do that, Dad."

"Why not?"

"It was snack time. And besides, that's tattling."

Jack has always had mixed feelings about the adult aversion to 'tattling.' Sometimes tattling amounts to annoying truthtelling. Better an innocent child gets blamed than somebody *snitches*, I guess.

"So what happened after snack?"

"Daaaaad . . ."

"What?"

"I don't wanna talk about it 'cause you'll be mad."

Jack is shocked, *shocked*. "Connor Larkin Kassel! I promise I will not be mad."

Connor exhales into the receiver. "OK, we talked about *God.*"

Well . . . okay, yeah, fine, Jack is a little mad. But it's a Lutheran school, so he figures he'd better get on that acceptance curve. "Connor, there's nothing wrong with talking about God. Remember what we said about that?"

"*We* didn't say anything. *You* said."

"Okay, what did I say?"

Connor, in a singsong. " 'It's fine to talk about God as long as you can make up your own mind.'"

"And it would be just as wrong if I said you *have* to think there is no God as it would be for Mrs. McIntyre . . ."

"McInerny, Dad."

". . . for Mrs. McInerny to say you *have* to think there *is* a God. You get to make up your own mind by thinking." And that's where Jack gets mad, since he knows there's likely to be no such open presentation going on from Mrs. McIntosh.

"And Callie had to stay in from recess even though she didn't even break that toy."

"Uh huh. And what else happened to day? Anything you really liked?"

"Oh! We got measured, and I grew almost two inches since school started! I couldn't even believe it! Two inches! Some of the kids didn't grow, and some even got *shorter*."

"Con, that's great! Wow, how are you growing so fast?!"

"I don't know, Dad. I guess God just wants me to grow."

Uhhhhhhh huh. Deeeeeep breaths. In, out, in, in, in, in . . .

"Daddy?"

Happy happy chirpy voice. "Anything else happen today except for you growing so tall because of all the good food you eat and all the exercise you get and the fact that your Dad is six two?"

"Oh. You're mad."

"I am not mad!!" Jack does a single normal breath cycle. "I am not mad, sweetie. Why would I be mad? Anyway, what else do you want to talk about?"

"I watched ZOOM and learned how to make a little volcano with just vinegar and baking soda and a little volcano."

"And he said, 'I don't know, Dad. I guess God just wants me to grow.'"

"Doh!"

"Exactly. *Doh*. And some of the other kids didn't grow, which means I guess that God didn't *want* them to grow, which means there's something *wrong* about them, doesn't it, if God doesn't love them as much as he loves *me*, and I better keep saying my prayers and loving him hard without any doubts and praying for Davy to stop doing whatever he's doing to piss God off, but oh, maybe it's because Davy is black, or gay, or a Jew, or something else that God hates, and maybe God wants me to hate Davy too, the short little bastard, and everyone who's like him."

"Oh my God!" Brian laughs. "Take a breath, Jack! So what are you gonna do about this calamity? Are you yankin' him out of that school?"

Jack massages his eyes. "I can't do that unilaterally. Becca and her mom want him in there. Well no, that's not true. Her *mom* wants him in, and Becca wants to look like a *gooood* Christian daughter."

"So get him out of there! What's wrong with you? You sit here whining like you have nothing to say about it. Your *mother-in-law* should be in control? Get him out! Be a man!" As soon as the last three words are out of his mouth, Brian cringes, glancing furtively around the bar for faculty colleagues. None.

Whew.

Jack takes a deep drag on his cigarette and blows a plume straight up. "You know how the Christian default works. Two Christian parents raise a little religious automaton."

"Uh, Jack, your child doesn't have two Christian parents."

"I'm getting there. The Christian default kicks in if only one parent is Christian, because the other defers, usually because he doesn't care or has trouble explaining why Granny died, so hey, might as well be safe and fill the kids with fear and hate and death and ignorance posing as love and life and truth."

"You get way too worked up about this crap."

"You don't get worked up *enough* about it. If you had kids you'd have to deal with the feeling of seeing a great one like Connor standing at the top of that slippery slope with all the ignorant bastards behind him poking him with crosses. He has this fantastic probing mind that's being told there are certain things you just plain accept."

"So yank him out."

"I might! For now at least I'm *out* there owning my beliefs, not sitting passively like you, snickering and doing nothing."

"Tell me you didn't just say you're 'owning' your beliefs. And oh, you're out there all right, whining hard into your pint glass about your Lutheran son and doing nothing about it. And then there's that bold little postage stamp on your door. 'Some people aren't religious,' or whatever that said. *Hooooooweeee!* What a heroic gesture." He laughs again. "You're a hypocrite, Jack. You lecture me and Scott and Connor and Becca one-on-one, but you don't have the courage of your convictions to go public. It isn't that big a deal to me, but it is to you, and you just run away from it."

"So what would you do in my place?"

"I'd do exactly what you are doing—but that would be consistent for me, so I wouldn't gnash my teeth about it. I'm a pragmatist. I like my job. Well okay, I don't like my job, but I like *having* a job, so I try not to piss on the Pope's hat while I'm teaching here, especially not with *Ex Corde* around."

"You know about this *Ex Corde* thing too?"

Brian looks at Jack scornfully. "Do you *go* to faculty meetings, Jack, other than the danced ones? We've been talking through the *Ex Corde* implementation for two years! Anyway, my point is that you are an idealist who acts like a real-ist, and that's chickenshit stuff." Jack is now up to three chickenshits. "I would *also* do nothing, but that would be a consistent position for *me* since I haven't been an idealist since the bombing of Cambodia. So it seems to me that you have a choice of being who you are, completely, and taking the con-sequences, or being who *I* am, completely, and dealing with that mess."

Jack inhales a handful of popcorn as an excuse to not respond for a while.

Standing at his office door at seven-thirty the next morn-ing, Jack has to agree. What a wussy attempt. The Mill quote takes up less than a quarter of the halfsheet it is on, which is lost in a sea of expired conference announcements, arcane journal articles, and political cartoons from two years ago. Scott and Brian only saw it because they've both stood wait-ing at his door to go to lunch or coffee, looking for something to read to pass the time until Jack, always late, shows up.

Since posting the quote, Jack has felt a little surge of defiant integrity as he walks around his floor of Bronte Hall, past the office of Marge Funk, historian, Presbyterian, whose conversations alternate between piety and complaint. The piety alternates between bland praise statements at the end of sentences ("I think I'm gonna make it through another week, praise God") and hummed hymn tunes. Complaints alternate between her salary and her students. Comments about students tend to end in italicized racism as often as not. "And she strolls into my office after missing three weeks in a row and asks if she can retake the midterm! Can you imagine? Never contacted me, never apologized, just didn't show up for three weeks. And whenever she was there, Jack, she was always asleep after ten minutes! *She's black, by the way, and pregnant for the second time."*

Jack would boldly engage Marge in a cheerful hello each morning as if she had read his halfsheet and was struggling to respond to his display of fearless integrity. Now, standing at his own door, he realizes she has certainly never seen it. The location of his office, last door on the left side of a dead-end hall, couldn't possibly help.

He thought he was shouting from a balcony. What a boob.

Forty-five minutes later the door has been stripped bare. The quote is enlarged and reposted and joined by a companion:

> The day will come when the mystical generation of Jesus, by the Supreme Being as his father, in the womb of a virgin, will be classed with the fable of the generation of Minerva in the brain of Jupiter.
>
> Thomas Jefferson

So it begins. Every day Jack spends hour after hour searching the pages of the great canon of disbelief, pacing a furrow into his shabby office carpet, one volume of Voltaire or Russell or Ingersoll in his hand and thirty others scattered over the desk, the chair, the floor, reading passages aloud, arguing points to see if they endure, cursing when the clock calls him away to class or a meeting. Every day he adds another carefully-selected quote, or two, or three to his display. Every day he takes a reading of Marge Funk, his canary in a coal mine.

Nothing.

By the end of exam week, the door is full of nothing but humanist quotes and essays, jamb to jamb. A page from Freud's *Future of an Illusion*, another from *Age of Reason*, Carl Sagan's *Demon-Haunted World*. H.L. Mencken, what a fantastic wiseass: *"The liberation of the human mind . . . has been furthered not by dunderheads but by gay fellows who heaved dead cats into sanctuaries and then went roistering down the highways of the world, proving to all men that doubt, after all, was safe—that the god in the sanctuary was finite in his power and hence a fraud."* The superhuman Hume. Lincoln, that's always a surprise to somebody. The ranting Ingersoll and the rational Russell—*"I cannot, deny that religion has made some contributions to civilization. It helped in early days to fix the calendar, and it caused Egyptian priests to chronicle eclipses with such care that in time they became able to predict them. These two services I am prepared to acknowledge, but I do not know of any others"*—Woody Allen and Mark Twain *("It ain't the parts of the Bible that I can't understand that bother me, it is the parts that I do understand")* and Kurt Vonnegut. Homer J. Simpson for fun *("Lisa, if the Bible has taught us nothing else—and it hasn't—it's that girls should stick to girl's sports, such as hot oil wrestling and foxy boxing and such and such."* Jack wisely takes that one down after about ten seconds' reflection. He just might survive stepping on God at CSB, but step ye surely not on Woman). Gloria Steinem and Elizabeth Cady Stanton, both of them campus buildings and feminists *and* atheists, how *nicely* that works out—the whole Top 40 of the unbeliever's pantheon.

He reserves a place of honor for his all-time favorite balls-out rant:

> We have heard talk enough. We have listened to all
> the drowsy, idealess, vapid sermons that we wish to
> hear. We have read your Bible and the works of your
> best minds. We have heard your prayers, your solemn
> groans and your reverential amens. All these amount
> to less than nothing. We want one fact. We beg at the
> doors of your churches for just one little fact. We pass
> our hats along your pews and under your pulpits and
> implore you for just one fact. We know all about your
> mouldy wonders and your stale miracles. We want a

"this year's" fact. We ask only one. Give us one fact
for charity. Your miracles are too ancient. The witnesses have been dead for nearly two thousand years.

Robert Green Ingersoll

There's consistency for you Finnegan, thinks Jack as he turns
around to survey the cacophony of disbelief on his way out
to Christmas break, a wild jumble now overflowing the door
onto the adjacent wall, running five feet up the hall. Waggle
your pragmatic finger at me, will you. There's the full, passionate embrace of deep conviction. Jack feels the warm,
self-righteous glow of the sanctimonious backbencher flood-
ing his body, that indescribable mix of indignation, integrity
and impotence.

Wait.

He leans back against the opposite wall in the abandoned
hallway and slowly slides to a sitting position, looking up at
his display.

Damn, *look* at this. Look what the bastards have forced
me into. His eyes move slowly from left to right, top to bottom, taking in the enormity of it. I'm a shrill, single-issue,
ranting, howling *evangelist*. They forced me to the ranting
fringe with their stupidity. I'm a rational middlist and they're
making me look like a screaming lunatic. Can't let them do
that.

He pulls his keys from his pocket again, unlocks the door
and emerges ten minutes later with another quote. Big Picture. It isn't just about one issue, after all. Here's the real
point, he says aloud as he tapes it centered and high on his
door in the last remaining open spot:

> "The best thing for being sad," replied Merlin, be-
> ginning to puff and blow, "is to learn something. That
> is the one thing that never fails. You may grow old and

trembling in your anatomies, you may lie awake at
night listening to the disorder of your veins, you may
miss your only love, you may see the world about you
devastated by evil lunatics, or know your honour
trampled in the sewers of baser minds. There is only
one thing for it then—to learn. Learn why the world
wags and what wags it. That is the only thing which
the mind can never exhaust, never alienate, never be
tortured by, never fear or distrust, and never dream of
regretting."

T.H. White, The Once and Future King

Okay folks. Respond to me now. *Ex Corde* me. *Engage.*

8

Goldenmiller's Tale

So we keep asking, over and over,
Until a handful of earth
Stops our mouths—
But is that an answer?

Heinrich Heine, *Lazarus*

FEDERAL BUREAU OF INVESTIGATION
FIELD REPORT
TOP SECRET–EYES ONLY

AGENT ID:001392
SUPVSR:001294
OPERATION: RODIN
FILE DATE:03 APR 1992

SECOND MEETING OF THE EXECUTIVE
COMMITTEE OF THE REVOLUTIONARY PHI-

LOSOPHERS FRONT OF AMERICA (RPFA), 31
MAR 1992 19:00:00 HRS

Meeting began with call by Subject FALLOWS
for approval of minutes of previous meeting.
An objection was raised by subject SUVENAL based
on "the unreliability of memory as a reflection of
objective reality," referring at one point to the "representative theory of perception." A discussion of approximately forty-five minutes ensued, the content
of which is assumed* to be irrelevant to this investigation, after which the minutes were approved on a
voice vote.

Subject HARRISON-LEWIS objected to "the assumed validity of majority rule" in deciding such
matters by voice vote. A discussion of approximately
one hour and ten minutes ensued, the content of which
is assumed* to be irrelevant to this investigation. [It
should be noted that a division of the group into two
subgroups occurred at this point, one (led by
HARRISON LEWIS) apparently arguing a "natural
law" position and the other (led by WHITTIER) referring repeatedly to "legal positivism". This division should be watched carefully for possible future
exploitation.]

Subject FALLOWS announced that the topic would
be tabled for discussion at a later date. Subject
HAYDEN questioned FALLOWS' authority to do
so, as well as his authority as committee chair, citing
philosophers Godwin and Gorgeous (sp?) and doctrine of anarchism as a more appropriate model than
the traditional authoritarian governmental structure
that had been "instituted arbitrarily" for the RPFA.

Subject HAYDEN called for an immediate renunciation of all arbitrarily assumed authority within the organization in favor of a freely anarchic system "based
on Stirner's social model." Subject WHITTIER suggested that HAYDEN "suck eggs," at which point
the meeting disintegrated into several simultaneous
loud exchanges between individuals in twos and
threes, ending without formal adjournment at approximately 2110 hrs.

[POSTSCRIPT: Agent reiterates his request for reas-
signment. Inadequate knowledge of philosophical
terminology and ideologies requires an inappropriate level of assumption regarding relevance (see *
above), increases the risk of exposure and diminishes
effectiveness of reports re content of discussions.]

————END OF REPORT————

Midwinter is for the laying of plans, especially in the
gawdawful North. Resolutions race to the page. Limitations
are forgotten, if only temporarily. Wild, seductive possibilities strain at the leash, resentful of the forced confinement,
as twelve million eyes stare out through ice-glazed panes at
the Great Pause, lusting for its eventual end.

Becca, Connor, and the mother-in-law are in Long Island
visiting Becca's sister for the holidays, so Jack spends the
break at home in Saint Philip like a newly-divorced philosopher would—thinking too much, rereading Hume, looking
through various college directories for Abby McWhatsit, planning for the coming confrontations and smoking like a Dutch
frigate.

Father Siberell is busy wondering if he added too much

yeast. In addition to three Masses each Sunday through Advent and Christmas, Scott has inaugurated not one but *two* radio programs at the feverish request of the management of KRST Christ Radio 1640 AM ("The Voice of Salvation in Southwestern Minnesota"). The first is a Sunday evening rebroadcast of the Mass with a running play-by-play commentary voiceover by Father Siberell and—in a stunning display of ecumenical fervor and imagination on the part of station management—color commentary by none other than the Reverend Lucian B. Delmore of King of Glory Lutheran Church (Missouri Synod) of Saint Philip. Father Delmore jumped at the chance to pretty much preach while sitting down, and Scott jumped at the opportunity for a straight man.

The other program is a call-in advice show three times a week titled "Ask Father Scott," pitched to the 14-18 year old female Christian demographic and nearly causing Jack yet another coffee-spewing event the first time he heard about it.

Father Siberell has picked up a disciple of sorts to help out with the running of the burgeoning ministry, one Haley Gilbert, sophomore music major at Saint Bernadette from small town Wisconsin. Jack knows Haley from last year's Intro course. Quiet, thoughtful, devout, selfless, sunny of disposition (though well short of the slapping point), full of *agape*, as good and decent a Christian as Jack has known, with a simple, omnipresent pewter cross around her neck, Haley took the second semester of her first year off to work in Costa Rica with a Feed-the-Children type organization. Not that she broadcast that information—Jack heard it secondhand from her mother when he called to return her end-of-semester portfolio. Haley is among that 0.1% of Christians, Jack thought at the time, who actually might make the whole charade worthwhile—absolutely humble, absolutely sincere, actually doing good. Jack himself, among others, has gone downright misty at the sight of this simple, faithful child making the Sign of the Cross as she received the sacraments from Scott.

He was less than thrilled when he heard she was getting in so tight with Scott's little operation, since she is also just unreasonably beautiful—something Scott is likely to have noticed.

Tina's break includes two weeks at a writer's retreat in New Mexico, tearing through her feminist revision of *Man For All Seasons* before the retreat is half finished, then bouncing from cabin to cabin to solicit feedback from appropriately-gendered fellow campers.

Leonard the Poet spends much of the Christmas break rummaging through hundreds of boxes of old files and books in his tightly-packed Saint Philip attic, lit by a single hanging bare bulb, looking for the manuscript of an unpublished paper of his own authorship, one more than thirty-five years old but suddenly of the greatest interest to him. He is distracted in the task by nearly every leaf and volume he happens upon, pausing and pulling up a stool to lose himself in this or that passage of John Donne or Chaucer or the Venerable Bede, mouthing the luscious words or shouting them to the walls of the tiny space as he skips in giddy circles. Thus is an afternoon's task agreeably stretched well into the lifeless middle of an especially harsh January.

Leslie Erickson Mitchell-Robbins Moore and husband Bill pass the holidays in Colorado with the Family Erickson, Leslie chatting excitedly with cousins and aunts about the coming collision of good and evil at the College, snowhiking in the Rockies with her sister and learning the Lakota language from scratch on her laptop.

Carl Holtz has a family of six in Saint Jude. He's Santa Claus for the St. Jude Y, for Wallabies Department Store and for the Flickering Light Rest Home. Twice a week during the holidays he pops over to St. Bernie's to check for burst pipes and ice dams, then gets back to his regular schedule on January 3rd.

Genevieve Martin's sister Sister Mary Virginia joins her for the holiday in the Dean's comfortable two-story Victorian in Sleepy Eye. Due mostly but not entirely to Mary Virginia's injuries, the sisters share the firelit, Persian-carpeted space and a deep mutual affection in comfortable silence. As in their youth, the sisters spoke very little, for each has always seemed to know the other's thoughts without asking. It has been a particularly satisfying visit this year for reasons neither can articulate but both seem to agree upon.

Wanda Streamley spends the four-week break on a tour of European pilgrimage sites, beginning at Medjugorje and ending at Lourdes. The visit to Lourdes fulfills a longstanding dream of Wanda's. It was Sister Marie-Bernard, later Saint Bernadette, whose claims to have seen apparitions of the Blessed Virgin at Lourdes established the site as a destination for Catholic pilgrims. Some local villagers dubbed her "the stupid one," claimed she was bluffing about the visions. *Their* names have been forgotten, notes Wanda; and now, as president of the College that bears the saint's name, she is overcome with emotion at Bernadette's grave marker, weeping and praying as she reads the inscription in French and Latin:

Here Reposes
In the Peace of the Lord
BERNADETTE SOUBIROUS
Favored at Lourdes in 1858
With Numerous Apparitions of the
Most Blessed Virgin:
In Religion
Sister Marie-Bernard:
Deceased at Nevers
In the Motherhouse

Of the Sisters of Charity
April 16th, 1879
In the 36th Year of Her Age
And the 12th of Her Religious Profession

"This is my rest forever and ever.
Here will I dwell, for I have chosen it."

REST IN PEACE

Bruce Everell-Beers moved back in with his parents after graduation from Mankato State. He spends the holidays reading Adam Smith and getting very, very good at PlayStation2.

Helen Highwater attends the annual knitters' convention in Pittsburgh in the week after Christmas, something she heard about three years ago at knitnet.org but hasn't had the time to attend since her elevation from Dean of Health and Human Services to Dean of the Interior. Helen is a constant, rabid knitter. Over the course of the bone meeting she made a six-color mitten under the table, complete with illustrations from Norwegian folk tales, without raising the slightest suspicion or so much as glancing down.

Lilly's deep into her novel, writing fourteen hours a day in her little Mankato townhouse, rarely coming up for air. It is four p.m. on the 25th before she realizes it's Christmas. She still doesn't care terribly much—other than to begin building a character in her novel who is writing a novel so intensely he doesn't even realize it's Christmas.

Peter D'Angelo's in the home district, hanging out for spontaneous chat at just the right delis and holding a couple of town meetings on farm subsidies, then he and his wife and teenage daughters are off to Aruba while his staff lays the considerable groundwork for a late March announcement.

Dr. Bedford and her husband spend Christmas and early

January on a busman's holiday in Jordan visiting the archaeological site of Petra, a 2nd century city carved into the side of sandstone cliffs, something she has always wanted to see. In her absence, on January 8th, the final report on the bones is quietly released to selected government offices, the college, and Gustafson and Son Construction. It takes Rebecca Kassel ten days to get word of the report, then, on Saturday January 19th, two days before the start of the new semester, the Minneapolis *Ledger-Domain* runs her story on page one under a confusing headline:

State Says Bernadette's Bones Not Native
Native Healer Comes To Opposite Conclusion—
Resolution Uncertain
by Rebecca Kassel • *Ledger-Domain* staff writer

ST. PHILIP—The crisis at Saint Bernadette's reached a new stage recently as the Office of the State Archaeologist released the final report on the human remains found during a tunnel excavation last November. According to the report, two complete skeletons were eventually unearthed. The bones are those of two Caucasians, one male, one female, both in their late sixties or early seventies, both dead of natural causes in the mid-to-late 19th century. That would place the death and burial of the individuals well within the period of European settlement of the region and well after the founding of the towns of Saint Philip and Saint Jude, on either side of, and in close proximity to, the formation.

"It is unthinkable that Native Americans living in the area would create a burial formation this close to existing European settlements," says Dr. Ronald

Kingsley of the University of Minnesota's Native American Studies program. "And if they did, there would surely be ample written records in the two towns of the sudden appearance of such a structure. Considering the nonexistence of such records and the proximity issue, I think we can safely say this is not a Lakota burial site. It is a much older natural formation in which two Caucasian settlers were buried for reasons unknown."

In an unusual move, the State Archaeologist's office provided the bones for examination to Lakota Healer Edward Moon-River. Moon-River carried out a ritual vigil with the original femur. "I consulted the ancestors," Moon-River said, "and they told me without a doubt that the bone belonged to a Lakota tribal elder named Looked-At-Clouds-From-Both-Sides." He added, emphatically, "My methods have stood the test of the ages and are indisputable. The College must be closed and removed from this sacred site."

"I knew we should never have opened that can of worms," said a source within the State Archaeologist's office who wished to remain anonymous. "We should not have dignified that mumbo-jumbo by letting them look at the bone." State Archaeologist Dr. Leigh Ann Bedford, reached on vacation in the Middle East, had no comment other than an expression of regret and apology for the use of the derogatory term "mumbo-jumbo" by someone in her office.

Dean Genevieve Martin of the College administration stated today that the long-delayed construction will go forward as soon as the campus reopens on Monday.

On the twenty-first of January, with an air temp of twelve below and a wind chill twenty degrees worse, the earliest of the returning College community slowly, resentfully make their way from the east through the gates at the bottom of the wedge, past protest signs jammed upright in the snow-bank next to three apparent protesters in the form of cone-shaped piles of blankets with hats at the peaks. Carl and Gerard begin the sad parade at five-thirty, long before sun-rise, to salt and scrape the long walks. The first staff shift arrives in a muttering clump at 6:25 and disappears by fours and fives into successive buildings all the way to Admin, where the secretaries to the administrative offices are the last to get in from the cold.

The first member of the faculty to arrive, or so he thinks, is one Leonard the Poet. Leonard has chosen to walk to campus this fine day, clutching under his arm the manuscript he found at last the night before, tucked tight in the leather pouch into which it had been shoved more than half a lifetime ago. And every thousand feet or so of the mile-and-a-half walk, he peels back the leather flap to smile at the title page:

In the Shadow of Bernadette's Butte
A Centennial History of Saint Philip, Minnesota

© 1964
by Leonard Holdenmiller

One of the first acts of the newly-formed Saint Philip Centennial Committee in the summer of 1962 was to enlist young Leonard Holdenmiller, Ph.D.—brother of Harold, the town councilman—to write a history of the town for the forth-coming centenary of its founding by the Putter brothers. Leonard had thrown himself into it with all the spirit and stu-pidity of youth. And youthful spirit had been necessary to sort through the hundreds of boxes of unsorted records, led-

gers, diaries, receipts and loose documents in the basement
of the Saint Philip Town Hall, reassembling a history that had
never really been assembled in the first place. Oral history
alone had been thought by the Philippians to suffice for the
satisfaction of their posterity. *Fools*, Leonard thought at the
time, prematurely curmudgeonly and stoop-shouldered from
an affection for Francis Bacon and Christopher Marlowe that
would eventually coax him ever-earlier in literary time, to
the infancy of the English language. Only the written word,
he would often say, can trap fact and poetry alike in timeless
amber.

Now, walking to campus with the written word clasped to
his side, he smiles unattractively at the thought of his wisdom born out.

Youthful stupidity was also in play in '62, for he under-
took the project on the strength of a handshake. When the
Committee ran utterly dry of funds in late 1963, he was left
with two chapters to go and no compensation beyond the
overrated satisfaction of a job well done.

Charlatans, thought Leonard as he angrily copyrighted
the manuscript himself and shoved it in a leather pouch and
tossed it into his attic, refusing to donate the work to the
Committee.

In the summer of '69 the Town Hall mysteriously burned
to the ground, reducing all of the primary sources of Saint
Philip history to cinders. The press speculated that the fire
was linked to an antiwar protest earlier in the day. Whatever
the cause, high in his attic Leonard danced round and round
with his shadow and the manuscript, the last reliable link between present and past. *Screw me will you*, he thought. *Now
they'll have to come crawling to Lee-o-nard.*

When the bone was found and the Lakota began their
rumblings, Leonard chortled to himself. Generations of
Philippians and Judeans had managed to forget the origins of
the Wedge between them, the idiots, but he and he alone

had found and read the diary of Josiah Harrison Putter, lunatic founder of Saint Philip, describing the building of the enormous wedge in 1873 to block his brother's town from view. Leonard had always enjoyed the secret thrill of knowing the truth as others conjectured on the origins of the formation. Miscreants. Cretins. Dissemblers.

Assholes.

But the recent discovery of the bones and the claims of the Lakota are simply too much to resist. He and he alone holds the key to solving a mystery that but for his contribution might well have gone unsolved. I even know their *names*, he thinks with a little shiver of pleasure, as he stops for the third time, turning to page 344:

> *Two of the residents of the town, an elderly husband and wife by the names of Engebret and Margret Bergseth, died within a month of each other in the last weeks of building and, to contribute to the cause, were buried with solemn ceremony in the depths of the massive formation.*

Their names, he mouths with delight, *are Engebret and Margret Bergseth.* Not natives, these. The archaeologist is right—but the proof of the pudding is in the *writing*.

By 6:55 a.m., as Leonard reaches the campus, the Lakota protesters have mustered a small fire for warmth and are huddled tightly around it. He strides past, not without shooting a disparaging sneer at the protesters, and begins to make his way to the office of the president with his precious cargo. He looks over to the tunnel opening as he passes, and the idled equipment soon to be brought roaring back to life at his command.

Then, suddenly, he stops.

Sitting in a snowdrift in front of the massive blade of the bulldozer is a small figure, swathed in neon yellow Gore-Tex, holding a sign that says DIGNITY AND JUSTICE FOR

THE LAKOTA. On closer inspection, Leonard can see that this person is chained tightly to the machine. On closer inspection still, he can see who it is.

He breathes deeply and exhales slowly. Makes the tiniest squeak. Looks back and forth from the protesters to the protester, then down at the leather pouch under his arm.

But I know their *names*.

He reaches into the pouch, riffles the pages lovingly with his thumb, then turns and walks, faltering, back through the gate. Leonard Holdenmiller takes a final glance over his shoulder toward the bulldozer, then walks to the little protest circle and sits between two Lakota.

"Leslie, Leslie, Leslie love," he mumbles softly to himself as he feeds the manuscript, page by page, into the fire.

9

Lamentations

For in death there is no remembrance of you; in Sheol who can give you praise? I am weary with my moaning; every night I flood my bed with tears; I drench my couch with my weeping. My eyes waste away because of grief; they grow weak because of all my foes.

Psalms 6: 5-7

At 7:10, Tina-something walks through the gate, sees Leslie and squeals delightedly, bounding through the snow toward her like a giddy Malamute.

"Leslie, Leslie! How are you? How was your break? I missed you!"

Leslie blinks in surprise. She had no idea they were so close. "Uh, fine Tina, how about yours?"

"We start rehearsals on Thursday! I'm about to burst!" Tina says, vibrating with excitement.

"Well I can see that, Tina! Oh, oh yeah, I remember . . . this is the all-grrrl *Man For All Seasons*, right?"

173

"*Person For All Seasons,* of course," Tina corrects. "Yes!"

"That just sounds *so* exciting! You ought to think about getting it published—it has to be almost a whole new play with nothing but women . . ."

"Oh, it's powerful stuff all right." Tina drops to a squat. "Lady Tammy More instead of Sir Thomas More, you see, and Henrietta the Eighth on the throne! An 'if-I-ruled-the-world' kind of thing, it really ends up being. Very empowering." For a moment she drifts back into the world she's been rewriting for the last two months, then snaps out of it. "Oh well, I've got costumes to order, sets to prime, you know the drill." She pops to her feet. "I'll see you around!"

She starts to walk away with a bounce, then stops suddenly and turns back to Leslie with the well-meaning whisper of a confidant. "You know—I'm not sure you'll be able to keep sitting there . . . I think they're gonna use that bulldozer today."

And she's gone before Leslie can figure out what on Earth to say.

Jack Kassel arrives at 7:20, hunched against the wind, looking perplexed as he passes an apparently weeping Leonard the Poet squatting amongst the Lakota few. Moments later his puzzlement gives way to envy as he spots Leslie at the bulldozer. Head shaking in amusement, he makes straight for her through the snow, grinning as if walking toward his younger self, and is met with the smile of one who knows he knows she knows he envies her the crusade just a tad.

"Leslie, what the hell are you doing?" He grins and kicks a little snow on her skipanted legs.

"Hi Jack! What a perfectly awful thing to ask. Go away if you're gonna be all Establishment at me." She wouldn't think of brushing the snow from her pants, preferring to revel in that little extra bit of oppression.

Of the two of them, only Leslie is really dressed for the occasion, and Jack begins to rub his arms through inadequate sleeves. "Come on now, Leslie. You must know you're on the wrong side of reality here. The bones are not Lakota."

"That's strike two, Jack. Whatever happened to my comrade on the left? Mister Sequoia Hugger? You've been on the tenure track so long you've forgotten what it's like to *stand* for something. I'm on the side of dignity and justice here, read the sign," she says as she flaps it in his face. "You're on the side of the jack-booted *conquistadors*, I guess."

Jack's cheeks are not holding up well. "*I* am on my usual side, the left brain."

"Well, I'm in the left heart." Her satisfied expression makes it clear to Jack that she means that to be a full explanation.

Jack, resigning himself to the cold, plops heavily into the snowbank beside her. "So it doesn't matter to you what the actual truth is here?"

"Actual truth," she says slowly, as if considering the notion for the first time. "Sure, if there were really such a thing as actual truth, that would be fun to know, I guess. I don't put that first in line, but it would be nice." She blows a vapor plume with her breath. "Just to keep you Enlightenment types at bay."

"Well I have a very exciting piece of news for you, Leslie. We know the truth on this one. The science was not ambiguous. I looked at the report myself."

"I'm sure you did . . . with an Enlightenment bias."

"With an En . . . what on Earth is *that* supposed to mean? Okay, sure, I am seriously biased toward critical thinking."

"Well at least you admit it."

Jack splutters wordlessly at Leslie like the Skipper at Gilligan.

"There, that's more like it," she says. "Get in touch with

your inner rage. Or better yet . . ." Eyebrows up, head cocked at the precise angle of conspiracy. ". . . put that rage on the outside and *join* me." She rattles her chains enticingly.

"What, just 'cause there's a bulldozer available?"

"Oh, I see. *Trees* you'll lay yourself down for, but actual *people* . . ."

"Right on, you two!" yells Lilly, passing by on the walk. "Way to go! Stick it to the Man!" Leslie, and Leslie only, flashes a thumbs-up and a grin.

"Leslie, *my* bulldozer was actually *aimed* at trees. *This* bulldozer is *not* aimed at people. It is aimed at dirt," he says, pulling out a pack of Salems and handing one to Leslie.

"Okay, Enlightenment Man," she says, staring at the cigarette. "What about the cigarettes?"

He lights his own, sheltering the flame against the wind, then flips the lighter to her. "What about them?"

"It's 2002 and two Ph.D.s sit here smoking cigarettes. Is this a rational thing to be doing, given what we know about them?"

"It's not irrational, Leslie, it's stupid. There's a difference. If I denied the evidence, that would be irrational. But I acknowledge the evidence and do it anyway. That's stupid."

"Oh I see. Much better. And what I'm doing here on the front of a bulldozer is which, stupid or irrational?"

"Well, at least irrational, since you are denying the evidence that clearly invalidates your position."

"How do you know that? Maybe I 'know' the evidence and do this anyway, in which case I graduate to merely stupid in your court."

"Now don't put words . . ."

Two students yell "Go Dr. Kassel!" in unison, and Jack sinks down further into his upturned collar. Passersby, students, staff and faculty alike, rubberneck like freeway ghouls passing a wreck.

"The point, Jack, is that you should want to be on the

side of what's *right*, definition two, not just what happens to be technically *right*, definition one. Lord, given a choice, you'd pick the incidental 'truth' over the chance to stand by people who've been shit on for five hundred years?"

"I'm quite fond of the incidental truth."

"So was Hitler. He used your Enlightenment rationality to justify the Holocaust, didn't he? That was the final discrediting of . . ."

"So you're suggesting he used reason *correctly*? That what he did was in fact *rational*? The only way you can use Hitler to discredit reason is to suggest that he was in fact reasonable, which I'm not sure you want to do. He *mis*-used the Enlightenment, Leslie, for crying out loud. His reasoning was *flawed*. That doesn't mean you stop using reason and just pursue your own self-interest. Now *that's* more like Hitler if you ask me. The original postmodernist."

"This isn't in my self-interest, Jack. It's damn cold out here. This is about jumping on the chance to create a reality that is useful instead of waiting for your incidental truth to line up with justice. Do you *honestly* believe it's more important for something to be true than useful?"

"What, you're saying usefulness is more important than truth?"

Leslie looks genuinely aghast. "What kind of question is that? Of *course!* Truth is a matter of perspective, Jack, surely you know this. Your truth and mine obviously don't line up on this issue, so they won't line up in a hundred other ways. So whose truth do we go with? I'll take usefulness over that mess any day."

Jack feels physically ill. He squints and rubs his eyes as Leslie begins to go fuzzy around the edges, then shakes his head and fights hard to resist grabbing her ankles. "My truth and yours? Those are *opinions* you're talking about, not truths. Opinions vary; objective truth does not. If I think the world is round and you think it's flat, isn't at least one of us wrong?"

Leslie draws deep on her cigarette, already nearly gone, and blows out a long column of smoke. "I don't especially find a flat Earth useful, Jack, but if I did, I'd be all over it in a minute. And I find it useful to put myself in front of yet another machine rolling over Native Americans, whether or not the details of this particular moment fit neatly into your requirements for 'the truth'." She smirks at him. "And how *cute* to hear someone still using words like 'objective.'"

Jack hauls himself to his feet and brushes off. "The amusing thing, of course, is that you are trying to reason with me about the unreasonableness of reason."

Leslie gores him with a smile. "If that's your truth, Jack, that's fine."

Jack trudges out of the snow to the flagstone walk with a sour mood and a cold butt. It is 7:35 and the protest crowd is growing rapidly in size and volume. The drumming has begun in earnest, and Leonard, still in a daze, has wandered off. Jack stomps his boots clean and heads up the wedge to Bronte. He draws deeply to finish his cigarette and pitches the smoking butt into a snow-filled receptacle outside the door, which hisses appreciatively.

The building is empty; the sound of the closing door booms through the stairwells. Jack clomps up to his second floor office and is immediately taken aback by The Display. Seeing it for the first time in four weeks really amplifies the volume. He turns the key self-consciously, enters as if plowing through an angry crowd, shuts the door and leans against it for a moment. Two minutes later he is out again with a notepad and a small hand-lettered note, both of which he attaches to the door frame:

> *Please feel free to leave a note under my door*
> *in response to anything you see here. Open*
> *discussion is what this is all about!*

The first few weeks of the second semester are always the same: fear and inertia and loathing. Everyone is forced abruptly from pampered, gluttonous lap dog curled up by the fire to Iditarod sled dog. There's always some excitement in the September return to school, but autumn is a warm weather transition—and summer, while glorious, is never as hard to leave behind as Christmas. The contrast in the January return is just too heartbreaking to endure. Everyone looks it—with the possible ironic exception of the woman chained to a bulldozer out front, who looks like she spent the holidays resenting every vacation day that stood between her and her martyrdom.

Jack clicks his desk lamp on. Jean Poole, the humanities secretary, has dumped a pile of his accumulated mail on his desk. *So she's seen the door then*, he thinks. No, on second thought, probably not. Jean retires in one year and could not care less. I, on the other hand, retire in twenty-six years and could not care less.

Jean will probably make it.

He sits heavily and begins rifling through the mail, pitching catalogs, conference announcements and college memos, saving position announcements and anything else interesting. The pile shrinks quickly.

Near the bottom is a personal-looking letter addressed by hand with a Wisconsin postmark and no return address. That counts as interesting. He tears it open.

Dear Dr. Castle,

You don't know me, but I wanted to write to you to express my grateful thanks for something you have done for my family. My daughter Haley is a student in her second year at Saint Bernadette's. She has had the great privilege of working closely with Father Siberell this year as he builds his wonderful ministry. It has meant the world to Haley to

*find a place in the service of the Lord and her community.
I am told that you were instrumental in bringing Father
Siberell to St. Bernie's and wanted to let you know how
very much it has meant to us.*

*Haley's father passed away unexpectedly in early Novem-
ber, shortly after Father Siberell arrived. It was especially
hard on Haley—she's always been very close to her Daddy.
She spent hours and hours alone over Christmas, crying in
her room or out in the horsebarn tending the horse her father
gave her and taught her to ride. It broke my heart. I was so
worried about her. I do not know how she would have
made it through this difficult time if Father Siberell had
not been there to guide her. He helped Haley to find hope
and rejoicing in her father's salvation and eternal life and
to remember that we will all be reunited in the glory of God.
Without that hope I believe she might very well have left
college. I shudder to think of what direction she might have
gone if she had attended a secular college or one without a
caring priest like Father Siberell to take her under his wing.
Life without hope is no life at all. I am deeply grateful to
Father Siberell for reminding Haley of that and to you for
bringing him among us.*

*Father Siberell has a gift for spiritual communication,
something that Father Hillerman, God rest his soul, never
really had. He has used such inspiring words to reach Haley.
All she can talk about now is her upcoming "One-on-One"
Retreat with him. It sounds like such a wonderful and
inspiring opportunity the way she describes it—to spend
three days in a remote cabin with such a spiritual man as
her guide! She has felt such a void since her Daddy died.
Father Siberell told her to "expect joy like she has never felt
before," that she would "feel his love deep inside her as he*

fills her void." Such a poetic soul. What a beautiful man
he is to bring her his light in her darkest time!

I will never forget that you are responsible for bringing him
to us. May God be with you, Dr. Castle.

Dorothy Gilbert

No. No way. Not even *Scott.* Jack rereads the last two
sentences several times with varying intonations. Where did
she get this idea? I am *responsible*, she says. Then may God
be with me indeed. Jack is seized by a need to do something
and quickly decides to write a letter in response. Got to plant
a subtle seed here so she can figure out the obvious. *Lord*,
woman, look past your best wishes here. Read between the
lines. Scott, you sick, sick *bastard.*

He yanks open his desk file and retrieves the college
directory to get Haley's home address. Gibbs; Gibson;
Gieseke; Gilbert *Bonnie* . . .

There. **Gilbert, Haley Abigail. 17732 Hudson Way, Eau
Claire, WI 54015.**

Haley Abigail? Oh God. *Abby!*

No, wait a minute, he thinks, staring at the page, then the
blank wall in front of him. Haley is Abby Mezliay? Yes. Yes,
of course, she just *has* to be Abby. It all fits. Haley Gilbert is
his target. Got it, got it, got it.

Jack grabs the letter, storms out of the office, vaults down
the stairs and sprints down the icy Wedge at an unwise clip, past
a waving Leslie, through the phalanx of students coming in the
gates, and bursts in through the rear doors of Nurse Chapel.

Quid retribuam Domino pro . . .

Ohhh *shit.* Jack skids to a halt, his sudden arrival still echoing through the sanctuary as eleven kneeling nuns turn their heads to scowl. Scott, right in the thick of his eight o'clock daily traditional Latin Mass for the campus sisters, raises an eyebrow in amusement. Jack makes an apologetic gesture and turns to leave.

Oh Scott won't hear of it. "Please, Doctor Kassel, do join us! *Please.*"

Why you twisted little fucker. All eleven nuns change expressions on a dime and begin to gesture serenely for him to come forward. He hesitates, looks up at Scott's beatific half-smile, and slowly walks forward down the center aisle through the ranks of dark brown wood, shoes clicking on the tiled floor, more certain with every step that this cannot possibly be a good idea. He takes his place at the end of the third pew.

That well-modulated, well-projected, off-Broadway baritone resonates in the darkened space.

Quid retribuam Domino pro omnibus quae retribuit mihi? Calicem salutaris accipiam, et nomen Domini invocabo Dominum, et ab inimicis meis salvus ero.

Jack quickly realizes to his horror that he has joined the service just in time for Communion. The chalice is in Scott's hand as he makes the Sign of the Cross with the other.

Sanguis Domini nostri Jesu Christi custodiat animam meam in vitam aeternam. Amen.

Best to make a quick exit, Jack wonders, or to stay and refuse the host in front of eleven sisters including Joan Krenek—or to allow Scott to prove him a cowardly hypocrite by letting the Sacred Particle be placed on his tongue.

He stands and slowly processes forward at the end of the

line, still fumbling with options. It's been twenty years since he took Communion, out of respect for the faithful; he'd considered it an act of courage, integrity and respect when he finally made the decision to forgo the Eucharist. But at this moment—a moment unsurprisingly of Scott's creation—it is terribly unclear what the least disrespectful action would be.

Father Siberell continues with light around his head from the well-placed rose window.

Ecce Agnus Dei, ecce Qui tollis peccata mundi. Domine, non sum dignus, ut intres sub tectum meum: sed tantum dic verbo, et sanabitur anima mea.

Jack finds himself kneeling at the rail, unable to comfortably reason his way out. Maybe take the blood but not the body. Maybe the other way around. Before he can think, his mouth is open and his tongue feels the pressed edge of the host. He looks Scott directly and unforgivingly in the eyes. *Corpus Christi*, whispers Father Siberell through a self-satisfied smile. Jack's eyes close as he chews and swallows, fuming.

More Latin echoes through the chapel, and moments later the cool chalice is to his lips, the wine in his mouth. *Sanguis Christi*, Father Siberell lies, still smiling.

After the Mass, Jack waits ten minutes until the nuns have dispersed and Father Scott emerges divested and walks grinning toward the third pew. He sees Jack's expression and goes impish.

"Aww . . . Is sumfing bozzuwing Jackie?"

Jack glares hard. "That was in very poor taste, Scott."

"Yeah, they're a little bland, I know," Scott stage-whispers, "but you're not really supposed to criticize the wafers."

"You know *exactly* what I mean."

"Don't tell me you're a . . ." He claps a hand to his cheek. "Hey, it's your responsibility to skip the Eucharist if you aren't of the True Faith." A deep, mock shrug. "How's the priest supposed to know?"

"But you DO know!" He kicks up the kneeler with a bang that echoes for a good ten seconds. "You *do* know, Scott. When is the game not a game anymore? Why do you need to shit on . . ." He lowers his voice to a whisper. ". . . on everybody else's deepest convictions? And that little stunt was especially sick because you managed to shit on mine and theirs in a single stroke."

"Exactly! What a piece of *poetry* that was." Scott's voice has the pumped-up edge of a teenage crook, still jazzed after a petty theft.

Jack looks for something in Scott's face, something to redeem him. "How can you do this day after day? How? Your beliefs are in there too, somewhere, all shit-covered—if you have any left."

"Oh come on, Jack, don't be such a drama queen. Who got hurt by what we just did there? That was *funny!* The nuns don't know you're a heathen, and there's no God . . ." Scott's turn to whisper. ". . . there's no God to be ticked off by it, so I force Communion on you and it's just our little joke. Nobody got hurt there."

"*I* did, Scott." He takes a breath. "Why do you assume just because I don't believe what they do that I want to piss all over everything they *do* believe?"

"Why do you assume *I* want to?"

Jack *pffts* and throws the letter down on the pew in answer. Scott picks it up and flicks the folded page open.

"Hmm. Mm hmm. Mm hmm. Jack, this is one smart woman. And *available*, too."

"See, that's exactly what I'm talking about! You don't have any boundaries anymore, and people tend to get chewed up when they're around somebody with no boundaries." He leans in. "These are good people around here. Sometimes dense,

sometimes blind, but they don't deserve to be your playtoys."
Leans in further. "Especially not *Abby*."

Scott looks perplexed. "Not *who?*"

"Don't play that. I'm serious." Jack puffs up for the kicker.
"I know that Haley Gilbert is Abby Mezliay."

Scott freezes in gaping disbelief, then throws his head
back and guffaws, filling the empty space with the sound.
"So Haley is Abbe Meslier. Is that why you burst into my
Mass today? To 'confront' me with your big discovery?"

Scott says the last line in a mocking jeer, and Jack's de-
fenses leap up. "Read the rest of that letter!"

Scott does just that, hmming, then looks up at Jack. "Ohhh,
I see. You think I have designs on Haley Gilbert."

"No, oh no no. I really think it's God you want to 'fill her
void' with—if 'God' is your nickname for your schlink, that
is."

Scott grins. "Hey, that's good. It is now." He looks at the
floor and clasps his hands. "Jack, really, I'm a little . . . well,
dismayed. I mean it. You must really think I'm some sort of
top-flight prick."

"Prick might be a little strong, but not much."

Scott looks genuinely wounded. "Oh come on, Jack. I
thought we knew each other pretty well. You think I'm gonna
take advantage of a really good kid who just lost her father,
who's put her trust in me, who's helping me out with this
pain-in-the-ass ministry expansion, just for a roll in the hay?
If that's what you think, prick's a pretty mild word. I'll bet
you used better ones when you first got that theory together."

"Well, yeah. Sick bastard and twisted little fucker lept to
mind."

"There, see how fun confession is? Now it's your turn to
feel bad, since I would never in a million years do that to
Haley or anybody else. Where'd you get the idea I have no
moral compass? Just 'cause I like a thrill now and then? Have
I left corpses in my wake, Jack? Think about it—do I really

slash and burn ... or do I like extreme entertainment where no one actually dies?"

"So this whole priest gig is innocent fun, then, huh. What about wa-*chung?*"

Scott smirks. "Oh sure there's wa-*chung*. You know Lilly Galen?"

"You liar!"

"Like hell. And Tina-something in Theater? Oh, I've been a busy little cleric. But you'll notice that neither of them recently lost a father, and neither sees me—believe me, Jack—as some sort of a saint like Haley and her mom do."

"Yeah, her mom the widow, who's 'available,' like you just said."

"That, Jack, is *humor,*" Scott says. "Humor, Jack. Look it up. I like humor without boundaries, it's damn funny. I did not, you'll notice, actually call her mom up and jump her. That's not humor, that's *life* without boundaries. Don't mix up my talk and my walk so much."

"So then Haley isn't Abby Mezliay."

Scott chuckles softly and shakes his head. "No, Jack. She's not. You are so far off it's sad. How *fun* to have you so stumped." Scott stares off into the rose window, clearly pleased with himself. "Abbe Meslier is still the answer to every question and the key to the kingdom. But Abbe is not Haley. Keep working, you brainy little Ph.D. type philosopher guy—but not too long. Fourth quarter starts real soon."

"Hello Susan, it's Genevieve Martin at St. Bernie's ... Oh fine, fine I guess ... no, just stayed home in Sleepy Eye, took a break from this nonsense ... oh no, just my sister ... Yes ... sure. Oh, I bet that was a grand trip for you ... uh huh ... uh huh, listen, is Steve there by chance? Sure, I'll wait."

Sonofabiscuit lawyers. I can practically hear the clock running while I'm on hold. I should charge *him* for making me sit here and listen to Yann . . .

"Oh, hi Steve, Gennie Martin. Fine. I am holding in my hand the seventh consecutive cost update from Gustafson. It is February twelfth and we're up to $645,000 for a forty-three foot tunnel to nowhere. Even if it goes ahead right this minute the whole thing'll end up twice the original estimate, and I don't see it going ahead at all if we don't . . . uh huh . . . uh huh. Well, that's what I've thought all along, but Wanda's wanted to avoid . . . oh absolutely, I'm ready. I am so ready, Steve. Let me run it by Wanda and you get a public statement written. I'd love to get that equipment moving by Monday. Okay then. Good deal. I'll work a little magic on this end and we'll bust this loose."

The Dean sends an emissary to the bulldozer to negotiate a meeting with Leslie and drops in on Wanda's secretary to check the president's schedule for the day. Clear. *Good,* she thinks. *Halfway back to sanity around here.*

By one-thirty that very afternoon, Dean Martin and a chapped-looking Leslie Erickson Mitchell-Robbins Moore are sitting tense and smoldering across the table from each other in the president's office like Begin and Sadat, with Wanda Streamley as Jimmy Carter.

The Dean rises and strides to the window to look out over the snow as she speaks, a technique she's recently picked up somewhere. "It's over, Leslie, *finito.* The College stands to lose three quarters of a million dollars on this escapade of yours if we don't wrap it up. You've had your chance to make a point, and though I've never been sure what that point was, let's consider it made."

Leslie could not be more pleased than to be handed an ultimatum. "Dean Martin, with all respect, history is on your side but social justice is on mine. I stand by the oppressed against the oppressors."

"Just on general principle, regardless of facts?"

"Oh, major *déjà vu*, Dean. I had this exact discussion with Jack Kassel on the first day of my confinement. You are both under the misconception that there is only one truth here."

Mental note to promote that Kassel. Life is way too short for this frickin' postmodern bullhockey. "Leslie, have you taken so much as a peek at the archaeologist's report? It is very clear and very final. The bones are Caucasian and only about a hundred years old. This is not the site of Lakota burials. It is not. It is over."

Leslie strikes her crusader's pose. "NASA crashes two spacecraft into Mars and still you cling to science as somehow better than random guesswork. How do you account for the dreams of the two elders?"

"Familiar with the correlation-and-causation fallacy, are you? Or the more pedestrian concept of coincidence?"

"Are you familiar with the long history of white people confidently telling Native Americans what the truth is, and the fact that gosh it always seems to line up so neatly to the whites' advantage?"

They retreat to their corners and fume for a minute. Leslie imagines Sitting Bull massaging her shoulders and whispering strategy. Dean Martin imagines poking Leslie in the eye with a sharp stick.

Leslie softens her expression. "Dean Martin . . . may I call you Gennie?" The Dean's silent glare answers the question. "Dean Martin, I appreciate your 'scientific truth' as one point of view, but only one. The Lakota also have their truth. For them, these *are* native bones no matter what your science says. Who are we to say they can only be one or the other?"

"This is where I start to lose my patience, right around the time we step through the looking glass," says the Dean, scowling. "Are you suggesting that they can be *both* native and non-native at the same time?"

"I'm more than suggesting it, Dean. To say otherwise is to cling to discredited male, linear thinking."

"So Leigh-Ann Bedford is guilty of male thinking? How does this work here?"

Leslie sighs the sigh of a patient tutor with a slow child. "Dr. Bedford has been co-opted by the patriarchal establishment. She and millions of women like her were educated by males to think inside the male box, all straight lines and right angles. It is not their fault, but neither do we have to accept their limitations-by-proxy anymore than we accept forced limitations from men." She sits back, pleased.

"And me?" The Dean is seriously crimsoning from the collarbone north. "I suppose I am co-opted as well? Pray save me from my bonds, Dr. Mitchell-Robbins Moore. Lift the veil for me."

"That," Leslie says, soothingly, "is my sole intention here. Think of this as an intervention. Letting go of old paradigms is difficult, but the love and support of women who've made it out . . ."

"We're done here." The Dean says, looking around for that stick. "The protest is over right now. Look out the window and you'll see that your bulldozer is gone."

Leslie leaps from her seat. "What?! You called me up here on the premise of good faith negotiation while you undercut my platform outside!" She sputters in fury as she rushes to the window to see a bare bulldozer-shaped hole in the snow. "I can't believe the gall! I will fill that tunnel entrance with Lakota! How do you think that's going to play in the media, *Gennie!*"

"I've heard enough." It is the president, whose presence both combatants had all but forgotten. "It is clear to me that we have only one possible course of action."

Dean Martin looks at Leslie with the placid air of an impending victor.

Wanda continues. "The project will be terminated."

"*What?!*" the Dean roars. "Wanda, be reasonable! On what possible grounds?"

"Gennie, can we really live with ourselves if we add another chapter to the history of the white majority dictating terms to Native Americans and ignoring their perspective? Can we really say it is more important to us that this tunnel project go forward than it is to them that it stop?"

Genevieve Martin sits in quiet disbelief.

"Thank you Dr. Mitchell-Robbins Moore. The bulldozer will be back in place shortly so you can resume your symbolic post for the remainder of the day. At sunset it will be removed permanently, along with the rest of the equipment. You may announce to your friends at the gates that the victory is theirs."

"I know you're awake."

". . ."

"You forgot to switch your halo off."

". . ."

"Never did answer the Question of the Day, you know."

". . ."

"Ooo looky, there's an angel hovering over the TV!"

"Ha ha."

"I knew it. Now answer the Question."

"Mandy, I really have to get some sleep. I have a big test in my eight o'clock."

"And you can be asleep in two minutes, just answer my question."

". . . okay. Fine. Sure, if I was born in India I'd be a Hindu, I guess."

"And you wouldn't go to heaven."

". . ."

". . ."

"I think all religions are just different ways of saying the same thing. Love one another."

"Uh huh, right. But I think your Bible says, 'Oh, and P.S., believe in Christ or burn like a dry twig.'"

"I can't do this every night. I really have to get some sleep. I can't afford to fail this exam."

"Dodge, dodge. This is a much bigger test. Now do Hindus go to heaven or don't they?"

"I don't know. I'm not God."

"Oh, so as far as you know the Hindus are right and you are wrong. Maybe *you're* the one with a false theology. Maybe when you die, you are going to Hindu Hell."

"You are just plain rude and gross."

"Not an answer. Give me an answer. Isn't it true that you are a Christian simply because you were born into a Christian family and place and time?"

"God would have found me. I would have found God, even in India. I believe that."

"Based on what? What if you were in a little village and had never even seen the Bible or heard of Christ? It would've all just . . . popped into your head?"

". . ."

"Well?"

"God would find a way to save me. God would have popped it into my head. Good night."

"Strange that he doesn't seem to be poppin' into a lot of Hindu heads right now. A billion Hindus and not much poppin' to speak of. All of 'em just keep Hinduin' their thing all the way to Hell. I suppose God's-a-poppin' and they just *aren't listening*. Isn't that right. So they deserve what they get."

". . ."

"Or hey, uh-oh, there's that thought again . . . is it possible that *you* were the one born into a bogus system—and Vishnu, right now, is trying to pop the Hindu truth into your head?"

". . ."

"Are you sure you're listening, Haley? Are you listening for Vishnu?"

"..."

"..."

"..."

"..."

Winter semester plays out as usual. Time travels in circles. Temperatures fluctuate wildly between 10 and 20 below. The sun stays packed in clouds for five, six, seven circular days at a go. Strong men find themselves weeping at so much a tragedy as a yellow traffic light. Self-help books fly off the shelves. So Brian Finnegan is not surprised when he walks into the Cascade to find not only a high general attendance but also one Lilly Galen sitting alone in the back, head on hands on the tabletop.

He glides up silently.

"Well, you look like just the thing for my depression, Lilly Galen."

"Go away."

He sits down soundlessly opposite her. After ten seconds, she peeks out.

"Further."

"Sure you don't want to talk about it?"

Lilly sits up and sighs. "Okay, sure. Let's talk."

"..."

"..."

"Uh . . . am I supposed to start?"

"This was your idea, right? Talk."

"Hmm. Oh, okay, how's the book going?"

Lilly's head thuds back down on the tabletop. "Go away."

"Ah, writer's block, eh? Well, it's your second book, right? Classic sophomore slump. Everybody hits that, from what I hear. You'll pull out."

Lilly looks up contemptuously. "Wow. Oh *wow*. How'd

you come up with something so good so quick? 'Everybody hits that. You'll pull out.'"

"Have you tried going for long walks, getting away from the book?"

"Brian dear, the problem isn't 'writer's block.' The book is writing itself at fifteen pages a day. It's not a shortage of ideas, it's . . . it's something that . . . just happened."

"What . . . family thing? Personal?"

Lilly's look changes to incomprehension mixed with fatigue. "In the *book*, Brian. Julia, the central figure in the story, just *died* . . . very suddenly, very unexpectedly."

"Wow. Well, that's a good thing, right? So convincing even the *author's* walking around stunned! Just imagine the *readers!* That sounds like a powerful . . ."

"Brian, she's not supposed to die yet."

Brian waits for the other shoe, then makes with the international *yeah, yeah, so?* gesture.

Lilly tries again, adding her own urgent gestures. "She's not supposed to die yet! I've got over a hundred pages to go, all of which are supposed to be built around her search for a new crusade, a new connectedness after the failure of her marriage and . . . and I was planning on making this a *trilogy!* Two hundred and sixty pages into the first book she steps off a curb in downtown Chicago without looking, the *stupid* . . ." Lilly bursts into tears.

Okay, this is a new one for Brian. He looks uncomfortably around the bar at the dozen or so people who think they know what is going on. Considers explaining loudly that her fictional character just died, then thinks again. "So you . . . she died because you had her step off . . . wait. Lilly, you're the author. Rewrite the scene. Make the character *look* first."

Lilly's own look is back to contempt. "Not a fiction writer, are you. Brian, she *stepped off the curb.* She really did. Like you said, it is convincing. This 'character,' as you call her, steps off the curb carelessly because that's what she would have done in that moment. She's distracted by the phone call she just finished with her mother in Grand Island. Her mom brought up all of that old stuff, all the things they used to fight about every Christmas since the fire . . ." Her voice trails off. "She wouldn't have looked, Brian. And now she's dead and I'm screwed."

"Maybe she survived the accident."

"It's 5:15 p.m. on Michigan Avenue on a Friday afternoon in July. She is very dead."

"Well make it not Michigan Avenue! Make it not 5:15. This can't be that hard."

Lilly rolls her eyes and looks at her watch. "Okay, why don't *you* make it not 7:08 right now. Come on, Brian." Taps her watch face facetiously. "Come on, big guy. Change the time for me."

"Maybe the light was red when she stepped off the curb!"

"Red light. So what you're saying there is you've never been to Chicago. Brian, you don't even *know* Julia and you're having trouble facing the reality of her death. Imagine how *I* feel!"

Okay, Brian says to himself. Just shut up and climb on board. "Wow. Okay, I get it. Is there gonna be a wake?"

"I know you're trying to patronize me, but that's actually almost the right question." She rubs her eyes with the heels of her hands, then exhales hard. "The actual right question is whether there's going to be a *book*."

Hi Mommy!

I got the package—yummy yummy yummers. Mandy says thanks too—she snarfed the toffees, which I don't like as much as the other ones, so we're both pretty fat now.

I still feel like I want to tell you how sorry I am for the way I acted after Daddy died. It just wasn't me, I don't know— I just really felt so alone, Mommy, a scary kind of alone. I felt sometimes like God wasn't even with me, which I know how that sounds, but it was just terrible, I kept picturing Daddy lying there in the funeral. I would open my Bible every night and close it again after a few verses—it only reminded me of when Daddy would read it to me. Whenever I read my Bible before Daddy was gone, God's words would actually come out in Daddy's voice, it was the most wonderful thing. I don't think I ever told you that before, but it was always a great comfort to me. That way, Dad was with me everywhere I went. Then when he died, the words didn't have any voice at all, they were just words, like—please don't take this wrong, Mommy, I'm just talking my feelings to you—like God had died too, right along with my Daddy.

I don't know if I'm going to send this letter to you, I don't want you to worry about me, you really shouldn't, but I'll finish it anyway because it makes me feel better and then maybe I just won't send it.

But anyway! Thank You God oh Thank You God for Father Siberell! He is my rock and my foundation! I don't know what I would have done without Father Scott (which is what he lets me call him!). Our One-on-One Retreat last week was such a joy. We talked and talked and prayed together and did simple things like gather wood for the fire and clean the cabin, which the other people had left a mess, boys, I think. He has a crazy sense of humor that I didn't even know about, you know how people are different when their not all formal. And the ministry! I am so blessed that God led me here at this very moment, right when I needed something to pour myself into and when Father Scott needed someone to help out. What a wonderful opportunity to serve the Lord! When I'm in the chapel office or in the sanctuary or praying with Father Scott, all my worries just lift away. It is so glorious. Psalm 7:17, "I will give to the Lord the thanks due to His righteousness, and sing praise to the name of the Lord, the Most High!"

Remember our little joke about the Psalms years ago, when we'd pretend we were talking about a school and really be talking about a psalm, and people wouldn't know? Like I'd be angry about something and you'd say, "Haley, I think you need to go to P.S. 37 to learn about that," and I'd laugh and go look at Psalm 37 and you were always right, Mommy. Every time you were right.

But now, when I'm not with Father Scott or when there's not as much to do, Mommy, I find myself sometimes in P.S. 42, looking for God, and I don't know what room he's in, and I keep looking and trying to hear Daddy's voice and it makes me scared and lonely when I can't. P.S. 42 is the school I keep finding myself in, Mommy, and I don't want to be there. I miss you and I miss Daddy. Please don't worry about me. I am just as right as rain with Father Siberell to hang on to.

Luvvy duvvers— Your Haley

The sunless days creak by, stooped and arthritic. February clings to office walls, stubborn, relentless, selfish, the shortest month in no important way. June days go down like shelled peanuts, thrown back by the hot, salted half-dozen. But each and every February day in the upper Midwest is a great gob of flavorless, overcooked taffy, joylessly worked by weary jaws, swallowed with tearful effort, then followed by another, and another. And another. The concepts 'February' and 'brevity' mutually repel in northern heads. There are several candidates for shortest month, but none with an 'r' in the name. Much less *two*.

By the conclusion of her protest on the twelfth, Leslie Erickson Mitchell-Robbins Moore had spent twenty-three consecutive days chained to the bulldozer. Lilly gladly covered Leslie's classes and even took two one-hour shifts in chains each day so Leslie could shower and pee—a high-concept demonstration of usefulness if ever there was one.

Thus has the issue of the bones, begun in November, been stretched into an award-nominated twelve-article series for the elated Rebecca Kassel. Her thirteenth and final article on the story covers the faculty meeting on the 19th when Dean Martin finally announces, through gritted teeth, that the construction project has been permanently discontinued. The running tab has reached a point of no return, she explains. Gustafson and Son will be paid off from the deferred maintenance budget, so Cady Stanton's forward pitch and the library roof will go unaddressed until the next budget cycle, if then.

"In my opinion, the fact that the bones were determined scientifically to be non-native should by all rights have ended the controversy," she says to faculty over a rank of press microphones. "But the College has been bullied into submission by protesters who were more interested in pursuit of a particular political agenda than in the pursuit of the truth. Tuition will most likely go up next year to help offset the unplanned $845,000 cost of the construction start and standby, a cost that must be borne entirely by the College." She glares directly at Leslie Erickson Mitchell-Robbins Moore, seated triumphantly in the front row. "At the risk of showing my irritation too plainly, let me simply say that it should not have gone this way. I don't like it."

Driving home that night, Dean Martin's weariness is overwhelming. In the middle of the long unlit stretch of straight highway between Saint Philip and Sleepy Eye, she flips on the radio for company and hears none other than R. D. Shaw in a radio interview proclaiming that nothing has changed. The College is still standing on our ancestors' graves, is it not, he says, so the Lakota protesters have not dispersed and will not disperse until the last vestige of the College of Saint Bernadette is removed from the site. Even the college faculty is on our side, he says.

Dean Martin reaches over and clicks the radio off. She looks carefully in her rear view mirror for headlights and just as carefully up the ribbon of road before her, then suddenly snaps the steering wheel to the left and across the opposite lane. Her little black LeCar veers wildly to the opposite shoulder until she jerks the wheel back to the right. Shoulder to shoulder and back she swerves, over and over, screaming syntax free strings of obscenities on the level of 'damn,' 'ass' and 'crap' at the top of her lungs, tires squealing with each yank of the wheel. After about a quarter mile she corrects back to a single lane, feeling ever so much better.

Jack dutifully rotates quotes and arguments on and off his door display, waiting for comment or engagement from someone. Nothing. Every morning he steps over the space inside his door as if a note must certainly be there. Nothing. What a profound influence I'm having on the world, he thinks.

Sarcasm there.

Until one Wednesday morning when he has finally stopped stepping over nothing and steps on a handwritten note. His heart leaps into his throat as he scoops it up, closes the door and reads:

Dear Professor Kassel—

You don't know me, but I was just passing by your office today and I saw the quote from T. H. White on your door from Once and Future King. It is one of my all-time favorites. It made my day!

It is nice to know we have such good people in the philosophy department! Bye bye!

Ellen Latimer

Jack snorts. What the hell do you say to *that?* Thirty-two refutations of the existence of God and she comments on the one and only one that *isn't.*

After a moment's reflection he gives it a fifty-fifty chance of being a joke from Brian or Scott. The i's dotted with hearts are a little over-the-top.

The next Monday he steps on another one:

Dear Dr. Kassel,
I don't know if you remember me, but I took your Intro course last semester. You called me shapeless in a good way on the day you zoned in class. Anyway, I thought you should know that I and at least three other non-theistic students on campus have read your door display and think it is the best thing to happen around here since Saint Bernadette appeared over the wedge a hundred years ago.

Humor. Ark, ark. (Hey, there's <u>more</u> humor.)

Anyway, we need to chat, you and I. I'll be at the Starbucks in the Student Union at three today if you want to meet there. Otherwise I'll call you later.

Amanda Corelli

Ohhhhhhhh *yes.* Hello again, Amanda Corelli.

Jack somehow makes it through two shape sessions, then at three o'clock sharp walks into the conversational hum of Starbucks and sees Amanda at one of the tiny café tables. She's got that Berkeley kid look, he notes, that sort of intentional mishmash of clothing that proves you don't spend even one minute thinking about things less significant than institutionalized racism or globalization. John Lennon glasses with a slight rose tint. Wooden jewelry. Earth mother hair.

She sees Jack's approach and lights up. "You came!"

"I came," he says. "So. What have you been up to since last term?"

Amanda *pffts.* "Well, as riveting as that conversation might be, let's get down to business. *You* are an atheist."

Even after all these years, that still gives Jack a start. "Well, no, I wouldn't say that."

"Oh, uh . . . you aren't?" Amanda goes ashen, looking nervously at Jack over the little rose circles of glass. "I . . ."

Where exactly is this going, he wonders. "Put it this way. You believe in leprechauns?"

"Uh . . . no." She smirks. "I firmly renounce any and all belief in leprechauns."

"And so, if I wanted to fully and richly characterize your world view, do you think 'aleprechaunist' would do it?"

The tension falls from her face. "Aha, point taken. Okay, lesson number one, we're not atheists. So what are we?"

"Well, I *am* an atheist, but that's just the beginning. I don't know what your convictions are, so you can call yourself whatever you want. I'd rather be defined by what I think is true, not just what I think is untrue. I prefer 'humanist.'"

"Humanist? So . . . you believe in humans?"

"Uh . . . yes and no." There's that teachable moment again, Jack, get yourself organized. And turn off the filter—this is a friendly audience. "Okay, it's very simple. Once you set aside the mythology, you look at the implications of its *absence.*" Good so far. Keep going. "You look at the world for the first time as it really is—and it's this intoxicating, beautiful thing. So much more of a miracle *without* some mystical sorcerer at the helm. You bathe in that freedom and wonder for awhile—and then it hits you. There's this huge feeling of responsibility that sets in. No divine safety valve in this life, no escape clause into the next. We're responsible for creating the kind of world we want. Every moment suddenly becomes more precious, more fantastic, when you know this life is the only one. Every thing and every moment is lit with significance and incredible rarity. And you're struck with an overwhelming desire to make the most of it—to do it right." He pauses, pleased that it's coming out as coherently as it is. Talk about a rarity. "So for me, a commitment to reason is step one, which leads to atheism, step two, and *humanism*—well, that's the thousand steps that follow."

The cappuccino machine whispers in Yiddish.

Jack admits to an inner giddiness going on. The last time he really had this kind of discussion was twenty years ago with a very different Scott Siberell. Having it again, now, sort of conjures up the old Scott—that is to say, the young Scott—and redeems the current one in some strange way. He's born again, to coin a phrase, in this young hippie chick.

"Okay, great," Amanda says. "We're on the same page so far. So sum up your beliefs for me."

"You know, I hate to keep dissecting word choices here, but I'd stay away from the word 'belief' too, since most people believe this or that for no good reason. I like to say I have *convictions*, not beliefs. That means they've gone through some sort of critical process. They're based in reason . . . not . . . uh, what are you doing?"

Amanda is fumbling in her backpack. "I should be writing this stuff down." She pulls out a steno pad and uncaps a pen. "Okay. Now. What are your convictions?"

"No, please, come on. Put that away." He looks around skittishly. "This isn't an interview. We're just talking. Now where is all this going? Why'd you want to talk to me?" He gets a horrible thought and grabs her arm. "Oh shit, hold on, this *isn't* an interview, is it? You don't write for *The Wedge Issue*..."

"Oh, no! Oh my gosh, no. I just... well, I wanted to run an idea past you." She takes a breath, then starts spinning it out. "We want to start a student atheist... er, well, let's say a student *humanist* association on campus. I know three other students who would join right away, and there have to be a lot of others. And the thing is, we need a faculty advisor. Required by the student government constitution. And we've been looking for one for two years, Deena and Stacey and Randi and I. We're sick of talking to each other—preaching to the choir, you know. We wanna big it up. Shake this place up, get a little Enlightenment going."

Jack ponders that for a moment. "All right, say we wanna 'big it up.' What makes you think a Catholic college will tolerate a humanist student group? And more important, do you think I'm ever going to get tenure if I'm part of it?"

Amanda's crest falls a bit, knitting her brow on the way down. "That kind of thing would stop you?"

High on Jack's shoulder, an itty-bitty Brian appears, taunting softly in his ear: *Coward. Hypocrite. Idealist-who-acts-like-a-realist. Chic-ken-shit.*

Jack takes a deep breath and admits to himself that this might be just what he's been hoping for, just what he's needed. "No, I suppose I'd actually do it anyway. I've been looking for a little something different lately. Maybe getting fired would do it for me." The customary tray of dishes is dropped in the kitchen, followed by the federally-mandated smattering of applause.

Amanda lights up hard. "Cool. You said yes. This is *so* good. Oh gosh this is good. We're on. I'll get the papers together and run them by your office tomorrow." She stands in a burst. "Thank you for doing this. Wait 'til I tell Randi, she's gonna flip out . . ."

She glances down and stops suddenly, seeing a look of dread on Jack's face. "Oh, Dr. Kassel, I'm sorry . . . I . . ." She sits and calms herself. "Look, I know this might get a little weird for you. You've got more to lose than we do. Please don't worry about it—we'll do it right. Nobody gets fired if we keep it cool."

Oh is *that* what you think.

As a deer longs for flowing streams, so my soul longs for you, O God. My soul thirsts for God, for the living God. When shall I come and behold the face of God? My tears have been my food day and night, while people say to me continually, "Where is your God?" These things I remember, as I pour out my soul: how I went with the throng, and led them in procession to the house of God, with glad shouts and songs of thanksgiving, a multitude keeping festival. Why are you cast down, O my soul, and why are you disquieted within me?

Hope in God; for I shall again praise him, my help and my God. My soul is cast down within me; therefore I remember you from the land of Jordan and of Hermon, from Mount Mizar. Deep calls to deep at the thunder of your cataracts; all your waves and your billows have gone over me. By day the Lord commands his steadfast love, and at night his song is with me, a prayer to the God of my life. I say to God, my rock, "Why have you forgotten me? Why must I walk

Dale McGowan

about mournfully because the enemy oppresses me?" As with a deadly wound in my body, my adversaries taunt me, while they say to me continually, "Where is your God?"

Psalms 42: 1-10

10

Acts

The Bible teaches that woman brought sin and death into the world, that she precipitated the fall of the race, that she was arraigned before the judgment seat of Heaven, tried, condemned and sentenced. Marriage for her was to be a condition of bondage, maternity a period of suffering and anguish, and in silence and subjection, she was to play the role of a dependent on man's bounty for all her material wants, and for all the information she might desire. . . . Here is the Bible position of woman briefly summed up.

These teachings in regard to woman so faithfully reflect the provisions of the canon law that it is fair to infer that their inspiration came from the same source, written by men, translated by men, revised by men. If the Bible is to be placed in the hands of our children, read in our schools, taught in our theological seminaries, proclaimed as God's law in our temples of worship, let us by all means call a council of women in New York, and give it one more revision from the woman's standpoint.

Elizabeth Cady Stanton

852-MCGO

(STUDENT 1 *drops script on table in front of her.*)

STUDENT 1:   I'm a little uncomfortable with this, Tina.

TINA: That's because you've got to throw yourself into it, and you're not! This is the cutting edge*! (She slaps her clipboard down on the tabletop.)* Come on, people, this is more important than just another go at the same old thing. If you haven't bought into it, the audience won't either.

STUDENT 1:   I guess that's my point. I'm just not buying it.

TINA: *(sighs hard)* That's because you've lived your whole life knowing *A MAN for All Seasons!* You've had this male-dominated world drummed so far into your head by the original version that you can't imagine your way out!

STUDENT 1:   But I've never even *heard* of this play before.

TINA :   *(exasperated)* Be *actors*, people! If I asked to you imagine yourself on Vega VII dancing with squidlizards in six dimensions, you'd consider it a method-acting challenge and be all over this. Why is it so hard to deal with a simple gender switch?

STUDENT 1:   Because it just doesn't . . . *(She stops and exhales)* I don't know.

(Tina claps twice)

TINA: All right, people, this is a simple first read-
             ing. Let's just take it again and pretend our
             imaginations haven't completely imploded
             here. Start with 'It is more than any woman
             could bear.'

(Cast continues, devoid of enthusiasm)

HENRIETTA VIII   It is more than any woman
                  could bear.

TAMMY MORE   *(admiringly)* You are not just
                  any woman, my Queen.

HENRIETTA VIII   Have you thought any more
                  about—about my relationship
                  with Lady Catherine?

TAMMY MORE   It is all I can think about.

STUDENT 1:   See, it sounds like I'm coming on to the
              Queen!

TINA: *(irritated) What* are you *talking* about?

STUDENT 1:   *(in a seductive voice) You* are not just *any*
              woman, my Queen. Oh, and about your re-
              lationship? *(She leans seductively across the
              table toward* STUDENT 2. *Sultry sotto voce.)*
              It's *all* I can *think* about.

(STUDENT 2 *purrs erotically and feints a bite at the nose
of* STUDENT 1. *Cast bursts into peals of laughter)*

TINA:　　　　　*(irate)* So it's homoerotic, is it? *(she has shouted over the laughter, which ends abruptly)* Why wasn't it homoerotic when it was Thomas More saying it to Henry the Eighth?

(The cast is silent, as if contemplating a damn good question)

STUDENT 1:　　*(weakly)* I don't know, but it's different. It's just . . . it's *different* when it's women. I don't know why.

TINA:　　　　　It is *not* different. You're just seeing the world through the eyes of men. Now take it back to 'Have you thought any more,' and try to be *people*, not men.

　　　　HENRIETTA VIII　Have you thought any more about—about my relationship with Lady Catherine?

　　　　TAMMY MORE　It is all I can think about. But my Lady, I cannot be a party to the execution of your wife . . .

STUDENT 1:　*(whining)* Tina . . .

TINA:　　　　*(snaps)* Not interested! Go on!

(STUDENT 1 *growls in frustration*)

　　　　TAMMY MORE　It is all I can think about. But my Lady, I cannot be a party to the execution of your wife, though it places us at odds and thereby grieves me deeply.

HENRIETTA VIII	Well might you grieve, Tammy, for you take a dagger to my heart with your stubborn insistence! I don't know whether to rage or beg, to fall at your feet or cast you in irons.
TAMMY MORE	I beseech you, your Majesty—cast me in irons, take from me my name and fortune—only leave my honor, my conscience. That alone is more precious to me even than your good graces.
HENRIETTA VIII	Oh I know, Tammy. *(sighs)* Would that I could proceed without sullying that accursed conscience you wear like an amulet. *(Her voice softens)* For though it stands between us, you would not be who you are without it. And that . . . *(she cups Tammy's chin in her hand)* would be a loss above all others.
TAMMY MORE	I am relieved beyond measure. I thank Your Grace for your willingness to proceed without my paltry consent . . .
HENRIETTA VIII	Proceed without . . . You sorely misapprehend my

meaning, Tammy. I can NOT proceed without it! *(she growls in frustration)* Why is it so difficult for you to see? I seek not divorce as such but the annulment of a travesty! Catherine was my sister's widow. I only seek to reverse my own sins.

TAMMY MORE   I'm afraid I don't . . . understand.

HENRIETTA VIII   *Scripture,* Tammy, think of Leviticus: "Thou shalt not uncover the nakedness of thy sister's wife."

STUDENT 2:   Now wait a minute! That's Leviticus upside down! You can't have lesbians quoting Leviticus! Verse twenty-two calls homosexuality an abomination! And what about Romans 1:26? And First Corinthians . . .

(Her look changes from indignation to pride when she realizes the cast is looking at her, impressed. She beams childishly, clearly pleased with herself)

Well *I'm* a theology major.

TINA: You are also supposed to be a woman, and an actor! Let's focus on *those* for the moment, shall we, and leave all the side issues out of it. *(Seeing the open mouth of* STUDENT 2, *cuts her off before she can protest)* Shh! Go on!

TAMMY MORE	But that Lady Catherine should pay with her life— that I cannot justify. There seemed ... *(she looks into the distance)* ... at one time there seemed such genuine affection between you. And she has borne you children ...
HENRIETTA VIII	*Sons,* Tammy! Sons all! Of what use are sons when one is marching toward eternity? They are good boys, Tammy, but without a daughter—without a daughter, *I am without a soul!*

(Cast members look up from their scripts slowly, then around at each other as if gradually becoming convinced. TINA smiles and motions for them to continue.)

II

First Peter

Hain't we got all the fools in town on our side?
And ain't that a big enough majority in any town?

Mark Twain, *The Adventures of Huckleberry Finn*

" . . . Which is going to put us solidly over the seventieth percentile for white blue collar urban males over 55."

The congressman sits in the silence into which he's been pressed, elbow on the table and cheek cradled in palm, listening for the second unhappy hour to the dronings of Robert Dole Wanamacher, idiot great-nephew of Bob Dole by way of Dole's sister Norma Jean. All of twenty-three years old, heir on his Wanamacher side to the Wanamacher Fresh and Frozen Foods empire, who was told nonetheless by his father Cedric III that he better damn well go out and learn some lessons in the school of hard knocks if he intends to be handed the company Cedric Johannes Wanamacher II built from a family egg-laying concern into a multinational food conglomerate, by cracky, which inheritance was made all the less damn well likely from Cedric III's p.o.v. when "that stupid pusspie of a son of mine" failed to gain admission to a single respectable college, ending up instead at Bob Jones University, first in political science, then in math, and four undistinguished years later needing a few phone calls from great-uncle Senator Bob Dole before finally ending up in nominal charge of demographic research for the campaign staff of Minnesota Second District Representative Peter D'Angelo, owner of the abovementioned cheek, elbow, and diminishing attention.

"Moving on now to the outstate working-class high-school educated female 40 to 45 stripe, we see that . . ."

"Bob."

". . . we are in a bit more difficulty, most polls placing us in the . . ."

"Bob."

". . . high thirties at best, a situation we should be able to remedy by targeting four key issues in the . . ."

"Yo Bobbie."

". . . early campaign, specifically (a) farm subsidies, (2) educ . . ."

"BOB!"

Bob Dole Wannabee, as his BJU friends called him, squeaks high and loud at the interruption, unintentionally hurling his laserpointer at the screen. "Oh. Uh, I'm sorry, Congressman. Did I . . . say something wrong?"

Peter D'Angelo remembers the elder Wanamacher's considerable generosity and passion for the right kind of politics and so refrains from answering the question directly. He gradually lets the pressure out of his head as if blowing tar through a straw.

"Bob, Bobbie, you've done a . . . really wonderful job here. Why, you've got it all laid out for us, don'tcha? Look at all those pie charts. How can we go wrong with *all, those, pie charts?* Especially that one chart that shows us pulling, what'd you say, fifty-two percent in a three-way race, if the Senate election were held today?"

"Yes sir, and that's a conservative estimate."

"Ah, just the kind I like. And this woman, the likely Democrat, Susan Goldberg, she's looking at, what did you say, twenty-six?"

"Tops!"

"Tops. And our governor, the honorable Mr. Ventura, you've got him around thirty-six percent right now by your calculations, is that right?"

"I think he'd be lucky to even get . . ."

"Which is a lotta percent altogether, don't you think, Mr. Wanamacher?"

"I . . ." Bob scrambles for his pointer, which has gone out. "It . . . well, you've got the most, which is all we care about, right, sir?" He tries a weak *heh-heh.*

"Fifty-two plus twenty-six plus thirty-six . . . how much did that come to at Bob Jones U?"

The soft, incessant trill of telephones in the next room.

"Uh, well, the same as . . ."

"Here in D.C. that's one hundred fourteen percent, Robert."

Bob D. Wanamacher looks at the screen and makes calculating clucks with his tongue. "Well, uh, we're . . . we're anticipating a really large turnout."

" . . ."

"I . . . well, there's something wrong with the numbers, I guess."

"No, the numbers seem to be doing their job, Bob, just standing where they were put and all. But why don't you go away now and push them around a little differently."

"I'll do that sir." Bob picks up a two-inch stack of overheads, which predictably slide onto the floor in a translucent flurry.

"Leave them, Bob."

Bob leaves them and goes. D'Angelo swivels his chair to face his campaign manager. "You've got to be joking with this kid, Michael."

"Well, it's a favor for You-Know-Who. Dole stumped for you a lot in '98 when you were in deep trouble, remember? And this kid's dad is a big contributor."

"These are not things I don't know, Mike, but can we bury him a little deeper in the structure here? Jesus, we've got to know what our numbers are, for fuck's sake."

Mike scribbles in his planner.

D'Angelo continues. "Now if I remember correctly that was about 25 grand in polling data he screwed up. Can you get your hands on the raw data and figure anything out?"

"Well, I already did a little looking on my own and, I'll tell you what, I can actually sympathize with our little friend there."

"How's that?"

"Well." Mike takes a deep breath. "It's that same damn thing that's been mucking up elections since Bush-Gore. The country's split down the middle on every workable issue you can think of, and I'm not talking 60-40, Peter. Heck, I'd give my right wing for a 60-40. This is the damndest thing I've ever seen, sometimes 50-50, sometimes 51-49, but not much better than that. And Minnesota's right in line with the rest of the nation, look, pro-choice, 51.6%, pro-life 48.4%."

"Margin of error?"

"Plus or minus three. Which swamps it, so it's a meaningless result, nothing to exploit. Capital punishment, look at this, *fifty-fifty* over seven polls. Gun control, never beats the margin of error no matter how you ask the question. Gays, affirmative action, trade, taxes, everything is a complete toss-up."

"That's bad."

"Oh it gets worse. Generally we can find one side that's

more energized than the other, more motivated, right, so we get the turnout even if we don't dominate in the issue itself."

"And? Where's the heat?"

"That's just it, *no heat*. None to speak of. When we get down to the 'strength of conviction' subquestions, the consistent response—now I mean on every issue, Peter, and on any side of the question—the consistent response can be summed up as," he shrugs, *"eh."*

"Eh?"

"Yes. Nobody gives a damn. It's the economy, stupid—uh, you know what I mean, sir. Except we're on the flipside now. In '92 that's where the heat was, but now, well, the economy's better, the Cold War's back there someplace with the French and Indian War . . . No real fear and very little loathing, no hunger in the middle class . . . no boogeyman except Osama bin Laden, and it's tough to really put the opponents in bed with him. So the chadknockers are picking their convictions by flipping a coin, pretty much. It's just ugly. This is an unnerving time to be in our business, Congressman, I'll tell you that."

"This better be leading to something I don't know, Mikey. I swear, if we end up in a hand recount again I'm gonna have somebody's . . ."

". . . so I've been combing through the numbers for days now, looking for something to hang our hats on, running issue profiles through the computer—and the damndest thing popped out of the pack." Mike reaches into his planner and pulls out a single sheet of paper. "Look at this."

Polling Compilation Data 11/14/01–01/26/02
McPherson-Donnally Research Group, Inc.
SUB-SELECTIONS: Profile 1F
[Poll1: 2311 respondents]
[Poll2: 1944 respondents]
[Poll3: 2078 respondents]

Combined respondents = n = 6333
SD + /–3.22%

1F SUMMARY (4 questions selected)

38. Do you believe in God?	YES = 93.64%
72. Would you vote for an admitted atheist?	NO = 83.18%
91. Is a candidate's morality important?	YES = 88.92%
107. Is religious faith an important element in the development of morality?	YES = 87.34%

"One hundred fifty-five questions in all, Congressman, every one of them splitting down the middle with no real heat, no loyalty to one side or the other—except these four in the eighties and nineties. Well I thought I had run the numbers wrong at first, but I hadn't—this is the real thing. There might be something there for us."

D'Angelo's eyes flit back and forth over the page. "And the strength-of-conviction numbers?"

"Same thing, eighties and nineties."

D'Angelo looks up from the sheet, aglow. "Jesus, Mike. Why the hell did you let me sit through that goddam moron for over an hour?" He looks back down and unfurls a positively lunatic grin. "We've got everything we need *right here.*"

"Well now, I don't know about that, Peter. This is interesting, but there's a lot of flux in the . . ."

"Mikey, Mikey, Mikey. Don't you see it?" His eyes are set for deep gleam. "This is not just interesting. You know Goldberg's gonna melt away, she's too far flaming left even for the damn liberals. *Nader* even called her dangerous, for shit's sake. She'll end up under twenty. But the centrist Dems will jump to Jesse, not to me, and he'll swamp us with low fifties. So he's the only competition, Mike. Put it together, son: what do these numbers mean for our friend Jesse The Body?"

The dawn's early light slowly spreads over Mike's face. Oh my.

D'Angelo is on his feet, pacing. "You remember Jesse's *Playboy* interview, don't you: 'Religion is a sham, a crutch for weak-minded people.' I'll go ahead and call that a vulnerability, looking at this."

"But you're really suggesting we go with a single-issue campaign? That's death, Peter. Focus that tight and you'll pull thirty percent with the best of issues."

"Not if it's THE issue, babe. Clinton did it in '92. Remember 'It's the Economy, Stupid?' And that was a high-sixties issue at *best*. Can you think of another issue in America that pulls down these numbers? Ninety percent of Americans don't agree on *squat*. You capture a ninety-percent issue, even an eighty, you own the election. This election is about *God*, Mike. That's it. Divert every question to the God question. Peter D'Angelo is God's candidate. Don't spell it out, of course, just get the strong implication out there. I've seen you do that—remember that Reynolds thing? If you pulled that off, this will be a cakewalk. 'Do you think God wants you to vote for Jesse? A vote against Peter-of-the-Angels is a vote against *God*.' " D'Angelo rubs his hands together. "This is our classic light bulb moment, Michael. There's one in every winning campaign, and this is ours. Do you really think a plurality is going to even *risk* voting against God?"

Peter has always been able to convince him of anything, and now Mike is fully aboard. "Not if Saint Peter tells them not to!"

D'Angelo hoots and clamps a hand on Mike's shoulder "Now see, Mr. Michael Lutz, *this* is why I feed you. Saint Peter, that's fucking *brilliant*. Leak that one to the friendly talk-radio shows next month. Saint Peter. What a goddam *romp* this is gonna be. *God* I love it when it's easy."

Ten minutes later, Mike Lutz marches out of the Rayburn Building into a raw February late afternoon. Eight blocks down C Street he blows through the campaign office door, straight past three humorless envelope-stuffing volunteers and to his desk. He pulls out a sheet of paper and a huge black marker, quickly writes a few words in huge, black letters, strides to the giant bulletin board, tacks it up—and stands back with arms folded to drink it in:

IT'S THE OLOGY, STUPID

12

The Epistle of Thomas

But where's the man who counsel can bestow,
Still pleased to teach, and yet not proud to know?
Unbiased, or by favour, or by spite:
Not dully prepossess'd, nor blindly right;
Tho' learn'd, well-bred; and tho' well-bred, sincere;
Modestly bold, and humanly severe,
Who to a friend his faults can freely show,
And gladly praise the merits of a foe?

Alexander Pope, *An Essay on Criticism*

There's a little teaser-thaw going on as Jack Kassel
tiptoes across the puddled walk in front of Admin.
Unnaturally early thaws are not occasions for rejoicing in
Minnesota; they only serve to convert harmless sidepiled
snow into sidewalk ponds that refreeze solid in a few days
and for the rest of the winter. February and March pedestrians are lucky to stay upright for more than a hundred feet at
a go until the more serious thaws of actual spring.

Amanda Corelli has exciting news, she says, and Jack's gut coils as he enters the Starbucks, scrapes his boots on the mat and sees her seated at a back booth, smiling and waving the piece of paper he fully expected.

"We got the thumbs-up!" she yells across the room. A few disinterested heads turn in pairs, then return to their low, rumbling conversations.

Jack smiles weakly and gives a little thumbs-up of his own as he shuffles to the register. He drops a dollar and change on the counter, picks up a mug of coffee and walks to the booth.

"That's great," he says halfheartedly, clearly unconvinced of the greatness of the whole thing. He slides into the booth, looking warily at the letter folded on the table.

"What's the matter?" Amanda asks. "We're on! Isn't that awesome? This is what you wanted, isn't it?"

Oh, to only know what I want. "Let's say I've been around here long enough to have inklings. Let me see the letter." Amanda's smile drops to a puzzled squint as she slides the letter to him.

Jack reads carefully from the top, realizing that he hadn't read what he signed before she sent it in. Application for CSB Official Club Status, yada yada, Saint Bernadette Humanist Association. Amanda Corelli, president, Randi Delaney, vice president, Stacey Rios, treasurer . . . Dr. Jack Kassel, faculty advisor. Purpose: to provide CSB students with an opportunity to read and discuss humanist writings; to provide a social network for student humanists; to provide a campus-level organization to interact with local, regional, and national humanist organizations; to foster campus dialogue over the most important issues of human inquiry; to educate non-humanists about the humanist perspective. Weekly meetings, yada yada. He scans down to the bottom: ORGANIZATION APPROVED AS PROPOSED. And then the kicker, a handwritten note from none other than Wanda X. Streamley:

*This is such a wonderful idea, Amanda! How heart-
ening to see this kind of student interest in the humanities.*

Oh *crap*. What is Wanda doing signing off on this? He
looks up at Amanda, who is almost incapacitated with silent
convulsions of laughter.

"Amanda . . ."

She attempts to speak. "She . . . she thinks it's . . . she
thinks it's a *humanities* club." She takes a deep breath and
recovers. "Nice Catholic girl Wanda Streamley approves the
first atheist student organization at a U.S. Christian college
without even knowing she's doing it. That's poetry."

"You like that, do you."

"Yes!! Dr. Kassel, for all we know she would have said no
if she knew what this really was! Now it's approved, so they
can't exactly rescind it without looking pretty darn foolish."

"I'm not thrilled that this is starting out with a strategy of
embarrassing the administration . . . wait a minute. What do
you mean, first in the country?"

"Yes! I looked into it. First at a Christian college! And if
the Administration weren't so embarrassable, by the way . . ."

Jack's face goes white. "Amanda . . . No. We can't do this.
Not this way." Brian appears on his shoulder and Jack flicks
him three tables away into a mochaccino.

"What?" Amanda's smile is totally gone, mouth agape.
"Dr. Kassel, what are you saying? We are *in*, it's a done deal,
and you want to *dump* it?"

"You really think it's a good idea to do this by stealth?"

"We didn't do it by stealth! We didn't misrepresent anything on that form! She's the moron who doesn't know humanism from humanities."

"Ah . . . before you go knocking Dr. Streamley around,
need I remind you that you first heard the word 'humanism'
fully two weeks ago? Were you a moron right up to that moment? This is not the way to proceed. Don't you see?" He

leans in. "This is just what the religious expect from the non-religious. Do this and you fuel their argument that Christians have a monopoly on virtue."

"We did not do anything deceptive."

"That is not how it's going to look. That note from the president tells you exactly what they're thinking, and that obligates you to clarify."

"Well what if she hadn't written that note?"

"But she *did* write it, Amanda."

"And we can't pretend that she didn't? She won't even remember what she . . ."

"Which I'm sure you know is not the point! We know what she actually thinks, so that's what we deal with. We deal with reality. That's what this is all about."

She sinks back into a pout. "I can't believe this."

"Amanda, what's the right thing to do? Forget the outcome you want: what's the right thing?"

She smolders, then lets her shoulders fall. "Oh *fine*, I'll write a letter clarifying the whole thing."

"Okay, now. Did you use the Ten Commandments to figure out what was right? Or the Sermon on the Mount?"

"*Pfft.* Take a guess."

"Here's my point. Swing a cat in the chapel this Sunday and you'll hit a Christian who'll tell you that you can't possibly know right from wrong without scriptural guidance. If not for the Bible we'd be slaughtering each other in the streets."

"Morons."

"No, Amanda, that's way too easy. They're wrong, but they're not morons. You've got to at least acknowledge that they're trying to do the right thing."

"Well, they miss that mark an awful lot, don't you think?"

"Again, beside the point. The more articulate ones will even tell you that. They know they're flawed, they know they're sinners, but they say they're forgiven and they continue to try harder than they would if they didn't have that book."

"Yet I don't believe in God or the Bible and I haven't murdered anyone in weeks."

"That's because you borrowed your morality from the Bible."

"What?!"

Jack is stonefaced. "What do you say to that?"

"I say bullshit!"

"And they say you're wrong, and you say bullshit, and they say it's okay, God forgives you. 'Bullshit' is a weak defense. Gimme something else."

Amanda slouches even further, then suddenly bolts upright. "Okay. The Golden Rule. It's in every religion and philosophical system on Earth."

"They all borrowed it from Jesus."

"Bullshit!"

Jack takes a long swig of coffee.

"Okay, fine," Amanda says at last, reslouching. "Okay. Confucius lived five hundred years before Christ. *He* didn't borrow it from Jesus."

"There you go."

"And Hinduism, and Buddhism, they've all got the same basic moral code, and they all predate Christ."

"Now that's an argument. And there's less murder in the streets of almost any non-Christian country on Earth than there is in Christian America. What's stopping them if they don't have WWJD bracelets?"

"Okay, I got it. Stronger than 'bullshit.'"

"Don't miss an opportunity to show that you and I have just the same moral compass as any given Christian. And that," he says, poking the table with each word, "is why you clarify this misunderstanding instead of taking advantage of it."

She *pffts* again. "As if a Christian would do that."

"And again, beside the point. Some would and some

wouldn't. But *you* have to be completely above-board, you've got to be twice as straight and narrow to be judged half as good."

She sighs and nods. "Okay, fine. I see where you're going."

"Look, I know what it's like to be in your position. I was there, and I screwed up at every turn. It didn't help that there was nobody more experienced sitting across from me who could walk me through this, so I made all the mistakes and took all the consequences. For years I thought I was the only one who thought what I thought. Then halfway through college I had a roommate named Sc . . ."

Jack stops abruptly. Well we can't go there, can we now.

". . . uh, I had a roommate with the very same convictions. I'll tell you, it was like a cool drink of water, finding someone else to talk to . . ."

"Yeah, that's what Randi is for me. You've got to meet her soon, she's incredible with all this."

His eyes have glazed for a moment, locked in the past, then he snaps back, unaware that Amanda had spoken at all. "Not that he was any more together than I was about the whole thing. He was a wild man is what he was, but brilliant . . . and just a little further down the road. *He* knew we weren't alone in disbelief, not by a long shot. Every couple of weeks a book would suddenly appear on my desk, on my bed, in my backpack—David Hume, Bertrand Russell, Voltaire, Thomas Paine, Montaigne. It was a great time. He's the reason I took up philosophy, that roommate—well, him and the Reynolds Effect, I suppose."

"The Reynolds Effect?"

"Oh, never mind that. Anyway, it was so liberating to be out that I made every stupid adolescent mistake there was to make. Uh, no offense to any adolescents present."

"None taken. I'm twenty."

Jack smiles slightly. "Of course, forgive me. But I was

still an adolescent, since *I* was a mere nineteen. I was loud when I should have been quiet and quiet when I should have been loud. I felt like an idiot and looked like one a hundred times. I debated from the hip, without preparation. And I didn't listen, so I couldn't respond. I used arguments without knowing what supported them, or if anything supported them at all, and did more damage than good."

Down goes the traditional tray of glasses in the kitchen, and the kitchen crew alone gets the applauding done.

Amanda looks into her coffee. "So if this is a time for restraint, why do I feel like climbing up to the chapel roof and yelling, 'I'm not a Christian!!'? You say you know what it's like to be in the box—and then suddenly see the lid open. It's fantastic. Well, your office door was the lid coming off for me. I know how I must look from where you're sitting, but . . ." She looks up. "It just feels like I've been headed to this moment for years. I don't want to throw it away."

"Amanda, that could have come out of my mouth! I feel exactly the same about this thing. And don't get the wrong idea about how you look from here, by the way. You are way ahead of where I was, *miles* ahead. Believe me, if College Jack were sitting across from you, there'd be no question about who should run this show. You're more centered, more articulate, more passionate . . . You know who you *are*, Amanda." He shakes his head, remembering. "But now, from this seat, twenty years later . . . well, this Jack knows a little about what's around the next curve." He winces inwardly to think of the hoot that Scott would give if he heard him say that. *You're great at the post mortem, JJ, always have been—but let's face it, you generally don't know what's happening until it's over, am I right? Look at Daddy, Jack—am I right?*

Got to keep these two apart.

"Well I appreciate the advice. Just like you think back on College Jack, I've got Pre-Teen Amanda to deal with. I'm doing all this for her as much as for me. That's when the whole Christian thing started falling apart for me, about twelve years old. I'd watch the church folks say one thing and do another, 'til finally I just couldn't buy the package anymore."

Jack smiles slightly. "Well, that's fine, I guess, if it got you where you were going anyway. Still weak, though. Their hypocrisy doesn't disprove their claims."

"True. I guess it was the admissions policy for heaven that really did it. I couldn't see God letting all of them in on a technicality and not me."

"That was an early one for me too. But you need to get beyond that pretty quickly to the whole beauty-of-truth idea I talked about in the Intro course."

"Oh yeah, the CRACK," Amanda recalls with a smirk. "We had a lot of fun with that one outside of class. Like the unique ability of plumbers to reveal great truths."

Okay, that's funny. "All right, I can think of a few more. Very good. But the point is that the God hypothesis doesn't have that *elegance* it would have if it were true. All religions are the same, just spackle in the cracks of our understanding. Wild guesses made into lovely stories. Look at the Greek and Roman myths. I ate them up as a kid. And I knew that everyone knew they were just attempts by poor, silly, dumb, ancient folks who lived way over there and way back then to explain the world. We'd outgrown the fables, I knew. The sun isn't Apollo's chariot, of course: it's a star that began burning when a god said *Let there be Light.* Man was not created from clay by *Zeus*, he was created from clay by *Yahweh*. Hades didn't restore Euridice to life, *please*. That would be absurd. Jesus *did*, of course, restore Lazarus to life. That's different. We know *these* things are true because they were written *here* instead of over *here*. By Mark instead of Ovid. By Paul instead of Homer. What morons we were before. How wise we are now. The underworld isn't guarded by three-headed Cerberus and rounded by the river Styx: it's a place called Hell, where demons torture people who refused to acknowledge that a particular prophet was the son of that light-commanding god. How could we have been so ignorant before? And we don't *all* go to that underworld when we die, only bad guys like Gandhi and the Dalai Lama do."

"What's the dolly llamadoo?"

"Whatever he wants, I'm sure. But the point is that really significant truths tend to have that loud CRACK of clarity and self-evidence once they're finally articulated. They disperse fog, they don't create it. Like the structure of DNA. Fog, fog, fog, then CRACK, the double helix, and we've got unlimited visibility. Same with heliocentricity."

"Sun-centered solar system."

"Right. Ptolemy thought the sun and planets orbited the Earth and came up with a complex table of calculations to explain it. Mars moves across the sky, you see, stops, regresses, stops, then continues forward. Different formulas for all the planets. Okay, I see. Geocentricity. So physical reality is inelegant, complex, absurd." Jack reaches into his shirt pocket, pulls out a cigarette and places it, dangling and unlit, between his lips.

"Then fourteen hundred years pass. Copernicus suggests the sun might be in the middle. Heliocentricity. CRACK. Clarity, simplicity, elegance."

Amanda sits back to enjoy a show clearly not over. "Testify, brother."

"Oh stop that. One more: scientists and journalists in 1919 gathered in little corners of the globe to witness the total solar eclipse that would confirm or refute Einstein's General Theory of Relativity. Einstein stayed home. Measurements of gravitationally-displaced starlight around the sun confirmed the theory precisely."

"A veritable *crack* epidemic."

"And the press clamored for answers. How could he stay home? How could he stand the suspense? How could he not have *been* there?"

"I was wondering the same thing."

"That's the beautiful thing, Amanda. The rumpled little guy smiled this patient smile at the press folks and said, 'You needed a demonstration to remove doubt. I needed no such demonstration.' Isn't that just a lovely story?"

She takes a moment, playing with the pewter bracelet orbiting her wrist. "It's just unbelievable. I'd have been there."

"Sure, me too, of course! That's the difference between Einstein and us. I figure that whatever it is in me that would make me 'have to be there' is the same thing that keeps me from coming up with things like relativity." Jack's voice and gaze drift off together. "Lovely, lovely, sexy thing, the truth. Once you fall in love with that kind of truth you just can't buy the God thing. It's just dripping with nonsense." He polishes off the cup. "Truth comes in a much more elegant package."

"Which brings us back to the Question of the Day: do you want to kill our best chance of getting that message out by writing a 'clarifying letter'?"

Jack shakes his head. "Amanda, you must have heard something in the last ten minutes." He sighs hard. "Okay." He drifts for a moment. There's a story she needs to hear, but it is so beautiful, so fragile, such a treasure to him that he hesitates. Twelve years of casting pearls before swine, he thinks, and a guy can be forgiven a little hesitation.

Then he remembers the Voltaire class. Amanda the Shapeless sits before him. All right. She's earned The Story.

He begins cautiously, watching her as he speaks. "September of 1860, Thomas Henry Huxley carried the body of his four-year old boy, his Noel, into his study and closed the door. He'd watched a fever ravage his son, watched as he thrashed and cried in his bed for two days, and finally held him as he died. He had wept over the boy for an hour before carrying him into the study and laying him gently on the desk. He sat in the chair with his hand on Noel's hand, then reached into the desk drawer and wrote in his journal—wrote about how much he loved his son, how devastating his loss was, how much he wanted him back. He'd given up theistic illusions years before, so he knew there was no by-and-by when they'd be reunited. He was face-to-face with the implications of his convictions: real, irreversible loss without any soft-pedaling fantasies to comfort him."

Amanda listens in complete silence. For that reason, and that alone, Jack continues.

"He got letters of condolence, hundreds of them, all of which he answered with a line or two of thanks. Except one," Jack says, looking Amanda dead in the eye, "a letter from the Reverend Canon Kingsley, Chaplain to the Queen, who had written that he himself could not face the loss of a loved one without knowing that that person would live on in another existence. Fortunately, he said, he had that assurance. So, Huxley old bean, he wrote, now's the time for you to throw away that blasted agnosticism of yours. Come to faith and be comforted in your time of loss."

"I hope Huxley kicked him in the balls."

Jack exhales hard. "No. Don't do that. He should be faulted for caring? For doing the best he could with what he believed to be true? Amanda, I understand that reaction, but you've *got* to bury that. Kingsley could've sat smug in his rectory and said, 'God hath dealt a mighty blow to the unbeliever,' but he didn't say that. He showed complete integrity within his own beliefs. You want to be respected for acting within your own convictions, you have to respect somebody like Kingsley for doing what he did. Think about it: if a Christian really, truly believes the unfaithful are bound for Hell, and then just sits back and snickers—well, that would be reprehensible. They must try to save us from ourselves."

"I don't know if I can buy that, Dr. Kassel. I just hate evangelism, more than anything."

"Did you ever try to convince a friend of your own convictions?"

Just thirty times in the past week, Amanda thinks. "Sure
I have. I do it all the time."

"Then you're an evangelist, Amanda. And that's good.
The nonbelievers I can't stand are the ones who sit quiet and
smug, smirking at all the 'idiot' believers around them. That
kind of non-believer is of no use. They don't have the courage of their convictions. A big part of growing up intellectually is learning to respect your loudest opponents for the courage of *their* convictions, even if they have every fact wrong.
Rail against them for *that*, sure, but you've got to respect
their integrity for living out what they believe to be true."

Amanda removes her glasses with a sigh, folds and pock-
ets them. "You know, I really don't want that to make sense—
but it does."

Jack sets down his coffee and smiles. "That was well put,
Amanda—and again, miles ahead of College Jack." He
reaches into the tattered leather briefcase at his side and draws
out an even more tattered piece of paper, clearly folded and
refolded many times. "At the moment of his most unbear-
able pain, Thomas Huxley held on to his integrity. He couldn't
accept Kingsley's offer of false consolation, and he told him
so—powerfully, but respectfully." He carefully places the
paper on the table between them. "You seem ready to throw
your integrity away just for the sake of a two-bit campus club.
That's a pretty thin reason. Huxley held on to his in the depths
of his grief over his son." He slides the paper toward her.
"You have got to focus on the truth or they'll have you for
lunch, Amanda. They've been in the driver's seat for two
thousand years because so few people can keep that tight
focus. Huxley could. They'll drag you into every tangent
they can draw, and it'll work, like it always has, if you lose
your focus. Huxley knew that. Kick and scream and bite and
claw and work your way through distractions and feel-good
mythology and superstitions and crappy thinking and wishful
thinking and accusations and namecalling and all those zeal-

ous, self-assured, smiling evangelical faces until you find the truth. Respect their zeal even as you refute their errors. And every step of the way, remember that going after the actual truth is all that matters. Everything else is a sideshow."

Amanda reaches out, draws in the paper and slowly opens it. *My Dear Kingsley,* it begins. It is a handwritten copy of Huxley's response to the canon. She looks at Jack and guesses correctly from his expression that it was written out by College Jack, years before—and that Jack has very mixed feelings about handing it to her.

"Thank you, Dr. Kassel. I really appreciate seeing this."

"To tell you the truth, I'm glad to have someone to show it to. There's a lot there."

She walks through the slush, slowly, reading the letter as she makes her way down the Wedge to Steinem Hall.

My dear Kingsley—I cannot sufficiently thank you, both on my wife's account and my own, for your long and frank letter, and for all the hearty sympathy which it exhibits—and Mrs. Kingsley will, I hope, believe that we are no less sensible of her kind thought of us. To myself your letter was especially valuable, as it touched upon what I thought even more than upon what I said in my letter to you. My convictions, positive and negative, on all the matters of which you speak, are of long and slow growth and are firmly rooted. But the great blow which fell upon me seemed to stir them to their foundation, and had I lived a couple of centuries earlier I could have fancied a devil scoffing at me and them—and asking me what profit it was to have stripped myself of the hopes and consolations of the mass of mankind? To which my only reply was and is—Oh devil! truth is better than much profit. I have searched over the grounds of my belief, and if wife and child and name and fame were all to be lost to me one after the other as the penalty, still I will not lie.

The longer I live, the more obvious it is to me that the most sacred act of a man's life is to say and to feel, "I believe such and such to be true." All the greatest rewards and all the heaviest penalties of existence cling about that act. The universe is one and the same throughout; and if the condition of my success in unravelling some little difficulty of anatomy or physiology is that I shall rigorously refuse to put faith in that which does not rest on sufficient evidence, I cannot believe that the great mysteries of existence will be laid open to me on other terms. It is no use to talk to me of analogies and probabilities. I know what I mean when I say I believe in the law of the inverse squares, and I will not rest my life and my hopes upon weaker convictions. I dare not if I would.

Science warns me to be careful how I adopt a view which jumps with my preconceptions, and to require stronger evidence for such belief than for one to which I was previously hostile. My business is to teach my aspirations to conform themselves to fact, not to try and make facts harmonise with my aspirations.

Science seems to me to teach in the highest and strongest manner the great truth which is embodied in the Christian conception of entire surrender to the will of God. Sit down before fact as a little child, be prepared to give up every preconceived notion, follow humbly wherever and to whatever abysses nature leads, or you shall learn nothing. I have only begun to learn content and peace of mind since I have resolved at all risks to do this.

I know right well that 99 out of 100 of my fellows would call me atheist, infidel, and all the other usual hard names. As our laws stand, if the lowest thief steals my coat, my evidence (my opinions being known) would not be received against him. But I cannot help it. There is one thing people shall not call me with justice, and that is a liar. As you say of yourself, I too feel that I lack courage; but if ever the occasion arises when I am bound to speak, I will not shame my boy.

HENR. VIII Everyone in the kingdom sees what you yourself are blinded to! How is it that this is so?

T. MORE It is my own failing, Your Majesty, nothing could be more clear than this. Why would you need the support of such a one as I?

HENR. VIII Honesty. You are an honest person, plain and simple, and moreover known to be so. Think of your rarity, my friend, *think* of it! Some follow me because they follow the crown I happen to wear. Some follow because they are sharp-toothed hyenas and I lead their pack. Others follow because they were born to follow anything that moves. And then there is you.

T. MORE I am heartsick to be such a disappointment to Your Grace.

HENR. VIII For honesty? No. That kind of honesty, why, it's like cool water in the desert. (claps) But enough of this! Did you chance to hear the tune the sackbuts played at my entrance?

T. MORE   *(Smiling)* Might I suppose it was your own
               composition?

HENR. VIII   *(Smiles back)* You guessed! That's too bad. Now
               I'll never know what you really think. Though
               I love praise, yet I love truth better.

13

The Book of Ruth

Train up a child in the way he should go: and when he is old, he will not depart from it.

Proverbs 6

As I looked around, I realized it was going to be wrong if I stole the shoes. So even though I knew I would'nt get caught, and even though I wanted them alot. I did'nt steal the shoes. And that was the beginning of my moral developement.

Now there's some first-class self-exploration, thinks Jack, massaging one tired eye. He finds the margin at the bottom of the last page and writes:

Good work overall, Missy. Now for the final draft you might consider doing the assignment.

Now now, Jack. He scratches it out solidly with a growl and rewrites:

Good work overall, Missy. Now for the final draft you might consider looking into the reasons you knew in that moment that it was wrong to steal. Clearly it was not a matter of consequences, since you felt you would not be caught, so there was some moral imperative at work. I need to see some conjecture on the imperative and some of its possible sources. See if it is possible as well to tie the several examples together into a more cohesive whole.

Or better yet, drop the class. Take a hike. I could use the ten extra minutes per batch of papers to scratch myself.

One, two, three, four, five, six, seven . . . damn. About eleven to go. Not gonna make it.

Jack pulls himself to his feet and walks to the refrigerator. He finds a Guinness and walks back to the living room to toss two more pine logs into the woodstove, sending up swirls of sparks and embers. He drops back into the recliner with a groan and swings the pile of papers onto his lap.

Jack scans down the first page of the next paper. Oh, my, what have we here. Gwendolyn Pierce. Purple phrases, dramatic, overwrought. He gets a picture in his mind of the student most likely to be Gwendolyn: quiet, cornered-looking, with the furtive eyes of the accused. Yes, that's the one, he thinks, I'm sure of it. I remember her whispering it during introductions on the first day. *Gwendolyn.* Damaged-looking little Gwendolyn.

He reads with a mix of scorn and trepidation—and sure enough, by the third page she's into the kind of serious self-revelation Jack knew was coming and would rather not hear. Oh here we go, he thinks, when he sees the name "Jesus" popping up several lines down:

I audition for a solo in the second-grade choir. No one, least of all myself, thinks I can do it. My voice

was too quiet and I rarely spoke. How could I survive
in front of an audience?

"Tell me," sings my friend Charity, "Do you love
Jesus?"

"Yes, I love Jesus," I reply confidently, aching to feel
that love and to show my fervent belief that it was
true. I love Him, and He loves me in return. I am
worthy of Him.

Two pages later, what has been a standard conversion
fable takes a turn that catches his attention:

As the years passed I began to see myself as the Church
saw me: dirty, fallen, unworthy. Christlike pain is a sign
of God's love, they told me. But your sins accumulate
like silt in a river. You will go to Hell if you do not
change your ways. Only the immolation of Death can
end the pain and cleanse the world of your sinful acts.

I do not want to hear this, I do *not* want to hear this. Now
I have to work up the 'appropriate response.' What did they
say in that damn workshop last year about 'responding to the
student in need' . . . I swear, if this heads into some suicide
attempt, I am going to scream.

To share the pain would only have been to bring the
anger of a vengeful Church on my head. God knew I
was unfit to live. I sank further and further into the
darkness of my own creation, knowing there was no
way out, no way to reverse the flow of the river or to
cleanse its waters. I was lost.

I sank into a deep depression. Finally, on an ordinary

sunny day, I fell into the hole that fate had been digging. If you have suicidal feelings, they say, tell a trusted adult. But 'trusted adults' do not want trustees. They live by the rule of hear no evil, see no evil, and speak no evil. I was only an annoying mosquito buzzing in their ears. Now I find myself peering into rapidly cooling dishwater, looking for the last dish. Fate dealt my cards that day. It was a knife, a long shiny knife.

Aw, *shit. Shit, shit, shit.*

It glinted in the sunlight like a million-dollar smile. But the smile held no promises. I turned my hand over and calmly scrutinized my wrist. My blood had flown uninterrupted for too long; it was time to dry up the river. I oh so carefully led the knife across my wrist. Nothing happened. The knife was too dull. The smile wasn't even worth ten dollars. It had barely made a scratch on my wrist. I desperately squeezed it. A puny drop of blood leaked out.

I could try again, I could press harder. I was afraid. I was afraid of the pain, I was afraid of Hell. I knew I deserved it, but I was too terrified to follow through. The sun rose on me, and I realised that since my final destination was Hell anyway, who cared what the church said? It was my life, not theirs. The soil beneath the seeds of my dreams began to warm.

Jack sits back and tosses the paper onto the end table. He throws his head back and drains half of the beer in one go, then looks deep into the fire. A few minutes pass before he picks up the paper again and writes.

Gwendolyn—This paper is powerful and authentic, with a distinc-

tive voice and a strong message. I am concerned that the prose occasionally overpowers the content and muddies the point in some places, but a bit of revision should remedy that for the final draft. See me for guidance or go to the Campus Writing Center.

Also—If you'd like to have a non-Christian ear so you can talk through any of the issues raised in this paper, I'd be happy to provide that ear. My extension is 4775.

"She is fit to be tied, Jack. She is not a happy camper, and you're the one who knocked her tent down, to hear her tell it."

"I've been very evenhanded, Becca, you know that. He's not getting a party line from me any more than . . ."

"Wait . . . Jack, she wants to talk to you."

"Becca, no. This is something you and I can . . ."

"Good evening, Jack."

Oh joy. "Hello Ruth. How's tricks."

"Let me presently get to the point. I am not pleased about the filth you've been feeding my grandson. Every Monday after he spends a weekend with you he is just full of hateful un-Christian thoughts and words, and I intend to put a stop to it here and now. You have no right to . . ."

"Ruth, please calm down. Just tell me what he said."

Jack's already heard a few complaints, filtered through Becca, about Connor's rolled eyes during Grace and offhand comments about Jesus being just a man—but nothing yet that would account for the fire now shooting out of Ruth's mouth.

"That boy has taken to responding to the name of Our Lord by saying, 'God is just pretend, you know,' every time the holy Name is mentioned in this house! Lord forgive me for even repeating such a thing. And I don't think he's getting that rubbish at the Calvary School, nor from his mother, which leaves you. I want it to stop this instant, this *instant*, Jack Kassel. Do I make myself quite clear?"

"Ruth, I have never encouraged any sort of disrespect for the church. On the contrary, I always tell him to keep an open mind . . ."

"Which you and I both know is fancy philosopher's language for rejecting the church. I don't care how you try to muddy the waters with your fancy words. You are to stop discussing these things with him. If he has questions about God or the church, you are to refer him to myself or my daughter or his teachers at . . ."

"And what if he has questions about the world, Ruth? What if my son asks me where the trees come from, or where he comes from, or what happens after we die—all questions he has asked already—what then, Ruth?"

"Those are all theological questions answered by Scripture, and therefore out of your area of expertise. You will refer such questions to us, period." Jack can hear she's as puffed up and righteous as she gets, which is saying something.

He takes a breath and proceeds anyway. "What about the possibility that scriptural answers to those questions are incorrect?"

"THAT, Jack Kassel, is precisely what I am talking about! You are constantly lecturing us about 'feeding him one perspective,' about doing his thinking for him, then you turn around and do the same thing."

"Oh give me a break, Ruth. That would contradict everything I stand for. I just let him know there's more than one opinion on these subjects, that's all. I want him to retain that message until he's old enough to think it through on his own. I wouldn't indoctrinate him to my point of view any more than I want him indoctrinated to yours. I just want the questions to remain open until he's . . ."

"And we're back to fancy language again. 'Open questions'

indeed! Do you really want him to end up without any moral fiber whatsoever? Haven't you read *anything* by Charles Colson?"

Jack fumbles for a cigarette and comes up empty. "Put him on the phone, Ruth. I'll talk to him."

". . ."

"Ruth?"

"Hi Daddy."

"Hey, Con. How are you doing?"

"Well, Gramma's really mad at me, I think."

"No, Connor, she's mad at me, not you. You don't have anything to feel bad about. Remember when I . . ."

"Get to the point, Jack!"

"Ruth, get the hell . . . *get off that extension* so I can *talk* to him!"

"You tell your father what you said about Grandmama's *Bible!*"

"Ruth, I swear to . . ."

He hears the click. Connor begins to cry.

"Aw sweetie, it's okay. Please don't worry. This is all gonna be just fine."

"Daddy, I want you to come home to be with me."

Jack's heart turns inside out. "Punkin, I'm right here with you on the phone. Tell me what happened today. It'll be okay."

Connor takes a deep breath. "Well Gramma was reading her Bible and I said why was she always reading that Bible . . . and I said her Bible was stupid."

Oh. Yes, that would do it. "I see. Ruth, you still there?"

". . ."

"Hey Ruth, I was baptized last Sunday."

". . ."

"She's in the bathroom, Dad. Did you say you were baptized?"

"No, no, Con, never mind that. Now why did you say her Bible was stupid, sweetie?"

"Because it's all just made-up stories, and she thinks they're true."

"How do you know they're made up, Con?"

"Well aren't they?"

"That's not what I asked. How do you *know* they're made up?"

"Well, that's what *you* think, isn't it? And you teach in college."

"You know, Connor, even people who teach in college might be wrong about something once in a while."

"So you think you're wrong about the Bible?"

"No I don't. I think I'm right. But Gramma thinks she's right too, and so does Mom and Mrs. Mac-il-hackysack or whatever. What's important is for you to make up your own mind, and to take your time about it. I don't want you to just believe what I believe without thinking about it."

"I thought about it a lot, Dad, and I really *do* think God is pretend."

Well what do you do with that. So did I, every step of the way, Con. Who am I to say you have to be confused for a while.

"Well, why do you think that, Con?"

"Because for one thing, astronauts went way up into space and never saw God."

Oh okay. Easy one. "But people who believe in God say he's a spirit, not a person you can see, so they wouldn't see him."

"But Mrs. McInerny says we were made in God's image, so he should look like us, right? How can he look like us and still be invisible?"

Jack never ceases to be floored by the things that come out of this kid. "Well, they'd say that's one of the mysteries of faith, I guess, Con." At which point Jack starts wincing and dancing around noiselessly, pounding himself in the head with his free hand.

"Oh, okay. Then I guess there is a God."

Uh oh, too evenhanded, Jack. "Well now you're sure the other way, huh?"

"Yeah, I guess so."

"And why is that? Just 'cause we can't prove he isn't real?"

"No . . . well, I guess 'cause he helped write the Bible."

"Okay. But the Bible has the names of a lot of people in it who said God helped them write it, but how do we know they're telling the truth?"

" . . ."

"Con?"

"I guess we don't know that. So okay then, I guess God is pretend."

"Wait a minute, sweetie." Jack feels like a spectator at Wimbledon. "I think what you really want to say is, 'I don't know.'"

"But you don't say that, Dad."

Mm hmm. "Well, that's true, I don't. But I did for a lot of years while I was learning about it. And I went to church and I listened, and I read a lot of books, and I talked to people who knew a lot about it. And then, when I was about twelve, Connor, I finally decided what I thought was true."

"But you still aren't sure?"

"No Con, I'm not sure. You can't ever be sure about some things, but after you learn as much as you can and think about it a long time, then you can say what you think is true. I just don't think you've spent enough time yet to say that."

"Oh. Okay. But what am I supposed to say now?"

"You might not like the answer, but it's the best one. Are you ready?"

"Yes."

"You say, 'I don't know.'"

"Rrrrgh!"

"Con, I know you don't like that, but it's wrong to say you know something when you really just kinda think something's true. That's a bad thing when anyone does it. Okay?"

"Okay."

"So you be respectful of people who think different things, and that means you don't call Gramma's Bible stupid, okay?"

"Okay, Daddy."

"Okay. Put your mom on the phone, would you?"

"I'm already here, Jack." Jack nearly jumps out of his skin. "I've been on for about two minutes."

"Wha . . . What is *with* you people? Can't I have a private conversation with my son?"

"It's the private conversations that are getting you in trouble, Jack, but I'll tell you, that one was pretty wonderful."

"Well, I'm not sure your mom would agree."

"I don't care. If that's the kind of input he's getting from you, I'll go to bat for you on this end all the way."

"Well, that is all he gets from me, I swear. I just want to keep his mind receptive."

"Speaking of receptivity."

"*Hel*–lo."

"Just kidding."

"Goodbye."

ALEX   The Pope is not worthy of your defense!

MORE   The Pope? Perhaps no. But the Papacy? The theory holds that the institution of the Papacy connects us to Christ.

ALEX   *(with disgust)* A weak and corrupted connection at best.

MORE   Certainly weak, certainly corrupted, yes.

ALEX   So you'll risk life and reputation, all for a
                theory?

MORE   *(angrily)* Hold there! The Succession is—
                (calming, interested) why yes, it's a theory,
                not tangible, nothing you can hold or carry.
                But what's important is not whether it is the
                truth but whether I in fact believe it is, or
                more to the point, not that I *believe* it is true,
                but that it is *I* who believe. I trust I've con-
                fused the matter properly?

ALEX   Entirely!

MORE   Good. Clarity, at the moment, is what I
                need least of all.

14

Revelation

Imagine there's no countries
It isn't hard to do
Nothing to kill or die for
And no religion too

>   from *Imagine* by John Lennon

Imagine there's no countries
It isn't hard to do
Nothing to kill or die for
And no religion too—except your own

>   from *Imagine* by John Lennon,
>   as paraphrased on a national
>   televangelical broadcast,
>   March 1985

52-MCGO

"**B**less me Father for I have sinned. It has been three weeks since my last confession. I have taken the Lord's name in vain almost continuously since then."

"Excuse me?"

"Well, it's because we're heading into midterms. I know that's no excuse, but that's why."

"And you intend to stop this, do you?"

"Oh, sure. My last test is Thursday."

"One Hail Mary should do it."

"Thank you Father."

". . ."

"Bless me Father for I have sinned. It has been four days since my last confession."

"And?"

"Well, this is a little awkward."

"I'm listening."

"I have had impure thoughts for a man of God."

"Uh huh. Tina, is that you?"

"I'm pretty sure you're not supposed to ask that, Father."

"And I'm pretty sure you are Jewish."

"I have to change dinner to seven."

"Okay. One Novena for that."

"Yeah, whatever. Don't be late."

". . ."

"Bless me father for I have sinned. It's been, what, about two years since my last confession. Um—well, I've got a list here."

"A list?"

"Yeah. Would I be able to just leave the list, or do I have to read it to you?"

"Well I can't really know what your penance should be without hearing your sins."

"Come on, they're all pretty small, it's just a lot of them."

"Look, I'm sorry, it's company policy. Just start reading and I'll stop you if I've heard enough." Scott has taken to

removing his heavy seminary ring during confessions and
spinning it like a top on a small wooden shelf below the screen.
He makes a game of grabbing it a millisecond before it stops
spinning and clatters to rest and is already twelve for twelve
in this session.

"Okay. I took the Lord's name in vain twice."

"In two years?"

"Yes . . . why, do you need dates?"

"No, I don't need . . . look, is the whole list about like
that?"

"Well . . . no, not really. There are some deadly sins further down."

"Skip to the deadlies."

"Okay, uh . . . well, a lot of gluttony last Christmas."

"Uh huh."

"Uh . . . Father? If a person were hypothetically, uh . . .
well, *bulimic*, and brought most of a gluttonous meal back
up . . . I don't suppose that like erases the sin of gluttony?"

"No." Now I remember this one. "In fact, the Lord might
well consider forced vomiting a desecration of the temple of
your body. Add that to the list."

"Oh boy. Okay, avarice. Four times avarice. Same time
of year."

" . . . "

"Six sloths."

"Listen, can I just assume the whole list of deadlies?"

"No . . . well, no envy that I can remember, anyway. I
guess the main thing is lust."

Clatter. Goddamit. I was on my way to a record.

"Lots and *lots* of lust. I don't have numbers. All in my heart,
no action, though . . . but I think I still have to tell you."

"True. And that's it?"

"I'll come back if I remember more."

"Fair enough. Hold on a sec . . . carry the six . . . okay,
we've got three Hail Marys and three Our Fathers."

"That seems a little light."

"I don't actually need a second opinion."

"Are you sure? I really worry sometimes about getting to Judgment and finding out I'm short."

"I keep good records—all in triplicate, of course. You'll be covered."

The confessional door clicks open, clicks shut. Ten minutes of total silence, the steady muffled *thunk* of the Lakota protest drum at the gates, and the naturally somnolent atmosphere of the warm confessional do their collective work. Scott rests his head against the soft dark wood, eyes closed, and he is gone. The nine o'clock bell sounds, signaling the end of the confessional hour, but Scott is off dreaming of his days as a jazz drummer, except that he was never a jazz drummer, and certainly not for the main lounge in the Playboy Club in L.A., but there he is, just finishing a kickass solo with indecent tray-laden Bunnies gliding by. Ohhh, those fluffy little tails. Now the bass solo kicks in, and he drops down to just the ride cymbal, tick-aTEE-tick-aTEE-tick-aTEE-tick-aTEE . . . The Bunnies are whispering hotter, *hotter!* you guys are on FIRE tonight, tick-aTEE-tick-aTEE, *hotter, hotter,* tick-aTEE-tick-aTEE-tick-aTEE-tick-aTEE-tick-aTEE, *hahther, hahther,* tick-tick-tick-tick-tick-tick . . . .

"*Father?*" Tick, tick, tick, tap, tap, tap, tap. "Father?" The cymbal turns into a confessional screen, the drumstick an insistent finger. "Am I too late?" Someone, probably not a bunny, is whispering insistently. "Are you in there?"

Father Siberell comes to. "Yes, I'm here," he mumbles. "What is it?"

"I've sinned. I've sinned."

"Are you crying, my child?" She is, and Scott sits upright. "Tell me what it is. You are safe here."

"I'm so sorry, Father. Bless me, Father." She's distraught, maybe a flight risk, Scott figures. He knows most of the Catholic students on campus by voice but the whisper is impenetrable.

"There is nothing God cannot forgive." Scott has mastered the system so completely that he has begun to believe it himself while he wears the collar. Ultimate method acting. There's a certain self-contained beauty to it, he thinks, though only as drama. The fact that it's more than just drama to those on the other side of the screen is as incidental to his performance as knowing the audience bought Shakespeare when he did *Othello*. "Whatever you have done is washed clean when you come to Him with an open and repentant heart."

"I used to think that was true." She begins to sob convulsively. "But it's *not*."

Well, well. Scott is intrigued. "Whatever would make you think that, child? Jesus assures us that all is forgiven of those who confess freely. Even *murderers* have His complete forgiveness if only they repent. What could you have done that is worse than *murder*?"

Her voice drops even lower. "I . . . I can't say it. I . . . this was a bad idea . . ."

She's gonna bolt, think fast. "Just say it all at once and it will be done. You will be on the path to forgiveness. Remember that the Grace of God and eternal salvation is granted to each of us, regardless of our sins, regardless of our actions, so long as we accept Jesus Christ as Lord and Savior . . ."

The other side of the screen suddenly erupts into uncontrollable weeping and the door flies open, banging against the side of the confessional. The running squeak of sneakers makes its way around the corner and out the side door before Scott can get the damned latch open on his side. By the time he runs to the chapel door and scans the gates, the walks, and the snow-covered labyrinth, she has been swallowed in the midmorning crowd.

The wicked, in the haughtiness of his countenance, does not seek Him. All his thoughts are, "There is no God."

                                         Psalm 10

"Can we go ahead and get started?"

Jack and Amanda decided a quiet beginning was best for the Saint Bernadette Student Humanist Association, so Amanda and her friends had spread the word without posters or announcements. Now, as he scans the first meeting, Jack sees that it isn't the philosophical coffee klatch he'd envisioned. As Amanda quiets the group, assembled in the third floor lounge of Curie Hall, Jack assesses them one by one. He recognizes Randi in the front row from Amanda's description of her, committedly preppy in dress and demeanor, so the other two sitting excitedly next to her must be Stacey and Deena. They land sartorially somewhere in the continuum between Randi's breast crest and Amanda's handknit Ecuadorian torso sack. Anthropologists digging the four of them up would have no trouble placing them in evolutionary succession. Behind the three Jack counts eleven others in attendance, with no more than one or two missing the opportunity to make some visual statement inviting the world to kiss her ass. There is hair the color of a road cone; there is hair the unmistakable color of blood. In the second row is a young woman with hair of a completely natural mouse-brown, cascading down in two lovely braids from either side of a scalp shaved completely bald on top. One T-shirt announces that the wearer is a RECOVERING CHRISTIAN; another simply says SEE YOU IN HELL. Jack stops counting at forty-six visible piercings. Only two are in earlobes, both belonging to a skeletal wraith in the back row. These particular specimens consist of a fishhook at one end of an industrial-grade chain which then wraps tightly around the wearer's paper white neck several times before ascending to a large packing staple hanging from her other ear. On close examination, Jack notes that two of the attenders are apparently male, probably some boyfriends forced to tag along; another minute confirms that they are in fact boyfriends of each other. Not that there's anything *wrong* with that.

"Okay, uh, hello everyone. I'm Amanda Corelli, and this is the first meeting of the Saint Bernadette Student Humanist Association . . ."

Her voice curls up into a huge grin and rises an octave as she completes the sentence, eliciting frenzied clapping and a high *"Woooooo!"* from her three supporters in front. Jack realizes with a tinge of regret that he has never once himself "wooed" and vows to find something wooworthy and woo at it very soon.

"I am the acting president of the Association, until we can have an election, of course, and this is Dr. Jack John Kassel, our faculty advisor . . ." Her voice has curled again, and for the second time in twenty seconds The Three find something worth their *woo*. Jack does a two-fingered salute and immediately hates himself for it.

"Now our first order of business is to meet everyone and find out what brings you to this meeting. Maybe you can each give a little personal history, sort of an 'unfaith story,' I guess. I'll start. Okay." She clears her throat dramatically and lowers her voice. "My name is Amanda . . . and I'm a humanist."

"Hi Amanda!" her backup trio yells in unison, and then . . . all right now, the wooing is getting to be a bit much, Jack decides. A dynamic is developing that isn't good: the room is splitting 4-to-11. Jack silently uh-ohs at the growing chasm.

"When I was a little girl I considered myself a Christian because that was what good little girls were. Then I began to notice that the Christians I knew didn't really act all that, well, *Christian*, if you know what I mean."

"Testify, sister!" yells either Deena or Stacey. Oh, that's where she got that dumbass, adolescent thing, thinks Jack. And the Eleven are just as pleased as I am. I'm not gonna make it through this.

"Then I started reading the Bible..."

"Booooo!" they roar, then giggle, yes *giggle*. Jack looks around for a sharp stick.

"... and noticing that the Bible is just full of rape and murder and genocide! God says 'Thou shalt not kill,' then he tells Jehu to slaughter the seventy children of Ahab and put their heads in baskets at the city gates—just because their father worshipped a different god! Second Kings ten!"

To their credit, the three remain silent. Several of the rest sit up a bit more attentively.

"And after Elijah 'proves' to the prophets of Baal that his God is a real God and theirs is a false one, and they *admit* it, and fall down on their knees to *worship* him, God tells Elijah to kill all four hundred of them! And after beating another tribe in battle, Moses, on the order of God, tells his people, I know this one by heart, from the book of Numbers, 'kill every male among the little ones, and kill every woman that hath known a man by lying with him; but all the women-children that have not known a man by lying with him, keep alive for yourselves.' In other words, kill the little boys, kill the women who've had sex, and keep all the little girls for your sex slaves! This is what we call The Good Book! Read it yourself, I'm not making this up!"

This is a very quiet room.

"So anyway, I decided that this book just couldn't have anything to do with a God I wanted any part of. So at the age of thirteen I declared to myself that I was an atheist."

Jack counts to eight, and right on the mark Randi bounces once in her chair.

"Okay, I'll go! I had a great history teacher in junior high who taught us about the Enlightenment and it just grabbed me from the beginning. I started reading Voltaire, like everything by Voltaire, and then . . ." She takes a deep breath. "And then I found Thomas Paine's *Age of Reason*. Oh . . . my . . . *gosh*. It is just not possible to see the Bible as any sort of valid source of information once you read that book. That was five years ago, so I was sixteen. And I believe in evolution, which is another reason I just can't buy the Bible stories."

Jack cringes hard and visibly. Don't say you 'believe in evolution,' it makes it sound like a damn faith system. You don't say you 'believe in' gravity, do you? You don't say you 'believe' that a year is 365.25 days long. Once the evidence is in, you *know* it. It's hard enough to get Amanda to use the language right, now I've got fifteen . . .

Stacey/Deena stands. "Okay. The problem for me was always the fact that there are so many religions on Earth and they're all different and it doesn't seem like a real *Gawd* . . ." She puts a contemptuous, adolescent spin on the word "God" that makes Jack roll his inner eye. ". . . would give the *Truth* to only certain people. The whole system is just too inefficient and unjust: so I get born into a Christian country and I get salvation and go to heaven, but some schmuck in Outer Mongolia only finds out how to get to heaven if a missionary happens to pass through town? I don't think so." Oh she's got more. "And what about all the billions of people who lived *before* Christ? Do they get a free pass into heaven, or are they just kept out, or what? Plus what about life on other planets, which it seems pretty likely now that there has to be, given the size of the universe? Was there a Jesus that went to every planet to save its creatures, or are we special? And did we have savable souls before we evolved into humans, or was there some moment when God said, 'Okay, they look like me now, I'll give 'em souls'? And if we were savable before Christ, then what was he here for? And if we were savable before we were human, what about chimpanzees now—why aren't they going to heaven? And if he *did* wait until we had evolved to a certain point, does that mean that one generation was saved but their parents *weren't?*"

Wow. She had about five of my top arguments in there. I like this Stacey/Deena person. Then she blows it by putting her hand over her face in an *oh-my-gosh-I-didn't-mean-to-go-on-and-on* blush-and-giggle.

Deena/Stacey takes over and turns out to be the most sober of the four. "I'm a history major. I've always been interested in how we know what happened a long time ago and all the ways it can get mixed up. I also had a great history teacher in high school who really walked me through the whole idea of textual evaluation and verification of source authenticity." To her credit, she doesn't follow this overt display of competence with the blush-and-giggle. Jack likes her best. "And once I had that knowledge, the Bible just fell to pieces. The Gospels were written by people generations after Christ who didn't have direct contact with the events they described, which puts an oral transmission link in there. Oral transmission tends to elaborate and deify legends, in this case literally. So Jesus swims really well and in a hundred years it becomes walking on water. Or he fixes Lazarus' sore throat and the friends of the neighbors of the grandchildren of those present hear that he raised him from the dead. His disciples remove the body to Galilee, which if you look at the traditions of the time is very likely, and we end up with the empty tomb story.

"The clincher for me was the words of Jesus. He never once directly claims to be the Son of God, and three of the four Gospels don't even suggest it. Jesus never indicates that he wants to be anything but the best Jew he can be and that he wants to teach others to do the same. Period. Every historical indication is that Paul invented Christianity, lock, stock and barrel, well after Jesus was dead, as a new moral code for the Gentiles."

Over half of the Eleven are in various states of pissed-off disinterest at this point. One of them stands.

"I'm Kat, and I'm an atheist because Christians are majorly fucked up."

Sits.

Her friend raises a fist and shouts, "What she said." Someone in the back says *fuckin-A* and raises the handsign that with one finger snipped off would be respectable Hawaiian for 'hang loose.' The extra index, though, makes it either plain old teen rebellion or devil horns, Jack knows, depending on who it's attached to. Jack looks at the gesturer and decides against simple teen rebellion.

This isn't good. This isn't what it's supposed to be, this is something else, Jack thinks, some sort of Stick-it-to-the-Man festival I don't want to be a part of. He makes sober eye contact with Amanda, whose dazed expression could mean just about anything. Get control of this damn thing, Amanda Corelli, he thinks, hoping the message comes through in his eyes. *Do* something.

Next up. "My name is Cyndy. I went through twelve years of goddam Catholic school with nuns and their fuckin' rulers whackin' me in the head and tellin' me I'm goin' to Hell. I didn't need to read no fuckin' Mister *Pain* or whatever the fuck to know how screwed up the ass they were." She turns to her friends and mocks, "Oh . . . my . . . *gosh.*" They *woo* derisively and Randi goes hydrant red.

And these kids are at a Catholic college because . . . Jack quickly pulls back from that thought, since it could be lobbed at him too. In fact, he's already lobbed it at himself, many times, and so far has managed to duck. Maybe I'm wrong. Maybe they don't all have to be the sphinctered-up philosophy geek I am. A little tolerance of diversity, that's what I'm doing here, sitting with my thumb up my ass. I'm quietly celebrating diversity.

With nothing to do but scan and self-justify, Jack has begun to decide the Eleven are not really an undifferentiated mass of social protest after all. The next one rises with an elegant attitude of self-respect and benignity that quiets the room again. "My name is Light. I and my sister Witches," she gestures to her right, "are of the Bernadette coven of Wicca. We are here to support your group and to educate others about our own religion . . ."

"Where'd you park your fuckin' broomsticks?" It's the Catholic schoolgirl, who bares her teeth and punches the offered fist of her friend.

"..which obviously needs doing, I see," Light continues. "Wiccans reject Christianity, as do you all, both for its untruth and for the ways in which it persecutes those who turn from it and seek truth elsewhere. We worship the Goddess and her consort, the God, while recognizing that they are only minor deities, subsumed in a higher reality that we as humans cannot yet perceive. Our own guiding principle, the Wiccan Rede, is *A'in it harm none, do what thou wilt*—an ancient Celtic philosophy that predates and presages the Christian Golden Rule."

"Wussy hypocrite lesbos," shouts a male voice from the back row.

"And I see my Satanist friend Void wishes to be next," Light says. "Please, Void, by all means."

A wall of metal studs rises in the back row with a human body hanging off the back of it. "Yeah, I'm Void, like the lesbo said, leader of the Saint Philip grotto of the Church of Satan, Reformed. And this is Walter." He gestures to another pile of metal at his side, which raises and lowers an arm heavy with bracelets in acknowledgement. "We're also here to straighten out all the screwed up things people think about us Satanists. For one thing, there's no Satan with horns and

stuff, it's not a person, it's a force of nature. And we have a
Golden Rule too, the one the lesbos took theirs from. It's
'Do what thou wilt shall be the whole of the Law.' You know,
act like everything you do would be what everybody has to
do. So we have a fuckin' great time, is what ends up happening." Walter nods heavily. "That includes lots of Magick, including sex Magick. We believe you gotta live out your lusts
and desires. You should spend your energy doin' the 'seven
deadly sins' with every consenting adult you can get your
groin up against. So Light knows when I call her a lesbo I'm
really sayin', 'Right on. Sex it up.' I'll fuck anybody in this
room who wants it, right now. When we vote for a new president, forget about the lesbos up in front and vote for Void!
These meetings'll end up all over the floor!"

He sits with a huge, crooked smile, then stands again
abruptly. "Oh and by the way, Satanists don't hurt kids or
animals, that's a bunch of Christian hate crap. We respect life
above everything else, okay, and little kids and animals are
the ultimate expressions of life. Well, kids, animals, and
fucking." He sits again.

Well, that's nice, thinks Jack. I celebrate your differences,
you damned freak. By now Jack is a mess of contradictory
impulses, most of which are saying *stop this before somebody
puts an eye out.* But the strongest impulse—the one that says
*you can't always choose your friends, Jack, can you really afford to
dictate the terms of disbelief, who the hell do you think you are,
anyway*—that impulse keeps him seated and silent.

Three remain, one of whom suddenly pales and flits out
the door as her turn approaches. Two remain and stand together.

"Hi, I'm Carla . . ."

"And I'm Rachel." Rachel takes her seat again.

"We are . . . well . . . oh *shoot.*" Carla decides to just spit
it out. "We're Jehovah's Witnesses."

Okay, now *that's* a quiet room. Even Jack sits up a little.

She shrugs. "I mean, our parents *think* we're Witnesses. We were raised as Witnesses. We doorknocked. We've been friends for a long time, Rachel and me, and we started talking when we were about, what, twelve?" Rachel nods. "We started sharing doubts about the church, just with each other. It's always been this kind of secret thing between us . . ." Rachel looks up at Carla with a little trepidation. "And now it's really just, just so *weird* to be talking about it out loud to a bunch of people who aren't Rachel, I dunno . . . It's weird to hear all this, you know . . . all this *anger*, 'cause I know it's kind of directed at us, sort of. But not really, I know. I mean, we're not . . ." She looks at Rachel, who looks down. "Well, we don't really know what we're doing here, I guess. We just wanted . . . somebody else to talk to . . ." Her voice trails off as she considers the menagerie around her. Her knees bend and she slowly lowers herself into her seat.

Amanda sends an uncertain glance Jack's way. He nods almost imperceptibly and raises his eyebrows just enough to say, *Keep going, I guess.*

"Well all right, then," she says. "This is a pretty . . . *mixed* group, so the first thing we're gonna have to do is, uh . . . well, come to some consensus about what the Humanist Association is going to be about. Right? Does that sound like a good idea to everybody?"

Complete silence as the constituencies bounce bad karma off each other.

Stacey/Deena raises a hand. "Maybe Professor Kassel can start us off with a definition? Of humanism, I mean."

The sound of a direct invitation to speak jolts him to his feet. Okay, he thinks. I memorized a good definition for just such an occasion. Now's the time.

But as he scans the group, all eyes on him, that other impulse—the Silencer—wins out. "You know, ordinarily I'd suggest that, too . . . but this group is so diverse, I—I just don't want to put any arbitrary boundaries on it up front. Let's let it find its own level." Whatever that's supposed to mean, he thinks, you damned feeble bastard. He sits again.

Years afterward he'd look back on that as the moment of the Big Mistake. Chaos theorists might one day trace the causal path of the eventual hurricane back to that moment of the beating of a butterfly's wings—or more to the point, the moment when the chickenshit butterfly folded his wings and did nothing. A much older Jack Kassel would lie in bed once in a while, mouthing all the things he should have said in answer to that question, knowing in retrospect it might well have driven out the ones who needed driving out. Kneel only before Reason, sweet, precious Reason. No Goddess, no God, no Satan-force, no "Magick." No damned bullshit guesses plucked out of the dark. Now how hard would it have been to just spit that out right then, instead of being so damned "all-inclusive." If I'd just managed that little bit of spine, he would always think, maybe everything could have turned out differently.

❧

"Still waiting."
". . ."
"Still waiting."
". . ."
"You wanna lifeline? Wanna buy a vowel?"
". . ."
"Calling Halo Gilbert. Saint seraphic, hear my pleading."
". . ."
"Unanswered question about to be declared unanswerable."
". . ."
". . ."
". . ."

Dale McGowan

On Friday night, the eighth of March, the Reverend Tobias J. Halliday of Charleston, South Carolina sins and sins good. Not that he wasn't already an accomplished sinner—oh he's sinned before, he'll tell you true, many, many times, and built himself a national televangelical empire out of the wondrous cycle of sin, repentance and forgiveness. Twice a year like clockwork—just coincidentally always on a Friday night during the spring or fall ratings sweeps—T. J. Halliday is caught in the sack with another in a series of prostitutes and/or wives of friends or colleagues. The Saturday papers reliably predict his demise each and every time—this time he's gone too far, this is beyond the beyond, you can only ask forgiveness so many times—and on Sunday he weeps for the cameras and gnashes his teeth and tears at his pompadour and swears he doesn't deserve God's endless love, but there it is, praise Him, praise Him in His ever-lovin' Mercy and Grace—and the ratings rocket and the contributions flow, and the choir and the Mighty Wurlitzer soar to Heaven locked in precious Gospel harmony.

One Friday two years ago it was a soprano in that very choir, wife of T.J.'s lifelong organist, and her tears rained on the stage along with those of the Reverend, as her husband—wearing an expression that suggested he was a tad behind in his forgiveness work—led the rest of the choir to Heaven, locked in precious, perfect, radiant Gospel harmony.

Six months ago it was the entire soprano section, at once, God bless him, and the stage was almost dangerously slick with the tears of repentance and infinite joy. And the ministry only grew and strengthened, planted in the soil of that joy and watered by those very tears. Why, he must be God's own prophet, some reasoned, to survive bedding the organist's wife and then those eight sopranos...

On Friday night, the eighth of March, the very congrega-

tion that had found the soprano section an acceptable receptacle for Halliday's affections nonetheless found the tenor
section a bit harder to reconcile.

Not even the ABC lawyers could believe their luck when
they came across a specific anti-sodomy clause in the anti-
quated contract Halliday had signed thirty-nine years before,
and by midday Saturday the network yanks Halliday's national television contract, leaving themselves with a gaping
time slot in the middle of Sunday morning and the need to
keep a weekly audience of 6.1 million holy rollers from bolting to Charles Stanley and NBC. Show "The Greatest Story
Ever Told" in two parts for the next two weeks, growls the
Director of Programming to his religious programming team,
but if we coast through Easter without a new preacher-show
and piss off six million good old Christian ladies, you can just
plan on kissing their blue-haired asses goodbye and your jobs
along with 'em.

The frantic nationwide search for a ministry that is ready
for the major leagues ends on Tuesday morning when the
weathergal for the Minneapolis ABC affiliate points the car
of a sleep-deprived network scout due southwest and toward
the ministry everybody's been abuzz about for the past few
months.

And on Wednesday, March 13, 2002, Father Scott
"Francis" Siberell arrives at the office of the affiliate in Minneapolis to sign a contract with the American Broadcasting
Company for a Sunday morning national network telecast
entitled "Live from Nurse Chapel with Father Scott Siberell,"
60 commercial-free minutes at the golden hour of 10 a.m.
Eastern for a trial period of fourteen weeks beginning just
eleven days later on March 24th—Palm Sunday.

All proceeds, of course, to be carried straight to the Throne
of Yahweh.

Haley precious,

I know you're so busy right now in the middle of the semester, but I sent a package to you a few weeks ago with some little treats and new pens and such and haven't heard back from you. Now that's fine, of course, I don't mean to be a nag, I just want to know you're all right. I hope the package didn't get lost, since I also put in some of those toffees you like so much and I was hoping you'd get them before midterms so you could have a little sweet treat during all your hard work.

We still haven't really had near the snow we have some years, which I'm grateful for since I have to shovel it all myself now of course. Little Tom next door, I guess he's not so little now, he helps out whenever we get a really big storm, but he's busy at the furniture store now, he's assistant manager, I think he said, after just two years. He said to say hi to you, of course, he's still so sweet on you Haley it's just too much, God bless him.

I must say I do think I'm a little prone to worry lately, I hope you don't mind that too much, but this house is pretty empty now, what with Randall in New York and your Daddy gone, so it gives me too much time to think, I guess that's the thing. But it just surprised me to not hear from you, you usually pick up the phone or write so quickly. I'm sure it's just the ministry and your exams and such. Please don't think I'm being too much of a nag. I shouldn't be so fearful—maybe I need to spend some time in P.S. 49, Why should I fear in times of trouble (tee hee).

I know how hard all this has been on you, Haley. I wish we could have talked more at Christmas, but I know you needed time alone. Now I hope you are surrounded by your friends—your Godly friends mostly, Haley, I must say I wasn't too happy to hear at Christmas that you would still be rooming with that Mandy person with her saying those faithless things to you and questioning the Bible like she does! Maybe the Lord has placed you with her to open her heart to His love. I just wish He wouldn't put so much on you at once, what with your Daddy and the demands of Father Siberell's ministry and your classes and then a godless Philistine in your own room! Oh dear, do forgive me Haley! Listen to me go on. Well, I always know that He would not ever give you more than you could bear. He is just and loving. You are safe in His hands, so long as you trust in Him.

Oh dear. I just read what I have written so far and I'm just a meddling nag! I can't find a Psalm for that, so I'm on my own (tee hee). You take care of your precious self, Haley Abigail, and I'll just get some more of those toffees in the mail to you soon.

Luvvie duvvers,
Mommy

"What was wrong with the first one? I thought it was *great!*"

"Oh come on, Amanda! We don't have a Humanist Association, we've got a freakin' powder keg. You and your three friends and the two Witnesses are about all I can handle, to tell you the truth. Remember what I said about working your tail off to avoid fulfilling the assumptions of Christians about non-Christians? Well believe you me, Void and Walter pretty well sum up the worst of those assumptions."

"Now listen to you and *your* assumptions. I happen to know Void. He's all bluff and posturing, it's just a gimmick. He's a thrillseeker, that's all. He loves to mess with other people's heads, but he's harmless."

Okay, that's two time bombs on campus posing as harmless thrillseekers, one with a fake halo and the other with fake horns. Jack lowers the phone from his ear, then raises it again. "Well once again, beside the point. You will never have an opportunity to sit the Christians down in one room and explain how very harmless Void is. They'll take one look and yell 'SEE?!' at the top of their lungs and call for an exorcist. He's not what we need in this group."

"So, 'not our kind,' is what you're saying?"

"Oh, cheap shot."

"How is it a cheap shot? Look, I'm learning a lot from you, but you've got to be willing to learn from me, too. You sound awfully Christian when you start judging people by their looks."

"Amanda, I believe I was judging by his stated life philosophy, which is pretty much to mount everyone he meets. That doesn't play well among the Godlies."

"And *that's* our goal? The goal of the Humanist Association is to impress the *Christians?*"

"Well, at least one goal of the Association should be to demonstrate that we're as normal and moral as the next bunch. Oh and by the way, why is he even eligible for membership? This is a student organization!"

"The charter for all student organizations permits associate membership by non-students. Good try."

"He's not a humanist, Amanda, not by a long shot. You don't substitute one set of crazy fictions for another. Look, I'm not trying to boot anyone, but I think we should anticipate concerns from . . ."

"From the Christers. I know. But it's just like I said when we first talked, Dr. Kassel: we use that Golden Rule connection to show we're all on the same foundation. Didn't you hear the Satanist creed? I was pretty impressed, myself, it's practically the Golden Rule word for word! Same with the Wiccan one, they're all pretty much the same thing."

"Uh, no. Think back to the Intro course and listen to the language. I wrote down both credos. The witch said . . ."

"She has a name. It's Light."

"I'm sorry. Light said *A'in it harm none, do what thou wilt* —which implies that there is an objective concept of harm, or maybe even that the *other* person could be the one who decides whether she's been harmed or not."

"And that's a problem?"

"No, and that's my point: the Wiccan Rede prohibits Wiccans from doing harm. That's a pretty positive philosophy. But the Satanists, listen to this: *Do what thou wilt shall be the whole of the Law.*"

"Basically the same thing."

"Oh Amanda, come *on*. It says 'do whatever *you* want, so long as *you* are willing for that thing to be universally done.' It gives the individual complete control over defining morality. If I'm a nihilist, I think it would be just great if everyone became destructive, anarchic thugs. I'd love to watch all them cities burn. There's no safety valve there, no shared assumption that keeps us grounded and allows us to trust each other."

"But Void's not like that."

"Fine. But if he literally follows his creed, he could become like that tomorrow if he wants. Christians harp on and on about non-Christians having no grounding morality. Someday I hope to take this group out of third floor Curie. We can't associate Void with rational humanism or the whole thing goes in the tank."

"So what if he said, 'Okay, I'll agree to the literal Golden Rule as a guiding principle of membership in this Association' ?"

Jack thinks for a minute. Maybe we could also ask him to

lose the 200 steel hoops and ball bearings and scalp studs. Jack doesn't say it, knowing the end of that argument. "Well, that would be a start, I guess."

"SNAP goes the trap! Okay, my turn to be the professor. Since the Golden Rule says 'Do unto others as YOU would have them do unto you,' *it* is *also* a system that permits the individual to define what is moral. If I love to experience pain, which some people do, and I torture *you*, I'm morally in the clear."

Ho ho *ho*. "That was actually a nice little trap, Amanda. Well done."

"Still needs an answer."

"Okay." Jack is reeling from the first decent attack he's ever heard on the Golden Rule. Surely there's a way around that. "Look, there's a nice concise humanist statement I should've read last time. If we can get everyone to agree that that's what we're about . . ."

"It'll never happen. I know which one you mean, on your door, and it'll never happen. Look, I don't think the way to start out is by pushing people away or by fitting them all into your own skin. If they feel like they belong, they'll stay. If they don't, they won't."

He sighs. "All right, fine. We'll go with that and see what happens. No statement of common principle."

And that would be mistake number *two*, notes Jack-in-the-Future.

"Okay. Now the club charter requires us to have elections within a month of the first meeting. I think we should do it at the next meeting, just take nominations from the floor and go that way."

"Fine. And the rest of the time?"

"Well, let's start picking texts and discussing them. Randi wants *Age of Reason* first."

"Yeah, I remember, she's a big fan. 'Oh . . . my . . . *gosh*.'"

"Oh, she would *kill* you. I should let you know, Randi

looks all harmless and prepped out, but you do *not* want to get on her bad side. You think Void is someone to worry about, good *gourd.*"

"Okay, fine. But I'm not sure we want to throw them right into Paine. I was thinking about Hume's 'Of Miracles' . . ."

Amanda laughs. "Oh, Dr. Kassel, you are such a *professor.* You think Hume's gonna go over with these guys better than Paine? At least Paine is good and pissed off at the church. Hume is just this big, fat guy sitting back and going, 'Oh, indubitably, there must be a uniform experience against every miraculous event, blah blah blah.' They'd be . . ."

"Uh, danger, young Corelli."

"Oh. Oh, that's right. You like the fat guy."

Jack's all right, really he is. "Okay, let's do be user-friendly at all costs. Maybe the best thing would be starting through the Humanist Anthology. Lots of little excerpts instead of one long text. How about that."

"Yeah, I've been going through that myself, I have it right here. I do have some thoughts."

"All right, shoot."

"Okay. If we go through beginning to end, we start with a whole bunch of ancient Chinese guys and we're gonna lose half the group."

"Can I pick which half?"

"Ha ha. Anyway, I think we should start a little more recent."

"Fine, what, like Lucretius?"

She laughs again. "Oh my *gawd*, you are such a *geek*, Dr. Kassel. I'm actually thinking past the second century, *hello.* Like maybe starting with H. L. Mencken. He's a crowd-pleaser, nice and irreverent . . . and modern."

"No, you can't do that. We've got to have more background or it looks like disbelief pops out of thin air. Go back about three hundred years and we can just intro some names and ideas at the next meeting, then have them read up for the time after. I don't have my copy of the Anthology here. Read me some of the names in the table of contents and we'll figure out where to start."

"Okay, after the Chinese guys. let's see . . . Epicurus, Seneca. Oh wait, I'm way back. Pliny the Elder, Epictetus . . . hey, wait a minute, then there's a huge gap in the middle, like a thousand years with no names."

"The burning years. Montaigne's probably next."

"Yep . . . Michel Montaigne, Giordano Bruno, Benedict Spinoza, Abbé Meslier, Adam Smith, Thomas Paine . . ."

"*Aack! What?*" Jack's heart leaps into his throat. "*Wait! Wudju jussay? Wuwuzat?*"

"Thomas Paine."

"No no, back, back! About three names back!"

"Benedict Spinoza. Abbé Meslier."

" . . . "

"What, did I pronounce something wrong?"

" . . . "

"Dr. Kassel? Hello?"

" . . . "

The Wedge is a blur of white and brown as Jack flies down it and through the gate. A record eleven minutes after he left his office, he throws his front door open and tosses his coat on the couch. In seconds the Anthology is whipped open to the page:

ABBÉ MESLIER (Jean Meslier)
1664-1729

The Abbé Meslier was appointed curé of Etrépigny in Cham-
pagne, at the age of twenty-five, and remained there until

his death forty years later. As a vigorous campaigner against
the social injustices of his day, he was in frequent conflict
with ecclesiastical and civil authority. But this did not
prepare his parishioners for the discovery, after his death,
of three signed copies of a manuscript entitled Mon Testament, *which contained a scathing denunciation of Chris-*
tianity. 'I did not,' said the Abbé, 'wish to burn until after
my death.'

The Abbé's Apology to his Flock

It was not from cupidity that I was led to adopt a profession
so opposed to my convictions: I obeyed my parents. I would
have enlightened you sooner, if I could have done so with
safety. You are my witness that I have never exacted the
fees that attach to my office as curé. I discouraged you from
bigotry, and I spoke to you as seldom as possible of our
wretched dogmas. I had to carry out the duties of my office,
but how I suffered when I had to preach to you those pious
lies that I detest in my heart! What remorse your credulity
caused me! A thousand times I was on the point of breaking
out publicly and opening your eyes, but a fear stronger than
myself held me back, and forced me to keep silence until
my death.

It is no use saying that the Gospel stories have always been
regarded as holy and sacred, and that they have been faithfully preserved without any tampering. It was common prac-
tice among the writers who copied these stories to add,
delete, or alter the text as seemed good to them. The Christians themselves cannot deny this; for St. Jerome (translator
of the Vulgate) said explicitly in many places in his Pro-
logues that the text had been corrupted and falsified, having already been through the hands of many people who
added and cut out as they pleased; with the result, as he

said, that there were as many different readings as there were different texts.

Which all goes to show that there is no firm basis for the authority claimed for the canonical Gospels. Those who say that these books are divinely inspired must admit that they know this by faith alone, faith which makes it impossible for them to believe otherwise. But how can faith (or in other words, blind credulity) establish the authority of the books that are the ground of this faith? What folly is this?

The main purpose, we are told, which God had in mind when he sent his son down to earth in human form, was to take away the sins of the world, and to destroy the works of the devil. Jesus promised frequently that he would deliver the world from sin. Was there ever a falser prophecy?—- as the present century bears witness. It is said that Jesus came to save mankind. Mankind, indeed! If an army of a hundred thousand soldiers is made captive, and some ten or a dozen men are ransomed, one does not say that the army has been ransomed. What are we to think of a God who comes to be crucified and to die to save the world, and who leaves so many nations to damnation?

On what do the Christians pride themselves? Their moral code? It is the same at bottom as that of all religions: but cruel dogmas have sprung from it and taught men to persecute. Their miracles? But what people have not had their miraculous stories, and what wise men have not rejected them? Their prophecies? Have they not been falsified? Their conduct? Is it not often infamous? The establishment of their religion? But has it not sprung from fanaticism and been sustained by intrigue? Their doctrine? But is it not the height of absurdity? I hope, my friends, that I have given you a sufficient protection against these follies.

Jack lowers the anthology slowly and stares into space, still breathing hard, his mind awash with conflicting reactions. It's an elegant plan, Scott, a brilliant plan. Simple in a complex sort of way. And this time, Jack thinks, *I've got it right,* I'm sure of it. I beat the clock, Father Siberell, I figured out your damn master plan before the buzzer, you sick freaking *genius.* The enormity of it becomes clearer the longer Jack stares, and the book falls unnoticed to the floor. The reaction—God, how can you even imagine the reaction? How can you know what will happen? And that's part of the point, of course, of *course.* He has to have been planning this for *years. Who would ever have the patience to see this kind of thing through?* This is why he went to seminary, why he built this whole mega-ministry. This is why it make any sense at all for Scott Siberell to be a priest—and now, in fact, it makes *perfect* sense. *Everything* fits. This is Scott's Big Thrill.

CRACK.

15

Judges

My soul, sit thou a patient looker-on;
judge not the play before the play is done:
Her plot hath many changes; every day
Speaks a new scene; the last act crowns the play.

Francis Quarles, *Epigram–Respice Finem*

"**S**o."
    "So!"
"How goes the flock-tending?"
"Oh peachy. Borderline dandy, really."
"Uh huh." Jack glances casually around the Cascade, pretending sudden interest in the old wooden floors, worn down soft. "And the big foray into televangelism, that's shaping up?"
"Oh sure. ABC's doing a fine job. They said we're looking at nine million viewers, if you can believe that. You know, the regulars plus the Only-on-Holidays-Christians plus the sickos who just wanna see a new show crash. My personal faves."

"Uh huh." When to spring it. When.

"What's on your mind there, JJ?"

"Oh, well . . . a lot less than last week, actually. Finally cracked a certain puzzle I've been working on."

Scott looks up, interested. "Do tell."

"Thinkin' maybe I should string you along for a while."

Scott descends into his glass. "Be my guest, like I care."

"Oh fine, be a prick in my finest hour. Okay, here goes. Abbé has undergone a sex change."

Scott's brow buckles with pleasure. "I'm listening."

"She's a man . . . *he's* a man."

"Ding ding ding! He is indeed! And I'm still listening." His eyes, how they twinkle.

"And *you're* a man."

"Why Jack, I'm flattered."

"And unless I miss my guess, which I don't, that's not where the similarities end. But you intend to do him one better."

"Well, well. Am I to take it you've heard the crack on this one?"

"You, Scott Siberell, are planning to do what a certain Abbé Meslier did about three hundred years ago, but *you* will be live and in living color. Feel free to nod all the way through this. You're planning to go on national network television on Palm Sunday in full priestly vestments and tell nine million of the faithful that they're full of shit."

"You know, I was beginning to think my faith in you was misplaced this time, but you pulled it out in the final seconds. Talk about your Hail Marys!"

"And you, the Happy Heretic of my youth, hatched this plan, what, six years ago, seven years ago, and went through *seminary*, and built two consecutive ministries, and made hospital visits, and heard confessions, and performed the last rites, and . . ." He leans across the table. ". . . and forced *Communion* on me, all as a prelude to this?"

"Not just prelude, JJ—*foundation*. I've been building the foundation for seven years come this July."

"Jesus."

"Meaning?"

"Meaning it's the most beautiful thing I've ever seen."

"Well shoot, I'd love to disagree, but . . ."

"The *discipline* to pull this off! The *focus* you had to have, my God, Scott! It's a work of genius, I must admit."

"Well, I'm relieved. I was a little worried you'd think it was . . ."

"And you can't do it."

"Come again?"

"You just can't do it, Scott. You must not do it. Sure, the twenty-one-year old revolutionary in me says go for it, burn the fuckin' church down, but the next minute I remember I *grew up*."

"Yeah, well, that's an overrated development."

"You said yourself you don't leave bodies behind. Nobody gets hurt, right? Just harmless thrills. Well this *is* a thrill you're talking about—it gives me a rush just to think about it, really it does—but it's not harmless, and even you should be able to see that."

Scott waves a dismissive backhand. "Apples and oranges, Jack. If this was just a thrill it'd be a different story, and yes, I'd be breaking my own rules. But it's so much more than that. And even *you* should be able to see *that*, you condescending ass. This is about living out your convictions, Kassel. Think back again to the twenty-one-year olds we were. What would they say if they were in the room with you waggling your great big grown-up finger at their convictions? They'd friggin' puke."

"And then they'd walk up to my office and see the quotes on my door . . ."

Scott laughs loud and derisively and bangs the table too many times. "You and that damn pathetic little door!! I can't believe you think that amounts to *shit!* Jesus, Jack, you sad little man, open your eyes! You tape up a bunch of hundred-year old quotes from *other people* on a door at the end of a dead-end hallway on the second floor of a building on the campus of a nothing little dog crap college in the middle of nowhere and then crow about living your *principles?* You probably sit in your office with your heart all a-flutter at the thought of Marge Funk saying something abou . . . oh, I *knew* it, look at you! Oh, Jack, Jack, *God* it *kills* me to see you like this. You're in serious need of a demonstration of living one's principles, my little friend. I'm talking to nine million Americans Sunday after next, and Monday morning they're all gonna be talking about *me* and what I said to their faces."

Jack opts for the lowered voice in a feeble attempt at reclaiming a little dignity. "Look. A lot of these people think you walk on water, Scott, and even though one of them is my ex-mother-in-law, it's just wrong to shit in their outstretched hands. That's all. It's just wrong."

"Oh get some *perspective*, Jack. Yes, some feelings are gonna get hurt, sure, but I had to earn their confidence or I'd have never made it to this day. This is the Catch-22 we've always been stuck in, you know that. As long as they think we're a bunch of fringe lunatics, then nothing we can say makes a dent in the status quo. And we all just limp along, one generation after another, up to our armpits in this damned ignorant mythology, grinning like gremlins and crossing ourselves, mouthing pieties, looking for Noah's Ark and hidden messages in Revelation, plugging our ears to keep out any *real* knowledge of the universe, trying to figure whether God wants us to *stone* gays or *crucify* them, I can never quite remember which, and whether it's okay to do that on the Sabbath, and whether it's certain words or certain deeds or certain thoughts or some other damn thing that gets us into heaven ahead of the other guy—and we keep at it, generations without end, because brains and balls rarely hang on the same person. We are wasting *time*, Jack, that's the worst of it. There are tens of millions of people out there spending their precious minutes and hours and years studying ancient ramblings in excruciating detail, memorizing Psalms by number and learning not one damn thing about loving their neighbors. We are wasting time that could be spent building the next world *right here*. Why do I have to give this speech to you, of all people—you wrote it! When we get this damned Christian millstone off our necks, civilization will just *soar*—morally, ethically, intellectually, materially. We'll look back and slap our palms to our foreheads in stone cold disbelief that we actually thought that was a *moral* system we left back there, much less *THE* moral system. I want that world sooner, not later, and I'm willing to break a few eggs to get it. I realized I had to be one of them, I had to be on the inside to even be heard. I could have been a Methodist or a Baptist or whatever I wanted—but I chose the priesthood because of the Catholic pretense of being a 'questioning faith,' don't you just love that, and for the unbelievable authority Catholics grant these guys and everything they say. I speak for God, you know, Jack, which will make the whole thing far more effective than it would be coming out of the mouth of a pale little Protestant pastor who speaks for the church deacons and the ladies' guild. So I secured the most potent platform I could get, then built ecumenical ministries that used Protestant tactics to broaden the audience appeal. It's been hard, Jack, I can't tell you how hard, but now I'm here. For fourteen weeks I will have the national ear."

"Oh use your head. ABC will pull the plug forty-five seconds into your tirade."

"*One*, there are no plans for a tirade. That'd be rather self-defeating, don't you think? Confirms the ignorant assumptions of the many about the few. No, Jack, this is an attempt to give the nation the same, quiet, compelling education you and I had to find on our own. And *b*, I have an ironclad contract that specifically prohibits ABC from pulling the plug based on content."

Oh. Oh my. Jack thought he was impressed *before;* now Scott smiles at Jack's expression, which signals his growing awareness of the totality and inevitability of it all. "They were absolutely desperate to find a slot-filler after Halliday went down, Jack, so they gave me everything I asked for, including that. Ironclad, JJ. They pull the plug and I practically own the network the next day, I'm not kidding. You should *see* this contract. So yes, over the course of three months and change, I will lead the faithful —gently, Jack, very gently—I'll lead them out of the woods and into the light."

There's the standard tinkle of glass and rumble of conversation all around, and the nasty sound of sleet has begun tapping at the windows, but it all seems far more distant than usual to Jack. He's almost out of ammunition, but not quite.

"You're talking about 'them' like an undifferentiated mass, not like individuals." He pauses, then delivers his last salvo, looking Scott straight in the eyes. "What about Haley Gilbert?"

Scott knew it was coming, but it still has an impact. "Haley will be fine."

"Oh what does that mean, 'Haley will be fine'? You don't know that. She's going to be devastated. She thinks you hung the moon."

"*She* thinks I hung the moon, *they* think I walk on water. They all think a god made the world and Heaven's waiting for them. Wrong on all counts."

"You can't pretend someone like Haley doesn't make it harder . . ."

"She makes it *much* harder!" Scott yells, louder than he'd intended, and the bar goes quiet.

Until someone yells, "That's the way it's *supposed* to work, buddy!" and the whole place woos and claps.

Scott fires the little good-humored-finger-pistol at the

comic and continues quietly. "She makes it much harder, Jack, but it's game day after six years of training. The stakes are too big. I also believe I'm helping make a better world for her kids and for their kids."

"And she'd agree with that, would she?"

"Oh what difference does that make? Seriously, what the *fuck* is that supposed to mean? And anyway, don't think I haven't been thinking about Haley from the beginning. What do you think that 'One-on-One' retreat was all about? Her faith was almost gone after her Dad died, it really just about did her in. I've spent the last five months building it up again, stronger than ever . . ."

". . . just so you could knock it flat again. That's great."

"Dammit Jack, will you listen to me? I built it up so she could weather what's about to happen. Haley is . . ." Scott pauses to consider his words. "Jack, she's a special kid. She has something that I've just never seen in a person before. And wipe that damn look off your face, that's not what I'm talking about. She's good, Jack, she's actually, honestly good, deeply good. It's a magnificent thing to behold, so glorious and rare I almost didn't recognize it. No ulterior motives, not a situational thing, not a Girl-Scout goodness, not Christian make-believe goodness. The Real Thing. It transcends the faith system she happens to be wrapped in. But because of who she is at the moment, I knew she'd need the trappings of that system to weather what I'm going to do, so I slowly built her faith up again, rock-solid. Now it's strong enough to . . ."

"Scott, her faith is built on *you!* Reread that letter from her mom. Haley's personal theology was built around her dad before he died. When he went, she nearly lost it—until she jumped to you, Scott. You *must* know this already. If you go south on her, she's back in the pit, and without the trust to jump to somebody else."

"I can't let myself . . ."

"And then multiply that by the thousands who've been going to your Masses or hanging on your every word on the radio and you begin to see what you're about to do. Ever look into their eyes when they're shaking your hand on the way out of the chapel?"

"No, I try not to, actually."

"Good thinking, 'cause I don't think we'd be having this conversation if you did. What you are talking about doing is not ethical. It's not moral. It's not right."

Scott looks Jack square in the face. "I'd much rather have you with me on this, Jack. I really would. That's why I was especially thrilled to see the St. Bernie's job open up when it did so I could do my thing in your backyard. I thought that'd be a poetic closing of the circle we started at Cal. And now you're takin' a little of the thrill away, I must say."

"Scott, I need to hear you say you won't do this, at least not here and now. Go somewhere and hurt people I don't know."

"Oh, okay, I'll wait until the next time I built a megaministry from scratch and get a national TV contract. No way. This is it, now or never. You haven't made enough of a case for never, so it's now. It's *now*, Jack."

"I'll pull the plug on you if I have to."

"Oooooo, will you *really?*" Scott sneers, his expression pure amused contempt. "And how are you gonna do that? You, the very picture of potency, what are you gonna do? Gonna put a little note on your door, saying 'Father Scott is an atheist'? Be my guest. And if Marge Funk sees it and comes to me, my serious off-Broadway credits kick in and you're left looking quite the flaccid little dink. The higher you go, the more flaccid you swing. I'd love to see the Wanda trying to decide what to make of you—and that's what it would amount to, you know. I don't want that anymore than you do. So just save yourself the effort and sit back and enjoy the show." He stands and drops a ten on the table. "Bye bye, Jack. Thanks for another riveting go-round."

Scott turns and walks out the front door into the early crackling sleetfall of a developing ice storm. Jack waits a decent interval before dropping another ten on the table and going out the same way.

And Randi Delaney, sitting alone in the next booth, waits an interval even more decent before lowering her hand from the *o* of her mouth, collecting her scattered books and papers and bolting out the back.

The ink is hardly dry on the "Live from Nurse Chapel" deal when Mike Lutz enters the House floor and whispers to Representative Peter D'Angelo that he's gonna love love *love* the venue they've chosen for the announcement of his bid for the Senate.

"It's a pulpit."

"That's your big breakthrough?" D'Angelo whispers back. "A pulpit? BFD, Michael. Right symbolism, wrong scale. Too damn local, unless it's the pulpit of the National Cathedral."

"Better. Much better. It's a pulpit in our district on national television, live, coast-to-coast, ABC. They're thinking at least six million viewers on any given Sunday you choose, so we could shoot for mid-April and have a sweet downhill ride into the convention."

"I'm sorry, Mikey, did you say something after 'national television'?"

"Look, can we step out into the hall?"

They do, and Mike spells it out, the whole meteoric rise of the Siberell star, the caravans of cars stretching for miles, coverage in the *Ledge*, fainting parishioners, SRO crowds. A tent-revival kind of authentic American religious phenom, hard to believe he's . . .

"A PRIEST? Mike, you have got to work on getting the key info up to the front of the sentence. It has to be Lutheran if it's a Minnesota thing. Catholic is the wrong angle for Minnesota."

"But this is already *working* in Minnesota! Lines of cars for miles! And this guy is the least Catholic priest I've ever seen, he's got the shouted amens and the tearjerkin' faith stories and a little white-girl choir that sounds like the Old Time Gospel Hour of Power! That's the beauty, Congressman, we reach *everybody* with this guy. And he's young and good-looking, so we'll grab the Thornbirds vote among soccer moms, that's another ninety-percent subgroup. Everybody's loves him—well, everybody but the damned atheists, of course, and they can take their five percent and sho.."

"And paste it right on Jesse's chest. I'll think about giving this Subaru guy a shot at hosting my announcement if I like him on the phone, but I don't want to hear you badmouthing the atheists again, Mikey. That five percent is just as important to us as the thumpers. You trot off to your office right now, as a matter of fact, and get somebody from your staff on the line to the Minnesota chapters of American Atheists and the American Humanist Association to line up endorsements, loud ones."

"I don't get it."

"For Jesse, you idiot! Act like you're after an endorsement for me and watch them fall backwards in their chairs and start chanting Jesse's name from the floor. Get 'em on video if you can, saying his name as many times as possible with the word ATHEIST plastered up in the background. And pick the gnarliest goddam ugly-ass atheist you can find. Shouldn't be hard."

"I get it."

"Good! Oh and Mike—Mr. Robertson does not need to know about this priest idea. He'll blow a damn gasket if he sees me in bed with the Catholics, and I wanna put that off until after the announcement. Got it? Not a word. Not that he's gonna run crying to Ventura or Goldberg, but I don't need any grief from him."

"Got it."

"And I want a report typed up and on my desk tomorrow morning entitled 'Why No One Including Pat Robertson, Ralph Reed, nor Peter D'Angelo Should Lose Any Sleep Over Saint Peter Announcing for Senate from a Catholic Pulpit."

"Got it."

Now to find Siberell and convince *him*.

Ninety minutes later, Mike hangs up the phone in his office and turns, pumping his fist in the air, to Bob D. Wanamacher. "Yes! I can't believe it! *Everything* is going our way on this thing."

"Who was that?"

"That," Mike says, his face consumed by a grin, "was Father Scott Siberell of Saint Bernadette's College. Peter D'Angelo will announce his candidacy from the pulpit of Nurse Chapel at Saint Bernie's on *national television*."

"Sweet!"

"Yes, especially since that starts to build Peter's national profile for the 2008 Presidential bid."

"You're kidding! The White House?!"

"Oh I kid you not. You backed the right horse, Bob Dole Wannabee. Your uncle's dream is gonna come true by proxy in the person of Peter D'Angelo, and it all starts at itty bitty Saint Bernie's." Mike spins in his chair. "And I'd be the natural for press secretary, don't you think? Man, you should have heard this Siberell guy, Bob, he was *ecstatic* about the idea, just over the top. Must be a big GOP man . . . oh, and wait 'til you hear this: you know what the best thing is?"

"What? What?"

He stops spinning on a dime, facing Bob. "The best thing of all is the actual day of the announcement. Peter's going to announce for Senate from a pulpit on *Palm Sunday*. That means another fifty percent onto the viewer total for one thing." He takes a moment to mentally congratulate himself. "But you also can't beat that for resonance. If Palm Sunday in a pulpit doesn't read like an endorsement from Jesus H. Christ Himself, I don't know what does."

By closing time on the Thursday before the Sunday before the big day, Father Siberell has assured multiple nervous telephoning staffers for both the American Broadcasting Company and Republican Representative Peter D'Angelo that he, Scott Siberell, has never, ever been accused of being too Catholic.

The second meeting of the Humanist Association has a very different feel to it from the start. Amanda and the three keep shooting electric looks at Jack that he would take for flirting if he weren't a rationalist. At least six more in attendance, Jack notes, plus the one who had fled before introducing herself last time, back for more. The new blood is split down the middle, with three on the Void/Light/Walter side of things and three who are almost as nattily attired as Randi. *Spies*, Jack thinks darkly, possibly Mormons, so very many teeth. Be thankful: could have been six more Voids.

Amanda loses control of the meeting almost immediately

when she suggests a quick overview of the Humanist Anthology.

"First we vote!" It's Walter, suddenly in fine voice.

"Oh, that's fine, if you . . . that's fine. I was going to do that at the . . ."

"First we vote! Void for President! Hail, Lord Void!"

Amanda is in full fluster. "Okay I, um, we have little pieces of paper so we can have a closed . . ."

"Speeches!" Yells Walter. Jack liked Walter better as a silent, brooding hulk. "Speeches first. Void first."

Void stands. "No no, I defer to Miss Corelli." He gestures graciously and sits.

"Oh I . . . I didn't plan to actually give a . . ."

"Void by acclamation!"

"No! Well, I mean, we're supposed to open the floor for nomina . . ."

"I nominate Void! Hail, Lord Void!"

This is actually good, Jack decides. This kind of Nazi crap will scare the normals and Amanda will keep the seat. Oh shit, I *assume* Amanda will keep the . . . Of course she will. Of course, oh *shit*. One, two, three, four, five, six, seven, eight, nine, ten secure votes for Amanda, right, if we can assume this goes pierced one way and unpierced the other. Ten out of, oh shit, *twenty?* No. Twenty-*one*. Does the advisor get to . . .

"Okay, Void is nominated," says Amanda. Jack notes a peculiar smile on her face. Oh, she thinks this is *funny*, does she.

Stacey and Deena and Randi in unison. "We nominate Amanda Elizabeth Corelli! *Wooooooooooooooo!*"

"Okay, Corelli," Amanda deadpans. "How do you spell that?"

Ha ha. Jack needs a joint.

"Other nominees?"

The Witnesses end up nominating each other, which is

just too damn cute. So they'll vote for each other and Amanda loses two of the ten. Time to dissolve Parliament.

"Okay, speeches, I guess, and I'll go first you said? Okay. Okay, uh, hello everyone. I'm Amanda Corelli, and I'm running for president of the Saint Bernadette Student Humanist Association."

Woo.

"And, well, for one thing, this whole group was my idea. Oh and Randi's, and Stacey's, and Deena's . . . and I just want it to be the best it can be! I will listen to your thoughts and concerns and try to really make this an association that belongs to everybody, not just to a few people."

Oh, stirring, Amanda. Jack will now settle for a damn clove cigarette.

"Void?"

"Hail, Lord Void!" Oh shit. Walter, Light, the other Witches . . . in fact the whole pierced contingent from last time, plus the three new pierced ones, plus . . . oh shit, the Mormons—so, not Mormons then, I guess . . . eleven all together shout the salutation, rise in unison, clap their closed fists hard against their chests and shout again:

"Hail! Hail, Lord Void!"

Lord Void, clearly both accustomed to and pleased with the melodrama, rises and strides to the front of the room.

"You may be seated." And they are, clattering like a Roman legion on the way down. "This is simple and quick. I am Void, and when I am your president . . ."

"Hail, President Void!"

Jack would feel better if they'd crack a friggin' smile, but they are not unserious.

". . . when I am your president, everybody will do what they want and believe what they wanna believe! Now Mandy's a great chick, don't get me wrong, and an awesome lay, let me tell you . . ." Amanda shoots a terrified look at Jack, who is way behind in processing already and doesn't

need this development. "... but you can see she's a little ...
structured. Right? All right. Not Void." The voice goes up
forty decibels. "You wanna lay on the floor, you wanna swing
from the lights, you wanna bring a box and crank it to ten, do
it! Do it! Build a fire in the middle of the floor! Feed off each
other's electric mayhem. This is the opposite of church, man.
Instead of a moment of silence we'll have a moment of fuckin'
bedlam. This is all about gettin' together and makin' something happen. It doesn't matter so much what it is, just make
something go down and you know you're alive. *Vote Void and
know you're alive!*"

"Hail, Lord Void!"

It's a landslide. Void pulls in the Witnesses, for God's sake,
and Amanda ends up with all of four votes. So much for the
Humanist Association, thinks Jack. But Void, in a fever of
transition gentility, insists that Amanda lead the first half of
the meeting as she had intended.

"Well ..." She is still reeling. "I don't think it makes
sense, really. I was going to assign some readings for next
week ..."

"*Pssshhtt!* You're kidding," Void says. "So much for voter's
remorse."

"Could I say something here?" It's Jack, far too late. "I'm
a little concerned this is ending up off the mark for our organizational charter. We claimed to be a humanist group based
around readings and discussions of ..."

"Well, there's a new sheriff in town."

"But even the new sheriff is supposed to follow the laws
that ..."

"Then there's a new Führer in town! A benign dictator.
No friggin' homework."

Amanda looks pleadingly at Jack, whose expression is
undecipherable. "Well," she says, "you might as well take it
then, Void."

Void snaps his fingers and the soothing sounds of

Megadeth issue from the speakers of an industrial-strength boombox under Walter's chair, volume ten, bass ten. Five people slide out of the room and walk down the corridor together, dazed.

"Dr. Kassel, I'm . . ."

"You *slept* with that?"

"Not my finest moment, okay?" Amanda shoots back, agitated. "You want me going through your sexual history with a searchlight?"

He decides the question is rhetorical. "Well, I'm not sure what our options are, but as long as the association charter has our names on it, we've got to keep coming back. You guys know those Witnesses?"

"No," says the one Jack has now learned is Deena. "Why?"

"Because if we're going to pull this thing back into line somehow we've got to have more than just the five of us. Why don't you try to find out who they are and see if Void's bodyslam in there is what they came for. Somehow I don't think so. And if there's anyone else you can peel off, try it. Even the Witches, I don't know."

They exit into the still, cold Saturday night.

Jack is seriously tired. "Amanda, you've got to try something. This isn't what I signed on for, you know that."

Amanda wheels around hotly. "Yes, I know that! Of *course* I 'know' that!" She runs her hand quickly over her hair. "You think this is what *I* had in mind?"

"No, I know you didn't . . ."

"This was *everything* to me, Dr. Kassel! *Everything!* This was my chance to find a place here, to be who I really am, finally, *finally!*"

Randi puts a hand on Amanda's shoulder. "It's gonna work out. There's nothing fatal yet. Talk to Void."

"Talk to Void? Randi, do you remember what he's like? Everything's a game, everything's a joke! This doesn't mean a damn thing to him!" She suppresses a sob with a guttural roar and begins pacing hard.

Deena and Stacey, bouncing slightly to stay warm, watch quietly.

Jack is a little intimidated, and at a loss for intelligent words, so he starts talking. "I . . . I don't think this is really unsalvageable, as long as we know what *we're* about and keep our heads a little. Why don't you call Void this week and arrange to . . ."

"Dr. Kassel, you know . . ." Amanda stops, searching for words. "You've really been . . . just *great* to help us get this thing going, but . . ." She looks up and into his eyes. "I feel like you're *hiding* behind me. I honestly get the feeling you are. If you only spoke up in there, just once . . . I know you think you're letting us fight our own battles . . ." She looks down, then up again, tears welling. "I'm sorry, I'm just upset. It's true what you said: you've *been* here before. But there are ways, Dr. Kassel . . . there are ways I honestly feel like I'm further along than you, like I'm willing to get outside my comfort zone to act on my convictions, and you . . . I don't know. I just feel like . . . I really need you to be more than you are. That's the best way I can think to put it. I need you to be more than you are."

She turns to walk away, and the others follow, leaving Jack to deal with his beloved truth.

Monday morning finds Jack standing outside Dean Martin's enormous mahogany office door like a kid called to the principal's office. A Sunday morning phone message ordered him to appear at eight a.m. Monday to answer a few questions, and Jack has practiced his responses all the way up the road from Saint Philip. This was not the intention when we formed the organization. Void is an outside agitator. Yes, we will dissolve the group and reform as a reading group only, for students only, yes, yes. I couldn't agree more. And no more music. He has to dissociate himself entirely from the whole debacle in order to save the concept of a sober, reasonable, philosophical investigation of serious and important ideas.

He pushes the door open and is met by no fewer than nine gray, unsmiling figures sitting stock still around the huge conference table. Oh God, *Stonehenge* wants to talk to me, Jack thinks as his knees nearly give. He manages to walk in and take his seat at the near end of an endless plane of cherrywood.

On his immediate left is the Dean herself; to her left is Thing One, then Sister Joan, then Thing Two, each Thing looking like she accidentally swallowed an eyeball and doesn't want to let on; on Jack's right is none other than Scott 'Francis' Siberell, putting his serious credits to use; a man unknown to Jack, surely not a good sign; a frail and trembling student who looks somehow familiar; the admin secretary; and, at the far end, directly across from Jack, sits President Wanda X. Streamley herself, wearing a look that Jack has never, ever seen before.

Suddenly, Jack recognizes the student and is overcome with horror and confusion.

Gwendolyn.

"Dr, Kassel, thank you for joining us." Dean Martin's voice is completely calm, Jack notices, something he'll go ahead and take for a good sign. "I think most of us know each other. Dr. Kassel, you know Gwendolyn Pierce from your Ethics course. And this is her father, Raymond Pierce."

Jack nods. Raymond Pierce himself moves not a fraction of an inch, eyes locked on Jack, who searches his files for the word to describe Mr. Pierce's expression, settling at last on *abhorrence.*

"Might you have an idea why I've asked you here, Dr. Kassel?"

Yes, Jack has an idea. Run like hell.

He sits in silence for several seconds, working through branching tree diagrams in his head, deciding at last that little Gwendolyn was that pale, fleeing figure who had abandoned the humanist meeting.

Then he remembers.

"The paper. Does this have something to do with a comment I wrote on Gwendo..."

"You're damn right it does!" Mr. Pierce, still locked on Jack. "My daughter, you see, is still somewhat *naïve* about the ways of the world, and when someone asks her to..."

"Daddy..."

"Shut up, Gwen. When someone asks her to write a paper exploring the darkest recesses of her inner life, she ups and does it. And she is rewarded, in turn, with an accusation that she is not a *Christian!*"

"I don't recall leveling such an accusation."

"It's right here on the DAMN PAPER! Are you calling me a LIAR, you son of a..."

"I think we can proceed amicably, and in fact I'll insist on it, gentlemen," interrupts the Dean, uncertain herself whether it is true. "Dr. Kassel, might you be able to articulate what you intended with your comment?"

Jack, still frantically revising his prepared remarks to fit the new crisis, is again relieved by her tone—which again amazes him, since her voice usually aggravates his reflux problem.

"Yes, well, I was concerned by the, uh... *distress* evident in Gwendolyn's paper, including an apparent recent suicide attempt..."

"None of your business! None of your damn business, she's fine now, that was a stupid stunt and she knows it. It was some damn thing she read about on the damn Internet, right down to the 'million dollar smile,' all a bunch of Goth garbage is all. Her mother and I have enough on our hands fighting *that* trash without then having some godless heathen pagan atheist son of a rip trying to recruit her away from the Lord . . . and at a Catholic college!"

"Recruit her? *Recruit* her? For what?" Jack spies the moral high ground and heads straight for it. "I was doing what we are urged to do at workshop after workshop, offering myself as a sounding board, intervening when it appears that a student might need an ear . . ."

"Not just any ear! A *Christian* ear, for God's sake," says Sister Joan, clearly exasperated. "Isn't that self-evident?"

"And when a student appears to have attempted suicide as a result of the pressure and judgment she felt from the church, do you really feel it's appropriate to send her back to the church?"

"Heavens, *yes!* Only there can she be assured of God's forgiveness."

"She specifically said she felt she could not be forgiven."

"She's *wrong* about that, Dr. Kassel," says Joan. "And the people to let her know she is wrong are Christians, not . . . *others.*"

"Now I'm not a psychologist . . ." Jack pauses. "I'm not a psychologist, but it seems to me just as important to listen to what she *perceived* to be true as to whatever happens incidentally to *be* true."

No, Jack can't quite believe how that came out, either.

"And, if I am not mistaken, there is in fact at least one unforgivable sin in the Christian system."

"Nonsense," Joan says disdainfully, and the Things titter like Munchkins. "There are no sins that stand beyond redemption."

Jack takes a deep breath and looks at Scott, then back to Joan. "What about disbelief?"

All sit motionless for six to eight seconds. "You are playing word games," Joan declares at last. "Christian sin and judgment take place within the context of Christian belief.

Faith itself is not subject to judgment, since it is presupposed."

"Exactly. Presupposed. The assumed default. And what if it is presupposed falsely?"

Raymond Pierce jumps to his feet, enraged. "Are we going to sit here playing philosopher games or am I gonna see this man's head on a platter?"

"I'll allow it," says the Dean, dropping Mr. Pierce back into his seat with a well flicked index finger.

Jack persists. "Is it or is it not an unforgivable sin to lose one's faith?"

Joan leans forward. "If one's faith is lost, one presumably no longer believes the system is valid and would therefore not be driven to desperate measures out of fear of consequences."

"But this assumes a sudden, complete loss of faith without remorse. What about a slow slide, a slow erosion of faith—probably much more common? What if the faith goes *before* the fear of judgment does?"

No comment.

"That," says Jack, "is precisely what I thought to be the case with Gwendolyn. Christians see that person in the middle and rush to restore the faith. I see the same person and rush to remove the *fear.* Either way works, wouldn't you agree Father Siberell?"

Wanda Streamley interrupts God-only-knows-what Scott was about to say. "Your idea works well as philosophical theory, Dr. Kassel, but eventually that faith will be essential as we stand in the presence of the Creator and are judged." She smiles that smile of absolute certitude. "Non-Christians are quick to emphasize our fear of the Lord in their many criticisms—and yes, our God is a fearsome God. But our fear is a trembling confession of the awesome reality we will all one day face at the Throne, not a fear of some contrived phantom—and the Church provides an infallible shield from that fear in the total absolution of those who seek it in the name of the Christ."

Which, Jack thinks, brings us right back to the same question. But I see we are out of time. Many thanks to our guests . . .

"Dr. Kassel, being a regular attender of faculty meetings, I assume you are familiar with the *mandatum Ex Corde Ecclesiae*," says Dean Martin.

"I am," Jack answers, suddenly grateful for the snotty tutorials he received from Brian and Scott in the Cascade. The Dean's delivery is still calm, but the content is beginning to make his cigarette-reaching arm twitch.

"Among the most important modern organizational principles is the need for any institution to know what it is about. We speak of mission statements, vision statements—at bottom, they're all the same: they are attempts to define who we are. The College of Saint Bernadette is a Catholic women's college. Our dual focus, then, is our Catholicity and our commitment to women. *Ex Corde* is an attempt to solidify the focus of our Catholic identity as an institution. It is a reasonable but firm document that, in its foresight and wisdom, anticipated and forbade precisely the sort of thing we are discussing this morning. We are collective signatories to that document. If there were no other reason for calling you to task for your comment to Gwendolyn, this one would be sufficient. It is a blatant violation of our Catholic identity to 'offer a non-Christian ear' to students, regardless of the situation."

Jack is impressed by the fact that the Dean appeared to go out of her way to characterize this as some sort of contractual issue, nothing more. He interprets that as an invitation to shut up and go away unscathed—and foolishly declines.

"I believe there was a third term in your description," he says, "that was overlooked: this is a Catholic women's *college*. And the nature of a college at its best is an open . . ."

"... marketplace of ideas," the Dean says, finishing Jack's thought. "If you are determined to lapse into clichés I can certainly tilt with the best of them. But every institution also designates certain ideas as *cognita non grata*, am I right? We don't welcome white supremacy or human enslavement or flat earth theories into our classrooms, do we?"

"I'm not sure I like the implication that..."

"... that secular humanism is equivalent to those? Don't be absurd. But the point is nonetheless made that every institution has the right to exclude some ideas as inappropriate to its self-concept. There are no truly open 'marketplaces of ideas.' Many of the left-leaning institutions who so pompously claim such a title are among the least tolerant places I know. Think political correctness. When we, as an institutional element of the Roman Catholic Church, exclude statements that run counter to our own assumptions, we do something far less authoritarian than many of these nominal 'marketplaces.' Now we can argue forever about whose world view is correct in which aspects, but..."

"No, we can't. That's just it. We can't argue if all opposing points of view are muzzled. And the students only get..."

"Can't you *understand?*" It is Thing Two, speaking in a palsied but somehow forceful voice. Everyone in the room is completely shocked to hear her speak at all, and Thing One is on the verge of a stroke over it. "Can't you simply leave us this place, this one place for ourselves? Can't we have one place that we don't have to defend from your, your *onslaught?* Your *arguments?* Your 'collisions of ideas'? Is it so terribly wrong that we have these few islands in the midst of all the corruption and coarseness and ugliness of the secular world, a few places where we can live out our beliefs? Must it all be a part of your incessant intellectual chess game?"

Jack is cowed into humility. I don't know the answer to that, he thinks. "I am just trying to live my own life with a little more integrity, a little more honesty. I'm trying to be who I am in-

stead of pretending to be something else, that's all." If only the
real Scott Siberell were here, he'd have the perfect defense of
the concept, but he's terribly busy being someone else.

"What I think we're all trying to say here, Dr. Kassel, in
one way or another . . ." It is the current Scott Siberell. ". . .
is that you may not realize how much these students look *up*
to you. Some of your philosophy students, why, I'm sure they
think you '*hung the moon.*'" He carefully avoids eye contact
with Jack, staring instead at the ceiling, hand to his throat.
"And when you find yourself in contact with a student whose
faith is in doubt, well you never know how much of her remaining, fragmentary faith might be built around *you*. Then
if you 'go south' on her, Dr. Kassel, she's 'back in the pit'—
and often without the trust to jump to somebody else."

Jack feels the very last of his tolerance for Scott Siberell
slip quietly away.

"Can we have your simple assurance, then, Dr. Kassel,"
asks the Dean, "that there will be no repeat of any such thing
as this, so long as you are employed by this College?"

So help me God, he considers saying, then chooses, "You
have my assurance."

"How about an apology for Gwendolyn and her father?"
adds Scott, one eyebrow cocked.

Jack decides he is in a poor position to actually pile-drive
Scott. He turns to face the Pierces. "You both have my sincere apologies for any distress I caused by my comment."

"We will be watching you, Dr. Kassel," says Dean Martin. "Thank you for your time."

MORE   I know the law, Cavendish, the law, not
              what's 'right or wrong.'

CAVENDISH   Just as I always thought—you place a higher value on human law than on God's!

MORE   Ridiculous, Cavendish, and more to the point, untrue. Navigating the wild seas of right and wrong, there's a skill far beyond me. But in the forest of law, why, there's hardly a person can follow me there.

CAVENDISH   *(pointing after the departing ALEX)* While you talk, she's gone!

MORE   And go she should, if she were the Devil herself! She's broken no law.

CAVENDISH   So now you'd give the Devil benefit of law!

MORE   Oh I see. You'd mow every law to the ground to get to the Devil, would you?

CAVENDISH   Without a second thought!

MORE   Or a first one, if I may say so. For when the last law lay broken at your feet, and the Devil turned on you—where would you hide, what with all your protections laying strewn about? Yes, I'd give him the benefit of law, for my own sake.

ROPER   Again I say: the law's your god!

MORE   *(Wearily)* No, you fool, *God's* my god . . . But I find Him rather too *(bitterly)* subtle . . . I don't know where He is nor what He wants.

As the others file out, Raymond Pierce still glaring hard at Jack, Jack remains in place, as does the Dean. When at last the president leaves, Dean Martin turns to the slouching Jack, hands folded on the table before her.

"I have not the slightest interest in pursuing this kind of thing, but I also have no choice in the matter."

"I see."

"I will now offer you my apology for ridiculing the marketplace of ideas. It is also among *my* highest values."

Jack sits up with a puzzled expression. "Then why . . ."

"Because everything else I said still stands, that's why. I walk a very fine line here, Dr. Kassel, trying to keep this place . . . well, *open*, first of all, but also viable and vibrant and alive with intellectual integrity. And I do *not* accept that that ideal is mutually exclusive with the ideal of a college in the Catholic tradition. The very first colleges were Catholic."

"And the very first scientists were alchemists. Not a terribly strong argument."

"Well speaking of weak arguments, sir, your desire to live your life honestly rang a bit tinny from here, given the way you got your humanist club certified."

He swallows hard. "What do you mean?"

"And there's another blow. I'm afraid Diogenes is walking right past you, Jack. You know very well that Wanda thought you were forming a 'humanities club,' yet you went right ahead and took advantage of the misunderstanding when you could have clarified it."

"Believe it or not, Dean, I asked someone to clarify that. Did the letter ever . . ."

"Right, Jack. Anyway, I think you'd best realize there was a little truth in everything that was said in here, including Sister Vera's plea to just be left alone. *And* your implicit plea to engage like hell. But the bottom line, I assume you realize, is that you've received your only warning. Please don't force my hand on this. More people in this room than just Raymond Pierce wanted to see your head on a pike today. Next time I will lop it off and stick it on top myself."

At the precise moment Dean Martin finishes her warning shot, Carl bursts into the office, breathless and wide-eyed in plaid coat and ear-flap cap. "Dean Martin, you've got to come see! The most amazing thing, Dean, the most amazing thing I've ever seen in all my life!"

16

Signs and Wonders

The coming of the lawless one will be in accordance
with the work of Satan displayed in all kinds of coun-
terfeit miracles, signs and wonders . . .

2 Thessalonians 2:9

"**D**irections! Give me directions, Carl!" yells Dean
Martin, sprinting outside as fast as the ice will
allow, sensible shoes flying out at angles like a speedskater,
outpacing Carl as he shouts her toward an American elm between Admin and Bronte. She takes the corner, the tree comes
into view, and she stutters to a panting halt in front of precisely what she feared: a feminine image, somewhat severe,
almost medieval, elegant and evident in the lines and ridges
of the tree bark. Genevieve lunges at the tree and begins
furiously stripping, scratching, and peeling the image from
the trunk with her fingernails.

"Gennie!" says a panting voice arriving behind her. "What
on *Earth!*"

301

Wanda Streamley, intrigued by the Dean's sprint past her office, followed close on her heels, arriving at the elm too late to see the (apparent, *alleged)* image but too early to miss Gennie Martin scratching at the tree trunk like a cat in heat.

"Oh. Hello Wanda."

"Gennie?"

The Dean, still short of breath, manages to gasp, "Oh, uh . . . aphids. Aphids, not good. Not good."

"Well . . . my goodness, Genevieve! You do run a tidy ship, dear." She turns and walks back toward Admin, past a very confused and slightly miffed Carl Holtz.

"Dean Martin!" he says, bewildered. "Why'd ya do that, Dean? Why? It was beautiful!"

"What was beautiful, Carl?"

"The . . . there was a . . . like a picture there, on the trunk, it was . . . well, you saw it, Dean!"

"I don't recall seeing any such thing, Carl. Just aphids." She begins walking back to the Admin entrance.

Aphids? he mutters to himself—- then shouts after her, "It's March!"

"Well then, by May we'll have quite the problem, won't we Carl, if we don't get right on it," she says over her shoulder. "That's all I'm saying here."

Carl scratches under his hat and slowly walks away, mumbling mild Norwegian curses.

Never a good sign to be this exhausted by nine in the morning, thinks Dean Martin as she drags herself back through her office doorway and slams the monolithic door behind her. She walks straight to her desk and retrieves a jerky from the top drawer, then on to her beautiful semicircle window—one of many reasons she adores and retains this office—for a long, restorative gaze out over the snow-covered campus.

A task rendered impossible by the frostpattern face staring back at her from the windowpane.

She lets out a short shriek and stumbles backward into her desk. After a moment she steps forward cautiously to peer at the face. *Good Lord. What on Earth is going . . .*

A knock at the door. "Gennie dear . . . Gennie, may I have a word?"

Oh God it's Wanda. The Dean freezes in place like a teenager smoking weed in her bedroom.

"Are you all right? May I come in?"

Dean Martin looks back at the face—assuring herself that the 'gotcha' expression is purely in her own mind—then in the direction of Wanda's voice.

"Uh, one minute, Wanda, I'm . . . one minute, please." Twelve years ago she took over this office and specifically declined the offer of curtains for the window. What could ever compel me to draw them shut, she had said.

Marian apparitions, maybe?

"Gennie dear, I'm a bit concerned about you . . ."

Suddenly the Dean seizes on an idea, dashes to the casement window and cranks it open. Pivoting on pinions at the bottom of the semicircle, the window opens inward with a *ssshhhhhhhhooooooo* and a bracing rush of frigid air. She reaches abruptly for her coffee mug, pauses a split second—then flings the steaming brown liquid over the frozen pane.

Crack.

She cranks the window closed rapidly, sets the mug on her desk and walks quickly to the door, opening it as casually as she can manage.

"Yes, Wanda, what is it?"

Wanda peers over Genevieve's shoulder into the office, brow knit tight. "May I come in?"

"Well of course." The Dean steps aside reluctantly and Wanda enters, eyes roving and head turning.

"Well I thought I heard . . . oh my goodness, Gennie, what in Heaven's holy name happened to your beautiful *window?*"

The Dean looks for the first time at a window coated with what is to all appearances a root beer Slushy—and an enormous crack running diagonally from eleven o'clock to four.

Uh . . . aphids?

"You know, Wanda, I've been wondering the same thing. I think perhaps an unfortunate bird, possibly carrying, uh, carrying something . . . wet and . . . *brown* in its beak, flew into the window, poor thing."

"Oh! Oh, the poor, poor *thing!* Oh, Gennie, how *awful!*"

"Yes, I know. I'll call Carl right away."

Wanda begins shaking her head dejectedly. Gennie puts her arm around Wanda's shoulders, purring consolations as she leads her back to her own office.

Once Wanda is safely delivered, the Dean returns to her own office and closes the door. She shoots a hard glance at the window as if at an adversary, then grabs her coat and pulls it on. Moments later she is stalking the south flagstone walk along the green, looking over her high wool collar at any and every potential host medium.

There.

Another frost pattern, this one on a ground floor Hildegard window. She walks to the image, calmly pulls a credit card from her coat pocket, and scrapes it to oblivion.

Six minutes later it is there in the fragile blanket of snow covering a bush at the entrance to Monty Hall. A terse shake of the bush does it in, and she is off at an ever-quickening clip, the click of her boot heels muffled by the thin veil of snow covering everything, mind spinning uncomfortably but focused, still focused, still mission-driven.

In the Monty Hall foyer, it's an arrangement of posted notices on the bulletin board. *Is it my imagination,* she wonders, *or is the look getting the slightest bit of a pissed-off quality* . . . her breathing becomes shallower as she reaches up to—

Three students suddenly burst through the double doors at the top of the small staircase, chattering and omigawding right past her and out into the cold.

After a moment, her heart starts beating again. *Oh this is ridiculous, I feel like a damned pervert or spy or something.* She recovers her composure and turns back to the board. Removing all of the unauthorized postings manages to scramble things nicely.

Something in the back of her mind pushes through a crowd of competing thoughts, asking the earlier *What on Earth* question in a sheepish Oliver-Twist soprano. The Mission elbows it back to the cheap seats as Genevieve Martin takes the little staircase up into the building two at a time, throws open the double doors herself and starts to break into a light shuffle-run, through the halls of Monty zooming.

Jack Kassel leaves the Dean's Office, only barely wondering what the maintenance guy had been so lit up about seeing that he would go straight to Martin about it. He'd planned to make a quick stop in the Admin men's room to liberate the coffee that had gotten him to the eight o'clock meeting—until he remembered he was at Saint Bernie's, where no man pees quick. Mother Anna Cordion oversaw the installation of indoor plumbing early in the century and specifically requested a five-to-one ratio for women's and men's rooms. Generations of Bernies have sighed with deep satisfaction at the sight of scores of men, dancing subtly in lines snaking out into and down hallways all over campus. By the time Jack found the Admin men's room, in a closet-sized corner room in the sub-basement, and did his business, the bark had already flown off the elm and Dean Martin was back in her office caffeinating the window.

The short walk back to Bronte promises to be uneventful, and Jack, like a fool, believes it. He walks with head down and the Dean's Voice ringing in his ears. Then, as he approaches the door to Bronte, he looks up and sees It:

The St. Bernadette
Student Humanist Association
[President Void Shakespeare, faculty advisor Dr. Jack Kassel]
INVITES YOU TO ATTEND

one unholy **HELL** of a meeting

bring your > > > URGES!!

bring your > > > RAGE AGAINST THE MACHINE!!

leave your > > > INHIBITIONS!!

and your > > > CATHOLIC GUILT behind!!

↗ ↗ ↗ ↗ ↗ ↗ ↗ ↗ ↗

GETINTOUCHWITHYOURDARKSIDEGETINTOUCHWITHYOURDARKSIDEG
ETINTOUCHWITHYOURDARKSIDEGETINTOUCHWITHYOURDARKSIDEGE
TINTOUCHWITHYOURDARKSIDEGETINTOUCHWITHYOURDARKSIDEGETI
NTOUCHWITHYOURDARKSIDEGETINTOUCHWITHYOURDARKSIDEGETIN
TOUCHWITHYOURDARKSIDEGETINTOUCHWITHYOURDARKSIDE

Unholy Saturday, March 23, 2002 · Third Floor Curie lounge
7:00 pm - ???

ARE YOU READY??????

Jack feels the distinctive pang of a pike being inserted into the base of his skull.

He reads the poster three times through, hoping with each pass that something will rewrite itself.

Maybe this is the only one on campus. Could be.
He rips it down and starts running.

By ten o'clock, Dean Martin has covered every floor of
Monty, Curie, Hildegard, Admin, and Bronte. Nothing to report since the Monty bulletin board—nothing except the odd
sight of Jack Kassel running frantically through the Curie lobby
with a ream of loose papers under his arm. Feeling the strain
of the past hour's intensity, she walks into an empty classroom on fourth floor Bronte and collapses in a desk-chair,
head on folded hands.

After a while her breathing calms, her pulse slows to normal. She gradually straightens up, and sees, in the center panel
of the recently-washed chalkboard, a face—beautiful, feminine, severe, almost medieval—in the streaks left by Gerard's
sponge.

Her head drops back to the desktop in exhausted bewil-
derment. After a moment's quiet reflection, she begins to
pray.

*What are you telling me, Lord? What does this mean? What
am I supposed to do with all this?*

She hears only that silence—the same silence that has
rendered a lifetime of prayers rhetorical.

*My Church, Lord . . . your Church, tells me to act on the basis
of an informed conscience. I am assured that in doing so I remain
blameless for whatever that conscience leads me to do.*

" . . ."

She breathes in deeply and lets it out in a burst.

*My conscience tells me this is not real, Lord, that this is only a
projection of their hopes and my fears. Please guide me, Lord.*

" . . ."

Genevieve Martin sits very still for a full minute—then

stands slowly, walks to the board, picks up an eraser and scrubs the image away.

Just after eleven o'clock, Jack passes two students in front of the Student Union, engaged in a top-of-the-lungs, nose-to-nose argument. Plenty of bitch-this and bitch that, but no contact. How lovely. He walks on.

Another student jumps from behind a column and thrusts a piece of paper at him:

> **You were just a witness to an incident of lesbian domestic abuse . . .**
> **WHAT DID YOU DO ABOUT IT ??????**
>
> **This episode of guerilla street theater education brought to you by the St. Bernadette Gay-Lesbian-Bisexual-Transgender Alliance.**
> **TINA, adviser**

He looks up at the student's face, now consumed in self-righteousness, then back at the two performers—now silent, arms crossed, staring back—then back at the slip of paper.

"Oh, I see," says Jack. "So she doesn't *have* a last name?"

"What?!"

Jack comes to. "Nothing. Nothing. Thank you." *And* I'm *a threat to Catholicity*, he mutters as he canters off.

By eleven-thirty, Jack is exhausted beyond description, breathing hard and aching all over. He stops at last on a bench in the library entryway and is collecting himself, organizing the mass of papers into some semblance of order, when Amanda Corelli walks by on her way into the library.

"Oh, hi Dr. Kassel!"

Jack puts up his hand and manages to gasp, *"Amanda!"* He takes a few more breaths to regain control. "Sit down, please."

She does. "What is it?"

He slaps the pile of posters down on the bench between them.

"Oh. Those. Yeah, I saw that. I figured you'd be pretty freaked out."

"Oh, did you? How insightful, my goodness, you've only known me for, what, six months, and already you know that I would be freaked out by LOSING MY JOB?!"

"Hey, don't go postal on me, bucko. This is Void's thing now. I don't have any control over what he does. Voice of the people and all."

"Why don't you climb back into bed with the son-of-a-bitch, that seems to get his atten . . ."

Her face goes stricken with disbelief. "You did *not* just say that. You did *not* just suggest to one of your students that she *fuck* somebody to get . . ."

"No, no, *dammit* Amanda, lower your voice," he hisses, looking back and forth, smiling unconvincingly at eavesdropping passersby. "No, I didn't mean that, I'm just upset."

"Sexual harassment and all that, you know."

"I know. I'm sorry, I'm sorry I said that. But I'm looking for a pound of your flesh, too, not just Void's." He grits his teeth. *"You never wrote that letter!"*

"What lett . . . oh, *that* one. The 'clarifier.' No, I guess I didn't."

"You guess you didn't. Amanda, I am on the Dean's List right now, and *not* in the happy way. And *you* are one of the people who put me there! She called me on the carpet this morning, made me look like a damned idiot by mentioning *exactly the thing I told you to address in your letter*—and right after I had made a high-and-mighty speech about being allowed to live my life with integrity."

"Ooo, ouch."

"Yeah, *ouch*. It was made clear to me that one more screwup will get me fired. And these—" He punches an index finger repeatedly into the top of the poster pile "—these have all the marks of a first-class screwup. With my *name* on it, a touch I especially appreciated."

". . ."

Jack picks up the top poster from the pile and scans it with contempt. "And what is this, his last name is really *Shakespeare?* What the hell is that?"

"What, you thought his first name was really *Void?*"

Jack slaps the poster back on the pile. "You, Miss Corelli, are going to redeem yourself by helping me scour the rest of the campus until there's not a single poster left anywhere. I've already done Bronte and Admin, Curie, Hildegard, but I haven't even been to the dorms or . . ."

"I can't do that, Dr. Kassel."

"What, you have a class?"

"No, I have a conscience. I'm not in charge anymore. You still have a title in the club, so you can do what you want, but Void's the president now. I'm just a member."

"Oh," he snorts. "Oh that's rich. Suddenly all full of conscience are you, Amanda? I could have used a dose of your conscience to write that letter while you *were* still president!"

"Dr. Kassel, I'm sorry you ended up in a bad situation because I didn't write that letter, but I still think it was the right decision. Otherwise we would never have been able to . . ."

"To what? Been able to what?" He grabs a handful of posters and holds them in Amanda's face. "Create *this?* Well Heaven forfend we ever did something that allowed me to hang on to some integrity *and* wiped out the platform for our friendly neighborhood Satanist."

"Now you're stereotyping again, Dr. Kassel, you can't just . . ."

"Amanda, if you aren't helping me, you're slowing me down. I have a pitiful little career to save. Goodbye."

Jack scoops up the pile and begins to walk out.

"Dr. Kassel . . ." Jack stops and turns with a look of lost patience. Amanda walks to him and, without meeting his eyes, slowly extends a tattered piece of paper, folded and unfolded many times. Jack takes it silently and watches as she walks away.

FEDERAL BUREAU OF INVESTIGATION
FIELD REPORT
TOP SECRET–EYES ONLY

AGENT ID:001392
SUPVSR:003781
OPERATION: RODIN
FILE DATE:13 NOV 1999

FIFTY-THIRD MEETING OF THE EXECUTIVE COMMITTEE OF THE REVOLUTIONARY PHI-LOSOPHERS FRONT OF AMERICA (RPFA), 11 NOV 1999 22:15:00 HRS

Meeting began as always with call by Subject FAL-LOWS for approval of minutes of previous meeting. Objection raised as always by subject SUVENAL based on unreliability of memory. SUVENAL was immediately shouted down and subsequently left the room, shouting in what seemed to be Latin or Greek.

Subject WHITTIER called for resumption of ongoing topic regarding planned armed insurrection against the government of the United States.

Subject FALLOWS called for justification of such an insurrection under Just War Theory. Subject WHITTIER interrupted, claiming no such requirement for moral justification exists, citing "consequentialist/intrinsicist" and "act-utilitarian" moral arguments that mitigate against the need for or possibility of morality in war. [AGENT INTERPOLATION: PLEASE RECONSIDER MY URGENT REQUEST FOR TRANSFER OUT OF THIS ASSIGNMENT. I AM WILLING TO PUT SAID REQUEST IN THE STRONGEST POSSIBLE TERMS OUTSIDE THE FORMALITY OF THE REPORT FORMAT. PLEASE GET ME OUT OF HERE.]

FALLOWS suggested that a revolutionary action without an articulated justification would not receive the support of the population and would therefore fail, noting that "the justice of our position is self-evident and will be recognized." Subject JOHNSON noted that any concept of objective justice was highly suspect, and that their grievances were based on the highly subjective experience of being a disenfranchised philosopher—an experience not shared by the bulk of the population and therefore understood only "tertiarily," whatever the hell that means.

WHITTIER shouted something about ends justifying means and was hit in the side of the head by an eraser thrown by HARRISON-LEWIS, who then shouted "Utilitarian!" and was shouted down by several individuals, including HAYDEN, who referred to HARRISON-LEWIS as a "pencilneck dipstick" or something similar.

HARRISON-LEWIS suggested that HAYDEN "suck eggs," at which point the meeting disintegrated into several simultaneous loud and occasionally physical exchanges between individuals in twos and threes, ending without formal adjournment shortly after midnight.

[POSTSCRIPT: IT IS THE STRONGLY-HELD OPINION OF THIS AGENT THAT OPERATION RODIN CAN AND SHOULD BE DISCONTINUED, IMMEDIATELY, WITHOUT DELAY. OVER SEVEN YEARS OF CLOSE OBSERVATION HAVE LED THIS AGENT TO THE INESCAPABLE CONCLUSION THAT THE RPFA COULD NOT COOPERATIVELY BOIL WATER, MUCH LESS CONSTITUTE A THREAT TO THE SAFETY AND SECURITY OF THE UNITED STATES GOVERNMENT.]

————END OF REPORT————

17

Our Lady of Victory

The Quarterly *Desert Candle* carries this story of a West
Texas Visitation:

Week before Christmas, 1996.
Juanita in her kitchen at Fort Stockton,
making tortillas for her family's dinner,
her mind not on the meal but on her son
(died in the line of Border Patrol duty some years before)
and of how terribly lonely Christmas would be without him.

                    When she sat
at table with her family ready to eat,
she served a few tortillas and then noticed
one in particular: "When I went to eat it,
I saw the donkey! I saw the ears and head,
and then the legs, and then I saw the Virgin
Mary riding, holding the Baby Jesus!"

It seems to her that even in West Texas
Jesus comes visiting sometimes,

that in this Blessèd Tortilla was writ
the Word of God.
So she kept this epiphanous tortilla,
which lightened the burthen of her grief somewhat,
and has it still.

When, recently, in Alpine,
the Desert Candle made a photocopy
of the tortilla, the contrast in the print
clarified the image enough to see—
well, look for yourselves, examine the tortilla:
the burro, Mary, Jesus, AND JOSEPH TOO!

To the Editor, *Desert Candle:*
Sir, your article concerning the tortilla
with revelatory powers was really no big deal.
I have at home: a partially cooked chupatti
showing a living likeness of the Buddha;
great Krishna limned in a popadam; a nacho
clearly depicting Jupiter enthroned;
Mahomet's profile on a Hershey Bar;
and all Olympus in a blueberry muffin.

from the poem *Marfan* by Peter Reading

Tuesday afternoon brings an annual obligation the Dean
simply hates—the March Midwest CollegeFest, a
three-day orgy of shameless self-promotion to late-shopping
high school seniors featuring over 600 participating colleges
and universities in ten Midwestern states. This year Dean Martin is to be accompanied by Coach Phaire, hot after new field
hockey prospects, and Diane Tomitcha and Lisa Carr, the current overeager twenty-somethings in Admissions. The Dean

gave careful and covert instructions to Latifah to reserve seats with at least ten rows between her and the two little gleeboxes, solely to avoid conversations that might be hard on the cheekbones.

Coach Phaire always flies first-class and pays the difference herself.

What a shame we can't sit together, Dean Martin moans to the two birdcalls-with-legs as they board—perhaps a bit too sincerely, for both immediately manage to chirp and twitter their ways into seat swaps with the two silent-looking men on either side of the Dean.

Genevieve Martin sits with a thud and immediately immerses herself deep into C. S. Lewis' *Mere Christianity*, eyes glued to the page with focused intensity, raising a single finger of *not-now-not-now* whenever one of the two gets a superneat idea for conversation.

Gerard is mopping up the water in Leonard Holdenmiller's office when he sees it. This winter the mold revived more quickly than usual after his New Year's Day window opening, so he tried again around Groundhog Day. Now, in late March, it's back and looking ambitious.

"You all need another lesson 'bout who's in charge here?" he says, smiling at the fungal civilization. "This ain't your office, you know. I'll just clean the slate again, teach you a lesson, you ain't learned nothin'." He moves to the window and starts to work the crank, stiff and stubborn as the floodgates of Heaven, he reckons. When the window is half open, Gerard catches a distinctive shape out of the corner of his eye, out on the green, so clear in fact that it startles a *Sweet Jesus!* out of him. He slaps the soaked towels into a bucket and races down the hall and out of the building, stopping with the amazing sight in full view.

"*Sweet, sweet Mother of God!*"

The hotel is every bit the opulent palace one would expect in an airport business lodge. But the Dean arranged for her own room—and no roommates for the birds to swap with. That counts for opulence at this stage of life. She kicks off her shoes, pulls a container of Slim Jims from her luggage and throws herself on the bed, which responds with that satisfying double-bounce. She dangles one Slimmy from her mouth, grabs the remote and punches buttons until CNN comes up.

". . . press secretary confirmed that President Bush had indeed intended to call for sanctions on Serbia when he said 'The U.S. shuns surfing in sangria.'"

"In religious news, a small Catholic women's college in Minnesota was the site today of what its president called 'rapturous joy' upon the appearance of what is claimed to be an apparition of the Virgin Mary."

Dean Martin bolts upright in bed, jerky jutting like a petrified tongue.

"The College of Saint Bernadette, located roughly 200 miles due southwest of Minneapolis, is a quiet campus, and was seemingly unprepared for this level of national attention. The image itself is unusual among such so-called apparitions in that it is enormous—over forty feet high and thirty feet wide—and rendered in a semi-permanent medium, the branches of a hundred-year old oak tree in the center of campus."

The Dean rises slowly to her feet, eyes riveted to the image provided by a circling news helicopter as she walks toward the glowing screen with disbelief and a rising pulse. The bare, snow-rimmed branches of the huge oak at the top of the college green form a startlingly detailed three-dimensional human head. I never noticed that before, she thinks. The nose is clearly and artfully rendered, and the mouth and eyes, all framed in a graceful drape of feminine hair. The effect is striking, the look somewhat severe, almost medieval in its aspect—and definitely triumphant. Beautiful. Our Lady of Victory, this one.

"The Blessed Virgin has chosen the College of Saint Bernadette as the site of her most glorious Visitation!!" Oh Lord, it's Wanda; Genevieve Martin holds her breath and listens from a helpless distance. "She calls the faithful to gather, gather at this place as the Holiest Week of our year approaches! Surely she will reveal her blessed will to us if only we will gather and listen! So come! Come, all ye faithful!!"

Joan Krenek's bookends begin singing the eponymous carol in the background as CNN cuts back to the anchor and a stunning development in the hogbellies market. Fully two minutes pass as the Dean continues staring at the TV, glued to the bed, jerky erect. Somehow the tree is still there on the screen, the nuns still singing, giving her time to think.

She clicks off the remote and falls back onto the bed, staring at the ceiling.

You're the one who made me a skeptical thinker, Lord. If I were a more credulous sort of gal—I'm just not, You know that—but if I were, I might consider this the answer to my earlier question.

I'd prefer not. I add that just in case it matters. I'd rather this were still just a projection, Lord. This kind of thing doesn't lead to anything good, You must certainly know that if I do.

Okay, tell you what. If this is just another projection of their hopes and my fears, and not a message from Your Holy Mother . . . say nothing.

". . ."

Well that's a relief.

If I needed another reason to skip dinner with the birds, she says aloud, this is it. She calls Room Service, has the front desk put a block on her phone, hangs the DND on the knob.

And just in time, it turns out, for within three minutes of

the broadcast she hears the approach of excited twittering in the hall. They flutter about her door for half a minute, then fly away in search of a seed bell or some such. Mercifully, thinks the Dean. I need some time here.

The next morning she is out of bed, showered, fed by Room Service, and stalking through the auditorium foyer at 6:05 a.m., miles ahead of all other exhibitors. But not ahead of all the student shoppers, as she can tell by the excited, late-adolescent treble buzz coming from the auditorium proper. She walks in to see 600 unattended booths and a single serpentine line of no fewer than two hundred young women, some sitting, some standing, weaving from the back of the auditorium around the center island of displays. She follows the line, nodding and smiling when necessary. Halfway into the halflit space she spots their destination ahead, a single exhibit stall, as of yet unmanned. Must be Notre Dame or Purdue, she thinks. Why the megaschools even bother coming I haven't a clue. She pulls out her glasses and squints to read the distant banner over the popular stall:

The College of St. Bernadette

A Catholic Liberal Arts College for Women • Saint Philip, Minnesota
Founded in 1895

Dean Martin stops in her tracks and looks up and down the line with a growing dread realization. Crystals. Flowered crosses. Actual *guitars*. Peasant dresses. Expressions of utter contentment and joy.

Oh shit. It's *them*.

"Look, here she is!! She's from Saint Bernadette's!!" someone shrieks, pointing at Gennie Martin's nametag as the line erupts into screams and quickly wraps around the startled Dean, shouting questions and acclamations.

Please take my name! Take my name!
I want to be with the Blessed Mother!
How can I get a message to the Blessed Mother?
Has the Blessed Mother spoken yet?
I am prepared for the End Time!
I want to be a Bernie!
Praise God in His Heaven!
Have you had visions?
Has she spoken to you? Tell us! Tell us!
Praise Jesus, Saviour of the World!
Do your dorms have single rooms?
Praise Mary, Holy Mother of the Living God!

Everything goes fuzzy for awhile.

When she comes to, Genevieve Martin finds herself weaving through traffic on Michigan Avenue at sixty miles an hour in her little rental car, pedestrians diving for safety as she deadheads to O'Hare.

Date: Tue, 19 Mar 2002 23:51:15 -0500
Subject: Its me again
X-Attach:

Where are you??? PLEASE, I need to talk to you, its really important, and I can't find you anywhere. I tried to leave messages on the phone but your voicemail is full. PLEASE tell me where you are, thanks

"So we meet at last! Please, please sit down. I must tell you there's some damn fine work of the Lord being done out at your place, just colossal stuff. And I know as well as anyone that it doesn't happen by itself. You're a man who gets things done, and I like that."

"I might say the same for you, Congressman. I've been a close follower of all you've done for the past twenty years. No one contributed more to making the Reagan years what they were. I and a lot of others will never forget the stands you took then. Never."

"You're too kind, really Father, it was a team effort . . ."

"Oh, you're too *modest*, Congressman! It was always clear who the point man was. Every time another Democratic big-government tax-and-spend scheme was rolled out to feed those God chose to make hungry or to house those God chose to make homeless, it was Peter D'Angelo rolling it right back in!"

"Well, I've always considered myself a public servant first and . . ."

"And you and James Watt, why, we would never have discovered what really was under all that timberland if the D'Angelo-Massey amendment didn't give the green light to . . . oh, what was it you called it then, that delightful turn-of-phrase . . . ?"

D'Angelo smiles, remembering. *"Displace."*

"That's right . . . to *displace* the wasted wildlands that were just sitting there covering up the cornucopia of our God-given national resources."

"You know, no matter how long I serve my country, it still humbles me to hear from those whose lives I've touched in some small way."

"Oh, no small way, Congressman. You touched my life and influenced my values more than any other public servant of your generation. And I never dreamed I'd be given the opportunity to return the favor. Never in my wildest dreams."

"Yet here you are, in the nation's capital, sitting in my office, working out the details of the greatest political favor of which I am currently in need."

"A dream come true."

"Is this not a great country, Father Siberell?"

"God bless America!"

"Long may it wave!"

The first car arrives at 7:25 p.m. Tuesday night, just an hour after the CNN story broke. Inside is a family of six that piled directly into the station wagon in Saint James and drove straight to the College, leaving six steaming bowls of succotash and a roast chicken on the dining room table for the cat.

At 9:05, the first out-of-state plate rolls in on the back of a 1981 Dodge Aries "K" from South Dakota, calico rust-on-white, papal flag flying jubilantly from the antenna.

By ten o'clock the line is nearly continuous, a double snake of headlights stretching into the darkness toward the eastern horizon. Horns sound intermittently, clearly expressions not of anger or impatience but of uncontrollable joy and anticipation.

By dawn, just over twelve hours have passed since the CNN story, and it is clear to all involved that a happening is happening. A happy camp of refugees has sprung up in the darkness, filling and finally overflowing the parking lot, simultaneously conjuring and dwarfing memories of past such camps— Hoovervilles, Woodstock, Camp OJ—with a monumental scatter of cars, tents, shrines, handpainted signs, craft displays and souvenir tables under a dull gray sky. No Twin Cities television station is unrepresented, so a skyline of satellite dishes and antennae lends the camp a third dimension and an air of technological sophistication and terrible relevance.

A small detachment of the Saint Philip Police Force sits, amused and warm, in a running squad car, the traffic control they were dispatched to perform rendered unnecessary by the incessant *please-you-gos, no-you-firsts,* and *God-bless-yous* among arriving drivers.

And—passing slowly through each gate on foot, three abreast—lines of solemn people, emitting a regular series of gasps as each entering sextet catches full sight of the image of the Virgin Mary, Mother of God, Our Lady of Victory, smiling down upon them from the top of the gentle slope. Each line continues up its respective flagstone walk, joining at the top of the wedge and feeding a silent, undulating circle beginning about twenty feet out from the trunk. Many of those present are deep in prayer, some clutching rosaries, many crossing themselves repeatedly, most in some degree of quiet, overwhelmed tearfulness. There is a steady, somehow apologetic click and flash of cameras. An almost imperceptible but definite hum thought at first to be a manifestation of the holy presence is later realized with some disappointment to be the collective whir of a hundred videocameras.

After viewing the Head for a while, certain of the faithful split off and walk gingerly back down the mud-slick wedge to do the labyrinth, now completely visible in dead grass after a week's thaw. A continuous, tight line weaves, slow and halting, around the pattern to the hopelessly-packed center. Thus does the solitary journey to Jerusalem come to resemble the line into Space Mountain on Labor Day weekend.

Around the miraculous celebration, the College does its best to function as if it were just another Wednesday. But by late morning, several members of the faculty are independently circling the circle, including among others a fascinated

Jack Kassel, a snide Brian Finnegan, and a transfixed Joan Krenek, each in search of a different confirmation.

By 11:30, the miracles have begun in earnest. Mrs. Frieda Groot of Bemidji, Minnesota finds the rosary she lost seven months ago, tucked beneath the front passenger seat of her Buick Riviera. The Lundgren twins simultaneously get over the nasty sore throats they've been trying to shake for four days. Carl Holtz's wife Gertie opens her mailbox to find a letter announcing that she may very well have already won ten million dollars. The air temperature hits forty-one degrees, a full four degrees higher than the prediction. And miraculously, less than eighteen hours after the news broke, Edgar Dorfman Enterprises of Minnetonka opens a concession trailer offering no fewer than six silk-screen T-shirt designs with the day, date and photo of the miracle and your choice of a half-dozen scriptural or liturgical quotations for just $27 each, $32.50 for long sleeves.

All proceeds, of course, to be carried straight to the Throne of Yahweh, minus expenses.

Jack Kassel, circling at the periphery, feels compelled to gawk at the crowd like a passing motorist at a ten-car pileup on a sunny afternoon: fascinating, compelling, unusual, a little grotesque, and, as far as he is concerned, utterly without explanation. Every face, every one without fail, without exception, is locked in beatific calm. Every gesture of every person is slow, flowing, as if the whole wedge were immersed in twenty feet of clear gelatin. The occasional cries of children are only cause for their parents to scoop them up and radiate profound joy over the very miracle of life. "Peace" is the preferred greeting offered Jack by passing beatifs—very hippie, very Berkeley, he notes—though "Joy" is a close second, followed by "hey."

In the relative open spaces outside the circle are the Gliders, young women all. One favorite procedure is to glide several steps forward then *rise-on-toes*, then several steps again and *rise-on-toes*, ad infinitum. The more imaginative add a twirl every few cycles, and some a high kick right after every third *rise-on-toes*. Arms move in what seem to Jack to be stereotypical little-girl ballet gestures, probably gleaned from a childhood in the tutu line of the local Nutcracker. One young woman glides by, early twenties at best, under a purple velvet Renaissance Faire cap, long narrow feather arcing gracefully downward into the small of her back. In her outstretched hand is the long, light branch of a tree—presumably not snapped off the Mother of God—which she sweeps through the gelatin ahead of her as she glides, left to right, right to left, on the periphery of the crowd, brimming with unbridled peace and absolute certainty that this, this precisely, is what she is meant to be doing at this moment.

Walking casually is made nearly impossible by spontaneous Kneelers. Jack sees one Glider go right over a Kneeler and into a positively gymnastic somersault recovery—which trippee and tripper both clearly recognize as a miracle.

Deep within the circle itself are apparently several Ecstatic Screamers. Every three minutes or so, one of them, overcome with Spirit, shouts something to the effect of "The Queen of Heaven is our hope of Peace!" or "Mother Mary, intercede for our troubled world!" One erupts so near Jack that he jumps.

"Ah, Dr. Kassel, you must be enjoying all this immensely."

Again Jack jumps. It's the Voice of the Dean on his other side. "Oh, Dean, hello, you startled me! I . . . what do you mean?"

"Well, I imagine this is what you think we're all about, we fools. I would probably think the same in your position."

"Oh no. Well, at least I've never seen you yourself as the charismatic type."

"And in this context, I'll take that as a compliment."

"Intended. Of *course* I don't generalize this to all Christians or even all Catholics." He notices her pursed lips and eyebrows. "And I'm guessing from your expression that you are less than thrilled. Or else you just ate a serraño pepper and don't want to let on."

"I," she says, drawing out her words for emphasis, "am less . . . than . . . thrilled. Well understated, Dr. Kassel."

"Good exposure for the college, though, yes?"

"Good exp . . ." She swallows it. "*No.* Exposure yes, good *no.* I want just about exactly what you want for this college, Dr. Kassel, believe it or not, that it be a place alive with *mind.* A thinking place. If you know *that* and then think *this*," she gestures flippantly at the tree, "is going to please me, well, then, your skull isn't exactly alive with mind, either. *This,* right here, not your little rational humanist group, *this* is Genevieve Martin's personal nightmare. One sidestep like this can overturn twenty years of building toward an actual college here. Entropy is a real force, you know. You've got to fight to keep the nuts from taking over, no matter what your particular battle is, 'cause there's nothing to be done once the lid's off. That's what lids are for. I stopped watching this pot for one day, *one day,* and here's where we are." She looks him hard in the face. "What kind of students or faculty do you think are even going to *consider* this place from now on?"

"What kind," Jack asks reflexively, needlessly, envisioning lids spinning end over end, flung high by the pressure in their pots.

The Dean makes a slow sweep with one upturned hand. "Look around you. Just look around. Here's our future, Dr. Kassel. Not good news for your *Weltanschauung* nor mine. Prepare to revise your lectures to cover the philosophy of mystic revelation."

She *pffts,* then turns to begin working her way through the crowd toward Admin. A few steps away, she turns around again. "And by the way, Dr. Kassel—don't think any of this changes what we talked about. Your escapades are less welcome than ever now." Oh, don't dare try that look of puzzled

innocence, Jack Kassel, she thinks. She glances around, then
steps back within discreet range. Looks him dead in the eye.

"Just what do you think would happen to these happy
crusaders if they bethought themselves amidst the very spawn
of Satan, hmm?" Her eyebrow slowly ascends, erasing as it
goes any hope Jack has that she is merely being droll. "Trust
me here, Jack. This little gathering is a double-edged sword.
Swings one way, off with my head. Swings the other, off with
yours. It is in your considerable interest to keep the sword
still," she says, softly—"for when it comes right down to it,
Dr. Kassel, and that blade starts moving—let's just say I have
a real talent for controlling the direction of swing."

She keeps her gaze locked on precisely as long as needed
to ascertain Jack's total comprehension—about two seconds—
then breaks it, turning away to disappear in the crowd.

A deep dread begins to tighten Jack's stomach as he thinks
of the upcoming meeting of the association. And his mind is
without form. And Void.

He begins to slowly orbit the outer edge of the circle,
looking at the tree from every angle, and runs into Brian doing the same.

"Brian."

"Jack."

". . ."

". . ."

"Okay, Dr. Finnegan. What do you make of this?"

"Well, I can make a hat, a brooch . . ."

Jack looks up at the tree. "Seriously, give me a rational
explanation."

"For what, Jack? The tree? It is a tree. Trees are indig-
enous to Earth. They grow in many shapes."

"But you've got to admit this pretty clearly . . ."

". . . looks like a human head? Sure. Always has. There
are precedents, you know. See 'Man in the Moon'—*also* not
an actual person, according to stunning new research."

"Well this is a little different, wouldn't you say? You aren't saying it's *always* . . ."

"First of all, look closely. There's no left ear. Would God leave off his mom's left ear? And the eyes are pretty Picasso-esque at best. The whole right side of the face is melting like she's had a stroke. Maybe she has, I dunno, she's a couple thousand years old."

"So explain why we suddenly see it so clearly if it's always been that way."

"That tree has always looked a little face-ish, Jack, I thought so the first winter I was here. But you can't see that when the leaves are on, right, and in the middle of winter most of us have our eyes down hard to the ground to keep from slipping off the damn Wedge. And I said it looked a *little* face-ish. Then what special event happened last week that might transform the shape of a tree? Think back, Jack. Harp music and waaaaaavy lines . . ."

Oh yeah. The ice storm.

"An ice storm, Jack, and it sheared off a dozen branches on that one tree—which happened to be the dozen that made the difference between sort of face-ish and the Mother of God. Pretty funny."

Jack looks up at the tree again and sees the fresh breaks for the first time. Deep down a tiny disappointed sigh he'll admit to. "What about the possibility that God sent the ice storm in order to sculpt the tree this way?"

"Uh huh." Brian waits a moment for the other shoe. "Well, I'm on my way to lunch. You going?"

"No, not yet."

Brian shuffles off toward the Student Union.

Not that I spend a lot of time wishing for God, Jack thinks, but a little mystery—just an occasional shadow on the face of rational certainty, once in a while—well, it's not a bad sensation while it lasts, but I guess I wouldn't want to live there. I guess.

At noon the chapel bells ring the assembled into a deep hush. The campus undergoes a transformation, evident to all present, as something beautiful begins to happen. It is, like most truly beautiful things, a combination of intention and circumstance—part creation, part evolution. As the bells go silent, a lone voice in the crowd begins singing the *Ave Maria*—Schubert's—gloriously, reverently. *Ave Maria, Jungfrau mild.* A few voices join, then all, flowering into full four-part harmony, perfect, unrehearsed. Many seem to know the entire text, others just the tune, singing *ooooo*, making a sound like a glorious human pipe organ. Babies sit silent in their mothers' arms. Several grown men suddenly burst into uncontrollable weeping.

And only now, somehow, in the midst of the exquisite sound, does Jack begin to see the wheelchairs. Dozens of them, scattered throughout the crowd—each with a form, frail and blanketed against the cold. And crutches, and leg braces—how did they manage to get up this grade, Jack wonders. To his right he sees a little girl in a flowered dress, maybe ten years old, holding a crucifix and clutching her mother, who weeps and sings and clutches back, her other hand placed gently atop the girl's bare scalp. It also becomes evident to Jack that not all of the adults are twenty-somethings in velveteen caps. Many, even most, are older, much older, seventies, eighties, often supported at the elbow by someone. Many are stooped so severely Jack again wonders at what must have been a perilous trip up the Wedge. Some tremble with palsy. All are singing, every one.

And just as the song reaches its reluctant end, the sun breaks and bathes the campus in a sudden glowing warmth, and everyone hugs someone. Even Jack. Beautiful serendipity.

Or another miracle.

He stands completely still, eyes closed, absorbing the moment, the tangible feeling of goodwill and hope and optimism . . . what a glorious coming-together of intention and circum . . .

"Dr. Kassel," the voice startles Jack from behind, "now *how* you can hear that, and see all these wonderful souls gathered together, and feel all this joy," says Joan Krenek, as she wipes the tears from her eyes, "and still not believe—well, Dr. Kassel, I must admit it is beyond me."

Oh not *now.* Jack suddenly sympathizes with Sister Vera's plea to be left alone.

"Sister Joan, I . . . Look, I know very well how I must seem to you from where you stand. All I can say is that that was one of the most beautiful things I've ever been a part of, just . . . *spellbinding.* I don't know how to say it. I struggle for words, but . . ."

"The word you are struggling for, Dr. Kassel, is *God.*"

"Sister, with all respect . . ." Jack hesitates. "Joan, I don't want to violate this moment for either one of us with argumentation. Another time, perhaps."

"We're just talking, Jack. To be honest, I consider this a teachable moment."

Jack sighs hard. "Okay. Sister, I can assure you that a feeling of wonder and awe is not in the *least* incompatible with disbelief in God. I can attest to that. I experience wonder and awe on a regular basis. It's what makes life worth living."

"And? Then what do you do with that feeling?"

"I *experience* it, Joan. I let it wash over me. But the idea that I *must* respond to any feeling of wonder by offering thanks to an imaginary . . ." He sighs again. "Joan, I understand the impulse, I can't say I haven't felt it myself. But I am convinced beyond a reasonable doubt that the God of Christianity does not exist and therefore isn't waiting for my thank you notes."

Sister Joan contains a wave of revulsion admirably. "Beyond a reasonable doubt, Dr. Kassel? How is it that you have come to this certainty that has so evaded all the rest of us?"

"First of all, Joan, it is not 'all the rest of you.' I am not the only person on Earth with these convictions."

"Granted."

"And the answer to your question is this: I really, truly always wanted to know the truth about things, right from the beginning. I didn't want to deceive myself. So when it came to the question of God, I went to church—I went to churches in nine denominations, as a matter of fact. I read the Bible, over and over. I questioned, I conversed. I sought out the best arguments on every side. I studied science, but I also studied theology. I *prayed*, Joan, You know, I *still* pray on occasion, fervently, earnestly, tapping out an urgent request for anyone who might be listening. I have not stopped asking questions, even though no reasonable doubt remains for me."

"So why pray?"

Jack pauses. "*Unreasonable* doubt, Joan. That's all. That's how serious I am. Every sign in the universe points to a complete renunciation of the tenets of Christian faith, Joan. If you approach it honestly, it simply falls to pieces. But I keep the phone on the hook just in case I've missed something."

"That doubt in your mind is *God*, Jack!"

Sword or no sword, his patience for this sort of thing, wearing thin for years, is beginning to show bare patches. "So you suggest, Joan, that even the tiniest grain of uncertainty in every area of life should automatically be filled with *God?* And not just *a* God, but *your* God? Doesn't that strike you as the height of arrogance if you think about it for two seconds?"

"There are just too many 'coincidences' to say that your uncertainty is tiny. How is it, for example, that the life of Christ so perfectly fulfilled Old Testament prophecy? How does your rationalism deal with *that* kind of evidence!"

"How do I deal with the fact that the Gospel evangelists

sat with the OT in their laps and, what do you know, wrote the life of Christ in perfect fulfillment of OT prophecies? Are you *serious?*" His voice has risen sufficiently to draw more than a few stares.

Joan huffs. "Okay, this is indeed becoming argumentative."

"Uh huh. Like I said. Joan, look, I'm sorry, I really do want you to be free to make up your own mind. Goodness knows I would not force my process on you, but can't you acknowledge my right to proceed *my* own way as well?"

"My beliefs teach that your soul is in peril. I would be remiss in my Christian duties if I did not pursue your salvation, regardless of your own resistance."

True enough. Jack looks up at the tree. "Joan, if you are right and I am wrong, my soul will burn in Hell for all eternity. The fact that I know that and *still* hold the convictions I hold—the fact that I am willing to look Pascal in the eye and take him up on his Wager—doesn't that catch your attention just a bit? Doesn't it make you want to know what it is that is so convincing to me that I'll willingly take that risk?"

"To which I simply say that . . ."

"That your convictions are equally strong? Granted. Never denied. Not the point. The point is that you risk nothing by your beliefs. In fact, you believe that you gain eternal life through them. I embrace my views not because I stand to gain from them but because I'm convinced they are true, *despite* the consequences. If I'm right, it's oblivion. If I'm wrong, eternal peril."

"How horrible a choice!"

"Oh no, not at all. Well, your Hell doesn't appeal to me, but I'm well enough convinced that it's oblivion that awaits us to focus on that. And if you get your mind around what non-existence really, truly means, it's quite a lovely and elegant alternative to eternal boredom, I should say. You are . . . and then," *snap*, "you're not."

Joan's revulsion begins to froth over a bit. "You were right, Jack. A bit of the joy is removed from the moment."

"I'm sorry, Joan, really I am. I think we can both enjoy wonder as long as we don't get into each other's bubbles too much."

"Agreed. Well, I have obligations."

"It's been a pleasure, Joan."

"Yes. I suppose it has."

Date: Wed, 20 Mar 2002 06:51:35 -0500

---

i dont understand why you wont answer me, i dont know if i did something wrong or if its true what i have to talk to you about. i am so afriad, please call me. please

HAIL holy Queen, Mother of mercy, our life, our sweetness, and our hope. To thee do we cry, poor banished children of Eve. To thee do we send up our sighs, mourning and weeping in this valley of tears. Turn then, most gracious Advocate, thine eyes of mercy toward us.
And after this our exile show unto us the blessed fruit of thy womb, Jesus.
O clement, O loving, O sweet Virgin Mary. Amen.

Remember, O most gracious Virgin Mary, that never was it known that anyone who fled to thy protection, implored thy help, or sought thy intercession, was left unaided.

Scott's Thursday morning flight into Minneapolis/Saint Paul is rockier than usual but he barely notices. A religious man could be forgiven for imagining that God was not only in his corner but that the Big Guy had placed some serious cash on him. Six and a half years down, three days to go, and the added incentive of Peter D'Angelo's head on a plate—God, it's just too much to process at once. Just keep the head down, script in mind, focus, *focus*. This is when perfectly-thrown passes get dropped.

By the time the Wedge appears through his smeared windshield it's nearly four o'clock. He hoots to himself at the emerging profile of Marianapolis—the growth of which he's been enjoying via satellite— and wonders giddily what this development will add to the stew. Nothing but spice, he's sure. *Heat.*

As he weaves his car through the makeshift settlement toward the parking lot—recently half-cleared by the police to allow the campus to continue a semblance of normal function—he spots what he quickly decides is his favorite thing yet: a ratty-looking bus with five cheerleaders, yes cheerleaders, or the late-middle age equivalent, on the roof, dressed in gold lamé with white cowboy hats, jumping and kicking and leading pro-Mary cheers for the assembled throng:

> "Big **M**, little **A**, little **R**, little **Y**
> **M-A-R-Y,** *Queen on High!*
> Be with US in our little ol' BUS
> And again in the hour that we *die, die, die!*"

Their lock on Scott's affections is confirmed when he sees the faded lettering on the side of the bus:

Praise God and Hail Mary! From Tulsa, Oklahoma, it's the world-famous

Marianettes!

Award-Winning Liturgical Pep Squad and Drill Team

He leans out the window and woos from the bottom of his heart.

The chapel is exactly the mess he'd expected. ABC has begun installing the lights, microphones, and miles of cables that, for fourteen weeks anyway, will bring "Live from Nurse Chapel" to the nation—first just nine million, sure, thinks Scott, but Easter's gonna be thirty million easy. Word gets out, always does. Wait and see.

A total of eleven cameras will be installed, he has been breathlessly informed, including one they've dubbed GodCam, a fully-zoom-capable camera affixed to the ceiling, looking down benevolently on the altar and the host.

Scott walks into his office to a blinking light and thirty-six messages. Yeah right, he thinks. Later, if you're all very, very lucky, which you are NOT. *Heh.* E-mail is worse, eighty-one, *eighty-one*, son of a *bishop*, what the hell has Haley been doing? He shuts the computer down, grabs his coat and flips off the light.

Tomorrow brings still more Marians to the camp, now numbering nearly two thousand according to a brow-knitted joint press conference by the police chief and fire marshal. Wanda has found it impossible since the start of the Visitation to stay in her office or in a meeting for more than twenty minutes at a time. Fellow administrators have begun to complain that they glance down at their notes for reference, only to look up and find her gone. By the fourth day they've learned to go to the window and spot the whirling muu-muu—something of a challenge among the Marians.

Friday morning Scott's phone rings at 6:33. He swears and rolls over. Rings again at 6:37 and he puts the pillow over his head.

An hour later he checks messages. Latifah. Father Siberell, we've got messages for you piling up at the switchboard because your office voicemail is full, please get your messages, here are the ones that seemed urgent, don't expect me to be takin' your messages after today, empty your voicemail, Father, I've got Marians coming out the ears and don't need more to do, no disrespect, anyway, you've got three home visits that had been rescheduled while you were out of town, all of them for today, all in Saint Jude, Rita said you should have the addresses, where were you anyway for three days, nobody seemed to know. Okay. Some guy from ABC called the switchboard to check in with you because, as I said, your voicem . . ."

Message number two, Latifah, more pissed off, get a longer tape Father, no disrespect, anyway this ABC guy sounded pretty nervous because he couldn't talk to you right that minute, something about 'segment timings,' I don't know, not my job. Also a student was checked in to Saint Jude Medical Center late last night so you might want . . .

Beeeep. Scott smiles as he imagines Latifah's next words.

Father Siberell is collared and out the door by 8:15. Makes an end run around the Wedge and takes Z. Putter Blvd. into Saint Jude to polish off the four visits before going in to the mess in the office. Tucked just inside the city limits across from the Founder's Statue, the single-story Saint Jude Medical Center is his first stop. *Medical Center my high holy ass,* he always mutters as he pulls into the lot. Switches on Pastoral Baritone #4 and asks at Admitting which of the seven rooms might contain a St. Bernie's student who checked in last night.

Room 3, mutters the receptionist, gesturing with a pen without looking up from her papers, just that way down the corridor and left.

He thanks and blesses the receptionist, who seems unmoved, then walks down the short hallway to Room 3 and pushes open the door.

"Oh, sweet Jesus. Oh, sweet, sweet Mother of God!"

Hail Mary, full of grace. Our Lord is with thee. Blessed art thou among women, and blessed is the fruit of thy womb, Jesus. Holy Mary, mother of God, pray for us sinners, now, and in the hour of our death, Amen.

"She took an awful lot of pills, Father. This was not a cry for help, she was planning on checking out. She very nearly succeeded. She may yet, she's very, very critical. I don't think the last rites are out of the question."

Scott's eyes fill with tears as the respirator inhales and exhales and the pulse monitor traces the faint and unsteady heartbeat of Haley Gilbert.

"And I should hold back on this because why again?"

"Because I will lose my job, boom, one second after it hits the newsstand, with nowhere to go."

"And this is my problem because why?"

"..."

"Jack, I'm desperate here. You've got to give me something else then, another *major* lead, Dave has been leaning on me ever since this tree thing happened, he knows I have a husband at St. Bernie's . . ."

"Ex-husband."

"Thank you! Precisely why I'm wondering why I drop the story that could finally get me promoted just to save your neck."

"Okay, let me try 'father of your child.'"

"..."

"Uh huh. Thought so."

"What if I just profile the association without talking about Void? It would still make a great contrast piece to the whole Marian . . ."

"But the association *is* Void at the moment! That's the problem! And I call you up to cry on your shoulder a little, only to find out you want to make hay out of it."

"Okay . . . tell you what. I get to *make* hay or I get to *roll* in it. Which one. Your choice."

"Oh now *that* is sexual harassment, textbook."

"..."

"Nine o'clock."

"Eight. And you don't get a permanent extension. This buys you forty-eight hours. You fix up your little association into a—wha'd you say you wanted, a 'philosophers' coffee klatch'?—at the Saturday night meeting and I'll profile it nice and low-key for Monday. Lots and lots of euphemisms. But if Void is still boss on Sunday morning, I tell it like it is."

"Seven-thirty."

"Just get in your car."

"Father Siberell, this is Mike Lutz, campaign manager for Congressman D'Angelo. Father, the campaign got wind of that suicide attempt. Tragedy, of course, and apparently someone associated with your ministry, if my information is correct. Well, that needs to stay buried for a while, I'm sure you understand, at least until a few days after the annou . . ."

"This is Mike Lutz again from the D'Angelo campaign, your machine cut me off. I was just saying that this suicide attempt needs to be kept under wra . . ."

"Mike Lutz again, get a new machine, for Christ's sake! Oh, I'm sorr . . ."

father scott–i guess it was all true and thats why you wont talk to me any more. mandy always tried to say there was no god and i always told her no, she was wrong, and we would argue and sometimes i got scared because the things she said made me think maybe she could be right, and then i was so scared i thought i couldnt be saved because i wasnt keeping jesus in my heart but you always helped me find my way back. i didnt believe it when mandy told me her friend randi heard you talking in the bar about not believing in god and that you were going to do something terrible on the show on sunday. i didnt believe it then i went to my bible and your voice wasnt there any more. i couldnt hear you and i couldnt hear daddy and i couldnt hear god. why did you do this? why did you tell me those things if you didnt even think they were true? were you just making fun of me? why did you turn away from me? i dont know what to do. im sorry if i did something to make you turn away. im really really sorry, please dont hate me

Jack approaches Curie Hall on Saturday night with no real plan and little hope. The subwoofer thump of the music starts to work on his guts as he climbs the front stairs, the very sound and feel of rank stupidity and nihilism. The Lakota drummer, much further away, thumps in sync, perhaps in unspoken sympathy. Three Marians take advantage of the evening lull to do the labyrinth as it is intended—slowly, one at a time. A wall of intensity hits Jack as he opens the entrance door and forces himself toward and up the stairs and into the third floor lounge. The lights are off, save for a red strobe, and the room is pulsing with dancers.

Jack feels his way to the front, only to find Void enthroned on an enormous carved wood throne with three studded sidekicks on either side, muscular arms crossed.

"WHERE'S AMANDA?" Jack shouts over the throbbing bass.

"WHAT?"

"AMANDA CORELLI! WHERE'S AMANDA?"

"GONE! EASTER VACATION! ALL THE STIFFS ARE GONE BUT YOU!"

Oh. The last remaining stiff scans the room and confirms it. At least seventy bodies, none of them looking much like students, and not a single fellow stiff. Several of those present are clearly dancing at a very low altitude. A lone middle-aged stiff. He quickly runs three scenarios through his head for recapturing the association in this situation. Two won't work and the third involves several felonies.

Jack Kassel turns to walk from the room.

"HEY, STICK AROUND, DOC!" Void yells. "WE'VE GOT SOME KICK-ASS PLANS TONIGHT!"

He nods 'no doubt' over his shoulder and continues out the door.

By the time he's reached the college gate, Jack can no

longer hear or feel the music, though the Lakota drummer, ears unmolested from close range, is still apparently tuned in, thumping and smiling by his little gateside fire. The Marianettes are out in the camp in the midst of a fine bus-top show, with none other than Wanda X. Streamley herself up on the roof with them, tambourine high above her head, an expression of inexhaustible delight.

Jack lights a cigarette and continues walking into the darkness toward Saint Philip with visions of Marians and Satanists dancing in his head. About a half-mile east he stops, finds a roadside stump, and sits, looking back at the Wedge and the clear prairie sky behind and above it. Tries very hard to sit for five minutes without thinking so much as a single thought.

Can't do it.

That should be possible, shouldn't it, for me to just sit for five minutes and not think about anything? Come on. Buddhists do it. Mantra. Chant.

Ommmm.

Which is completely cheating, you're not doing nothing, you're using other crap to push out the original crap. Does not count. I should be able to clear all crap out of there for five lousy minutes, just five minutes of real mental oblivion. Here goes . . .

. . .

. . .

. . .

. . .

(Shooting star.)

Well that's not fair, like I'm not gonna register that. Try again.

. . .

. . .

. . .

. . .

. . .

(No shooting stars.)

Okay, fine. Maybe it's not possible. Descartes' fault, I guess. I stop thinking, I stop being. But I'd give a lot of cash right this minute to think of something other than Voids and Wandas.

You can't tell me that's really the choice, Wanda or Void. Brainless construction or brainless destruction? I'd swear there were other options once. Maybe not.

Man, it's getting cold.

Wait, another shooting star. Oh, hell, that was a flash of rhinestones from a Marianette boot heel. Then so was the first one, probably. Nothing worse than finding out what you thought was a shooting star was a damned rhinestone.

Oh.

Oh.

That's pretty much what Vera was saying, isn't it. Just leave us alone, she said. That's why they hate us so much. We take their shooting stars one by one and turn them into rhinestones. I'd hate us too.

Ooo, shooting star. No, really, right there.

I don't blame them for making up pretty stories, I guess. How can you blame them? We're on a little floating pull tab in the ocean of the cosmos; we're not here for any particular purpose; we live only as long as our bodies keep ticking and pumping and working just so; and eventually, no matter what we do, we're gonna die, and we don't know what happens then.

Is it rational to respond to all that with your eyes *open?* It's too horrible to stand, isn't it? So we close our eyes tight, make a wish. No uncertainty, no injustice, no purposelessness. Little world, one God, simple rules. Everything for a reason, even if we can't see it. We *matter*—in fact, we're terribly important—we are loved, and if we'll just buy the whole thing and stop looking for the man behind the curtain, the big reward: death is cancelled due to lack of interest. Sign me up.

Or maybe reality's just too *fantastic* to stand, too *wonderful* to grasp. Although what's the difference if you can't stand it, I suppose. I mean, look at the void up there—uh, I mean that vast nothingness. A dozen billion years, immense space sprinkled with lifeless elements, full of potential. Every possible chemical synthesis going on somewhere a trillion times over. Then—impossibly, or inevitably—amino acids, then proteins, then unicells, then multicells, then *Yo Yo Ma*. Forgive me if I find that much more wonderful than a Great Magician with a Yo Yo kit. And so now some of the rocks know that they *are*, that they exist. Matter that knows it exists—and knows that soon, very soon, after a quick look around, it'll be back in the ground, inert, unknowing. Too horrible, or too wonderful, I don't know. Ask Yo Yo. Which one is the rhinestone and which the shooting star, after all, the 6000-year old universe or one two million times older? All life created by magic, or all life related by blood? Eternal life, or terminal life? An afterlife Paradise that's a country club for the few—or no afterlife at all?

And is this really what I should be doing with my quick look around? Headscratching over the cosmos?

Better than big time wrestling, I guess. Better than selling widgets.

Shooting star. No wait, that's a steady glow, a steady yellow glow.

Star of Bethlehem?

Jack gets to his feet to the sound of applause not for him. Drumming. Muted wooing from the direction of campus. And a bright yellow glow at ground level, growing brighter.

A thousand feet closer he can see it's the Lakota fire, well-fed, growing into a bonfire, sparks flying skyward. Figures dancing around the fire, flashing light from every part of their anatomies. Shooting stars. Marianettes?

Satanists. Void. Walter. They're all out out of the Curie lounge and around the fire, jumping, writhing, dancing, singing, screaming, body studs flashing in the light, beating fifteen, twenty drums. Someone is playing a panpipe, two, three panpipes. Rattles, whistles.

Dithyramb. It's a damn *dithyramb.* Void did a little homework and worked up a pagan Bacchanal, minus the gutted goats and the gored bull. Well, not to jump to conclusions, I'm still a quarter mile away, Jack thinks. Not putting the livestock past him.

Reality sinks in. Goats or no goats, Dean, I'll go ahead and concede this as One Last Screwup. And I must say I shun the small screwups lately, he thinks as he walks, slowly but inexorably, making his way up to the edge of the Marian city. Nothing but the best, the biggest screwups for Jack, and this one in front of Wanda Streamley, what an elegant touch. Here's your story, Becca. Here's another thrilling debacle to watch, Scott. Another disenfranchised philosopher, Reynolds.

Here's to Jack Kassel Widget Sales, Dad.

The Marians have begun emerging from their tents and campers, slowly, rubbing their eyes in the bright firelight, uncertain. Marianettes peer through bus window curtains.

And then it happens. Wanda Streamley suddenly bursts from the crowd, tambourine high, muu-muu streaming behind her, and begins dancing, all around the fire, whooping and hollering, stomping, kicking, jumping. Void and the rest stop in momentary disbelief, then whoop back hard. An instant kinship is forged.

"Can't you *feel* it?" Wanda cries out in ecstasy, torso undulating madly once more, bright eyes made brighter by flames of yellow and orange. "Can't you just *feel* the energy here!!"

The Marianettes explode from the bus to join Wanda, yee-haa-ing for Jesus, hats waving high above their heads, lamé and rhinestones flashing like firecrackers. Hundreds of Marians shout dozens of praise-lets at once and rush forward to join the mosh-pit—dancers, drummers, pipers, presidents, cheerleaders, satanists, Catholics, Wiccans, Witnesses. And, in the middle, a lone Lakota protest drummer, dazed at first, then finally joining the band with reckless abandon.

A scavenging crew forms quickly, scouring the campus for branches downed in the ice storm. Six-foot branches, hurled by dark figures, scream and crackle as they meet the flames, swirling sheets of orange embers into the starfield above their heads.

"Can't you just *feel* it?" Wanda exults. "This is all about life, this is what we are here for! Celebrate the earth! Celebrate the miracle! Celebrate ecstasy! Praise Him with tambourine and dancing! Hallelujah!!"

18

Pauling's Letter to the Philippians

The two extremes appear like man and wife
Coupled together for the sake of strife.

Charles Churchill

I should've been a nun, he says, half aloud. *An anonymous pawn.*
Quiet, uncomplicated. On the periphery.
Nobody gets hurt.

Too late now.

He whistles appreciatively at the ascending earth.

No one was ever able to pinpoint the moment the flames began to spread, or who was responsible, or whether it was intentional or just the natural result of joy unbound. At one point I thought I saw another shooting star right over my head, but it was going *up*, which, I'm no astronomer, but that's not right. It stopped about a hundred feet in the air and dropped, straight at me. I jumped aside and it thunked into the soft ground right where I was standing, still burning.

Hockey ball.

Then another, and another. I looked at Void and Walter, who were looking back at me and laughing their asses off, standing in a pile of gathered hockey balls. Walter picked up another, doused it with lighter fluid, set it afire and launched it, wooing.

Quite an effect, actually. And I should have stepped in, I guess, and said *stop that* —but I felt so completely detached, outside of it all. An observer. Like I could no more step into it than I could step into *The Godfather* and tell Sonny not to take that toll road or Fredo not to get into the rowboat. It's more like *Look, they're doing this now, geez*—sad little chickenshit impotence, maybe, I don't know.

So now let's say it was a stray flaming hockey ball that landed on the roof of Nurse Chapel and started it burning. Except that the Marian girl with the velveteen hat was gliding again at this point, ecstatic, waving her light little branch ahead of her, all the ends of the branches ablaze with little flamelets, and she's followed by about four others, gliding, *rising-on-toes*, twirling, running, in and out and in and out of the gates with their own branches aflame, dropping burning bits of bark like candlewax.

And right then, or long before, or much later, Nurse Chapel began to burn. I don't know the order of things, how do you ever know something like that. Maybe the flaming hockey balls and branches came later. Maybe the Lakota had a hand in it, hell, they said the whole place had to go. Eyewitness memory, it's not worth a dime. Well perception, period, for that matter, Bertrand Russell can make you doubt the table in front of...

But I digress.

The whole thing could have been so much worse. But the students were gone for Easter break when Schlafly Hall went up and the tinder-dry dead grass of the labyrinth burned like a prairie fire over to Steinem and Monty.

For some reason, even though Monty Hall burned to a cinder shell, the office of Leonard the Poet up on the third floor was almost totally unscathed. A thousand books, a desk, a phonograph player, all of them still sitting up there, intact, steaming, in weird denial of the skeleton of gray ash all around them.

Wanda was the last to know things had gone bad. You could see that blackened tambourine at the end of her outstretched arm as the firefighters carried her out of the middle of the burning hockey pitch. She'd just followed the heat, dancing, whirling, drifting obliviously into the middle of the inferno, never a clue she was in danger.

Relax, she's fine.

Everybody's fine, in fact, just swell. Although nothing really affects a college quite as much as having the whole damn thing burn right to the ground. And it did, every building, every square foot except Leonard's office, burned to a crisp. No serious injuries, thank goodness, just a big fire and then no college. It sure shakes a place up to burn the place down.

Although a close second was the news about Scott. Everybody was shook up about the fire, but people walking around shaking their heads in utter disbelief during the following weeks were mostly trying to make sense of the death of Father Siberell. The night before his big television premiere, he goes *skydiving*, what *sense* does that even make. He'd never been skydiving before, according to the form he'd filled out at the Mankato airport, which must somehow explain why he died with a perfectly packed, fully operational parachute on his back. He just didn't pull the cord, how could he not pull that cord, it's right there, it's huge, you can't miss that handle.

Shooting star.

Strangest of all, perhaps, was standing outside the gates— as the Marians jumped in their cars and campers and pickups and trailers and drove like bats out of ironically hell as the giant oak popped and crackled and succumbed—and me just standing there with none other than Dean Martin. She'd seen the first news reports from her home in Sleepy Eye, jumped into her car and raced to campus, her approaching headlights a pair of diamonds sliding down the ruby necklace of the re-treating Marians. Thirty minutes after leaving home she was walking up behind me, silently, hands deep in her coat pock-ets, half-glasses reflecting the campus inferno blazing like the surface of the sun. We stood there without a word for a long while, watching both our futures remade by the flames. She'd have just stood there in silence all night, I'm pretty sure, but I couldn't. I had to say something.

"I'm sorry."

"Sorry for what."

"Well, don't you . . . isn't this really my . . ."

What the hell I was afraid of now, I don't know. Losing my job?

"Just since I'll wonder for the rest of my life, tell me. Did I do this?"

She looked straight at me like I was insane, which was oddly relieving. "No, Jack, give me a break. Not directly. No more you than me, anyway."

"You?"

"Both of us, you and I, we're the ones who left the lids off, didn't we Jack. Two different pots, but both of us left the damn lids off when we should have been sitting on them hard. I did try a lot harder than you, I must say that, but that's just because I saw the boiling years before you did. I knew what it could do and you didn't. Result's the same, though. If anything I'm the bigger fool for knowing better and still letting it happen."

I resisted the urge to ask why God was letting the place burn down.

"And now you're wondering why God is letting it burn. Aren't you?"

"I am not."

"Okay then, tell me why He is."

"Well . . . I don't know, standard wrath of God, I guess."

"No, Jack. You just don't have the knack for this. Sodom and Gomorrah, *that* was the wrath of God. This," she said, looking into the flames, "this is a *learning experience*. That's how it works. And it does work, Jack."

"And the World Trade Center?"

She looked me in the eye with an intelligence I haven't often had cause to associate with the faithful. "The point, Jack, is what happens now. You watch these people rebuild this place. Maybe not physically, or maybe so, but one way or another they'll rebuild their lives because their belief in a god gives them the strength to do it, to pick their butts up out of the ashes and get on with it."

Admin collapsed with a roar at just that point, fortunately, since I never know what to say to this sort of thing.

"And you have no idea what to say to that because God doesn't exist."

"I beg your pardon?"

"Or maybe he does. Or maybe he doesn't. And you think it matters, somehow, in some way, you think it *matters* whether he does or doesn't. Doesn't matter, Jack."

I tend to clam up when conversations do this kind of thing.

"Do you take Vitamin C, Dr. Kassel?"

"Uh . . . yes. I do, sure. It works."

"No it doesn't."

"I haven't had a cold in ten years except the one time I stopped taking it."

"It doesn't work, Jack, but it does. Look at the research, sixteen major studies in thirty-five years. Zip. Vitamin C isn't doing anything for you, Jack."

"But it . . ."

"But it *is*, right? That's correct. It's the placebo effect. Thirty years ago Linus Pauling said 'Vitamin C works to prevent or minimize the common cold.' He spent the rest of his life swearing to it. And he *had* to know it was a lot of horsehockey. His own *research* didn't back him up. But he held his Nobel Prizes up for the cameras and said, 'Believe me, it works. It works.' Nobody of equal stature called his bluff, and thirty years later, Jack Kassel Ph.D. is standing here telling me he hasn't been sick but once in ten years because Vitamin C works—even though it doesn't."

"Placebo effect."

"Right. So why would Pauling lie? Because that's the only way the placebo works. He lied to our faces—and the result has been a lot less suffering and pain because we *believed*. Doesn't work for everybody, but what difference does that make? If it works for half, or a quarter, or a tenth, isn't that better than nothing?"

"Huh. Where can I find those studies?"

"Wrong question! Read those studies and you might have the damndest cold of your life next week. Would that be a rational thing to do?"

Yes, I thought but didn't say. It might be stupid, but it isn't irrational.

You, gentle reader, might suggest the fact that I didn't say it this time speaks volumes. I say shut up.

"Why would you want to throttle the effect that's kept you well for ten years? Best thing for you to do is look at me and think, 'She's wrong. It works. I don't *care* what the research says.' And what I'm saying to you, Jack, is that it is also best for believers in God to look at you and think exactly the same. Because it does not matter whether God really exists or doesn't—all that matters is that you *believe* he does."

Look, shut *up.* Go read a different book.

"Tell me how it matters, Jack, when the college still burns down and the people still get up again, or it doesn't, or they don't, and *still* Christians make perfect sense of it all as a God-existing situation, no matter what, and get some benefit from it that they wouldn't have had otherwise. Read Job. The idea's the thing, the idea of God, and it always has been. You have to believe in the idea, and believe it with all your heart, and then it works. Doesn't much matter whether there's really a recipient on the other end of the prayer. Just pray. Doesn't matter if there's a heaven. Just live like you're trying to get into it. It works. Not all the time, not every minute, so don't even bother to throw that in my face."

"Wasn't planning to."

"Not out loud you weren't. Now I don't know if you've ever wrapped your mind around the reality of our existence, Dr. Kassel, but it's a terrible and a wonderful thing, really too much to handle. Once every few years I get my mind in a place where I feel for a moment that I grasp the size and coldness of the cosmos, that I can feel the earth spinning at 15 miles a second under my feet, that I can tangibly imagine the fiery death of the Sun, engulfing the planets, or my own death engulfing me. That's when I need help, and that's when I turn to the Idea." She took off her glasses and began to polish them with the hem of her sweater. "It's very simple to understand, really, but it's also fragile. You see, God is either real or He's the Great Placebo. What difference does it make whether we're in the control group or in the one with the real pill *if the placebo works just the same,* if the placebo stems the tide of fear and grief and loss and loneliness just as well as the real deal. You want to call the bluff, take the placebo away. You want to run into the churches and yell 'it's a sugar pill!'" She held her glasses up to the firelight, then put them on again. "You'll excuse me if I think that's a mistake. A placebo works only as long as the patient believes it does."

By this time the fire department had established a perimeter and we were behind it, watching the great ring of fire, all feeling inwardly guilty for how much we were enjoying its warmth. The Lakota drummer began a mournful, wavering, wailing song, beating his drum slowly, clearly a song of loss and loneliness.

I didn't know what to say. She had a point, I suppose, if the point of life is to flee reality and be happy, which, who am I to say that isn't the point. Except that it's *not*, of course, which isn't much of an argument. Which left me no real rebuttal beyond 'nuh *uhh*,' so there you have it.

"'I have to reply,'" I muttered under my breath, "'and as I have nothing really worth saying I talk a great deal, and am ashamed of myself afterward for having talked.'"

She smiled a little without taking her eyes from the flames. "Voltaire."

"Yes." I was impressed. Another kindred spirit. "Yes, Voltaire. Okay. So for the sake of argument, let's say you're right. Truth doesn't matter. What does that leave me, Dean?"

"Call me Gennie. I'm dean of nothing at the moment," she said with a toss of her head toward the burning campus.

"Okay. What does it leave me, Gennie?"

She turned to smile at me, just a little, just enough. "It leaves you your mind, Dr. Kassel. And as much a fan of mind as I am, I can't pretend that's anything but a consolation prize. You get to stand outside the clinical trial and know—or at least believe you know—who has the real pill and who has the sugar pill. But you've got the same disease. You live in the same reality as the rest of us. And once you've left the trial, you can never go back in. You can't pick up and pretend again that the placebo is real."

She turned to head back to her car, stopping after a few steps and turning back.

"I wish you well with it, Jack, really I do. That's a tougher road than the one I'm on. I wish you well."

(A prison cell, hours before THOMAS MORE's execution for treason. MARGARET MORE is pleading with her father to convince him to make the simple recantation that would save his life.)

MARGARET   I cannot see this as heroism! Self-sacrifice for noble ideas, in noble times and places— this I can see and admire. But neither this place nor this time is fit to huddle in the magnificent shadow of your principles.

THOMAS MORE   But to acquiesce to stupidity and ignorance—to let it divert your path, let it dictate the terms by which you meet the challenges of the times—Margaret, surely this cannot be what you wish from me. Neither could the God I know wish for me such a betrayal of my principles.

MARGARET   *(Emotionally)* Father, I beg you, be *reasonable!*

MORE   Well, in the final reckoning, it isn't a question of reason, but a question of love.

JACK KASSEL   *(walks out of shadow)* Now wait just a minute. You must be kidding with that. In one fell swoop you overturn your commitment to the truth in favor of a *platitude?*

MARGARET   Guard!

MORE   No, it's all right, Meg. *(To KASSEL).* Now, sir. A careful reader would note that my commitment has always been to the law, not 'truth.'

KASSEL   I am indeed a careful reader—careful enough, in fact, to notice that you've placed *truth* in quotes. Do you find law more compelling than truth, then?

MORE   Let us say I find the law more reliable. More fundamental.

KASSEL   More *fundamental!*

MORE   An example. Do we speak of the *truths* of nature, or the *laws* of nature?

C. S. LEWIS   *(walks out of shadow)* And another: Christ in the presence of Pilate. It was law that convicted Him; even Pilate confessed that truth could be disputed more readily than law.

TINA   *(unseen, amplified, an offstage director's voice)* Right, I remember that passage! Pilate says "But what is truth? Is truth unchanging law? We both have truths—are mine the same as yours?"

LEWIS   *(to the ceiling)* Uh, that's not the Bible, that's *Jesus Christ Superstar.* Bully for the support, all the same . . .

MARGARET   *(exasperated)* This is all very interesting, but there's a task at hand here! I must convince my father to save himself from execution!

He stubbornly refuses to make a simple renunciation to save himself!

CRITO   *(enters as LEWIS exits into shadow)* Talk
about *déjà vu*. There's just no reasoning
with some people.

MORE   Ah yes, Crito. I've thought a great deal,
perhaps immodestly, about the parallels
between Socrates' death and mine. His was
a good death, a death to be envied above
all others. I could never wish for a better
one. And you and my Margaret are of a kind,
both convinced that utility and practical
self-interest must ultimately outweigh the
principles around which one builds a life.
How grand to be young and certain of everything!

KASSEL   But whether you value law more than truth
or the reverse, you must concede that reason has been among your own highest values.

MORE   I must in candor say that you, Doctor
Kassel, are in a poor position to convince
me of the overarching value of reason after
losing that argument with Dean Martin.

KASSEL   *(indignant)* I certainly did *not* lose that argument!

CONNOR KASSEL   *(enters from shadow and pffts)* Oh *please*,
Dad. All you could say to the reader was

'shut up and read another book.' Hardly a compelling response.

KASSEL   Go to your room!

T. H. HUXLEY   *(enters behind CONNOR)* Actually, I found the Dean's last argument quite interesting. Made me think of religion in Darwinian terms for the first time.

KASSEL   I'm not sure I understand.

HUXLEY   Think of all the ridiculous *accoutrements* of the natural world: the peacock's tail, the giraffe's neck, the plates on the back of a stegosaur. All must confer an adaptive advantage, or away they'd go. It could not be otherwise with religion: patently ridiculous, manifestly false, yet surviving and thriving throughout the ages. So it simply *must* have some adaptive value. The whole idea of a *placebo*—that is, a beneficial lie— why, it actually helps to explain the whole matter rather nicely, don't you think? If it weren't somehow a good thing for the species, then it, or we, would have been gone long ago.

KASSEL   Well of course! How stupid of me not to have thought of myself. But I still don't like the idea of truth as some optional commodity.

HUXLEY   You don't *like* the idea? What on *Earth* has that to do with anything? I learned long ago to make my aspirations conform to facts rather than expecting facts to conform to my aspirations. You'll continue losing arguments until you do the same.

KASSEL   *(miffed)* I did NOT lose that argument! I . . . I just wasn't prepared for the direction she went with it. She actually suggested that the truth doesn't *matter*. I've never liked that kind of bald-faced utilitarianism . . .

HUXLEY   *Again* with what you like and dislike! Disliking her point is not the same as having an argument against it, and unless I yawned and missed it, which is certainly possible, you presented no counterargument.

KASSEL   Look . . . I can undercut any argument for the existence of God if we can just agree that it's the truth we're after, I mean, doesn't that go without saying? But to suggest that the actual truth just doesn't *matter* . . . well . . . I just . . . oh for crying out loud! The value of truth is so fundamental to me that it's self-evident, and self-evident values are always the hardest to articulate.

MORE   Which presumably gives you some sympathy for the Christian perspective.

KASSEL   I don't follow.

MORE   Because the value of *our* beliefs is also so fundamental as to be self-evident to *us*, and therefore all the harder to articulate. But I do admire your willingness to stand by your principles, regardless of the outcome.

KASSEL   *(sighs)* Well . . . I don't know about that. My outcome was pretty bad.

MORE   *(softly)* I would gladly trade mine for yours.

KASSEL   *(horrified)* Oh . . . of course. I'm so ashamed.

MORE   Oh don't be. Just one of the few pleasures on death row: you can make anyone else feel terrible for whining.

CONNOR   But actually, Sir Thomas, if you believe death is a doorway to Paradise . . . well, that has to take some edge off the tragedy here, doesn't it?

MORE   *(smiling)* It does indeed, young man. But I'd say it's an emblem of humanity—or humanness, perhaps—that few walk through that final door with total confidence. So much is a mystery, so little is truly known—or so say the philosophers. What arrogance it would be, then, to die with smug countenance, believing that one truly grasps what follows. I believe that God will welcome me into the next world, but I also believe that my understanding of that world and of that God is woefully impoverished. A little fear seems a reasonable response to that uncertainty, tempered though it be with trust and faith. Might I be so bold as to suggest that you, too, Dr. Kassel, will feel more than a little uncertainty as you reach for the knob on that final door?

BLAISE PASCAL   *(as he walks by outside the bars, jingling keys)* Place your bets, everyone! Last call. *(continues walking out of view)*

KASSEL   Well, of course. I'm the first to admit that I don't have all the answers ... and sure, it can be terrifying to contemplate. But I wouldn't choose instead to be couched in comfortable fantasies.

THE BRAHMIN   *(from the next cell)* Outstanding! Or complete idiocy, I don't know which. *(retreats into muddled contemplation)*

KASSEL   Well you surely can't call David Hume an idiot.

DAVID HUME   *(offstage)* Oh no, you leave me out of this!

KASSEL   You, Sir Thomas, admire Socrates in his final hours. For me there is David Hume. No deathbed conversion—just faced oblivion with wit intact. On his deathbed he joked with Adam Smith about what he might say to Charon to forestall his voyage across the Styx. "Have a little patience, good Charon," he promised to say. "I have been endeavoring to open the eyes of the public. If I live a few years longer I may have the satisfaction of seeing the downfall of some of the prevailing systems of superstition." And Charon would reply, "You loitering rogue!

That will not happen these many hundreds of years. Do you fancy I will grant you a lease for so long a . . ."

HUME *(storms in from the shadows, powdered wig akimbo)* Oh, what rubbish! Not the *Charon* fable again! I said nothing of the sort. Smith made it all up in that dismal head of his. Dr. Kassel, how is it that you can see the Gospels for the hagiographies they are, then turn around and accept that *utter* nonsense about my deathbed scene!

KASSEL I uh . . . it's just . . . *(sheepishly)* that's not true?

HUME Not a whit!

KASSEL *(distantly, with undisguised disappointment)* Oh. Well, I . . . I guess I just really *wanted* that to be true.

SCOTT SIBERELL *(dropping down to hang by parachute cords from the ceiling)* Jack, Jack! *Tell* me you didn't just say that in front of David Hume!! Who is this shell of a man I see before me? Is there nothing left of Jack Kassel?

MORE Don't listen to them, Jack. You are an honest man, honest even in your doubts and your errors. That's something to be treasured. As the Dean said, it doesn't make for a smooth journey *(glancing scornfully at Scott)*—nor for many loyal friends, I'd add.

PASCAL   *(comes to the cell door)* Time, Sir Thomas.

(MORE and MARGARET exit with the jailer; all others vanish except KASSEL and HUME, who begin to walk off together into the shadows.)

HUME   Just kidding about the Charon thing, Jack—jerking your chain a little, as it were.

KASSEL   *What!?* So you . . . you *did* say all that, then?

HUME   *(his voice now echoing from the darkness)* I did indeed. You can be just a little self-righteous, you know, Jack Kassel. I thought I'd make you feel a little doubt about something you were so cocksure of—and cocksure for no good reason, by the way. Teach you a good lesson. The fact that it happened to turn out true doesn't absolve you.

KASSEL   *(A little peevish)* Okay, got it. You're a funny guy.

HUME   Oh sure. I was a scream right to the end. Highly recommend it. Much better than jumping into Pascal's arms at the last minute.

(Curtain.)

Printed in the United States
31805LVS00001B/68